DOME 6

BY GAIL CARRIGER

Tinkered Starsong
Divinity 36 | Demigod 12 | Dome 6

The Tinkered Stars
Crudrat

The Finishing School Series
Etiquette & Espionage | Curtsies & Conspiracies
Waistcoats & Weaponry | Manners & Mutiny

The Parasol Protectorate Series
Soulless | Changeless | Blameless | Heartless | Timeless
prequel: *Meat Cute*

The Custard Protocol Series
Prudence | Imprudence | Competence | Reticence

Parasolverse Tie-in Books & Novellas
Poison or Protect | Defy or Defend | Ambush or Adore
Romancing the Werewolf | Romancing the Inventor
How to Marry a Werewolf
Dear Lord Akeldama (direct from Gail only)

AS G. L. CARRIGER

A Tinkered Stars Mystery
The 5th Gender

The San Andreas Shifters Series
The Sumage Solution | The Omega Objection
The Enforcer Enigma | The Dratsie Dilemma

Newsletter exclusives: *Marine Biology | Vixen Ecology*

DOME 6

TINKERED STARSONG BOOK 3

GAIL CARRIGER

GAIL CARRIGER, LLC

This is a work of fiction. Names, characters, places, events, and incidents are either the product of the author's imagination, used in a fictitious manner, or in the public domain. Any resemblance to actual events or actual persons, living or dead, is coincidental.

WARNING

This work may contain implied contact of a romantic and carnal nature between members of the same sex, opposite sex, sexless aliens, or more. If love (in its many forms) and love's consequences (in even more varied forms) are likely to offend, please do not read this book. Miss Carriger has the tame young adult Finishing School series, which may be more to your taste. Thank you for your understanding, self-awareness, and self-control.

Copyright © 2023 by GAIL CARRIGER LLC
Cover © 2023 by GAIL CARRIGER LLC
Cover design by Paul Sizer of Sizer Design + Illustration, PaulSizer.com

The moral right of the author has been asserted.
ALL RIGHTS RESERVED, including the right to reproduce this book, or any portion thereof, in any form.
This book is for your personal enjoyment only. If you are reading this book and it was not purchased for your use, then please purchase your own copy. In accordance with the U.S. Copyright Act of 1976, the uploading, torrenting, or electronic sharing of any part of this book without the permission of the publisher is unlawful piracy and theft of the author's intellectual property. If you would like to use material from the book (other than for review purposes), prior written permission must be obtained by contacting publisher@gailcarriger.com
The author strives to ensure her self-published works are available as widely as possible and at a price commensurate with her ability to earn a living.
Thank you for respecting her hard work.

Version 1.0
9781944751593

There were many battles fought bringing these three books into the world. Thanks to all who helped, in many forms and many ways, from typo fixers to Goliath tricksters and beyond. Would that we all could have our own Dome 6.

In the beginning, the Dyesi created the domes and the divinity.
　But why?

1

SIFT OF THE EARTH

"Are you sad Asterism didn't win?" Missit's gold-flecked eyes were earnest, staring up at Phex.

Phex paused at the entrance to the practice room. "Win?"

"The Best New Pantheon award."

Truth be told, Phex had already forgotten about the Divine Awards. Even though they'd ended yesterday. "No."

Missit wrinkled his nose in that utterly endearing way. "I am."

Phex's heart sank. Had he disappointed Missit?

Tyve stuck her head out from behind the curtain over the doorway. "Phex, there you are. Oh, hello, Missit."

"Are *you* sad about losing?" Missit instantly asked.

Tyve grinned, teeth pointy and menacing, but her tone was deferential. "Of course."

Missit clicked softly, affirmation and sympathy. "You know Tillam won our first year?"

"Yes, but there were fewer groups back then to compete against," protested Kagee, his silver head also sticking out from behind the curtain, on the other side of the doorway from Tyve and lower down.

"Tillam also got to practice together for much longer than we did, before debuting," added Tyve.

Missit held up both graceful hands and turned pleading eyes to Phex. "No need to be defensive. I was simply hoping you'd follow in our footsteps, that's all."

"Sorry, Missit," said Phex, voice low, meaning it. Perhaps they should have tried harder? Honestly, he hadn't thought winning awards was important.

Some of Phex's fear must have shown in his face, because Missit put a hand to his forearm. "I'm not mad at you. The voting system is clearly rigged!"

Tyve snorted. "Nevertheless, my brother is going to be insufferable about this." She and Zil had a contentious sibling relationship, or maybe *rivalry* was a better way of describing it.

"You realize that you don't *have* to follow in anyone's footsteps, right?" Kagee was clearly encompassing both Tyve taking her brother's path and Phex taking Missit's.

"Zil's are very graceful footsteps, though. Galaxy's best, some would say." Tyve was all sarcasm.

"Do you want us to be like Tillam?" Phex asked both Tyve and Missit, for clarification. "Because I don't think that's possible."

Kagee snapped, "Must we deal with your collective inferiority complexes right now?"

"Hey!" said Tyve.

Phex wanted to say that where Tillam and Missit were concerned, they... well, *he*... was inferior. It wasn't a complex, it was a fact. But Kagee looked like he might hit him if he did. And Missit would be upset too. Missit hated it when Phex talked like he was lesser. He *was* lesser, but Missit refused to believe it.

An acolyte came gliding down the hallway toward them.

Their latest assigned precatio was a slender, frenetic Dyesi with particularly flappy crests who seemed young and worried all the time.

Finding Missit talking with the demigods, it made a full obeisance – finger flick, crests way back, even lowering its gaze.

Missit looked faintly embarrassed by such obsequiousness but also realized he was still clutching Phex's forearm and dropped contact quickly. "No need, precatio. How can I help the divinity today?" Missit was very good at formal speech, but that only made the acolyte even more deferential.

"Your pardon, great one." Its cheeks went opaque with embarrassment. "It is not you. I am here to speak with Asterism."

Missit flashed a smile. "That'll teach me to assume it's always about me. Well, babies, better luck at next year's awards. I'll be off." Missit twirled and trotted away, presumably off to find the rest of Tillam.

Phex watched him go, gaze lingering on the Dyesi influence in his walk and the sway of his hips.

"At least he didn't call us *losers*," said Kagee, side-eyeing Phex.

Phex dipped his head, embarrassed to be caught yearning. Fortunately, the acolyte seemed oblivious.

"Shall we go inside?" suggested Phex politely to the Dyesi.

"Please," replied the precatio, crests wilted a little, presumably in relief at not having to deal with Missit.

But once they were inside the practice room, with all six of Asterism collected expectantly around the acolyte, the Dyesi became nervous again – even though they were lesser gods.

"Are you here to inform us of our next tour stop?" asked Phex gently, trying to prompt the poor thing.

"Are we expecting an imminent departure?" asked Fandina, following Phex's lead, tone softly polite and crests neutral, trying to put the acolyte at ease.

"Oh! No. Nothing like that," said the acolyte.

"We are not leaving right away?" Fandina was surprised. Indeed, they all were. It had been a whirlwind tour with very little rest time not caused by Fortew collapsing or Phex getting injured or similar medical emergency.

"We are staying *here* in Dyesi space?" Jinyesun was always one to pursue clarity in all things.

"Have we finished the tour already?" Kagee asked.

"*Already?*" Tyve pointed two fat-tipped fingers at Kagee. "It feels like we've been touring forever. What do you mean, *already?*"

Kagee ignored her.

"Is Fortew back in hospital?" asked Berril, concern causing her wings to rustle slightly.

Phex felt rather proud of them. Asterism had grown into itself, peppering acolytes with questions as if they had the god-given right. As if they were important. Which they *were*, even if they didn't win some stupid award. They had, after all, proved themselves on tour with Tillam. But their newly developed confidence came out as chatter and seemed to be driving the precatio into a panic. Its crests were in a permanent state of flapping, unfurling and folding back in distress at each new question. The lights of the practice room shining through the thin iridescent membrane caused little blue-tinged rainbows to appear and disappear on the floor.

Phex wondered if this was the acolyte's first big assignment – managing Tillam *and* Asterism. It couldn't be easy.

Finally, its crests paused and puffed, everyone stopped and waited expectantly.

The acolyte opted to answer them all simultaneously. "Not staying here, you *will* be leaving soon, it is only that you need to transfer ships first." It said this politely but without pause for breath.

Phex felt his stomach clench in pure panic. Were Asterism and Tillam being separated by the divinity? Was he losing Missit already?

"Why?" asked Jinyesun.

"New ship? Why *transfer ships*?" Kagee crossed his arms, not liking the phrasing, not liking the sudden change.

"Will Tillam be going with us?" That was Tyve asking the question Phex couldn't bear to. He wasn't sure if he was grateful to her for it. He found himself clenching his jaw hard.

The precatio's crests flattened at the fresh onslaught. Phex willed him to answer Tyve first.

Jinyesun and Fandina looked guilty over a fellow Dyesi's obvious distress, but Tyve, Berril, and Kagee were not disposed to give a new acolyte an easy time.

"We are accustomed to this ship and this crew," protested Berril.

Fandina pointed its crests at the precatio. "Let the acolyte speak."

Berril and Tyve pouted.

Phex's tension evolved to nervous caregiving – desperate for a distraction, he handed out flasks of water to the graces. "Occupy your mouths," he said.

He tossed a third water at Kagee, who caught it deftly, unsnapped the lid, and took an angry sip.

The acolyte's crests puffed. "Thank you, sun. All of you,

including Tillam, will be transferred to a larger spaceship. The tour is not ending."

Phex worked hard not to show obvious relief. Although his shoulders must have visibly relaxed. He and Missit would be together a little longer. He knew, of course, that they had an inevitable ending. They were from different pantheons, different backgrounds, at different places in their careers and life journeys. Not to mention the fact that the acolytes forbade romantic relationships. The divinity, the worshippers, the whole galaxy would be against them if they found out. Quite apart from that, who was Phex to hold the attention of a god like Missit for very long? But he was still pathetically thrilled that they weren't separating right now. Phex wanted to hold the undeserved happiness of Missit being his, and belonging to Missit in turn for as long as possible.

"Meanwhile, *you* must pack." The acolyte used the singular formal *you*, crests pointed at Phex.

"We all must pack, if we are moving spaceships," Phex corrected the mistake gently.

"Ah, no. You, alone of your pantheon, will be taking a shorter trip *first*."

Phex's skin prickled with fear. He was being singled out and separated from the others? "Why?"

"Your presence has been requested."

"My presence? Alone? By whom?"

"You *and* the great god Missit."

Okay, they would get to be together, but was this some new trouble Missit had gotten them into? Had Missit known this was coming? Was that why he'd popped up in the hallway on the way over?

"Your duet," the precatio added, as if that would explain everything.

Phex relaxed. "The divinity wants us to do another special performance?"

"Yes. Exactly. Less spectacular than the last, we hope."

Missit and Phex's duet had caused a *sensation* at the Divine Awards the night before. Mostly because it had quickly become not a duet. They had been joined on the dais by four sifters, making up the proper number six. Oddly distributed, but still six. But four sifters matched with two Sapiens, acting both grace and cantor, had produced a display on the dome like no other and never likely to be seen again. It had caused quite the ruckus, much to Missit's delight and Phex's chagrin.

"Just the two of us?" Phex clarified.

"Yes, just the two of you."

Phex relaxed even more. The original duet he and Missit had practiced, singing and dancing together in the old Sapien way, was not a godly thing. But it was spectacular and it was a lot of fun. He enjoyed what he and Missit could do together as artists almost as much as all the other things they did together. He was happy with another opportunity to perform the piece.

"Where do we go this time?"

"You have been honored by a formal request."

"Have we?"

"One of the *caves* has asked to witness you."

Phex was stunned out of his customary calm complacency.

Berril and Tyve both gasped.

"Dyesid Prime?" said Kagee, voice full of shock. "Phex is going to visit the home world?"

"Which cave?" whispered Jinyesun.

The acolyte looked at Asterism's two sifters. Three sets of

crests fluttered in some complex form of body language communication that Phex could never hope to understand.

"Not yours, demigods, apologies," said the acolyte to both Jinyesun and Fandina, highly formal.

"But the invitation would not have included us, even if it *were* one of our home caves," said Jinyesun, looking sad.

Fandina said, crests neutral, "It is probably one of the west caves. They are very forward-thinking. They often pay closer attention to the divinity as a result."

Jin clicked agreement. "Highest number of keyskins come from the west. Still, I miss the caves."

Phex hadn't thought until that moment that the Dyesi could get homesick. He'd always assumed that the divinity was simply what they all did. Well, what all the nymphs did, anyway. If your life's pattern included an obligation to explore the galaxy as part of your religious movement, did you have a right to miss your home planet? That seemed counterintuitive to an expansion model.

Suddenly, Phex was worried about Jinyesun in particular. How long had his friend been hurting and Phex hadn't realized? He'd taken pains to learn what homesickness looked like in Sapiens because he did not feel it himself. But he hadn't realized he should include the Dyesi in his assessment. What was it that made others feel better? Comforting memories? The food of their home worlds? A warm beverage? Conversation? Phex shuddered.

"Should I bring something back for you?" he asked Jinyesun and Fandina. "From the caves, I mean? Something you miss?"

Jin blinked huge eyes at him, crest tips folded. Finally, it said carefully, "You cannot bring colors back from the caves, Phex, you can only experience them in person."

Phex said, "I'm low cantor, of course I can bring color."

Jinyesun was jolted out of its sadness by amusement. Really, Phex was always making the Dyesi laugh, and he had no idea why. "You are so cute sometimes, Phex. Perhaps I should have said *beauty*, not *color*."

Now Phex was confused, so he moved on. "Missit and I are to dance in the caves of Dyesid Prime for the entertainment of the locals?"

"Yes. Is that not what I just said?" The acolyte was now both flustered and frustrated. Clearly, it was too new to its divine precatio duties to understand that Sapiens dealt with surprise poorly. Especially gods.

Phex frowned, "Will Quasilun be joining us?"

"Why would you want the protector imago?"

Phex tilted his chin. "Think very carefully about the phrase you just uttered, acolyte."

The Dyesi speckled and its crests drooped. "I do not understand, demigod."

Jinyesun looked away to hide amusement.

Fandina took pity on the new acolyte. "Quasilun is our *bodyguard*, precatio. Remember?"

"Your sun thinks a protector imago would willingly protect him from *other* imagoes?" The acolyte paused. Then its crests went flat to its head. "He thinks he *needs* protection from them?"

"Knowing Phex," piped up Berril, "he thinks Missit might need it."

Kagee sniffed. "How do you know he's not worried your beloved imagoes don't need protecting from Missit?" Kagee did love to throw soap in the soup.

Now all three Dyesi in the room had flat crests, gods and acolyte.

Kagee continued. "After all, the award show proved what Phex and Missit's voices can do together under a dome. From what I've gathered, your caves are merely domes in another form. Is it not a great risk inviting them to perform?"

Phex turned and looked at Kagee. "What are you doing?"

His high cantor pretended innocence. "Just teasing a bit."

The new precatio looked panicked, skin almost entirely opaque. "Should I request Quasilun's presence? Of course I should. Please excuse me. Meanwhile, please pack for a short stay, low cantor Phex, and meet me to disembark in one hour."

Phex bowed in acknowledgment of the instruction, but the acolyte was already dashing away.

"Happy with yourself?" Tyve asked Kagee.

"If our new precatio can't handle us, how will it handle Tillam?"

"Fair point."

"I guess I'm packing." Phex left the practice room, heading for their quarters. The others trailed after him.

"Don't worry, Phex. We can get the rest of your stuff to the new spaceship," said Fandina.

"Again?" said Phex. Because that was how his stuff had made it to this spaceship. Fandina and Jinyesun had done his packing for him. Frankly, if it had been him, he would have included more spices and that one spatula he really liked.

"Are you excited?" wondered Berril, bouncing up next to him and grabbing his hand. "You'll get to see Dyesid Prime. Not many non-Dyesi can say that."

Phex turned his head toward Jinyesun and Fandina. This was their home world. He was getting to see the planet that had birthed two of his best and only friends. That had birthed the divinity. He supposed that made it a kind of pilgrimage.

"Sure," he said. He didn't want to rub it in, especially not with Jin and Fandina right there. They, who had their beloved home so close but would not get to visit it. And he, who had no home at all, would get to visit yet take no comfort from the experience.

He wondered if Dyesid Prime would make him sneeze.

So far, every planet that he had visited had made him sneeze. He seemed to be allergic to planets.

Quasilun was waiting for them on the ramp of the transport ship.

Phex nodded at his bodyguard and removed his hand quickly from Missit's lower back. "So, you *are* coming along."

The murmel had declined to accompany them. She had done so by screaming her objection at the very idea of boarding a transport vessel, apparently on the basis of being a spacefaring creature and deeply suspicious of planets. Phex wondered if they made her sneeze, too.

Quasilun twitched their crests in greeting, then nodded in a jocular way. It was always odd, to see a Dyesi adopt Sapien mannerisms, but Quasilun was different from most Dyesi. The imago was comfortable in its own skin but also relaxed around other aliens in a way the nymphs of the species seem to find elusive. Phex wondered if it were a matter of age or life cycle or both. If, as the Dyesi got less flexible in their skin, they got more flexible in their minds.

"We can't have you two mucking about planetside without supervision," said the imago, leading them aboard.

"I thought you might feel that way," replied Phex.

"Who, us?" Missit batted gold-flecked eyes. "We're just harmless little ol' Sapiens."

Missit was the only one who didn't have to duck his head at the top of the ramp. The ship was not Dyesi-made – like most spacefaring tech, the divinity rented, borrowed, or bought. They sometimes decorated, but not with this one. Dyesi aesthetics extended mostly to the insides of their domes and the outsides of their gods. This transport was narrow and pointed, probably Cotylan-made – sleek with a dangerous aura, like a sheathed blade.

Quasilun gave a crest-droop of disbelief and secured the small cabin while Phex strapped down next to Missit in the port fold cots. An acolyte pilot came in and settled into the guidance niche at the back, watching Phex and Missit with interest out of the corner of one eye while it conducted prelaunch checks.

"Are you excited to go back?" Phex asked the god next to him.

Missit's mobile mouth twitched. "Not particularly."

Phex couldn't help his snort of amusement. "Bad as that, is it?"

"Not so much *bad* as very boring." Missit sounded like he meant it for a change.

"Do you think they invited us to relieve the monotony?"

"They invented an entire divinity to *relieve the monotony*. It's that bad down there," replied Missit, deadpan.

Phex hid a smile. "Isn't that the function of all religion? Alleviate boredom with ritual?"

"Phex, are you getting theological on me all of a sudden? You don't talk enough to be a theologian."

"Are they always like this, imago?" the pilot asked Quasilun during a lull in chatter.

"Like what?" teased the imago, strapping down in the starboard cot. Even made for two, it was too small for Quasilun.

"Irreverent." The acolyte began the wind-up for takeoff, and the ship rumbled softly.

Quasilun ascertained that both Missit and Phex were secure before buckling under their own net. They weren't going to fold, so Phex wondered why they needed to be strapped down. But Quasilun seemed intent on safety and Phex trusted his bodyguard.

"They are gods," said the imago to the pilot. "Those who are divine do not have to *respect* what is divine. That would be illogical. Gods cannot worship, let alone believe in themselves."

"If you say so, imago." The pilot managed to make even frozen register sound a little impolite.

Phex and Missit exchanged amused glances.

"I think I shocked our pilot," confessed Missit.

"Proud of yourself, are you?"

"Of course."

The transport ship launched off of Divinity 12 in soundless efficiency, leaving the small satellite moon behind. It zipped through the rings expertly, the viewscreen risk flashing factor trajectories, and the pilot engaging collision-avoidance protocols with consummate skill.

"Tell me what to expect from the caves?" Phex asked Missit.

"What do you mean?"

"How will we need to modify our performance for an underground venue? How will it be different from the domes I'm used to?"

"Always so practical, my Phex." Under cover of the netting, Missit risked poking two fingers through the mesh and against Phex's back. "Unfortunately, we won't know until we see the cave in question – since every cave is different. But our performance is adaptable and we will be given some time to practice in the allotted space beforehand."

Phex supposed that was good enough. He let the fingertips stay touching him, since there was no way they could be seen by imago or acolyte. Because Missit wanted it, of course, not because he, Phex, actually liked the reassurance of that slight contact. Never that.

He craned his head to look back at the pilot. "Why are we strapping down if there's no FTL?"

The Dyesi home world was too close to bother wasting resources on a fold.

Missit was the one who answered him. "It isn't easy to land on Dyesid Prime. There's a reason the surface is unoccupied by sentient life."

"Apart from the megafauna?"

"Yes, apart from dracohors."

"Fun."

Missit gave a pained smile. "No one with a lick of sense would settle on such a planet."

Quasilun said, sounding amused, "Hey, now, that's my home world you're insulting."

"Mine, too," said Phex.

"What?" that was the pilot, clearly very surprised.

"Phex is a naturalized Dyesi citizen. Technically, Dyesid Prime is his home world," Missit explained.

"I've just never visited it," added Phex, trying to be friendly.

The pilot gave a huff of amusement and then toggled the viewscreen.

Dyesid Prime filled it. As a potential, training on Divinity 36, Phex had seen the planet a lot. But only ever from a distance half-obscured by the dust, rock debris, asteroids, moons, and satellites of the ring they'd live within. While he was training to become a god, the view of Dyesid Prime had become part of the furniture, like a moving tapestry on the wall of his kitchen.

But up close, unobstructed, it was a new creature entirely. A sullen purple planet covered with swirling storm clouds. It was beautiful, looking as iridescent and as multifaceted as Dyesi skin but bitter and insane about it.

"Welcome home," said Missit, sarcastically.

Phex felt that statement in his bones. It was the first time anyone had ever said it to him.

He wondered if, after visiting this strange new place, he would feel homesick for the caves, like Jinyesun did. Or if homesickness was something that had to be earned, like godhood.

He started because Missit's cool firm hand cupped the side of his face. Apparently, Missit's arm was slender enough to fit through the holes in the net.

"Where did you just go?" the god asked.

Phex's arms were too big, so he could do nothing to break contact but turn his head away. He hoped the others hadn't seen.

Phex huffed, sounding the way the Dyesi did when they laughed, only his huff was a kind of pain. "Is it weird to be going home for the first time at my age?"

"Look at me for a moment," ordered Missit. His arm was back under the net.

The golden god's flecked eyes were suddenly all Phex saw, instead of Dyesid Prime. He wondered if home could be a person – a beloved stranger, instead of a strange planet. Were those flecks actually planets in Missit's eyes? Planets that he would become homesick for when Missit left him behind? Would he seek comfort in memories? Or had he already started? His throat ached with the need to kiss him.

"We are all a little lost, Phex. No matter where we are in the galaxy." Missit's hand was back, thumb running over Phex's cheekbone, pressing reassurance into his skin.

Phex wondered if, when humans took to the stars thousands of years ago, they did it because they were looking for something. Or if they did it because they were trying to leave something behind. Could all of them – gods, acolytes, Wheel, Dyesi, Agatay, Shawalee, Jakaa Nova – be divided into two types? The lost who were searching and the lost who were running away?

He was one of those who ran.

Missit was one of those searched.

Perhaps that was why, in this brief time when they crossed paths and got to be together, Phex felt like they were both still yearning. Perhaps he could excuse his own constant need to kiss, and touch, and keep, for it being nested in so much fear and starborn legacy.

But still, Missit shouldn't be obviously caressing him like that. Phex pleaded with his eyes for him to stop.

Quasilun had clearly been watching their interplay intently. The imago said, at that juncture, yanking Phex away from the specks of home in Missit's eyes, "Does the divinity know what you two are to each other?"

Phex felt the bottom fall out of his stomach.

Missit was militant. "What should they know?"

Quasilun huffed at them. "Keep your little secrets. The nymphs will figure it out or they won't. But are you prepared for the repercussions if they do?"

Absolutely not, thought Phex.

Missit only lifted his head to glare across Phex's bigger body at the imago.

The imago wiggled both crests in a suggestive way. "I won't say anything."

Phex was relieved, but he knew very well that didn't mean the imago was on their side. Just that Quasilun thought it would be amusing to see how long it took the acolytes to discover they were lovers, or for them to utterly expose themselves, whichever came first.

Dyesid Prime did indeed make Phex sneeze.

Even underground, he sneezed.

After a truly taxing atmospheric landing that left Phex's stomach somewhere in the vicinity of his left ear and Missit looking more green than gold, they made their way immediately down into the caves. The Dyesi city-warrens were deep below the surface of the planet. That far down, there was no wind or, presumably, pollen.

Still, Phex sneezed.

He supposed that there was plenty of vegetation throughout the Dyesi caves. Vegetation would appear to be his respiratory tract's one true enemy. Many connecting passageways were structurally supported by beautifully patterned root systems, with glowing tendrils dangling down. In many caves, enormous tubers formed the ceilings of immense chambers, big as any dome. It seemed Phex was allergic to the broad category of *living things on planets* – underground or not. Which was both annoying and amusing, because it meant that somewhere along the way towards engineering his supposedly perfect body, the Wheel had sublimely messed up. Phex liked that the Wheel had made such a tremendous mistake, even if he must suffer the nasal repercussions.

They walked through yet another massive cave full of pale globular tubers, each one three or four times Phex's own size.

"What are those?" he asked Missit, pointing up.

Missit was proving to be a willing font of useful information. "You know those, you've just never seen them growing before. Those are Dyesi spuds."

Phex was delighted to learn this. He'd cooked with multiple iterations of spud back in his potential days – spud flour, spud pasta, spud dough, spud thickener. Spud was the mainstay of the Dyesi diet.

Missit explained that above the ground, these were huge, lush plants, tall as trees, that extended their roots down through the topsoil so that these enormous tubers dropped into caves, forming the ceilings of the biggest ones. The spuds they encountered were various shades of white and yellow, giving the caves into which they grew a soft, pillow-like feel.

"Like walking inside a stiff cloud," said Missit, grinning and twirling about.

Phex privately thought that the tubers looked a bit like a blister he once got after wearing too-tight gracing shoes, but didn't want to pop Missit's fantasy. He watched with interest as resident Dyesi climbed up long ladders to hack off chunks of spud for food. No one said anything or approached them as they moved, sometimes by putt-putt, sometimes on foot, from one cave to the next, ever downwards. The putt-putts were kind of round and soft and globular, and designed for three nymph-sized Dyesi, so Phex had to operate it, since Missit was too small and Quasilun too large.

Most of the caves also boasted enormous hollow reeds that grew down through the soil like the spuds. These, Missit explained, were a different but equally vital plant that provided ventilation, light, and aeration.

There was a distinct smell to the caves, earthy and savory, like a broth made with root vegetables, coupled with a prevailing feeling of being slightly too cool and damp. It wasn't unpleasant, but it wasn't normal to Phex's nose or skin, either. He had grown up in the perennially dry air of artificial gravity.

"It's a lot less dim than I was expecting," Phex commented, a little incautiously.

Quasilun, who'd been letting Missit do most of the talking, pointed above to the ceiling of the high passageway they currently putted through. Millions of threads dangled down, each glowing a faint purple but together providing a warm wash of light. Phex wondered if they were artificial, like Berril's hair.

But then Quasilun said, "Glowworms."

Phex clicked understanding, even though he'd never heard of such a thing.

Missit grabbed Phex's arm, grinning cheerily. "There are bioluminescent veiled fungi in the spud caves, too."

"What language are you speaking?" It sounded like Galactic Common but Phex hadn't understood how the words went together.

Missit grinned at his confused expression. "Sparkly mushrooms. They're cool-looking *and* tasty."

"Have I used them for cooking?"

Missit nodded. "Dried as a powder. It's the base for lots of Dyesi soups. They stock the dorms with it on Divinity 36."

Phex nodded. He remembered it well. "Silkhorn?" He used the Dyesi word he remembered from the packages, a shiny bluish powder he often found himself adding to sauces as well as soup.

Missit clicked. "And there's the sweet green version from the north. You made a tea out of that. Although the Dyesi mostly use it as a colorant. There's a rare purple kind too, it's a little sour."

Phex nodded, he'd encountered that too, made it into a cold tea. "I thought the green was a kind of screwpine."

"Nope, also from sparkly fungi."

Phex was disposed to accept whatever peculiarity he was told was reality here.

They continued on, walking through the next set of warrens. So far, they'd only passed a few nymphs, who gave him and Missit funny looks and Quasilun all due respect, but few others. Phex supposed these nymphs were still too young to leave the planet and join the divinity. Or these were those few who did not wish to go off-world, and as such had probably never seen a Sapien in person before – let alone two cantor gods.

On Dyesid Prime, Phex was the alien.

Or maybe it was Missit, who moved like a Dyesi, liquid bones and smooth strides, but looked nothing like them.

Phex didn't feel confined or oppressed by the caves. He had thought that he might. The idea of being underground, with layers of rock, soil, vegetation, and megafauna weighing down the earth above him was unsettling. But it didn't mess with his head like he'd expected it to.

Apart from one or two domes on their tour, the caves were the biggest structures Phex had ever visited in his life. The fact that they were underground registered with his brain but did not frighten him so much as the concept had before they arrived. He supposed it was more dangerous to be trapped in a space station or spaceship than trapped in the caves of a planet with breathable air. At least here, in the end, they were not dependent on technology to survive, only earthwork structures and spuds.

The caves felt oddly safe to him.

He sneezed.

Missit gave him amused eyebrows. "You were raised on a space station. Are you allergic to everything that grows as a result?"

Phex made big puppy eyes. "I'm allergic to planets, apparently."

Missit patted him. "Poor baby."

Quasilun, who was leading them in a way that suggested extreme familiarity with the warren, huffed in amusement. Phex wondered if this was the imago's home or if, as a bodyguard, Quasilun had studied up on their destination and trajectory, or if every Dyesi cave system was just laid out exactly the same way.

"I guess this is the price I pay for an enthusiastic immune system," Phex said.

"Death to all dust?" suggest Missit.

"Plants on a planetary scale is not something the Wheel would consider when tinkering with my genetics," Phex explained.

Missit looked confused. "Wait, are you saying that there is no Wheel Prime?"

"Not that I know of." Phex paused to make the appropriate greeting to a small group of nymphs who seemed a little older and very excited to meet Missit in particular.

Missit made polite little finger-flicks in leu of crest-wiggles, while Phex watched their behavior patterns for clues.

So far, apart from the surroundings, things felt culturally very like they had on Divinity 36.

He, Missit, and Quasilun had been met and greeted by acolytes at the entrance to the cave, or he assumed they were acolytes, Phex supposed they could just be ordinary nymphs, no way to tell the difference. But their short robes were similar to acolyte formal attire, and the way they spoke and looked was similar. Most of the other nymphs they'd met since then had been wearing scraps of megafauna skin or nothing at all.

The entrance to all the various caves and passageways, including the one to the surface, were hung with skins, as Phex was accustomed to, both on Divinity 36 and their spaceship.

The transport ship and its pilot had not stayed on the surface. It was too dangerous to leave a ship parked on this particular planet. It wasn't even a matter of megafauna intentionally attacking. One of them could simply step on the transport and accidentally crush it.

Instead, Phex, Missit, and Quasilun would be retrieved in a few days.

The initial greeting party had left them to their own devices once they were inside the warren. Phex and Missit had automatically followed Quasilun, trotting to keep up with the bodyguard's long strides.

Now, finally, they were entering a cave bigger and more impressive than any that had come before. This one was teeming with Dyesi talking, playing, and moving about.

There, off to one side in an impressive group, were the breeder imagoes.

Even Phex could not hide his shock.

2

CAVE OF EVERLASTING SONG

Quasilun, as an imago, looked substantially different from all other Dyesi Phex had ever met. Nearly twice as big as the nymphs of the species, with hard pearl-grey skin that lacked iridescence, and yellow eyes. But Phex hadn't realized that the three imago types would *also* look different from each other.

Quasilun, as a protector imago, while different from the nymphs, was still clearly *a Dyesi*. Basically humanoid but stretched and elongated and entirely hairless, with those too-big eyes, expressive crests like fish fins off both ears, and a way of moving that spoke to joints that flexed in multiple directions.

The breeder imagoes, on the other hand, looked like they could have belonged to entirely different species. Some part of Phex had assumed the distinction was mainly gender and culture based, but it turned out physical appearance played an important role. He didn't know why he was surprised – physical appearance was *always* a big deal with Dyesi.

"They're massive!" Phex had to make a conscious effort to close his mouth, left open in shock.

Missit, who had lived with the Dyesi before becoming a god, found Phex's reaction highly amusing.

Missit corrected Phex's pronouns to the plural for *she*. "Those are all females. The ones you're looking at are actually smaller, younger imagoes. Those ladies can still fit through the passageways, and they have all come to visit this cave to see us perform, I suspect. See how the ladies are all sort of piled in and on top of that big pearl-colored mound? That mound is actually a matriarch imago. She'll shake them off once they're done gossiping. She'll be the one in charge of this warren, and the origin of our invitation. We will be formally introduced to her before we're allowed to do anything else here."

Phex had learned that imago breeders were classified as H10, which meant they were unable to leave their planet. Usually, an H10 meant that the alien could not breathe the same air as Sapiens. But in this case, it clearly meant that a matriarch breeder could not, physically, leave her cave, let alone the planet. The Dyesi became one with their caves because they grew too big to escape them.

The matriarch and the smaller female imagoes did look basically like Dyesi nymphs in skeletal structure and form – big-eyed and hairless – but like Quasilun their skin had a hard sheen to it. That skin was mainly shades of white and grey, lighter than Quasilun's, but even the smallest was at least twice Quasilun's height and girth. They were simply big – big like the megafauna above ground were big.

Several nymphs danced attendance on the matriarch and her visitors, polishing the ladies to a mirror-like sheen. Phex realized that they were primping before a party.

Phex felt a little embarrassed, like he'd stumbled into the wrong pantheon's dressing room.

"Should we be here?"

Missit grinned. "They're having a spa day."

"A what?"

"Never mind, sweetie."

"Where are the male imagoes?" Phex asked.

"There are a few over in that corner. They tend to be darker grey and smaller. There will be fewer of them in general."

"Why?" They looked very like the younger females, just a few shades darker, and like the ladies had no obvious genitalia or secondary sex characteristics. Or clothing, for that matter.

Quasilun, hovering behind them, joined the conversation at that juncture. "Because there are fewer of them after instar. Breeders number well over sixty-six percent female."

Phex wondered if that genetically impacted breeding numbers for survival. But figured it probably didn't, since the Dyesi seemed to be doing pretty well with regards to population. He supposed that it all rather depended on how many offspring could result from any given breeding session.

Ripping his eyes away from the imagoes, Phex spent some time just standing and looking around. He found the cave restful and pleasingly pretty. The nymphs, dodging in about the imagoes, made for elegant fluid purples, blues, and greens within a backdrop of imago grey and the grey of the cave itself.

Phex examined the cave walls, noting how different it was from those that they'd traveled through to get there.

This one seemed the most like a dome. It was a great deal less regular in shape than any dome he'd ever been in, as one might expect of an organically formed cave rather than a constructed edifice. But something about it still felt familiar. The reeds bringing in air and light were interspersed throughout, much like observation niches in domes. Instead of scale-like symmetrical panels neatly covering the interior, this cave was lined with huge irregular panels. But it still *felt* very much like dome technology. These were all slightly different shades of that familiar dormant pearly silvery material, but it was definitely the same material.

Phex wondered how they would reflect skinsift when each one started out a slightly different shade. Maybe the whole color-and-pattern experience was simply different down there. Phex did not understand how dome tech worked. It was a secret the Dyesi kept from everyone, even their gods.

Phex felt there was something beautiful about the cave's imperfections. It was not incurring the same awesome reverence as the cathedral domes, but instead had a homey, satisfying aura that made the space feel friendly and comforting.

The dais at the far end from where the matriarch and her friends lounged was equally organic and irregular in shape. Nothing more than a mesa-like boulder jutting up from the cave floor. It looked like it was flat enough on the top for them to dance, but Phex still worried about some of the choreography working there – his wall runs and flips had been designed for smooth-sided, regular-shaped domes. They really must practice before their performance. And how could they do so in such chaos as this cave, surrounded by curious Dyesi?

"Will they be staying here during our practice?" he wondered.

Quasilun said, "The matriarch never leaves. And the others will remain in attendance since they came expressly to visit her."

Phex nodded, nervous. He didn't want an audience to see him imperfect, stumbling, and making mistakes. He didn't even like it when Missit saw him do that.

"They will not mind seeing both practice and performance. The experience will not be ruined thorough lack of surprise," explained Missit, picking up on some of Phex's concern.

Quasilun clicked agreement. "That is not how Dyesi experience the divine."

"But our duet is *not* divine." Phex bit his bottom lip.

"It feels that way to me sometimes." Missit was being flirtatious.

"It is only a song and a dance." Phex looked to Quasilun for support.

"Nothing is ever simple when gods are involved." Quasilun, like Missit, could be sublimely unhelpfully sometimes.

Phex sneezed.

The earthy, savory smell was stronger in this cave. Also, there seemed to be a smoky quality. Phex wondered where the Dyesi kitchens were. "Do we wait for an introduction or can I go check the dais?"

"Impatient Phex." Missit sounded fond.

Phex was uncomfortable, not impatient. He needed something to do. Something useful. He wished he were making everyone drinks. Even if that took the form of some weird Dyesi kitchen. Practicing their duet would be the next best thing. At least it was familiar.

Quasilun said, "Wait," with flat crests that brooked no argument.

Phex tried to coach his own body into stillness, like holding grace.

There came a low, humming rumble, and then the dozen or so smaller females began to tumble to the side, revealing the enormous matriarch they'd been cuddling with in all her glory. She was lying on one side and had an upper arm the size of Phex's whole body. She was still humanoid, just almost sculpturally large. With that hard shimmery skin, it was as if she had been carved from some massive gemstone boulder that was part of the cave wall. She was similar in coloration and steeped in repose. A recumbent giantess, like some ancient rock-hone sculpture, essentially humanoid but awe inspiring and grooved into the earth as if she had not moved for generations. And perhaps she had not.

She was pretty. Stunning, even. For some reason Phex hadn't expected that. But there she lay, beautiful in the way Dyesi gods were beautiful, elegant and big-eyed, and perfectly sculpted by refined aesthetics, a living piece of art.

Quasilun did something then that they had never done before. They had been in and out of many caves and entrances throughout the warren thus far but never announced themselves.

Now, this time, the imago gave voice and title, loudly, to its relationship with the cave.

"Quasilun. Protector imago. Bodyguard to Asterism, pantheon of the divinity. I was born to these caves and I will die of them. For now, I return as friend to all Dyesi but no longer family."

Phex thought that was an interesting way of putting it. He wondered if all protector imagoes gave up their rights to a home cave, or if that only applied to those few who took to the stars.

The matriarch crested with slow formality at Quasilun but said nothing, waiting. Her crests, like everything else about her were enormous, like ship's sails, and while the membrane was still thin, it was no longer iridescent. The rainbows they cast over a whole corner of the cave were diffuse and soft and greyscale, like a pattern made of rain on still water.

Quasilun gestured Missit and Phex forward.

Missit stood slightly in front, and made his introduction to the cave. It mirrored the pattern already ingrained into Phex from entering rooms, first on Divinity 36 and then on the spaceship. So, he wasn't nervous.

Missit used frozen register, highly formalized. "Missit. God of the pantheon Tillam. I am a stranger to this place."

Phex immediately mimicked Missit's register and words. "Phex. Demigod of the pantheon Asterism. I am a stranger to this place."

The matriarch spoke then, her register frozen, her words loud and amplified by the cave. "Kumaimi. Matriarch of this place. I was born to these caves and I will die of them. Welcome to our home." Her voice was like Quasilun's, full and extremely musical with two distinct tones at once, as if two people were speaking in unison. Or as if two cantors, high and low, were harmonizing.

She switched registers then, lowering her volume, her speech turned casual as if talking to children. Phex supposed that is what he and Missit would seem to her – both by age and appearance. "You are both so cute. Missit, I know, is a child of the Hu-core home system, but you, Phex, to whom do you belong?"

Phex considered this, looked to Quasilun for help.

The imago's face and crests were neutral.

So Phex said, "To you, I suppose, if you will have me."

The matriarch looked neither startled nor offended – her crest stayed up and neutral, which Phex took as a good sign.

"Curious creature," she said. "But I have not met many Sapiens. What do you mean?"

"I am a Dyesi citizen. A former refugee," Phex explained.

"But you cannot be a Dyesi if you have no cave. There is no such thing."

Phex gestured with his hand to Quasilun, "And yet there stands a caveless protector imago."

The matriarch huffed a laugh. The Dyesi all around,

imago or nymph, relaxed perceptibly. All of them had been stiff-crested and tense until that moment. "Could you also protect us if needed, little blue Sapien?"

Phex knew that he could. He could sing the Dyesi into immobility, and presumably, he could sing them into motion. With Missit, in a dome, he was just that powerful. Hadn't Quasilun said that imagoes were the first cantors?

"With Missit, yes, I could." *I can also fight,* Phex wanted to add, but didn't. He didn't think the capacity for violence was valuable in the eyes of the Dyesi.

Matriarch Kumaimi huffed again. "Bold claims from one so small and thin-skinned."

"Is that not why you invited us to perform?"

The matriarch fairly sparkled with delight, and her crests went puffy. Apparently, even matriarchs found Phex amusing. To the Dyesi, Phex was nothing more than a small walking, talking joke – a jester god.

"My stars, this one is *adorable*, isn't he? I can see why the nymphs recruited him. And such pretty blue hair. Not that you are anything to sneeze at, golden child." Kumaimi pointed her crests at Missit, rustling the air in the cave and thus Missit's hair. "You are, after all, the darling of all the caves of Dyesid."

Missit preened. "Yes, I know. I don't mind it if you admire Phex. I too think that he is *adorable*."

"Missit," hissed Phex, embarrassed.

The matriarch only seemed more delighted with them both – her crests gave a little wiggle of pleasure.

Missit inclined his head to hide a broad grin and asked politely, "May we check out the dais and do some test runs, matriarch? Phex has never performed in a true cave before. He is nervous."

"So cute. Of course you may, sweethearts. And then

perhaps you both will join me for a nice meal?" It was not a request, but she was granting them a respite and a breather. Phex was grateful for small mercies.

"It would be our honor," Missit responded for both of them. Much to Phex's relief. He would far rather Missit did the bulk of the talking.

Kumaimi turned her attention back to Quasilun. "You may stay and entertain me in the interim, protector."

Quasilun huffed. "A poor and ugly substitute, no doubt."

The matriarch's crests did not deflate, so this was Dyesi humor. "I will ruin my eyes, then, for the sake of a dear old friend with much to tell me concerning the wide avenue of the stars."

Quasilun clicked, crests puffy. Were they flirting? "Do I get tea?"

The matriarch made some graceful gesture and several of the nymphs ran off. "Of course you do, dear heart."

Phex and Missit made their escape to the other end of the cave. There they ran through practice – just the dance components of their duet. Phex figured singing would be the same no matter the irregularities of the cave.

Fortunately, running this cave's wall was not so difficult as he had anticipated. Even more fortunately, those who gathered to observe seemed to find Phex's use of their dome as a kind of springboard-meets-exercise-equipment amusing rather than offensive.

The dais itself was actually fun. It was larger than dome standard, so they had to lengthen strides, but after half a dozen run-throughs, both Phex and Missit felt like they had it down.

"What were you doing up there?" asked one of the nymphs pertly, after they'd jumped down, sweaty and happily exhausted.

Missit took the container of drying sand it offered and brushed himself with it. "It is an ancient Sapien art called *dancing*."

"It is graceful, but it has no grace."

Missit cocked his head and said, in a challenging way, "Who says that beauty is the only thing with multiple facets?"

The nymph in question looked startled but not upset. "Is it like that with cantor, too?"

"Yes, indeed. For our performance later, we will also sing."

"Which is?"

"Cantor without skinsift."

"What's the point?" A different nymph came over then. Phex could tell, by the thinness of both Dyesi's bones and the way they were not so elegant as the others, that these two were very young nymphs. Perhaps only recently out of their first instar.

"Watch and you will see," said Missit, not bothering to hide a smile this time.

The two nymphs folded their crests, a posture that was almost subservient.

"Gods truly are magical creatures," said one.

"Are you like this because you are gods or because you are Sapiens?" asked the other.

Even awed, they remained curious.

Quasilun appeared. "You cannot expect gods to reveal all their secrets, younglings, especially when you have been called to witness their performance later. Surely, all secrets are revealed on the dais and not through mere conversation?"

"You are right, of course, protector. One should not try to understand art before experiencing it."

"Very good, little one. And now, please excuse us? These

two have been working hard for many hours – they must be fed. The matriarch, you understand, requests their presence."

The two nymphs immediately moved away. "Of course, protector."

Phex was grateful that his time on Divinity 36 had somewhat prepared him for cave culture. He had not eaten *all* the different types of Dyesi food – for surely there were as many different cuisines and variations as on any other planet, but he was at least accustomed to the Dyesi palate. He had cooked for Jinyesun, Fandina, and other Dyesi potentials regularly once. He knew that by most Sapien standards, the Dyesi preferred things less sweet and less salty. He knew that spud starch featured prominently in their diet, and that he himself was a fan of the mashed savory porridge variant. Phex found it comforting, and was delighted to see it grace their welcome meal. He liked how the porridge was served in a communal manner with various sour pickled vegetables and seared meats as toppings. This allowed him to simply pick and choose whatever he wished.

Still, there was more food set out before the matriarch and her guests than Phex had ever seen in one place in his entire life. The vast majority of it he did not recognize. He followed Missit's lead on the porridge toppings. He and Missit did not have the same tastes, but at least if Missit ate it, Phex knew it wouldn't give him indigestion.

The meat was gamey and similar to avian meat he'd eaten at one of their tour stops. Earth 10, maybe? He couldn't remember. Phex supposed this must be megafauna flesh. He'd had it before on Divinity 36, but never this texture or light brown color, so it must be a local species or different preparation technique. He wondered if megafauna had to be aged or treated to become palatable. It wasn't his favorite, but with such a long practice session and a performance coming up, he needed protein.

Dyesi did not drink while eating, but afterwards, Phex and Missit were offered a choice between saposi fruit juice (far too sour for Phex), corrosive dark, or cold water. Phex took the water, and was a little sad because the cool, clammy atmosphere of the caves made him crave something warm and comforting.

Missit bumped Phex's shoulder gently. They were seated together opposite the Matriarch's head, presumably a position of importance and dignity that should prohibit shoulder bumps. She remained on her side with the table stretching the whole length of her body. If she wanted something from the opposite end, the others simply passed it up to her.

Phex glared at the golden god. Was he never serious?

"You're missing your kitchen again. Aren't you?"

Phex looked down at his now-empty place setting. "How did you know?"

"You only sigh like that when you want to cook."

"Is the adorable blue one a chef?" Kumaimi looked intrigued.

"Only as a hobby." Phex jumped to correct any assumption of proper training.

Missit liked to brag about Phex a bit too much for Phex's comfort.

The golden god said, eyes sparkling, "He took it up while a potential, so he learned using lots of Dyesi ingredients but catering to mostly Sapien taste."

Phex muttered, "I cooked for Dyesi, too."

The matriarch seemed delighted with this information.

"How exciting! Was there anything of ours you found particularly popular?"

Phex said, "Spud, of course."

Missit waved an airy hand in a gesture not unlike a crestwiggle of dismissal. "Yes, yes, everyone knows about spud. But look here, Matriarch, he makes tea out of green silkhorn powder."

Phex added, because it was important, "I'm experimenting with the blue and purple varieties too."

"A *tea,* you say? How unusual. And the Sapiens enjoy this *tea*, do they?"

Phex was compelled to be honest, "Some of them. The purple seems the most popular when I can get it, but that could be the color."

The matriarch clicked with deep understanding, "The most important aspect, of course. Would you like some now? I understand corrosive dark is too much for most Sapien digestive tracts."

"It'll also keep us up all night." Missit occasionally enjoyed corrosive dark, but only ever drank it in the mornings in very small amounts with lots of added sweetener.

"Ah, of course."

But Phex was uncomfortable and hesitant to draw out the meal any more than necessary. "No, thank you, but you might try it with other visiting gods."

Kumaimi found that hilarious. "Dear, we don't *have* other gods visit."

Phex wasn't sure how he felt about that.

The matriarch added, "I was thinking about exportation. But we don't keep a stock of the green here, not my cave, anyway."

Phex and Missit slept in that cave, along with all the other Dyesi.

They were given their own couch puff, of the style so ubiquitous in Dyesi furnishings. It was more than big enough for two comparatively small Sapiens, and no one seemed to care that Phex and Missit cuddled together. In fact, most of the Dyesi seemed to prefer sleeping in communal piles. The matriarch and all the breeders of both sexes, visitors or otherwise, made up one large pile that may or may not have included sexual activities. Quasilun slept with them.

Phex decided not to think about it. The whole pile and its arrangement seemed like some grown-up thing he was too young to fully comprehend. He may be an adult by Sapien standards, but he wasn't an imago by Dyesi standards, and he was pretty certain he didn't want to be, either. Missit, of course, found Phex's obvious discomfort highly amusing.

"You're a prude."

A few of the nymphs indicated that they would like to join Phex and Missit on their puff. Not for sex, obviously, just for company or out of social obligation. But Missit made them feel highly unwelcome through a combination of hand-flapping, dominance posturing, and glares. Eventually, the nymphs all settled into other puffs, and merely directed observation, crest-wiggles, and commentary in their direction.

Phex tried not to overhear the gossip, but the Dyesi clearly meant them to, or didn't realize how good Sapien hearing was.

"Just look at their sweet little faces."

"Don't you just want to pet their hair, it's so pretty."

Missit was staring at Phex with twinkling eyes.

"I like how thin their necks are. Charming."

"They look like they smell good, don't they? Like skinless."

Phex had no idea what expression was on his face, but apparently, it was comical, because Missit clapped both hands over his own mouth and began shaking with suppressed laughter.

"Their round ears would be so much fun to poke."

"You can't just go around poking and petting humans, especially not gods."

"I can't help it, I just wanna, they're so cute!" One of the nymphs stood and approached them hopefully.

Missit stopped laughing and flapped furiously at it.

Its crests wilted and it returned to its friends. "Why do you think they don't want sleep company?"

"I read somewhere that some Sapiens pair-bond."

"How remarkable."

"That's even cuter. They can form emotional attachments? How adorable."

Missit hissed, in Galactic Common, "Phex, your face!"

Phex said, so as not to roll his eyes, "No wonder these nymphs aren't allowed to become acolytes yet." He poked Missit's ear, just to play with them.

"Don't start." But Missit's eyes were back to twinkling.

"But you're cute and can form emotional attachments," parroted Phex.

"I'll stop laughing at you. Promise." Missit subsided and stopped teasing him.

Phex relaxed into the puff as well, arranging himself so Missit could flop against him, head in the divot formed below his shoulder. "The nymphs don't like to sleep-cuddle off-planet, though. Why?"

Missit noticeably relaxed, tugging a soft woven throw up to cover them both entirely. "They do. Just mostly with each other. And that's only because they don't want to lead Sapiens on. They would prefer cuddling everyone and everything in general, I think, especially within pantheons. They'd probably love it if pantheons slept together in one big bed puff."

Phex thought of his own pantheon. Fandina seemed fine, but he sometimes worried about Jin, the yearning in its eyes. He'd thought it was homesickness – was it touch starvation instead? Had he been unintentionally cruel to his friend?

Missit continued. "Melalan and Yorunlee never sleep alone. But Tillam has been together long enough to know what they are and what they need. But with most Sapiens not understanding the nymph state, the Dyesi are scared of leading us on. They know we find them sexy."

Phex thought back to his interaction with the matriarch. "While they find us *cute*?"

"Mostly, just us gods are considered *cute*. We are, after all, tailored to their aesthetics. But ultimately, yes. They lump us in with skinless more than nymphs."

Phex felt almost offended. "We look like adorable tiny *children* to them?" He paused. "I look like an *infant*?"

"More toddler, I'd guess. Yeah." Missit nodded against Phex's chest.

"And to each other?"

"Other nymphs? Essentially, also kids. Hence the sexlessness of nymph state. It's gross or unthinkable to them to have sex with us or each other. Affection and cuddling, sure, sex, not at all."

They lapsed into silence while Phex processed that information. On so many levels, it made sense that the nymphs could not tolerate sex with Sapiens or each other. They were kids, they didn't want to think about it, and why should they? From their perspective, it was unnecessary and caused drama and complicated matters. Sex was imago business, and nothing to do with nymphs or the divinity that they had created. Sex was verboten in the divinity because the divinity was nymph business. So far as the Dyesi were concerned, Phex, Missit, and all the gods were also at nymph life stage, so they should act and be treated the same way. To the Dyesi, this would all make perfect sense.

Missit pressed his nose into Phex's neck, inhaling. "You smell much better than the caves. I forgot how musty they are."

Phex rubbed Missit's back. "Will I get to meet any skinless?"

"You might see some, but I doubt you'll be actively introduced. That would be lowering for you."

Phex didn't understand, but Missit sounded tired. It would be better if they just went to sleep. Understanding could wait.

He rubbed Missit's back until the god in his arms lost all tension, his breath softening and evening out. It took Phex much longer to fall asleep himself, but he enjoyed the luxury of getting to pet gold. It was nice to watch Missit in repose under the dim grey like of the caves, face soft and a little sad instead of capricious.

Weirdly, Phex found that the hardest part of trying to sleep in a Dyesi cave was not being surrounded by hundreds of alien strangers. It was the sheer size of the cave itself. It was the biggest space he'd ever bedded down in, and that was the problem. It almost didn't feel like he was *inside* anything.

As a child, he'd slept in air ducts and gutters, walls always close and tight around him. On Attacon, he'd had a tiny residential pod – more walls and more closeness. On Divinity 36, he'd had a niche, and on the tourship a tiny bunk in a tiny room. Here, it wasn't being surrounded by people that he found unsettling – it was the massive, echoing openness of the cave itself. A few strands of glowworms like misty purple stars were high above him. But that was the only real sense of space he got. The sheer emptiness was terrifying. There was no surety of anchor, so he could not doze off. There was only the sound of his own breathing and Missit's – those breaths leaking upward into a void.

When he finally did sleep, he did it feeling like he and Missit on their puff were adrift in open space. Each breath he emitted pushed them further and further into the unknown nothingness, like they were sailing eternity.

3

DOME OF THE IMAGO

The next day around lunchtime, the cave began to fill. Phex had thought it crowded enough already, but more and more Dyesi kept arriving. A steady flow persisted all afternoon, mostly young nymphs and breeder imagoes (the smaller ones who could still move around).

By midafternoon, everyone was sitting, and the only reason to stand was to fetch and carry snacks back to a group, use hygiene facilities, or something equally vital. Otherwise, it was too crowded, safer to stay seated.

The cave took on a festive air. It was both like and unlike the excitement inside a dome before a pantheon took to the dais.

The assembled Dyesi were looking forward to the show, but it was also clear they didn't expect the same all-encompassing experience that worshipers expected from a dome. They were excited in the way Phex's pantheon got excited when he cooked something new. For the art and the taste of it, for the novelty of the experience, but not because they anticipated transportive euphoria or all-consuming joy.

The Dyesi had come for a good time, not godfix. Phex

found himself a great deal more relaxed before this performance as a result. More relaxed than he ever had been under a dome.

The Dyesi simply wanted to enjoy themselves. Therefore, Phex and Missit could enjoy themselves too, if a show was all that was required of them.

They changed into their performance costumes and did their own hair and makeup.

They were waiting to go up onto the dais when Missit said, "Look, Phex, skinless."

A long line of orderly Dyesi were filing into the cave from an inconspicuous entrance behind the matriarch's huge body. These were much smaller than other Dyesi, about Berril's size, and they moved with a certain amount of awkwardness, which starkly contrasted to the normal fluidity of the species. Phex still guessed that these were on the older end of the skinless spectrum. They were all quite dark in color, muted greens and blues and purples, but Dyesi-shaped. Their skin did not show the hard sheen of the imagoes, nor the beautiful flexible iridescence of the nymphs. Instead, the skinless were matte-looking and also almost transparent. Their skin was so thin, the veins underneath were clearly visible – threads of black running webbed and meshed all over their bodies in an irregular pattern not unlike the roots that crisscrossed the passageways of the warren.

They looked thin and delicate. Phex could see why the Dyesi might be rabid to protect them. He thought one stiff breeze, like those that made him sneeze, would tumble them over. Frankly, him sneezing might do it.

The skinless all sat carefully on a row of puffs near the matriarch, eyes huge in their small, excited faces. They stared at Phex and Missit with true childish awe, crests focused intently, never having seen Sapiens in the flesh before, let alone gods.

Phex couldn't help but wonder how susceptible they were to his voice. He already knew that he and Missit, if they sang a dome properly, could control every nymph in that room. He could even damage some of the most susceptible sifters with a wrong note. They could also have a mass effect on nymphs – fight, flight, or freeze. What could they do to such fragile little creatures as the skinless?

He turned to Quasilun, who was lurking nearby, looking very bodyguard-like.

"Are the skinless in danger?" he asked. "From our voices, I mean?"

"I think that is what the matriarch wants to know. That's why you were really invited to this cave." Quasilun did not look worried. Which worried Phex.

"She is testing us on children?" Missit sounded horrified.

"She is testing children on you," corrected the imago.

"What if we injure them?" pressed Phex.

Quasilun looked amused. "You overestimate yourselves, godlings. By imago standards, your cantors are quite weak, especially without a full pantheon to back you. Besides, why do you think there are so many imagoes present here now? You think a Dyesi would risk a single child for any reason, let alone a group of them, out of mere curiosity?"

Missit looked mollified but Phex was still scared. After all, the Dyesi had let him songbruise *and* songburn nymphs in the past. Historically, they had never been careful enough with his voice – always underestimating what the Wheel had done to him.

And what about Missit? The Dyesi had made him into the greatest of all their gods – yet they themselves did not seem to understand the full scope of what that meant.

In the name of religion, he and Missit had been forged into weapons of art by a race of pacifists. Now the Dyesi wanted to test how dangerous that weapon was, by pointing it at their own young? Trust pacifists to be so ignorant of the destruction inherent in creation.

Phex said to Missit, "We have to be very careful up there."

But Missit was looking hard and driven. "No. We have to do our best and enjoy our own performance. Anything less would be an insult."

"To us or to the matriarch?" Phex wondered.

"To me," said Quasilun. "Why else do you think we carry the moniker of protector? It has nothing to do with physicality or violence. I am a living shield."

Phex understood then. Protector imagoes must be the strongest Dyesi cantors. Quasilun had come along to this cave not to bodyguard Phex or Missit but to protect everyone else from them.

Weirdly, that made Phex feel a lot better. He trusted Quasilun.

So, Phex and Missit climbed onto the wide stone dais of a true cave for the first time.

They sang an ancient song from the distant past, sourced on a planet many folds away, for a species that had evolved so far beyond that source, they had long since forgotten what it meant to be human. Or maybe it was just that the meaning had changed.

It was a good performance, if not a great one. Because the caves walls were so irregular, Phex messed up a few of his flips, none of the catches, though – Missit stayed safe. But Phex also realized, in those moments where he could pause to actually look out over their audience, that the cave's strange shape allowed *any* nymph present to skinsift the song. The way the waves of their singing bounced reflected colors off of all the sifters in their audience – like the petals of flowers scattered about. Stolen images made abstract but no less beautiful, patterns both on the cave and all around them. Like rainbows made by light through crests.

Everywhere Phex looked, the dome was a little different, a little less cohesive and more unique. It made him think of the swirling pollen on unfamiliar planets. Of old stars in new placements every time they completed yet another fold in the universe.

It was nothing like a dome and nothing like a pantheon, and yet also exactly like both. The technology was the same, that mysterious alchemy of the senses that turned sound into color, that made the music into motion patterned over alien skin. All of this caused by two small gods, no bigger than children, who sang and danced for no other reason than that they were good at it.

Just before the last chorus, there was a short moment when Phex was flipping to land, so Missit was holding the song alone, and Phex looked directly at the skinless.

They were standing and swaying together, all of them in perfect unison. Too perfect, like they were automatons, or artificially generated imagery, like their every movement was controlled by each note of the song. The hairs on the back of Phex's neck rose in horror.

Phex lifted Missit, opened his mouth, and let his low cantor join Missit's high – hating himself and what he could do in that moment. What he and Missit could force onto others, unintentionally or not, because they were doing it to children. His hands, even though they were touching Missit's molten heat, were clammy.

How different was he right now from those who had forced him to run the blades and clean crud for survival? How different was he from the ones who had forced him to bleed and fall and run again and eventually lose everything? He, like his past, was using kids.

They finished their song at last.

Phex set Missit down carefully.

Missit's hand was instantly on his face, tilting Phex's chin, gold-flecked eyes worried. "What happened there? Why are you so sad all of a sudden?"

Because usually, they enjoyed this part. Enjoyed the ending. Missit always did. Because Missit loved to sing in whatever form it took, and he loved being with Phex best of anyone, for whatever reason and for however long. And Missit did not think that something so wonderful and beloved could possibly hurt others.

Skinless.

Fixed.

They were done.

Phex did not think they needed to bow or receive accolades from the Dyesi – that was not the Dyesi way.

For once, he couldn't worry about Missit or Missit's feelings. Instead, he did a crudrat's run down the side of the cave and through the seated crowd until he was right before the skinless – all of them still standing, all of them eyes unfixed and minds unmoored.

"Are they okay?" he asked the matriarch, forgetting formality let alone frozen register.

"You were truly beautiful up there" was all Kumaimi replied. "I am so happy that I invited you."

Missit's small hand slid into Phex's and he squeezed. "What's going on?" he asked, ignoring the skinless and the imagoes.

"Why are they all so still? It's like they are stuck." Phex could not rip his eyes away from the skinless – so frail-looking, so fixed in place. Phex wanted to touch them, to shake them out of it, but these were Dyesi children and he was an alien in their midst.

Quasilun's voice came from behind him. "It is a kind of euphoria. It is a fine and healthy state. It means they are in good working order."

"They are not harmed?" Phex remembered formality and changed his speech pattern. Breathed a little easier.

"No. They are just starstruck for a while, transported somewhere else. They will come back when they are ready. You two did good."

Phex wanted to be sick.

The nymphs around them began to stir at that juncture. They also had been frozen in place, but seated and still, without the part where Phex's voice had made them dance. He had not forced them into movement, like he had with the skinless.

The imagoes, of course, had been unaffected. Quasilun always said that they did not feel godsong. Like the gods themselves, imagoes could only create it.

Phex realized then that the three life stages had each responded differently to his performance.

"Only two of you were singing the colors, and you still managed it. I am impressed. Very impressed." Matriarch Kumaimi looked pleased, her crests puffy. "Protector Quasilun, please extend my reverence to the acolytes in charge of these cuties. They have turned out a matchless set of gods. A true masterpiece from foreign worlds. Children from another species came down and transported a full cave to distant stars. It will be talked about for generations."

"The skinless are undamaged?" Phex asked again.

"Why is the little blue one so worried about my children?" Kumaimi asked Quasilun.

"He worries that his voice has hurt them."

The matriarch gave Phex a kindly crest-wiggle. Her enormous eyes went soft. "You are concerned for our young? You are a true citizen of Dyesid. But I would not have allowed them in the cave at all if I thought they could get hurt here."

"Please do not take offense, Matriarch. Or think Phex offered insult to your parental prowess." Missit said this quickly and with great formality, sinking to his knees. He tugged on Phex's costume to indicate he should join him.

Phex did.

But the matriarch only huff-laughed. "I am not offended by ignorance of our ways. How could he be expected to know what he was never taught? Quasilun, rectify this situation."

"But, Matriarch, he is not *actually* Dyesi."

"Neither is your little golden Missit, and yet he knows."

Missit said, tentatively, "Actually, I do not. I have just always accepted, because I grew up among you."

The matriarch's crests puffed in pleasure once more. "Such a good little god you are, so obedient. But I think it is fine. Show them."

Quasilun looked as if they did not want to, but still clicked in reluctant agreement.

Then the protector imago opened their mouth and sang cantor.

The two tones of its voice, bell-like, filled all the cave with sound. There was no song to it. This wasn't a performance. It was a kind of command. It was stronger and more powerful than anything Missit and Phex could do together. Had they been singing, Quasilun's voice would have cut through their song and cut them off, drowned them out. And Quasilun did that easily.

The sound of it sifted off of nearby nymphs almost instantaneously. It became colors not just on the walls of the cave but in the matriarch's skin, right there in front of them.

Phex glanced covertly to the side – the other imagoes were changing color too.

The skinless, who had until then not moved from standing, went in motion. They ran together, in perfect unison, around and behind Kumaimi's massive supine body until they were entirely hidden from sight.

"There they are protected from everything, including more cantor," Quasilun explained. "Her body can shield them from most every danger."

"Because she is the dome," said Phex. Staring at the fading patterns in the matriarch's skin.

Imagoes can no longer skinsift, Quasilun had said, but they could reflect the sift just like the caves did.

Just like the domes did.

Then Phex remembered what Quasilun and Kumaimi had both said when they introduced themselves and their relationship to the space.

I was born to these caves and I will die of them.
Of them.

Phex pivoted slowly, looking around and up, at the shapes making up the reflective panels of the cave, irregular in form and color. Panels that responded naturally to all the skinsift around them, almost as if they were linked to the nymphs below, interacting – as if the cave itself remembered what it was like to be alive.

Those panels were the carapaces of dead imagoes. There was no other possible explanation.

Walking back up the passageways through the warren to the surface of Dyesid Prime, Phex asked one last question. Even knowing he had figured out the answer, he wanted Quasilun to confirm his conclusion.

"Dyesi have door phobias because there are so many living inside each cave. If anyone panicked and caused a stampede, closed doors would result in hundreds being crushed or killed. That's why all the openings must be easily accessible, correct?"

Quasilun looked strangely amused. "That's as good an explanation as any. A bit culturally deterministic. Perhaps we don't have doors because we never invented the hinge."

"Isn't that just technologically deterministic?" wondered Missit, cheeky as ever.

Phex wasn't really one to discuss anthropological theory. "Godsong is used to keep them safe. The skinless. To control them so they do not hurt themselves or each other."

He thought that for as long as he lived, he would never forget how beautiful and fragile the Dyesi young looked. He might halfway love them already. He certainly felt protective of them. He suspected that was because they reminded him so much of Berril. Or maybe it was just them. The skinless simply did something to the adults around them. Activated instinct with their cuteness. Even in Sapiens.

Quasilun clicked confirmation. "For us, it's the nymphs, too. In the old days, imagoes would sing sift as a protective mechanism, turning any nymph around us into whatever color was needed for camouflage or protection of the young and the cave. Nymph is the most numerous life stage. They are the ones who are the most mobile, and were often used to physically defend the caves, back when we had to fight megafauna to survive."

"They're expendable." Phex winced, thinking about his

Dyesi friends, who were all nymphs. Thinking about how this meant that Fandina and Jinyesun were considered something lesser than the rest of their species.

Quasilun hissed a negative. "They *were* expendable, in the distant past. No planet has an unsullied history where survival is concerned."

Phex supposed that was true.

Quasilun continued. "Why do you think we let them out to play so much now? Once upon a time, they had to pay the price for our existence. We could think of no other reward than the freedom to explore the entire galaxy."

"And they developed the divinity as a result?"

"Creative little things, aren't they?" Quasilun sounded very proud.

Phex wondered if the imagoes ever once concerned themselves with what their nymphs had done *with* the galaxy that they'd been handed. If the imagoes cared that the nymphs had taken the very thing that was once used to control them and turned it into an art form that enthralled millions. "Did you ever stop to worry about what the domes were doing to us?"

"To who?"

"To Sapiens."

"Not really. Protector imagoes, as a rule, are only concerned with protecting Dyesi. Present company excluded, of course, since I am *your* bodyguard."

"Don't be silly, Phex is technically Dyesi. Plus, we know, in reality, you're really here to protect them from us," said Missit – his eyes were hard on Quasilun's face and he purposefully used low register.

Quasilun huffed in amusement. "Don't worry, I'll stop any fixed while I'm at it."

Phex wondered why it was that in exploring the vastness of space most every species ended up wanting to control it.

He wondered if what the nymphs were doing with the divinity and their domes, and the skins of dead imagoes, was intentional or instinct. If he and Missit sang because in their own way, they too wanted some measure of control over their destinies. If art of this type, shared and influential, was simply another, more beautiful means of conquering.

They returned to find both pantheons happily ensconced aboard a new tourship. Or not a tourship at all. Instead of a sleek if garish spaceship designed for rapid travel, light capacity, and divine expansion, their new digs were inside a ship ten times the size, ugly and clunky.

It was not the kind of thing Phex would ever expect to transport gods.

Looking at Missit's surprised face, he knew this kind of spaceship wasn't normal for Tillam's tours either. It was an awkward, lumbering, fat-bellied creature. It looked like it would lurch from star system to star system, its folds flabby and its presence mildly insulting to all who encountered it. It was not painted in sparkles and glitter – it was utilitarian at best, like plumbing turned inside out.

Phex, Missit, and Quasilun boarded, announcing their relationship to the space – strangers all of them. The ship hummed with activity, mostly Dyesi nymphs and a few other alien devotees moving at a rapid pace, undertaking various tasks and duties. There seemed to be a great deal of fetching and carrying of large objects, using drones, of course, but still... It was all *very* different from their previous spaceship.

No one noticed them at first, until Quasilun muttered about devotion to the divinity into their wrist ident. A few minutes later, a trio of flustered acolytes appeared before them, full of apologies and formal register. They were all unfamiliar faces.

"Welcome to the *Nusplunder*," said one, humbling itself

with a reverential tone before the two gods. The others followed suit. All three of them showed poor control over their crests, which wavered in discomforted excitement. Phex couldn't tell if they were nervous about Missit or Quasilun or both.

"We are thrilled to be transporting actual gods, especially ones as famous as Tillam." Well, that answered that question.

"And Asterism, of course," added one of the others, crests flicking hastily in Phex's direction.

"Don't mind me," said Phex, hiding his amusement.

Missit preened. "This ship is much bigger than normal for us."

"We are not, technically, official divine transport."

"No," agreed Missit. "You're a dome-construction vessel, aren't you?"

That made sense to Phex. A ship this big and clunky would be required to carry dome panels, scaffolding, and other technology designed to meet the physical demands of an expanding divinity.

One of the acolytes clicked in agreement. "Ship's complement includes builders, architects, and technicians. There is even an advanced acolyte aboard who is under divine mandate to become the sexton in a new dome. It's all very exciting."

"Don't pantheons normally arrive well *after* a dome is built?" asked Phex, choosing his words carefully. Then he added, to make sure they knew he was not worried for his own consequence, "Especially pantheons at Tillam's level."

Three crests instantly wilted a little. "We will explain shortly, we promise. Meanwhile, if you would follow us? We will show you to your quarters."

Phex wondered if the panels carried in the hold of this huge spaceship were the carapaces of dead imagoes, or if the regularity in shape and color to the majority of the panels used off Dyesid Prime indicated that the divinity had figured out how to artificially recreate their own dead? He thought it was probably taboo to ask. Most cultures had taboos around dead bodies. Although most cultures didn't use dead bodies for decoration, either. Not that he knew of, anyway.

Plastering the skins of the dead onto walls and putting them, literally, on display seemed somehow both more and less reverent than other mortuary practices. It explained why the custodians of the domes were called sextons, though.

"Do you think the food will be better?" wondered Missit softly to Phex as they trailed dutifully after the three acolytes, Quasilun bringing up the rear.

Phex gave him a dour look. "More importantly, will the galley be bigger?"

"More importantly, with the chef be stable?" shot back Missit, who was still upset that the chef of the last ship had fixed on Phex.

One of the acolytes perked up, its tone very devout. "Oh, you are the cooking god! We've heard about you. We have some of your ladles."

"From my old dorm on Divinity 36?" Phex had left most of his cooking equipment behind, odd that it would end up as part of a construction fleet.

"No. Your *special*-merchandise ladles."

"Ooo, Phex, you have signature merch already! Very well done." Missit crowed at him and clutched his arm in a paroxysm of delight.

Phex frowned down, pleased to see Missit so happy but confused beyond measure. "I have specialty ladles?"

Missit looked at the chattiest of the acolytes with teasing eyes. "Are they blue?"

"Of course."

Phex asked, worried, "Are they *good* ladles?"

The acolytes all looked collectively crestfallen. "Oh, we don't *use* them. We just hang them on the wall in the galley. They're too pretty to use."

Phex looked at Missit helplessly. "Since joining the divinity, this may be the single weirdest moment of my life."

"Poor baby."

Phex melted at the endearment, hiding his reaction, of course.

Missit turned the full force of his twinkle on the acolytes. "Do you think you might show us to our quarters by way of the kitchen?"

"The kitchen?"

Missit grinned cheerfully. "He's the cooking god, remember? He'll want to see the kitchen and claim a corner of it. And I want a tour of the ladles."

How *dare* Missit be so sweet? Phex glowered desperately.

"The low cantor of Asterism wishes to annex part of the ship's galley for his personal ritual use?" The greenest of the acolytes looked very confused, crest wilted.

"Is that a problem?" Missit's tone of voice suggested that it had better not be.

The acolytes quickly consulted among themselves.

Phex was about to step in and explain that Missit was teasing them, when they looked up, all three clicking at once.

The chatty one, who was a little pinker than Phex had ever seen before in a Dyesi, said, "It is a very big galley, for a spaceship. I am sure we can accommodate the cooking god's wishes."

Phex said, "Perhaps I can claim just the bit that's under the display ladles?"

The acolytes looked confused, but Missit laughed. "Look at you, making a joke. You're adorable."

"Stop it, Missit."

"This here is the pathway to the communal gathering area," said the bluest of the three, interrupting the ladle discourse to get them back on to the business at hand, a tour of their new spaceship.

Phex glanced around eagerly, but it pretty much looked exactly like all the other hallways they'd been through so far. Like the previous spaceship and the buildings on Divinity 36, there were no distinguishing markers to give guidance or direction. It would take him a while to learn how to get around this ship.

Missit turned to Quasilun, who was trailing them reluctantly. "You coming?"

Quasilun hissed softly, "I don't think you two will be in danger now that we're aboard – from the ladles or otherwise."

Missit blinked. "No one said you could joke or be cute."

"Quite right," said Quasilun. "I'll stop now."

"Do not scare me like that," admonished Missit.

"My apologizes. God Missit. Demigod Phex." Quasilun gave them an ironic little crest-wave that indicated the imago felt no remorse whatsoever, and then retreated down a different hallway, presumably on some grown-up business of great import. Quasilun may not have been on this particular spaceship before but was clearly familiar with the layout.

Phex and Missit followed their new acolyte minders first through the galley, which was indeed big for a spaceship and decorated with pretty blue ladles on the walls, and then on to their quarters, which were only a little bigger than those of the previous ship. Although this time, the two pantheons were housed next door to each other. At least Missit would have an easy time sneaking into Phex's bunk.

Asterism's quarters were not decorated with ladles.

Phex found this oddly disappointing.

Their respective pantheons were already in residence and, from the shrieking emanating from next door, so was the murmel. She clearly smelled Missit, because she came out into the hallway to reprimand him for having left her alone for an interminable *two whole days*. Dimsum was having none of that nonsense, and so far as she was concerned, the entire construction vessel should know her ire.

The acolytes informed them that on this ship, it would be inappropriate for gods to fraternize with the crew. They had been assigned a converted storage bay for practice and social activities outside of meals, and were granted access to the galley only at specific times. They were to be escorted by bodyguards whenever possible, who were billeted across the way. They were told that they must eat quickly and as a group and not linger in the galley, which made Phex sad. Fortew was already ensconced in the ship's medical facilities, which were vastly superior to the tourship. As a construction vessel with a large complement and crew, plus a first-contact mandate, the *Nusplunder* was regularly required to deal with trauma and illness.

Missit disappeared with Bob to go visit Fortew, Dimsum wrapped around his neck.

Phex joined his pantheon in their new quarters. It had roughly the same layout as their previous one, three bunks up the wall on each side, one set farther inside and close to the porthole, the other set near the doorway and opposite the hygiene chamber. Asterism had already elected to keep the same bunk arrangement, if the faces looking at Phex were anything to go by. Phex suspected this would hold for all their touring life together. These kinds of traditions took hold fast and were hard to break.

He plopped himself on the lowest bunk nearest the door. Same as before, he liked it because it was easiest to get into and out of but also because it was the first line of defense. That was the reason Tyve was on the bunk directly above him – she could jump down and help fight if needed. Kagee had the inside bunk lowest, so he could be backup and protect their weakest members.

The three of them hadn't discussed this arrangement, but Phex knew they all felt the same and that was why they'd each chosen to sleep where they had. The other three arranged themselves to accommodate this, probably without realizing why.

The three supervisory acolytes stayed to answer Asterism's questions, at Fandina's request. Apparently, Phex's pantheon hadn't really had a chance to quiz the acolytes yet, and now that they had their sun back, they were ready to try.

It was then that Phex finally realized that these three acolytes were different from the previous ones they'd been assigned. As expected, the chatty pink-toned one was their precatio, intended to manage the two pantheons. But the other two acolytes weren't the normal low-ranked lackeys. These two also held formal, even more highly educated divine positions than precatio.

Fandina introduced the green skinny one to Phex as a calator, trained to organize events, and the shorter one as a sacerdote, which Phex knew meant that it specialized in worshiper interaction. That last was both rare and unusual – Asterism had never had a sacerdote assigned to them before. Phex wondered if it meant their popularity had increased or decreased, or if the divinity anticipated trouble from believers, or if it had something to do with Tillam. Every option made him worry more.

"This spaceship is only for one tour stop," explained the

calator, who was taller than most nymphs and almost painfully thin, although not as tall as a protector imago. "We apologize that these accommodations and your practice spaces are not more luxurious. It is the price we pay for using this kind of transport."

"Why *are* we on a construction ship?" asked Tyve, sounding only mildly interested. Phex could tell from her eyes, though, that she was quite curious. She had probably tried to find out the answer already and been thwarted.

"Ah, well, yes, that has to do with our destination." The calator looked uncomfortable, cheeks speckled and crests a little wilted.

Phex stared hard at the acolytes. "It's our final stop on this tour, right?"

The precatio's crests flicked at him. "How would you know that, demigod?" Its eyes were big and purple and reminded Phex of the first Dyesi he'd ever met in person, way back in that cafe on Attacon 7.

Phex had been keeping track. "Not counting the awards performance and Dyesid Prime, this next stop would be number *nine*."

"A good number to end on." The acolyte, in customary acolyte fashion, answered Phex's question without really answering it at all.

"Are you holding out on us?" asked Tyve. "Does Tillam know *why* this ship and where we go next?"

"Yes, but not because they deserved to hear it first or because they are gods and you are only demigods." The sacerdote had a soft voice and an unusual accent.

"Why, then?" pressed Tyve.

"We think you will object."

"*You?*" Kagee looked up from his bunk, where he'd been

pretending to read the infonet and ignore the acolytes. The pronoun was ambiguous. "Which *you*?"

"Asterism," explained the precatio.

"We have the right to object?" wondered Phex.

"Of course. Just as the divinity has the right not to listen to your objection," replied the calator promptly.

Phex was beginning to wonder if this one had a sense of humor – that would be a first among the acolytes he'd met. Perhaps it had been assigned to Asterism and Tillam because of that quirk.

"Why would we object?" wondered Kagee.

"Is it not a *nice* place? Cold?" asked Berril.

"Ugly?" asked Jinyesun.

All three acolytes looked about as uncomfortable as Phex had ever seen acolytes get. As if they really did *not* want to tell them. But as they were departing soon no matter what, they should hardly care how a bunch of demigods felt.

Kagee finally said, "Forget it. We can just ask Tillam."

The precatio hissed a negative. "It should be us who bears the brunt of this decision. We have made it, after all." But then it fell quiet.

An awkward silence ensued, full of crest-wiggles too nuanced for Phex to follow.

Finally, the blue-tinged sacerdote spoke. "I'll tell them."

Its big eyes focused on Kagee. "We go to Agatay and the quarantine zone."

4

THE COST OF SALVATION

"Agatay!" Kagee jumped up out of his bunk at the name of his home world.

The acolytes' crests all straightened with something that Phex guessed was a weird kind of pride, even as they focused on a clearly agitated Kagee.

The sacerdote explained only slightly defensively. "Agatay has invited the divinity to build its first dome. Asterism will be the first performers in that dome, with Tillam following. It is quite the honor." The acolyte did not add that this would also make for the perfect symbolism around Tillam's final performance with Fortew. To have their last show together be in a new dome – how illustrative of sacred rebirth. A new dome, on a new world, would usher in a new era – expanding the divinity while simultaneously closing out an old pantheon. It was elegant and would appeal to the Dyesi's sense of temporal symmetry.

Even Phex could acknowledge the symbolism, but his attention was focused on Kagee, who was vibrating in agitation.

Kagee turned his head away from the acolytes to look at Phex almost desperately. "I can't go home."

Phex didn't know if that meant Kagee didn't want to, or would be killed if he did, or something in between the two. But he knew why Kagee was looking at him. Phex felt the same way about his home.

"The divine has no presence on Agatay and no support there." Kagee attempted Dyesi logic.

The acolytes only looked even more smug.

The calator said, "The divine didn't *use* to have support there. It's been a while since you left, grey god. Things change."

"Not *that* much, they don't," objected Kagee.

Fandina said, "What do we do?"

"Not go," answered Kagee, flat.

"Pantheons do have the right to object to tour stops," agreed the sacerdote.

"Would you like to lodge a formal objection?" asked the precatio.

"Would it do any good?" wondered Phex.

The sacerdote answered sympathetically but firmly, "No. But we can put you on record as objecting. You are, after all, still only demigods. You go where the divinity sends you, for you are the vanguard."

Phex wondered if demigods were a new version of the Dyesi's expendable nymphs.

"The divinity's number one objective is expansion," acknowledged Tyve, bitterness in her tone and the slump of her shoulders.

"Actually, that is our second objective, but it lends itself to the first."

Phex wondered what the first one was, but Kagee was

pacing the small bit of space between the lowered bunks in agitation. Back and forth.

"This is bad. This is very bad. A terrible idea, in fact." Kagee paused, close to their three new acolytes, eyes going from one impassive face to the next. Then, in desperation, he turned to Jinyesun. "Why would the Dyesi want to go to Agatay?"

But it was Fandina who answered. "The divinity wants to be everywhere. Anyone who wishes to be touched by the colors should get to have that experience once in their lifetime. Why would you deny your own people the transcendent beauty of a dome?"

"It's not my people I'm worried about."

"You think the Dyesi would be in danger?"

Kagee raised his hands to the heavens, rings twinkling in the artificial blue lighting of their quarters. He was obviously frustrated but trying to control himself in the presence of acolytes. This was an improvement – usually, Kagee would have lashed out or yelled by now.

Phex thought Asterism would be getting an earful from him later that night, though. Once they were in bed and alone, their high cantor would let himself loose to rant and complain about the situation.

"I think *we* would be in danger. I think Tillam would be in danger. Us gods are the ones being put at risk." He pointed his whole hand, as if it were a crest of accusation, at the calator acolyte. If it was in charge of events, it would be responsible for this whole plan to build a dome, and use it, on Agatay.

"Did you forget that gods aren't actually immortal? You Dyesi like to pretend that we are. But your imaginary universe and pretty monikers won't stop us from bleeding. From dying. Are you ignoring the lesson Fortew is teaching right now?" Kagee was being very blunt, using Dyesi informal register to the point of rudeness.

"You think Agatay would destroy gods!" The sacerdote's crests wilted and its eyes went very wide, suggesting it was genuinely shocked at the idea.

"Gods, worshipers, Dyesi, dome. All of it, all at once if they felt like it. They play only one game on my home world – politics. And they play that game violently."

The calator had apparently latched on to only one aspect of Kagee's rant. "Your people would destroy a *dome*?" It practically hissed, its crests low with fear and fury.

Kagee said, deadpan, "They have exploded more for less."

"They would *bomb* a sacred artistic space?" Jinyesun spoke then, and its crests were flat back in horror. Fandina too looked appalled at the idea.

Phex wondered sometimes at their innocence. Just because the Dyesi were a nonviolent species, they could not wander around the galaxy assuming everyone else was similarly inclined. Surely, they knew that?

Kagee gave a sigh. "*Nothing* is sacred on Agatay. Certainly not a glorified entertainment pod, occupied by gods or not."

The calator shook its head. "That's not possible. No one in the history of the divinity has ever intentionally destroyed a dome. That is a preposterous notion. It is, in fact, somewhat psychologically impossible."

"Have you ever put a dome where it was unwanted?"

"There is no such thing as an unwanted dome."

The sacerdote reminded them. "We have been *invited* to Agatay."

"By which faction?"

"Does that matter? We have an *invitation*."

Kagee looked at the three Dyesi like they were certifiably crazy. "Did you not research my planet at all? There is a noble history of mass killings, particularly in assembly areas. Bombings with high casualty numbers are frequent occurrences. My people make no distinction between military and civilian the way other cultures do. Everyone serves and everyone fights, and so everyone is considered a fighting force and a threat."

The sacerdote's crests went neutral. It looked like it too was attempting patience. "Yes, we know Agatay has a dwindling highly violent population. There is only one habitable continent on your home world, and that has kept your numbers suppressed throughout your planetary history, and this, in turn, has allowed and encouraged mass conscription."

Kagee said flatly, "We are a small population because we spend so much of our time killing each other. It is not a *nice* place, my home planet. Why would the divinity want to go there at all?"

"Because it is places like Agatay that need divine salvation the most."

Kagee threw his hands up into the air and collapsed next of Phex on his bunk. "You talk some sense into them."

"Well, now we know why they moved us to this space barge," said Tyve. "Closest thing to a tank that the divinity can get."

The calator said, "We go to launch a new dome into existence. That means we have to build it first. This is a construction barge. Is it not a great honor, that you will be the first to sing in a new dome?"

"Not if you're sending us to die there," said Kagee. "I left my planet specifically because of this kind of attitude. I don't believe that it is noble to die for a cause, certainly not someone else's."

The sacerdote still seemed, crest-wise, the most sympathetic to Kagee's distress. Nevertheless, it too was ultimately unmoved. "No? Well, gods are never believers, we know that. And the divinity does not think you will die for this dome. In fact, we think quite the opposite."

"Yes, yes, the divinity brings *salvation*." Tyve waved a hand in the air dismissively but she looked worried. Kagee had at least convinced *her* that this was a dangerous venture.

Berril hadn't said anything so far. She climbed down off her bunk and came to squeeze between Phex and Kagee, putting her head on Kagee's shoulder. Phex found her spicy sweet smell comforting.

Kagee grumbled at her but calmed down a little. At least he didn't jump up and start pacing again. "Does the faction who invited the divine to Agatay know that I am part of Asterism?"

The sacerdote answered calmly, "They know you're from Agatay. We think that pride is partly why they invited us. You are a popular cantor throughout much of the galaxy now, Demigod Kagee. Among Asterism's popularity rankings, you are second only to Berril – in the nearest divine sector to Agatay."

"You're telling me I have a high number of believers already in my home space?"

"It's common for the visually familiar to have highest appeal in any given sector," said the sacerdote, who should know.

Berril spoke up then. "That's why I'm always the most popular with chiropteran species."

"You're usually the most popular in general because you're adorable," said Tyve, stalwart.

Kagee didn't care much about popularity numbers. "I didn't ask if they knew *what* I was, acolyte. I asked if they knew *who* I was. My name. Did you tell them my full real name? Not my god name but the one on my ident?"

"Yes."

"Well, poop." Kagee put his head in his hands, slumping forward.

Berril stopped leaning on him and petted his back in little circles with her small hand.

"Could that mean the faction your family supports is in power?" asked Phex, who only knew how Wheel power struggles worked but assumed this was similar.

"Or it could mean exactly the opposite. Either way we are screwed, because I don't get along with any of them." Kagee looked up at the sacerdote with hard grey eyes. "Did the divinity recruit me because they saw me as representing an opportunity to expand to Agatay? Because that is a truly *terrible* idea."

"High cantor is *high cantor*. Market capacity and draw is always a secondary consideration, but primarily you are a god because we care about the colors you can sing."

Fandina said quickly, translating to make sure Kagee understood, "You were recruited for your talent, just like the rest of us."

"It wouldn't hurt, though, that you are a member of a species that has not yet accepted the divine into its culture." That was Jinyesun being brutally honest.

Phex didn't object or try to mitigate their blunt sifter's statement. Kagee could take it. But Phex still winced internally at the disappointment on his high cantor's face.

"Do you know which faction is currently in power?" Kagee asked the acolytes.

"No," said all three in unison, as though it didn't really matter to them. And it probably didn't.

"And the infonet won't have that information easily

accessible." Kagee sighed. "Not that it matters. It might change six times on our way out there and another two while the dome is being built."

"How long does it take to construct a dome?" Phex wondered.

"Only a few weeks," assured the calator.

"Weeks? We will be spending *weeks* on Agatay?" Kagee flopped backward on Phex's bed.

Phex, took a breath and stood, facing the acolytes. "You won't reconsider this plan? The new dome? Agatay? Us performing there?"

"The divinity has decided," confirmed the calator.

Phex clicked. "Then there is no further point in continuing this conversation. Please fetch us for the next mealtime, and we will discuss the practice schedule, travel times, and fold then – over dinner with Tillam."

The three acolytes looked relieved. They clicked and gave honorific crest-wiggles before hurrying away.

Kagee flailed about on Phex's cot like he was being fried in a skillet.

"Drama monger," said Phex affectionately.

"But Phex," whined Kagee, "this is *such* a bad idea."

Tyve made a sympathetic cooing noise. "I'm sure the divinity has had worse."

"I highly doubt that."

"We'll need to warn Tillam," said Phex. "And the bodyguards. I don't think the divinity is taking this seriously enough."

"Now?" asked Berril.

"No. Missit is gone to visit Fortew with Bob – best to do

this all at once, so you aren't fielding the same questions over and over again." Phex reached for a hair stick to put his hair up out of the way – he had nobody to impress at the moment.

"There isn't much info on Agatay on the net, Tillam is going to have questions," said Tyve.

"Probably do already, since they knew we were going before we did," added Phex.

"Well, some of Tillam." Jinyesun was likely thinking of Yorunlee who, didn't seem to be interested in anything at all these days. Phex worried about that sifter. Was it a kind of Dyesi depression or sorrow over Fortew or just its personality?

Phex flopped back next to Kagee and stared up at the underside of Tyve's bunk. "I'm still confused. I thought Agatay was like the Wheel. Too xenophobic for the divine to make inroads. I can't see why *any* political faction would benefit from inviting a dome to be built and the Dyesi to visit. Even with gods along. Especially with gods."

Kagee said, "We aren't as closed off as your home space. But there is definitely a strategy of some kind in play. From whoever invited the divinity. We need to figure out what it is and who stands to benefit. I wish I still had contacts back on my home world."

"You cut ties?"

"They were cut for me. Once I found out I was sterilized without my knowledge or consent, I would have cut the rest myself."

"If you're an outcast, why does it matter which faction is in power or who invited us?" Phex understood *outcast* to mean a person entirely unnecessary to the functioning of the main culture. As a Wheel outcast, he'd been considered a nonhuman – by default no part of any kind of power struggle because he had no power whatsoever himself. He had been useful as a crudrat, a tool for the function of a space station. Like a soup ladle. His identity, present or absent, had no impact on the station he'd occupied for the first ten years of his life. Clearly, Kagee's kind of *outcast* was materially different from Phex's.

Kagee explained. "I am still me. I still have the name and the blood connections. I was an active proxy before I left to become a god. There is power in being trained to protect and kill. I had help getting off-planet. I even still have…" He paused, as if searching for the right word in Dyesi. "… *friends* who I left behind."

Phex clicked, understanding a little better. He, after all, had none of those things.

Kagee was saying, much as he too was a refugee and an exile like Phex, that he still had tethers to his home – emotional, physical, intellectual. Kagee still *felt* something for Agatay and its people. Unlike Phex, who was indifferent to the Wheel – he had nothing and no one left behind. He hadn't had friends among his fellow crudrats. He hadn't been good enough to warrant even their respect, big-boned and comparatively clumsy. He hadn't been expected to last very long. Crudrats didn't make friends with those destined to die young on the blades. What would be the point of that?

Kagee continued. "This could either be my family using my godhood as a stepping-stone within their faction. Or it could be the faction itself using me for political gain. Or it could be our political enemies using me so that when the dome falls and this whole endeavor is a failure, I can be blamed, and my faction and family will lose power because of me. This is a no-win situation for me and us, no matter what. No one is thinking this through properly. Least of all the Dyesi."

Berril said, tentatively, "But Agatay knows divinity? I

mean, you heard godsong, Kagee, didn't you? Otherwise, why did you leave to become one of us?"

"It was all done in secret. We listened privately and got into trouble if we were caught. But there was a black market in godsong vids and beams. For all us fans on Agatay, it was a mere pipe dream to someday see a live dome in person. Those of us who worshiped did so in secrecy. We knew we would have to flee Agatay if we ever wished to meet gods, let alone become one. Circumstances drove me off-world. I never wished to become the first of my species on a dais. I certainly never expected to go home again representing for the cause."

Jinyesun said, "Yes, but there was more than just you back on Agatay. You said *we*, and you said *secret*."

Kagee nodded. "Me and some..." He paused, again like he was looking for the right word. "...*friends*." The Dyesi term sounded uncomfortable in his mouth.

Phex wondered what Kagee really wanted to say. Probably an Agatay word that had no direct translation.

"Perhaps now there are even more worshipers on Agatay? It's been a few years since you left. The divinity always monitors beaming demographics and numbers, especially in parts of the galaxy where the domes have not yet reached." Jinyesun did not sound worried. It seemed to be the least concerned and the least convinced of the danger inherent in their next tour stop. Jin had faith in the divinity and its power.

Phex was not reassured by this. He always thought of Jinyesun as particularly innocent. Jin didn't understand how bad the universe could get. It was one of the few things Jin didn't *want* to understand.

"You aren't worried that they're sending us, and Tillam, to the front lines?" Kagee asked their two sifters.

Phex shivered, a burst of dread fluttering his stomach as

he latched on to something Kagee had said before, to the acolytes. "Violent society. Plus, Agatay is ex-core with natural evolution."

Kagee stared at him. "Yes. Your point?"

"Would that include dark-matter explosions and dark-energy weaponry use?" he asked, but his skin prickled with certainty.

"Of course."

"Holy divine gods," swore Tyve, following Phex's line of thought and reacting appropriately.

"What?" said Kagee, annoyed with *them* now.

"I bet Agatay has particularly advanced medical operations designed for Sapiens with flawed genetic structures," said Tyve, whose family was, after all, in the medical field.

"Hey, now, what do you mean by *flawed*?" protested Kagee.

Phex blinked at him rapidly.

"Ah, right, I'm color-blind. I get your point. And yes, of course we do. Everyone knows the more violent the society, the more advanced the medical profession in order to compensate. We can't all be universal experts in plastic surgery or fetal genetic manipulation like some species I could name."

Phex, Jinyesun, and Fandina shared a look.

"If he hates his home world," wondered Jin, "why does he defend it so?"

"I don't hate it. I just don't want to go back. Phex, make your point."

Phex was a little annoyed Kagee hadn't caught on. Then again, it was probably too close to home for him to fully comprehend the ramifications of what his own people could do that was *good* for the divinity. Good for the galaxy, even.

"I bet a society such as yours is pretty great at treating non-baryonic bronchopulmonary attrition."

"Crud lung? Yes, of course. Ah. Fortew." Kagee paused, staring at Phex. "You think the Dyesi are building a dome on my home world because one god is sick?"

"It is a great excuse to send him there, and we have to wait around while the dome is built. He has time to get comprehensive treatment."

Kagee said to Jin and Fandina, "Your people are crazy. What a reason to go to a cesspit like Agatay."

"It's that bad?"

"It's worse than you could possibly imagine. Especially you two."

The two Dyesi did not take that amiss. It was not an insult that they could not understand the ugliness in the galaxy. It was a privilege. And they both knew it.

Phex sighed. "How are we going to explain this to Tillam?"

"Very carefully," said Berril.

Pretty much everyone said in unison, "You do it," to her.

"Bad news should come in cute packages," added Tyve.

Berril rolled her eyes and accepted her fate.

Phex said, "I'll go get Missit onto our side and check up on Fortew. Which way is medical?"

Fortew looked better than he had in a while. The move to the bigger ship was already having some beneficial effect on his system. He was wearing a kind of air bubble, which presumably the medics could pump full of benevolent gasses. It was like a shiny sphere over his whole head, generated by a tight collar. It was mostly filled with Fortew's hair, fluffing and floating about. It looked rather silly, but his cheeks actually had some healthy color to them for the first time in a long while.

The murmel, clearly in a magnanimous mood, was sitting in Fortew's lap, giving herself a good neck scratch with one of her back legs. This contorted her into a shape graces would envy.

"You look good," said Phex to the god, meaning it. He was aware of Missit, of course, right there like a gravity well sucking at Phex's attention, but he tried to focus on Fortew.

"Flatterer," said Fortew. "I look *less bad*, you might as well say. But I feel more comfortable than I have in a while."

"You know why we're on this ship and where we're going?" Phex asked.

"I do."

Phex nodded. "I have to pull Missit away for a moment. We need to talk to Tillam about this. It's serious, it should happen as a group. Missit can fill you in later."

"Is he this intense about everything?" Fortew asked Missit.

Missit waggled his eyebrows. "Yes, *every*thing."

Phex felt himself get hot.

Fortew looked cheeky and amused. "How does he kiss, then?"

Missit, conspiratorial, glanced at Phex to see how he'd react to them talking about him in front of him. "Like he's in a kitchen."

Fortew burst out laughing. The murmel chittered at him in annoyance for jiggling the lap she had rightfully claimed for murmel-kind.

"What?" Phex was both embarrassed and confused. Why were they talking about this stuff? Did Missit not realize how serious their situation was? If anyone could put a stop to this crazy divine plan, it was Tillam. The divinity wasn't going to build this dome if Tillam refused to perform there.

Missit pointedly turned to talk only to Fortew. "Thorough and deliberate and meticulous and caring."

"You make it sound like I'm doing the dishes," said Phex. Thinking that he kissed Missit like that because he liked the shape of his mouth and enjoyed the luxury of exploring it. The very mouth that at this moment was going to keep on talking and embarrassing him. His ears felt hot, even the surgically enhanced tips.

"No, it's great. I've never been the focus of anyone's intensity like that before." Missit was still looking at Fortew. "It's like being kissed by a waterfall. Relentlessly wonderful."

Phex wondered who else Missit had kissed for comparison.

Fortew looked wistful and sad. "That sounds nice."

Missit clicked. "It *is* nice. It's delicious."

Now Phex was really embarrassed and a little turned on. He was getting a glimpse into what these two must have once been like together – irreverent and a lot of trouble, but a lot of fun. Their dynamic must have once been magical, back before Fortew fell ill.

"I'm jealous," said Fortew, teasing. "He's young. I bet his stamina is excellent." Fortew was over a decade older than Phex and a major god. Phex could not possibly tease him back, even if he knew how.

"I'm not sharing," replied Missit, calmly.

"Do I have a say in any of this?" Phex asked, plaintive, trying to distract them.

"Hush, sweetie, the adults are talking."

Phex licked his lips and looked away from the two gods, frowned to hide a smile. Then he sighed and burst their bubble. "Do you realize that Agatay might have the best treatment options for Fortew?"

"The acolytes mentioned something to that effect," said Fortew.

"Yes!" crowed Missit, eyes shining, "Isn't it glorious? He might not die."

Fortew patted Missit's hand. "But if it's transplant surgery, I won't ever sing again."

"Small price to pay," insisted Missit.

Phex realized this was all for naught. It didn't matter what Kagee said about Agatay. If the divinity had already told Tillam that Agatay might be able to save Fortew, then Tillam would vote to go there no matter what, despite any danger. There would be no discussion. Phex couldn't fault them for that. If it were a member of his pantheon lying in that medical bay, he would make the same decision. If it were Missit... Well, he couldn't even think about that possibility.

"Never mind," said Phex to Missit. "You stay here." Were he a different kind of person, he would have added an endearment. But Fortew smiled at him and Missit blushed in such a way that suggested they both could hear the affection in his voice.

"You *don't* need me to come back for the discussion?"

"I just realized, there isn't really going to be one. Zil can fill you both in later."

Missit smiled winsomely up at him. "Okay, baby, see you at dinner."

"I'll make sure one of the acolytes comes to fetch you."

"Yay! Thank you."

Fortew cocked his head inside the bubble and narrowed his eyes conspiratorially at Missit. "Tell me more about Phex's *intensity*."

Missit took a careful seat on the bed next to him and

scratched the murmel between her ears. "What do you want to know?"

Phex said, quickly, "I'm going now."

They ignored him.

Phex went.

In the end, Berril and Kagee went to talk with Tillam without the rest of Asterism. Phex and Tyve went to explain the situation to the bodyguards.

As expected, Tillam would not side with them in objecting to visiting Agatay. Without Tillam's backing, they stood no chance of changing the divinity's mind.

Kagee returned upset but Berril was understanding.

"If it were you in that bed, Kagee, I'd take the risk too," she explained. "And you'd do it for me. You can't say you wouldn't."

Kagee looked like he *wanted* to say that. But this was Berril. Anyone else but Berril making the point and he would have denied their value in his life, true or not. But Berril was too sweet for that kind of rejection.

Kagee looked frustrated enough to cry.

Phex understood that feeling. The bodyguards had been equally obtuse, even Quasilun. Especially Quasilun.

The imago had seemed to find Phex's objections to Agatay amusing. As if he and Tyve were whiny children. Phex was a little humiliated by this reaction. Usually, the bodyguards, at least, took him seriously. They took his concerns about Asterism's safety and threat under advisement. They worried, just like he did, about the security of the pantheons. There they were, headed into the most dangerous situation yet, and the bodyguards were acting just like the acolytes.

They simply did not believe that anyone, no matter how violent the planet, would intentionally destroy a dome.

The dome was sacred.

The dome was special.

No dome had ever been bombed. No dome had ever been destroyed, not with worshipers and gods inside it. Not even empty. Because such a thing had never happened, everyone believed it never *could* happen. The bodyguards thought only in terms of danger from the fixed. They were not generals to strategize the idea of a whole political faction moving against them. Guerilla warfare and mass killings were beyond their ken. Phex could understand that – he didn't *want* to think about it either. But he trusted Kagee to know his own people far better than the Dyesi did. He had to assume this tour stop put them all at very great risk. But the more they tried to convince others, the less recourse they seemed to have.

Now they were all frustrated, and there was a prevailing feeling that it was Asterism against everyone else – Tillam, the acolytes, the bodyguards. It was as if they believed in some wild conspiracy, saw truth that everyone thought was hysteria.

"How long do we have before we are summoned for food?" asked Phex.

"A couple hours still," answered Fandina, checking its ident.

Phex said, because he thought it would make them all feel better, "You know where the new practice room is?"

"Of course," said Jinyesun – they had, after all been aboard longer than Phex.

"Let's go practice, shall we?" Phex suggested.

Kagee still looked annoyed, but it would do him good, too. He never realized how much singing always helped him relax, but Phex noticed after a session that his shoulders were less tense and he fluttered his fingers less.

"Yes, please," said Fandina, jumping down from its bunk.

Berril and Tyve were game. They were graces, always hungry for movement when they had been still for too long.

"Can we work on a new song?" Kagee asked, by way of agreement.

"I think that's a great idea," said Tyve, patting his shoulder.

Kagee grumbled at her. "Don't be condescending."

Tyve flashed one claw at him sarcastically.

"Let's go, then," said Fandina leading the way.

Phex was pleased his distraction tactic was working.

5

CANTOR GOT YOUR TONGUE?

That night, Phex made the rounds, tucking his pantheon into their new cots. He'd never admit such a thing out loud, but there was something innately satisfying about making sure his favorite people were safe in the dark.

Six of them in one small space should have been challenging, but they were as much a pantheon in cohabitation as they were up on the dais. Before bed, they conducted automatic duets, mirroring each other with personal ritual, sometimes together, sometimes apart, gracefully sidestepping and waltzing around, as they abluted before sleep. Phex always waited for the other five to go first before he washed up and dealt with his mass of blue hair. Hair was inevitably time-consuming for gods – they tended to have so much of it.

Then, after the lights cycled down, Phex made the tuck-in rounds. He checked the back set of three bunks first. Berril, in the top one, had a high metabolism and shivered easily. Phex had to make certain her blanket covered her properly. He tucked it in around her tiny feet, and she chirped at him happily.

"Night, Phex."

"You warm enough?"

"You ask me that every night."

"You get cold."

"I'm good, thank you."

"Fandina?"

The Dyesi was in the middle bunk, underneath Berril. But the sifter was already asleep. Dyesi dozed off easily, as if they never worried about anything. It was a gift Phex envied.

Kagee, in the lowest bunk, cracked one eye and glared at him.

Phex wouldn't dare tuck him in, but he did do a quick visual evaluation to make sure the high cantor was safe in his cot.

Kagee rolled onto his side and presented his back to Phex.

Phex turned to Jinyesun in the top bunk nearer the door. Jin gave him a faint crest-wiggle. Phex patted the Dyesi's shoulder gently. He didn't linger, though – Jin didn't like fuss.

Tyve, in the middle bunk, yanked him down for a sleepy hug.

"You have water?" he checked. She got thirsty at night.

"Mmm," she murmured, which he took as agreement.

Phex climbed into his own bed at last, satisfied that he had done his due diligence.

His bed felt cold and empty. Usually, Missit was already in it, waiting for him. Fortunately, he didn't have to wait long. Even though they were on a new ship, Missit had already figured out how to sneak around.

"You're all asleep early," said a golden voice.

There was a brief arc of light from the hallway as Missit pushed the curtain aside and came in. He unwound Dimsum from his neck and dropped her unceremoniously into Tyve's bunk. Both the murmel and the Jakaa Nova protested but settled. Dimsum curled behind Tyve's knees, and then proceeded to give herself a violent tongue bath, shaking the flimsy folding cot.

"Must you?" said Tyve to the blue beastie.

"Settle," growled Phex, using the old crudrat command.

The bath did not pause. The murmel had already forgotten that she'd once had to work for a living. Or she just liked to ignore Phex. Spoiled little thing.

"We aren't sleeping early, you're late," Kagee grumbled to Missit, but then fell, like the others, into tired silence.

One of the things Asterism collectively tried not to do was acknowledge Missit's presence at night. It was as if they were all still pretending he never showed up. As if he were a shared hallucination.

Phex made as much room as he could for the hallucination, and Missit squeezed himself in easily – as if he were smaller and less important than everyone knew him to be.

He tucked his cold feet between Phex's legs and arranged Phex's arm under his head in exactly the way he preferred. His hair was braided back, but strands still got caught on Phex's lips and chin. Phex wondered if they were strands of privilege or obligation.

"You're here again?" he said, into the hair.

"Where else would I possibly be?" was Missit's reply, but then he added, "Could we go somewhere else, just us, for a bit?" Phex could hear the pleading but also the desperation. He felt it too – they hadn't been alone together in days. It felt like just under his skin itched and Missit's strong hands were the only thing that might soothe it.

"It's a new ship, Missit."

"I know a place."

Phex was weak in the face of both their need. He

followed Missit out of bed and into the hallway. Behind them he heard Tyve snort.

Missit's *place* was a kind of storage facility. This being a construction barge, there were plenty of compartments full of tools, drones, and equipment locked down for transport. This one seemed particularly cluttered, full of secrets, smelling musty and neglected.

It was long and deep. The corner farthest from the curtained doorway was very dark and shielded from view.

It was cold, too, but Missit had already sourced and piled up a nest of Dyesi woven blankets. He pushed Phex down into them. Phex could easily have resisted but didn't, and got a lap full of squirming Missit for his acquiescence.

Phex swallowed Missit's needy noises with his own mouth – this place may be secluded, but it wasn't soundproof. He wondered if there would ever be a time when he could relax and hear what Missit's stunning golden voice sounded like in pure pleasure.

Missit's hands came up to bracket Phex's face. This was new – it warranted caution. Phex paused and pressed their foreheads together, listening to their rough breathing, unable to distinguish whose was whose.

Missit's eyes stayed closed. A moment of recovery? Phex absorbed that. The effect he had on this god, the way Missit felt in his arms, the pressure of their heads together. This transient gift.

Normally, Phex wouldn't have said anything – he would have allowed the distance and numbness to develop between them. This time, he asked.

"What is it?"

"I just want this every day. I don't want to sneak around. I don't want to try to be quiet, or hide in storage closets, or…" Missit was whining.

"But we—"

Missit cut him off. "I know why. I know we can't do it any differently. I'm not complaining just to complain. It's only, this is *it*. For me. This is the *thing* I want, more than the dais, I think, sometimes. This, with you, it's the only time I feel real, like I actually exist in my own skin, not just under a dome. The rest of the time, it always feels like I must be a god."

Missit leaned back, both hands still on Phex's face, then darted forward to peck Phex's lips so quickly, Phex had no time to respond. He waited patiently to see what the mercurial god would do next. Maybe not a *god* right now, just a boy?

Missit's eyes were now intent on Phex's. Phex really looked into them, not getting distracted by gold flecks, trying to understand Missit's expression, comprehend what he was trying to communicate.

To Phex, Missit was always a god, always something unachievable. Missit had descended to earth to fraternize with a flawed mortal like Phex. Confusing but acceptable as a temporary state. But in that moment, Phex understood, Missit saw him differently. Saw *them* differently. In the eternal quest for meaning, Phex had somehow become Missit's truth. Missit believed in him. Not like worshipers believed in gods, or acolytes believed in the divinity, but like scientists believed in the universe. Like travelers believed in the stars. This was pure trust, not wishes or fantasy, and more humbling and overwhelming than burning desire.

But if their being together was not something either one entirely controlled, how could they not, inevitably, betray that trust? This thing they had accidentally built had no foundation.

Phex turned away from those terribly mortal yearning eyes and scattered kisses down Missit's neck. He peppered

Missit's smooth skin with understanding. He closed his own eyes against the gold and the Dyesi-curated flesh, against the powerful voice and the cultivated charisma. With hands and mind he stripped Missit of divine raiments, of clothing and artifice. Missit became naked against him in all ways, grounded by him. The Missit underneath it all was lonely and lost, passionate and permissive, loving and trusting – and always had been. It wasn't Missit who'd held up godliness as a barrier between them – it was Phex. And that did both of them an injustice.

They were sneaking and hiding and risking everything. If they really did care, if they really did love, whatever form that took, it wasn't fair to either of them to think their relationship lesser by comparison to Missit's godhood. If Missit thought they were more important, then so would Phex.

Phex licked around Missit's collarbones and bit softly at his Adam's apple. He transferred his reverence for Missit's state to Missit's body. He worshiped like no divine believer ever could, because to do this properly, he had to trust that he and Missit were equal. He had to trust Missit.

Missit arched and pressed as close as he could get, eager and hopeful.

"Kiss me more."

Phex kissed, for the first time obedient to the boy, not the god.

The pantheon's practice room was a converted storage bay.

It was massive but not dome-shaped. It had been cleared of everything and hastily floored with something loosely resembling dais material. Phex would be unable to practice any of his wall runs or crudrat-based tricks, because nothing was curved properly. There was a sifting booth like the ones they'd learned in as potentials, so cantors could practice separately. Even though it was bigger than their facilities on the tourship, it was a much less efficient use of space. It would be challenging for both Tillam and Asterism to rehearse at the same time, let alone for Missit and Phex to work on their duet. They would need to set up a rotating schedule.

The space hadn't any dome paneling, either. Or, more properly, it did, but only one.

There was a single large panel of that pearly-grey reflective material that Phex had become accustomed to over the years. Now he knew this was a dead imago's carapace, its solitary presence seemed a bit eerie. It felt like the whole echoing practice chamber was a memorial to one dead Dyesi.

Phex hadn't told his pantheon about the origin of the dome tech. He wasn't sure how they would react. Jinyesun and Fandina already knew, of course.

"Look! How polite of them, they left us the keyskin," said Fandina, pleased to see the huge scale-like object leaning against one wall.

"It's a piece for the new dome?" Berril ran over to it in excitement, like she hadn't seen a million of them before. She unfolded her wings and ran her feathers over the surface, dusting it off. "How pretty it is alone, like gallery artwork."

"Leave it, please, Berril," said Phex, possibly a little too sharply. It creeped him out, her so close to death like that. He'd have to get over that feeling.

Jin gave him a funny crest-wiggle. Confused that Phex would be sharp with Berril, of all people.

Phex winced.

"That's not just any piece, that's the *keyskin*," explained Fandina. "It's the one that all the others will key off of. The keyskin is the one part of any dome that's actually native to

Dyesid Prime. From that, all the others for the new dome will be cloned."

Cloned, were they? Well, that explained how the insides of all the domes were a consistent color and shape, while the ones in the caves were not. It meant that this one panel alone was taken from a dead imago. All the others would be mere copies of it. It also explained how the experience inside a dome was so consistent and so different from the caves. Each dome was basically cut from the same cloth, but the caves were a patchwork.

Quasilun had said once that Fandina was destined to become a matriarch among imagoes. Phex wondered if Fandina was also destined to become a keyskin. If decades in the future, some other pantheon would be boarding a ship to travel to a dome made from the cloned carapace of *his* dear friend – a reflective eulogy to a pantheon long gone and a god of a previous generation.

"Is this due reverence?" Phex wondered. "Do you care that this is your future?" he asked his sifters.

"To bring color to an entire galaxy, can you think of a better afterlife?" Fandina was sanguine.

Jin's crests were neutral and the others just looked confused.

Dyesi logic in all things, even death. Phex wasn't even surprised.

Perhaps the domes were less graveyards than they were beacons of memory. Perhaps keyskins were odes to imagoes who never truly died but lived on to react to the skinsift of gods brave enough to perform under them.

"Let's get started," said Phex, not wanting to think about it anymore.

They spent a good hour working on a new song, before

deciding it was a little too much brain strain in this new practice room, on a new ship, newly reunited.

They switched to running through a regular rehearsal and well-known godsongs. Phex pretended to do many of his tricks, and struggled to make his marks when gracing as a result, because everything was timed to flips he could no longer execute.

They decided to cool down with one of Tillam's songs, just for fun.

Of course, Missit stuck his head in just as Kagee opened the first verse.

"Can I play?" asked Missit, of Kagee.

Kagee was still struggling to process an unexpected trip home. He had relaxed a little but not entirely, and was happy to be relieved of high cantor duties.

"I'm gonna go bask in the glory of having our quarters entirely to myself for *ten whole minutes*," he declared with a glower that suggested he better get *ten whole minutes*, or heads would roll.

"You can have fifteen," said Missit magnanimously. He deposited the murmel and shooed her away before taking Kagee's place on the makeshift dais.

"You really want to sing with us?" Berril was nervous.

"Are you sure?" pressed Jinyesun, equally nervous.

Tyve looked amused.

Fandina's crests shivered with excited nerves.

Phex couldn't fathom why they were still uncomfortable around Missit. Missit, who sneaked into his bed and shoved cold feet between his legs. Missit, who belched ridiculously loudly when the drinks were fizzy. Missit, who was never serious about anything.

Phex supposed that was some *other* Missit. Mortal Missit.

His friend and lover. This was Missit the high cantor, god of gods.

So Phex said softly, "Let's do it."

It was Tillam's song, and having been on tour with Tillam, Asterism hadn't performed it since their potential days. But Phex was accustomed to singing it now, so it was only the graces who had to reinvent their part of the equation.

Tyve and Berril didn't even try to imitate Zil and Tern. Although they probably could have done an adequate job. Over the years, Tillam's graces had toned down the complexity and acrobatic strain of their movements. They were getting older and they couldn't risk the flips and jumps and catches that came so easily to Asterism and its chiropteran. Besides, Tillam had always been a pantheon more about cantor than grace.

But even though they *could* do it, Berril and Tyve chose not to attempt the original choreography. Instead, they adapted bits and chunks of Asterism's other pieces, and then melded and combined these with some fun experimental moves.

The result was a performance that, under a dome, would have looked nothing like Tillam's original, although it didn't *sound* too far off.

Missit clearly had fun with it and them. He really seemed to enjoy recoloring his own old songs. It was as if, when performing with a different pantheon, he actually thought about and experienced his own godsongs in entirely new ways. A song he had been singing for over a decade could be given new life.

They could only see what patterns and colors they were creating in a limited way, when facing the keyskin. Thus, only at certain points in the performance did they even know what they were doing as gods. That was strange. Phex hadn't realized until that moment how much of the dome around him was something he reacted to, even if only by instinct and with his peripheral vision.

This turned out to be a good thing, since without a dome, there was no possibility of godsong or godfix, and they ended up not being alone after all.

Phex only really registered that they had an audience after they ended the piece. But seeing who it was and knowing what he and Missit could do with their voices together, he had reason to be grateful.

Most of the bodyguards had collected to watch near the entrance. Some of the spaceship's complement were there too, and all three of their supervisory acolytes.

"That was fun," said Missit, not really caring that they'd been observed, looking up at Phex with big, happy eyes.

Phex privately agreed.

Berril and Tyve were both smiling. Jin and Fandina were puffy-crested with delight. Everyone had enjoyed themselves.

"It's an honor to sift for you," said Jinyesun to Missit.

"Don't bother with ritual words, sweetie. We're all friends here." Missit grinned at the Dyesi. "One more time?"

"Yes, please!" called someone from the audience.

They did the whole song a second time. If possible, it was even more enjoyable.

Berril stumbled once but only grinned hugely, having to deploy her wings at an inopportune moment to keep her balance.

Then Missit changed the pace on them in the last chorus, so they all had to slow down. The graces looked a bit like they were wading through pudding, which caused both them and Missit to fall into a fit of giggles after the last note.

Jin and Fandina skinsifted beautifully through it all. It was a joy to get to simply watch them and not have his gaze constantly drawn to the glory of what they did to a dome. Just the six of them made for a simple, focused beauty, but beautiful nonetheless. It reminded Phex of the first time he'd seen a Dyesi sift in person – purple eyes and a cafe cupola on a forgotten moon in an obscure corner of the galaxy.

They stopped after the second round and stretched. Their impromptu audience gave them an impromptu round of applause – claps, yells, bows, or clicks, depending on their cultural background. Then they all left, quietly and efficiently, back about their duties.

Only the three acolytes came up to them. "That was rather enjoyable, thank you."

"We were only playing," explained Tyve, a touch defensively.

"That's good. Gods should have fun with the colors when they can. And gods are allowed to play with other pantheons on occasion. Interesting and divine things can result. We wouldn't want to stifle immortal creativity," said the precatio.

"As expected, Missit is wonderful no matter what pantheon he sings with," said the sacerdote.

Missit blushed and dipped his head.

Phex thought it was endearing that praise could still delight and embarrass Missit even after so long a god.

"Phex and I have been singing together for a while now. I am accustomed to his low cantor."

"Yes," agreed the precatio, familiar purple eyes delighted. "The divinity is lucky to have recruited a Sapien so flexible in so many ways. I understand he can also grace."

Tyve said quickly, "He can."

Phex hastily added, "Not good enough to actually *be* a grace. And only in a real dome."

"But you have a keyskin right there."

"It is the shape at issue, not the tech," Tyve explained, gesturing at the flat walls.

"Ah, well, I supposed we shall have to wait to see what you mean by that," said the green calator.

"You haven't watched any vids of Asterism?" That was Tyve, confused. Because surely part of Asterism's reputation was built on Phex's ability to shift roles and do grace tricks.

"Of course not. We acolytes get to enjoy the privilege of live performances, not to mention experiencing new and interesting variations on the divinity in action. It is why we do what we do. Getting to see something like what you just did in person – the great god Missit singing with demigods. *That* is why many of us join the divinity. It is a privilege we would not waste on watching mere recordings."

Missit pressed his lips together and made a very silly face at such a pompous attitude.

Tyve said quickly, "Well, I guess you'll have to wait and be surprised, then, next dome."

"Next dome," agreed the precatio with a click. "The new dome. It is all *very* exciting."

Phex said quickly, even though Kagee was not there, "Could we not talk about that? It's a delicate subject right now."

The three acolytes looked properly chastised. "Of course. Our mistake. You did state your objections. We shall try to be respectful of your wishes."

"Even as you ignore them," muttered Tyve under her breath.

"Tyve," warned Phex in a low, gravelly voice.

"Sorry, Phex," said Tyve.

Missit, sensitive to the mood, brought the subject back around to himself. "I did good, then?"

"Of course you did," praised the sacerdote. "When have you ever disappointed? Our great golden god."

"Please stop," said Phex, "he is more than enough to handle already."

"What?" the acolyte was shocked.

"You love it," said Missit.

Which was true. Phex kind of did love it when people said how wonderful Missit was. Or any of his pantheon. It was praise of his own abilities that made him uncomfortable.

Phex took a deep breath. "Dinner?" he suggested hopefully.

Everyone was at dinner except for Fortew. Seven bodyguards, five members of Tillam, and six of Asterism. There was no way for them all to sit together, even in the construction vessel's larger galley. Ladles or no ladles. So, they broke into groups. Phex ended up eating with Missit, Jin, Fandina, Kagee, Tern, Itrio, Bob, and the chatty pink-tinged precatio with the big purple eyes. The murmel lurked under the table hopefully. She only really ate crud, but she liked to taste whatever everyone else was eating – just in case.

Phex had never learned the name of the Dyesi with the purple eyes who initially recruited him, so he couldn't ask if the two were related or from the same cave. But he did wonder. He hadn't seen very many Dyesi with such dark purple eye color.

The precatio's name turned out to be Ohongshe, and it solved Phex's curiosity rather helpfully without prompting. "I have been eager to work with you, Demigod Phex, ever since I heard of your recruitment. I could hardly believe what my cousin told me of your abilities."

"Your cousin recruited me?" Phex was swimming in purple.

"Indeed."

"You must know what he can do grace-wise in a dome?" pushed Itrio.

"I do, although I have yet to see it in action."

"You are in for a treat," said Itrio, who took a kind of older-sibling pride in Phex.

Phex said softly to the Dyesi, "You and your cousin have the same eyes."

Ohongshe's crests wiggled. "We do, indeed." It lowered its voice conspiratorially. "Did you know Zalihan traveled to Attacon 7 expressly to recruit you? Can you imagine? My dignified, highly-placed cousin traipsing across the galaxy to some Podunk moon targeting a blue barista in an obscure cupola." Ohongshe hissed and huffed in a mixture of shock and amusement, presumably at its cousin's expense.

"Wait. *Expressly* for me?"

"Of course."

"How would anyone know I was there?"

"Ah? You mean you haven't been told how divine recruiting works?"

"Is it okay to know?" Phex had enough secrets of his own to caretake – he didn't want to be burdened with the divinity's as well.

"What does it matter if you know how we found you?" The precatio looked confused. "Not everyone is recruited the same way, but in cantors, it's not uncommon." It cocked a crest at Phex. "You used to sing along in that cafe of yours on that little moon. Didn't you?"

Phex nodded. "Well, I hummed a lot. I'd sing when it was empty. The cupola played the same godsongs over and over again. That's how I learned all the words to Tillam's stuff. And I didn't even speak Dyesi at the time."

Ohongshe clicked. "The cupola was listening."

"That's not creepy at all," said Phex, deadpan.

Missit snorted into his stew.

Dimsum made a trill of inquiry, stood on her hind legs, placed two paws at the edge of the table, and peeked over the top optimistically.

Missit bopped her on the nose. And she retreated again.

Ohongshe gave the Dyesi version of a shrug with its crests. "All the cupolas conduct vocal profiling on local populations. Why wouldn't they? Cantors are the hardest pantheon spots to fill. The divinity must always be vigilant in pursuit of expansion opportunities, and that includes new gods."

"The Dyesi came to Attacon 7 specifically for me?"

"We came to the Attacon *sector* specifically for you."

Phex wasn't entirely certain how he felt about that. The whole audition process that he'd been put through, had any of that even mattered?

Missit said, "Now you're making him feel uncomfortable."

Fandina added, "Our Phex doesn't like to put anyone out or feel special."

Ohongshe was genuinely startled. "Is that not odd in a god?"

"That is Phex for you, oddest god. So, how do you feel about working with us?" Missit intentionally changed the topic.

The precatio perked up. "I have been eager for the opportunity to manage Tillam for ages," it confessed. "You are such a significant pantheon, so talented. I came out of my first instar to a Tillam godsong, you know? Your voice was the first thing I ever heard as a nymph. It was a magical experience."

Phex threw a fried spud chunk gently at Missit, who was sitting across from him. The murmel went chasing after it. "Hear that, Missit, you're *magical*."

Missit flipped his hair. "Naturally."

Precatio Ohongshe was mildly shocked by Phex's food-hurling disregard for Missit's dignity. "He is your elder both in age and standing, should you not treat him with more reverence?" There was reprimand in its tone.

Phex didn't say anything. He didn't have to – Missit leapt to his defense.

"Phex never treats me like I'm a god." Dimsum retrieved the spud and presented it to Missit, who examined it for a second, then ate it without much apparent care for the sanitary nature of spaceships or murmels.

Kagee looked up. "Don't think you're all *that* special. Phex doesn't treat *anyone* like they're a god."

Missit smiled widely. "It's one of his many charms."

Phex thought that was interesting since he'd always *thought* of Missit as godly and only recently changed his feelings on the matter. He guessed he'd managed to hide that part.

The poor precatio looked uncomfortable. It clearly wasn't accustomed to such casual informality between gods and demigods. Phex wondered what it expected. Asterism and Tillam had been on tour together for months – of course they were relaxed around each other. Or maybe this was a Sapien thing. Or even just a Missit thing. He supposed Jinyesun and Fandina were still stiff and formal with Yorunlee and Melalan.

Also, in the end, Missit was closer to Asterism's age than he was to Tillam's, in behavior if not actuality.

Phex considered the possibility that he was behaving too comfortably around Missit in public, especially as they were supposed to be hiding their relationship. He shouldn't pay Missit too much attention, formal or informal, when they had three new highly placed acolytes watching their every move.

A fateful thought, as it turned out.

They left Dyesi space shortly thereafter. With the size of this new spaceship, it took them longer than normal to find a true void. Even fold felt sluggish and strange. Although Phex knew that wasn't how FTL technology worked, it still *felt* ponderous because of the size of the ship.

It took them nearly three weeks of a methodical lumbering through space and two more folds before they arrived in Agatay's sector, near the quarantine zone. They had to be particularly careful on the last FTL, folding in some distance away, since the quarantine zone was so dangerous. They remained fixed in space for a full day after the final fold. Quarantine-zone proximity required a series of test pings of varying types to ensure the AI singularity inside could not leach into their tech, infect it and, through them, the rest of the galaxy. Preventing the singularity from expanding was one of the only things the entire galaxy had ever agreed on in all of history – even the Wheel had signed on to avoid exposure at all cost.

Phex had never been so close to it before. He felt a kind of titillated horror, knowing the singularity was just out there, lurking self-aware technology. He was tempted to spend his waking hours walking softly and speaking in hushed tones. He didn't, but he was definitely tempted.

He wondered at the desperate risk Agatay had taken in deciding to colonize a planet so close to the quarantine zone. But then, he supposed it was entirely possible Agatay had been there first, before the singularity achieved self-awareness. He'd never been very good on the ancient history of fringe planets, and no one knew very much about the singularity except to avoid it at all costs.

It was during that final week of transport, as the *Nusplunder* crawled carefully and cautiously toward Agatay, that Missit and Phex finally got caught.

The new dorm and practice-room arrangements meant that for nearly a month, they'd managed multiple late nights in what Missit had come to call their *secret storage bay*.

They got careless as a result.

Phex was running his hands over Missit, ignoring the gold in favor of warm human flesh. Hands that had made thousands of drinks over the years were now thirsty for Missit's skin and silken hair. Phex basked in the novelty of it even though he'd gotten to do it many times before now. Missit arched and melted over him, making Phex think of starshine and impossible things, his heart squeezing with reverie.

One of the acolytes found them. Or perhaps had followed them.

Either way, it discovered them in such a position that there was no other explanation as to why they were there together.

They certainly weren't singing.

And they definitely were naked.

Even a nymph with no sexual identity knew what two Sapiens were about under those precise circumstances.

Unfortunately for them, it was Calator Heshoyi who caught them. There was a slight chance that Precatio Ohongshe or Sacerdote Chalamee might have been sympathetic, but the calator was straitlaced and stern and lacking all sense of humor or compassion. Also, Heshoyi was an old-enough nymph to know exactly what they were doing and a devout-enough acolyte to be seriously shocked by the fact that two gods were fraternizing, against all standards of divine decency and regulation.

Phex heard the skin flap open and felt himself go entirely cold. Even as he raised his head and his lips from Missit's neck, he knew everything was over. He met huge, dispassionate green eyes through the shadows of drones and construction equipment. His skin went from the warmth of melted gold to the cold, clammy prickles of the void.

Missit sensed the change in Phex's body instantly. He twisted around, hissing in regret when he too realized they'd been caught. He folded, crumpled for a moment as if he had been hit, and then recovered his divine grace. Dyesi elegance seeped back into his bones, and like he had all along, he converted it into a defensive mechanism.

Missit unwound his legs from Phex's waist, both of them knowing this was it, the last time – how unfair and how sudden and yet how expected and how just.

Phex had known all along that what they did was against divine law. That they did this because they were young and dumb and could not stop themselves. That maybe in some other lifetime or as some other species, they might have been strong enough to love without expressing it through touch. But while they were both creatures of the divinity, they were also both human, and victims of their own history which, for generations, made love manifest as desire. Even Dyesi shame had not stopped them from needing each other.

It was one thing to be wanted as a god and quite another to be wanted as a person. While Phex had been busy treasuring the divine in his arms, Missit had been busy learning humanity in Phex's. They'd lost what little sense they had in the pursuit of new parts of themselves that were only to be found in each other.

It was never going to last. Maybe Phex had hoped they'd

make it through all the way to the end of the tour – to be parted by circumstances rather than scandal. But that had always been a futile hope and he knew it.

Missit had been grasping at something ephemeral from the start – something he saw in Phex, a lonely foundation. Missit was less logical even than Phex in this, for all his choices had been lowering and dangerous and desperate. He thought Phex was something strong he could lean on and trust. He was wrong. Not because Phex didn't want to be that, but because Phex belonged to the Dyesi, even more than Missit did, and he wasn't allowed to be.

But his reaction in that moment was pure Missit – arrogant god, naked and annoyed. "What are you doing here?" he demanded of the calator.

But Heshoyi was having none of that attitude. The acolyte would not buckle before a god who had defied the divinity and defiled himself with his own actions.

"I heard the rumors, of course. We were warned before we boarded to watch you two closely. I did not believe it was actually true. Apart from everything else, that you, Missit, would choose a demigod. It's so entirely beneath you."

Missit was instantly furious. He said, Dyesi-crisp and painfully formal, "Currently, Phex is, in fact beneath me. Your point being?"

"You are angry, god? At me? By what right?"

Phex was ashamed and scared, but Missit was star-splitting mad. Phex could feel the rage vibrating the strong, fine-boned body still resting atop him. Maybe that was fear, too, but Missit covered it well.

Missit climbed off Phex and pulled on his robe, throwing Phex's own at him, violently. Phex stood as well and pulled it on – slower, feeling drained and sad and terrified.

"You'll be called for disciplinary action."

"We're almost done with this tour. You couldn't overlook it this once, wait until we've built a dome and made idiots of ourselves for a new species of sycophants? Surely, it would be easier to use us now and punish us later," Missit's beautiful voice dripped with venom.

It hurt Phex to hear it. Contempt was an ugly thing, especially in his starshine boy.

"Still unreasonably angry," said the calator, to no one in particular. It turned pointedly to look at Phex. "And what do you have to say in your defense?"

Phex didn't lower his eyes but he did look at the Dyesi's shoulder instead of its face. "Don't blame my pantheon. They had nothing to do with this."

"How long have you two been" —Heshoyi's crests flattened, uncomfortable with even the words— "*intimate*?" it finally decided on.

Missit looked militant. "Not long."

Phex said at the same time, "From the very beginning."

For Phex, it had always been since the start. Since Missit looked up at him with bossy, mercurial eyes in a crowd of potentials. Phex had known he was a god from the moment they met and the damage they could do to each other because of it. Phex had *known* Missit. Always. Phex, who hadn't known himself at all, who was a formless, feckless lost soul with no home and no family. He'd had the great good sense to let Missit love him. Certainly, Phex was a dumb, insignificant creature, but even people like him desired starshine and beauty. Who wasn't hungry for light and happiness?

Phex was like a child who had been warned not to touch that which he'd already grabbed on to, two-handed and clutching with all his might. Because if Missit saw him as a foundation, Phex saw Missit as hope. Because Phex had had nothing of his own in life until the moment flecked eyes looked up at him, and in that split second, he'd been offered everything, all at once. He'd become desperate and stupid and lost over that fact. Still was.

Now he was losing everything, all of it. Just like it started. All at once.

Phex did not know if he would regret Missit for the rest of his life or learn to be happy over the brief time they'd had together. But he knew without question that night, his bed would be lonely and his bones would ache for lack of Missit's weight, and the cold, sinking sensation in his stomach and his throat was starlight being snuffed out.

6

THE BURNING FLESH

The Dyesi weren't cruel about it. They wouldn't know how to be cruel about human love. Instead, they were simply cold and efficient and intent on separating them. Which was somehow worse. Had they been cruel, they could have been blamed – this way, Phex had no one to blame but himself.

They called a meeting the next morning – the three acolytes, Phex, Missit, Quasilun, and Bob. They took over Tillam's quarters while the pantheons were firmly guided to breakfast by the remaining bodyguards.

Phex had no doubt that Asterism and Tillam knew what had happened without having to be told. The fact that Missit had not been in Phex's bed that morning was telling enough.

Missit looked flushed and sour. Phex didn't want to know what his own face looked like, but his insides still felt cold and empty and sickened, as if the underside of his skin had become permanently bruised. He no longer itched with need, just ached with regret.

Phex and Missit sat on opposite bunks in Tillam's quarters. Phex wondered whose beds they were. Did Tillam assign beds out of fear like Asterism did? He hoped Missit's wasn't the lowest one closest to the door, because that was also the most dangerous. Too easily accessed.

The three acolytes stood inside near the porthole, and the two bodyguards stayed at the entrance.

Phex tried not to look at Missit. Tried not to want to touch him as badly as he did. Always, but also worse now that he never could again. Their knees were separated by barely a hand's breath. Phex imagined that if he turned and slid to the floor, he could press his face into Missit's outer thigh and forget about everything else but the warmth that might seep in to fill all those bruised, aching layers of him.

"Missit and Phex, you are accused of ungodly behavior including sexual fraternization in violation of the third divine precept. Do you deny it?"

"No," said Phex quickly, before Missit could make a fuss.

Missit looked at him with wounded eyes. "Phex."

What did Missit want from him now? Did he expect him to fight? What enemy? The truth? The whole of the divinity?

Phex looked away – busy becoming a disappointment to absolutely everyone.

"Is this what they call *shameless*?" wondered Sacerdote Chalamee.

"What point would there be in denial?" Phex was legitimately curious. Was he supposed to lie?

Oddly, in that moment, he thought about the teens back in his cafe. He envied them their petty dramas and small lives. It had all been so easy for them – flirting, relationships, love. For the first time since leaving Attacon 7, Phex wondered if he had actually given something up, something mundane but important, when he became a god. When he chose to become Dyesi. He hadn't lost his humanity, but maybe he had lost some important aspect of the human experience.

The Dyesi had taken what he and Missit had and made it

dirty. Back on Attacon 7, it would have been normal. But also, it wouldn't have been Missit.

"We are agreed it cannot be allowed to continue now that we know what is actually occurring?" Calator Heshoyi looked like it was still trying to recover from the shock of having discovered them in action. It was hiding its disgust only through pure Dyesi control and a great deal of formal register.

"They cannot be left alone together," agreed the precatio.

"All physical contact should be forbidden unless necessary under the dome," added the sacerdote. "The divinity demands a performance on Agatay. The pantheons must function until then. The bodyguards will be instructed on new protocols."

The calator assumed dominant posture in front of Phex and Missit, thin and green and cutting, crests stiff. "You two will refrain from all contact and communication not directly related to the divine, or you will be forcibly separated and confined. Your duet will never occur again."

Missit's laugh was humorless and bitter. "And *after* Agatay?"

"Your behavior and that of your pantheons will be taken under review and your future as gods reexamined."

Quasilun spoke up from the doorway, double-barreled tone mild, almost sympathetic. "I understand it is beyond your ken at this life stage, acolytes, but have you considered the fact that this may be the third beauty?"

"Unlikely," said the calator.

"They are far too young," added Ohongshe.

Quasilun hissed softly. "Remember they only *look* like children. They are actually older than you in many ways." The imago was fighting for them for some reason. "Phex and Missit carry in them imago power and imago status."

The calator was having none of it. "But they are not *actually* imagoes. Regardless. It would require emotional proof, probably the serum test."

Sacerdote Chalamee said, calm and soft, "Unfortunately, the statistical likelihood of permanent alteration to Sapien psyche as a result of that test is a high risk factor. Best not to damage any of these gods until after Agatay. We are already down by one."

"That's awfully kind of you." Missit swallowed hard and looked up at the ceiling.

"Will we be given the option?" Phex wondered.

"What option?" Missit's eyes burned on Phex's face – he was clearly not following, busy just being mad about the whole situation.

Phex thought that was good. If Missit stayed mad, that would carry him. Hold him together. Maybe he wouldn't be so badly hurt. Maybe he would come out of this whole mess unscathed. Maybe the burden and the consequences could mostly fall on Phex.

"To prove it," explained Phex.

"Prove what?"

"Whatever it is they want proved with a *statistically hazardous serum*," said Phex, imitating the sacerdote's cadence.

"Third beauty," said Quasilun, again.

"Third beauty is a myth you tell the skinless to help them sleep at night," snapped Missit.

"You've been hanging out with too many nymphs." Quasilun looked amused. Was the imago finding this whole situation *funny*?

Calator Heshoyi said to Quasilun, "It is irrelevant. The divinity has decided. You have your instructions?" It included Bob in this question.

Bob shifted, armored impassivity breaking into something that resembled annoyance. "When did *bodyguard* become code for *prison guard*?"

Phex was startled. At best, he would have thought Bob an indifferent observer of their affair. It was both endearing and painful to realize that the cyborg had, in a way, been on their side all along. Bob had probably been ignoring Missit's sneaking around, which explained how he'd gotten away with it for so long.

"Never forget you work for the divinity, not the gods. And to be frank, cyborg, who else would employ you?" The calator's voice was impossibly curt and cool.

Bob's eyes glittered but the cyborg shifted back, ceding the floor and the point, not best pleased about either.

In that moment, and for the first time, Phex actually hated the acolytes. Until then, they had been doing their jobs, but they didn't have to be mean about it. Certainly not to a bystander like poor old Bob.

Missit stood. "Are we done here?" He marched from the room without waiting for their answer, Dyesi liquid in his bones. Phex's gaze, despite everything, followed him, bruised and hungry.

Bob followed.

Phex looked down at his own hands. They had once poured drinks and they had once held liquid gold. Why did the memory of both make him so sad?

The bodyguards were instructed to watch the entranceways and prevent either Phex or Missit from leaving during sleeping hours. At daytime practices, they were allowed contact only when Phex was rehearsing with Tillam. Even then, the acolytes monitored them closely. Anything to do with the duet and dancing together was banned.

Of course that only made him want to touch more, a perversion of hormones. The rebellious teenager he'd never been was coming out now, responding to Missit's petulance and his own misery.

Phex thought they had been watched closely as potentials, but it was nothing on this. He wondered how long it would take for him not to be *aware* of Missit in that way that he was *aware* of pollen in the air – some other part of him chemically reacting to Missit's presence in any room.

Phex knew his pantheon was there, and he knew they were trying to be supportive. They didn't ask him directly what had happened or how he and Missit had been caught, but it was easy to guess. Asterism knew that in talking about it, Phex would only feel more stupid.

Berril and Tyve both tried to cuddle him as much as possible. But Phex was prone to flinching at any physical touch now, hyper aware of what the Dyesi didn't allow, platonic or not. Jinyesun did its best to offer quiet intellectual support, but Phex didn't have any questions to ask anymore. Fandina tried to distract and amuse, and Kagee to needle and annoy. Nothing really worked, but one part of Phex's numbness was still aware enough to appreciate that they were *trying*.

That first night, after the punishment had been meted out and the separation commenced, Berril tried to curl up with Phex in Missit's spot.

Phex gently turned her away.

His eyes were stretched and dry, eating into his face already. He thought that hugging her, when he would rather it were someone else, did a disservice to them both. Worse, he might start to cry, and he wasn't sure if he could stop once he started. So, he'd rather not start.

He hugged his own stomach hard instead. Using the strength of his own arms to try and control the quivering of his muscles and the desire to throw up. His hands cramped with the force of it, and no matter how hard he clenched, he still felt empty.

Kallow had once asked him on Divinity 36, when they were both potentials, if he would regret the part of himself he was giving up to become a god.

Phex had thought he had nothing to give up, because he conflated it with nothing to lose. Stupid of him. He'd given up the free will he'd never even utilized, like giving up a trick under the dome. He belonged to the Dyesi now and they would make his choices for him, for the good of the pantheon. For the good of the divinity. As *they* saw it. Because it was *their* pantheon and *their* divinity, in the end. Phex was theirs too, more than he had ever been Missit's.

Foolish that he'd thought he was allowed to want something for himself. Let alone something special like Missit. Foolish of Missit to give it to him freely, so much that he actually believed it. Believed in anything at all, let alone himself and his capacity for love. No wonder the Dyesi had built an empire out of belief.

Phex tried to hold on to the cool numbness of absence and not feel anything. Missit had said Phex was his anchor, but it turned out Phex was the one adrift without him. But he still got hit by small hot sparks whenever he saw Missit. Singing together felt like actual pain. It was cruel that they must still work together for Tillam's sake.

Phex wondered if this was the cantor equivalent of song-burn or if this was just what missing a lover felt like. His body had been burned where Missit once touched him. Like his scars, gone invisible but still there under a new layer of skin. As if the numbness were a false covering created by Dyesi artifice to help him forget what once had been. It wasn't working. He would never see gold again without feeling the absence of it.

They managed it. Of course they did. They were still gods. Performing was their job.

The divinity endured.

The divinity always endured.

More vocal about the whole situation was the murmel. Still under the misguided notion that Dimsum was Phex's symbiont, the acolytes kept moving her, shrieking in protest, every night from Missit's quarters to Phex's. She never stopped complaining, but also eventually learned to simply wait them out in a grumpy huddle in a corner. As soon as the lights cycled down, she scampered back to Tillam's quarters. Unlike the acolytes, the bodyguards let her. They were under no such delusion that she belonged to anyone but Missit. Or, more precisely, without having to share Missit with Phex anymore, that Missit belonged entirely to the murmel. Phex was embarrassed by how envious he was of the small blue beastie.

Phex managed his duties with Asterism because he was what the divinity had trained him to be, but the color had leached out of it. He felt as grey as a dead dome.

Missit managed his obligations with Tillam exactly the same way, by duty and habit. Although Missit behaved differently. He was a small ball of pounding anger most of the time now. While Phex floated slightly out of flux with everything, Missit crashed chaos through rehearsals and gatherings and conversations, lashing out indiscriminately – a tiny terror making everyone miserable. Both pantheons tiptoed around them, afraid of doing any more damage.

It was good that they had no proper dome to practice in, for it would have been an ugly thing. Phex had no idea how they were going to carry off an actual performance in their current state. He would have felt guilty because the others were scared and nervous, but even guilt couldn't penetrate his numbness.

Thus, with shadows permeating both pantheons, the *Nusplunder* limped into orbit around Agatay and an already-terrible situation became a whole lot worse.

First of all, no one greeted them as they entered orbit, and they were stuck without contact, waiting on the planet's whim for days.

Kagee said this was probably because whoever invited them originally was no longer in power and there was either chaos or indifference headed their way next. Or being ignored was just the opening volley in a power play.

Then, suddenly, the three acolytes disappeared and there seemed to be an inordinate amount of communication and negotiation. The acolytes had to became diplomats for a while, and the pantheons were confined to their respective quarters.

"I don't understand it either," said Kagee before anyone could ask him what was going on.

Phex finally remembered that he had a question. He was lying on his bunk, staring up at the underside of Tyve's. He did that a lot these days, lost focus and time without realizing it. He was idly fiddling with a blue decorative ladle. For some reason, Tyve had unhooked one and brought it to him. Perhaps she thought he would find it comforting. Phex thought it was a nice shape and there was something intrinsically satisfying about it. At least the divinity had gotten *that* bit right. He spun it about in his hands.

"Jin, can I ask you something?" he said, breaking the quiet. The pantheon had been very quiet recently. Phex worried that was his fault.

"Always, Phex," came Jinyesun's soft reply instantly, floating down from above.

"Quasilun said something about *third beauty*. What does the term mean?" Phex didn't mention when he'd heard it or that it had been connected to him and Missit and some kind of toxic serum. But if he was destined to take some potentially damaging test against its presence, it might be good to know if he actually had this third beauty or not.

Jinyesun, of course, was willing to help him understand. Especially as it was the first thing Phex had taken an interest in, in days. The Dyesi jumped down and sat carefully at the foot of Phex's bed.

Phex shifted his legs to accommodate. He sensed that Jin wanted to touch him more these days – some effort at care and offer extra friendship? An apology of some kind? Why should Jin apologize when this was all Phex's fault?

The sifter leaned against Phex's shins. "You know that in Dyesi, the word for *beauty* and the word for *love* are the same? But we divide beauty into three variants of sensation. *Skinsift*, which is to see and to know beauty – to observe love. *Songsift*, which is to hear and to understand it – to receive love. And *soulsift*, which is to feel and to believe – to give love. Soulsift is thought of by many Dyesi as a curse, because it renders the first two irrelevant. Once you have learned how to give, why bother with anything else?"

"Under the dome, we engage in all three?" suggested Tyve, her head appearing over the side of the bunk above.

"Very good, yes. But the exchange is not one of equals."

"We are getting it from our worshipers?" suggested Kagee.

"Quite the contrary. Every time we climb onto that dais, we pour out beauty like water from a pitcher. Any given congregation will mostly experience the first beauty, true worshipers the second, but only the most devout believers ever attain the third."

"And godfix?"

"That is the transformative power of all three at once, brief and remarkable, but it never lasts. It changes both the worshiper and the god, though, because it is one perfect moment of euphoria – and that is how love/beauty works."

Phex thought he understood the Dyesi concepts in play. Not sure he believed in them, but they clearly did. And with the divinity, that was the point – belief.

Jinyesun continued the explanation. "This is why we are called *gods*. Eventually, neither appearance nor talent will affect the belief of a worshiper, because the worship itself is the point. We Dyesi both fear and hunger for the third beauty. Few nymphs get to experience it in truth except as gods. But this is also why it is so dangerous to soulsift with another god." Jin didn't say it directly, but it was referring to Phex and Missit.

"Why?" wondered Phex.

"We emit beauty on the dais, all three forms, and hold nothing back for ourselves. What beauty we have left to share with another god is empty of all value. To love, truly love, is to give away yourself. Is that not terrifying?"

Phex wondered if that was why he felt so numb and empty. There was nothing *him* left. Could he sing colors onto a dome under such circumstances?

Kagee snorted. "To love, truly love, is more divine than

the divinity. And thus it makes the dome meaningless. That is the sad truth in your third beauty."

"Perhaps," said Jin, still looking at Phex.

Missit had said something similar about Phex once. About the way he loved. Phex thought about the empty exhaustion he always felt, late at night after a live performance. He didn't think he agreed, because all he ever wanted in those moments was Missit curled against him. And he knew Missit felt the same. He thought if they were both pitchers pouring out love, they might pour it easily back and forth into each other so that neither ever ran dry. They could give *more* of themselves to the divinity if they were together. But he wouldn't be allowed to test that theory, and Jin's face said this belief ran deep and devout.

Phex remembered the saying: *Gods cannot worship each other.*

Ironic that what the Dyesi feared with two gods coming together was the ruination of godhood and the chaos of pantheons destroyed by romantic relationships and break-ups. And yet the acolytes had wrought this exact situation for Tillam and Asterism through their own hard stance. Phex and Missit had been muddling along fine, and now that they were separated, it was like a migrating fracture in glass that could not be stopped. It was entirely possible both pantheons would shatter as a result.

During that hiatus, while they waited adrift for Agatay to accept or reject their presence, Missit actually managed to catch Phex alone for a moment in the galley. The acolytes absent for negotiation and the bodyguards lax out of discomfort afforded them a few precious minutes together.

Missit managed to spin Phex into a corner behind a net of dried herbs. His gorgeous face was pinched and drawn, his eyes red-rimmed.

To have him so close burned. Phex's hands reached to grab and support and balance by instinct, and then fell uselessly to his sides. He jerked away.

"We could, we could—" Missit started to say. The golden god was tarnished and lackluster, his hair was limp, and he probably wasn't hydrating properly. He definitely wasn't sleeping properly. Missit had always been a poor sleeper.

Phex pushed himself back as hard as he could into the cabinet behind him, feeling the hard edge dig into his spine like an anchor. Wishing he could fold away into the hull. Become a grey keyskin on the wall of a dome and not feel anything, just reflect.

"Don't, Missit."

"But, Phex!"

"What can we do?"

"Leave the divinity."

Phex imagined Missit without cantor. Missit leaving Fortew behind to die alone. Missit leaving his pantheon of over a decade. To do what? Walk among mortals? The most recognizable god in the galaxy? Unprotected? So many fixed coming after him. So many worshipers rabid with grief for his leaving them behind. Phex imagined abandoning his own pantheon, his family. He imagined leaving the Dyesi, the only ones who had ever wanted to keep him.

Phex whirled away and around, using a grace's spin. "Stay away from me," he said to Missit.

To his Missit. Who he wanted *so badly*.

He added, as if politeness might help either of them feel any less empty. "Please."

Missit did not try to get him alone again.

"Asterism will be part of our first-contact and planetary-landing party," the sacerdote announced, crests and skin-speckles entirely neutral. Too much control there – it was a little concerning. Phex snapped out of his general apathy long enough to be wary.

"We are not trained diplomats or divine ambassadors," objected Tyve.

"Gods are, by their very existence, both." Sacerdote Chalamee remained neutral.

"This is considered an honor," reprimanded Fandina, gently. "Not many pantheons get to take point on a new planet, especially not demigods."

"You have been specifically requested as part of preliminary outreach," the sacerdote added brightly, as if this might make it more tempting.

"They want to host a welcome congregation for Asterism? Already? Have we enough worshipers on the planet for that?" Jinyesun was confused.

The acolyte looked uncomfortable. "Not exactly. I admit it is highly irregular. But the planetary leaders have specifically asked to meet Asterism in person, as part of the dome ground-breaking ceremony."

"You really are going to build a dome on Agatay?" Kagee's voice was genuinely awed. All along, he had not believed they would even be allowed to enter Agatay orbit. His whole understanding of his home world was being shaken.

"The planetary leaders were particularly insistent."

"Diarchs. We call them *diarchs*, not *leaders*. Which faction is in power?"

The acolyte looked like it wished the other two were present. "One of them said she represented the Modal?" It paused, thinking hard. "And the other said he was Endant."

Kagee shook his head. "An alliance? Between the Modals and the Endants? Things really have changed on Agatay while I've was away."

"Are either of them connected to your family or faction?" asked Tyve hopefully.

"No. We're solidly Deduct. Have been for as long as anyone can remember."

"Us being here has nothing to do with your family, then?" Berril slid out of her top bunk to join Kagee on his. She covered his hand with her smaller one and squeezed. He rotated his to squeeze back but let go right away. Kagee did not like to be seen as needing support or reassurance. But also, Phex noticed, when Kagee talked about his home world, he tended to isolate himself.

"A dome request was always the least likely to have come from my family. We aren't particularly powerful, even within our own faction. And of all the xenophobes on Agatay, the Deducts are the worst. My leaving the planet to work for an alien species was a profound insult. I intended it that way. It makes more sense that I would be invited back as an embarrassment to them."

"But you are a *god*!" The sacerdote was genuinely shocked. A god, so far as the Dyesi were concerned, was to be revered. Especially by others.

Kagee smiled bitterly. "On Agatay, I am a mere proxy who abandoned his family and his lineage for the stars. I ran away. Already delineated. It means I'm probably expunged from the family line. I wasn't good for much before I left, but I should still have stayed behind to serve in whatever capacity *they* saw fit."

The sacerdote clearly could not, or would not, comprehend this perspective. Kagee changed the subject. "Did you happen to get the names of the diarchs?"

"We were not gifted with them during negotiations."

Kagee shrugged. "That is normal for outsiders – certainly with off-worlders, it's titles only. But they know me?"

"You were mentioned by name. God name. But your presence is expected. I would even say obligated."

"Asterism goes planetside because of *me*, specifically? Can I not go alone, then? It would be safer for the others." Kagee could be protective too, in his way.

Phex was proud of him for that.

"No. Asterism stays together. If this is a congregation, we *must* treat it as such."

"Standard divine practices are not going to work on Agatay." Kagee muttered, but he had said that already in many different ways, and the acolytes refused to listen.

No one was surprised that the sacerdote ignored him now, too. "The divinity does not deviate. We operate on this planet as we would on any other that has petitioned for its first dome. There are no exceptions."

"When the divinity falls, it will be because of its stubbornness." Kagee turned his head and looked out the porthole.

"Foolish cantor, how do you think we have lasted so long? Change is the provenance of individuals, not institutions."

Kagee hissed in resignation. Then clicked his reluctant acceptance, still not looking at the Dyesi. "When do we leave and what should we wear?"

"You have half an hour. As a local, we trust you will be able to guide your pantheon's attire." The sacerdote left their quarters without further ceremony.

Asterism panicked. They had only half an hour to primp and prepare.

Kagee said they should dress in their awards-show garb

for meeting a congregation on Agatay. He encouraged them to impress. "They pretend not to care, but appearance counts for a lot on my planet, especially among the elite. Luxurious fabrics are highly valued."

That meant Phex, Tyve, and Fandina put on their traditional Dyesi protector skins – gleaming scale-plated and reptilian. Black, red, and purple respectively. Frankly, Phex would have lobbied for them to wear skins no matter what. They were for show but they were also a kind of armor. Kagee believed that Agatay was dangerous, and Phex believed Kagee.

Jinyesun, Kagee, and Berril wore their long, layered filmy robes – Jin's teal, Kagee's greyscale, and Berril's pink. Her outfit melded the style of the robes with the reptile scales. All three sets of robes moved beautifully, but they weren't very protective.

"Kagee, should you wear something more defensive?" Phex asked, worried.

Kagee hissed disagreement. "I understand why you ask, but fighting leathers is what I used to wear all the time. I'm here as a god. I should look as different as possible from who I was before, both as a mortal and as an Agatay local. That too is a kind of armor."

Phex hadn't realized until that moment that clothing could make a political statement, but he trusted Kagee to know what he was doing.

"You're wearing all your jewelry, though?"

"When have I ever not?"

That was something – at least his friend was weaponized. "I'm taking my whip scarf." Phex's tone brooked no disagreement.

"That is a very good idea," replied his high cantor, brushing his long, silvery hair into a waterfall of shine.

Berril's small voice piped up. "Are you actually okay with all this, Kagee?"

Kagee's lips twitched but he only pulled on his second robe. "The fact that it's not my family calling me home actually makes it easier for me to go."

Phex thought that sounded like pain, not relief. Phex understood. He too knew what it was like to be unwanted.

Kagee continued. "The diarchs being from different factions is a big change. It might be considered a beneficial thing. But that they have united over a dome is very strange. I cannot comprehend the game in play until I know a lot more about the players and the current political climate. To do that, I need to visit the planet."

"That's why you're not objecting more to this congregation," said Tyve.

Kagee clicked. "At this point, we just need to survive this insane Dyesi plan. And to survive on Agatay, we need information about the elites."

"Admit it, you're curious." Only Tyve would dare tease Kagee when he wore that expression.

"This is my home planet." Kagee pulled on his final robe, settled the various folds so all the layers showed, and cinched the waist tight. Rearranged his hair to fall properly.

Phex thought that he had never cared at all which progenetor family was in power at any one time on in the Wheel. Life had never changed for crudrats. It must be different for proxies. Perhaps he and Kagee were not so alike as he had once thought.

They boarded a transport ship, looking fabulous, and landed on the surface of Agatay as part of the first official divine party ever to visit. In this way they became ambassadors of the divinity but also of the whole rest of the galaxy.

The mantle weighed heavily on Phex, or it would have if he'd had the will or the energy to care.

This would be the first time anyone on Agatay had ever seen a Dyesi in person, let alone a chiropteran. Sacerdote Chalamee, Quasilun, and all six of Tillam's bodyguards accompanied Asterism. It was possible that they too represented races and modifications never before seen on Agatay.

They were met and surrounded by more soldiers than Phex had ever seen in one place. And they were transported from the dockyards to the capital city in actual tanks.

Visiting gods was a military operation on this world.

The capital city was a mountainous organic mess of beautiful stone edifices, overgrown with vegetation – great swaths of it destroyed rubble. There was a prevailing aesthetic toward flora, verdant and lush, crawling around and over meticulously fitted and carved stone blocks – brutalist contrasted to organic. Phex liked it, although he knew very little about architecture. And then scars – craters and empty, bombed-out patches, stone-fresh and barren.

They watched the city roll by out the tiny slit of a window in their tank. There would be stunning architecture and then sudden piles of refuse or abandoned fields. A few times, they passed the underground guts of a building now filled with water, plants, and wildlife like some watery grave. For a big city, it was remarkably empty of humanity. Those few people they saw in the streets moved quickly with their heads down. They remind Phex of crudrats on space stations – scuttling from one hidden, unwanted place to another, afraid of being noticed.

This was a city at war. It was human ingenuity pitted against human destruction – order versus entropy.

It made Phex and Berril wince. Kagee looked complacent.

Tyve was interested. The Dyesi were confused. The bodyguards increasingly tense.

"What do they do to each other?" asked Jinyesun, shocked by the destruction. Its huge eyes flicked from recent piles of fresh rubble to the old forgotten and never rebuilt – it was all a sad testament to a certain kind of hopelessness.

"This is exactly what my home city is like, too," said Kagee, quietly.

Phex wondered if Kagee might claim that the capital had once been beautiful. Then realized if it had ever been a complete or whole city, that would have not been during Kagee's lifetime.

"Where is all the color?" he asked Kagee. Because this place wasn't dim, like Dyesid, but it seemed somehow faded. The plant life, for example, was green but not a very *vibrant* green. It was as if the whole planet had been washed out.

Kagee laughed. "Like I would know."

"Oh. Right. Sorry."

It was Jin who answered Phex. Clearly, the sifter had been wondering the same thing. "Infonet says *spectrum issues*. Agatay's sun is a blue giant. Apparently, that has something to do with it. There's also something unusual about the atmosphere. It may be filtering the light in some way."

The capital building was a fortress – star-shaped, crenellated, rock cut, and impenetrable. It looked ever more impressive as they approached. Phex suspected that was the point.

Phex wondered what such a fortress *couldn't* survive, because it would take a lot. Earthquake, tornado, flood, firestorms, all the crazy planetary weather he had read about and never experienced would be nothing to this building. Or it felt that way.

Guards in different uniforms, a mix of two colors and styles, escorted them from their tank through the echoing, empty halls of the building that governed the destruction. *Impenetrable* also meant *lonely* – Phex understood that all too well. He wondered how much of the planet's population was left.

There was no congregation waiting to meet them.

The reception chamber was massive and echoing, designed to impress visiting delegations but now more like a mausoleum to the absent than a testament to any living civilization.

Part of this feeling came from the fact that there were only two people waiting for them.

Svelte and slight and grey like Kagee, the Agatay were a pretty people by Dyesi standards, but even garbed in what amounted to the planet's highest ceremonial dress, they were made *less* impressive by the echoing emptiness of the room they stood in, not *more*.

There were guards with them, of course, still and stationary, dotted about the circumference of the room, but otherwise, it was just the two diarchs waiting for them.

A soon as they were close enough to see their faces, Kagee gave a funny little hitching gasp and stumbled slightly.

"What mockery is this?" he hissed low and in Dyesi, to no one in particular.

Phex took his elbow to steady him. "You know them." He was not surprised.

Kagee looked up at him – his eyes were pained in his face. Phex knew that look. Those were his eyes every morning. Those were Missit's eyes whenever they actually caught each other's gaze. That was heartbreak looking up at him.

"Those are my exes," said Kagee, beautiful voice cracked and shaken.

7

BE STILL AND KNOW DIVINITY

"Exes? Plural? Both of them?" Phex mentally flailed.

"Naturally. At the same time, too." Kagee looked smug, but then again, Kagee always looked a little smug.

"Well, this isn't going to get messy at all." Phex addressed the smugness.

But Kagee seemed to take that as a compliment. "Worried that I'm stealing your thunder?"

Berril perked up. "Do Agatay relationships group-bond like my species?"

"Agatay is nonrestrictive on bonding dynamics. For genetic reasons, non-monogamy is encouraged." Kagee spoke almost tonelessly, as if he were reciting something he'd had to memorize as a child. Or maybe it was that he was still dealing with the shock of his exes just standing in front of him, in charge of the whole damn planet.

The exes were smiling shyly at them. Well, at Kagee.

The Dyesi were very confused.

Phex brought them back to the current situation. "Are they the reason you left?"

"No, but they're half the reason it was considered a good

thing I disappear permanently at the time. They are way above my status, especially as a proxy."

"Kagee," pressed Phex because there was something the high cantor still wasn't telling them. "What's the other half of it?"

Kagee grimaced and tilted his head. "They didn't want to let me go."

"And?"

"They are probably the great loves of my life."

"Ah." Phex understood that, so he shut up.

Tyve said, "Well, recalling you via divine mandate is one way of getting revenge on you for breaking their hearts."

"Who says I was the one who broke it off?" Kagee was trying not to look at the hearts in question, half-facing his pantheon with his back to the diarchs.

"We know you very well, Kagee, of course you did the breaking," shot back Tyve, having none of it.

Asterism was speaking in rapid informal Dyesi, difficult for anyone not fluent in the language to follow. "What the hell happened while I was away?" Kagee asked his pantheon, presumably without expectation of an answer. "How did those two, of all people, end up the Diarchs of Agatay?"

"Wait, aren't you all different factions?" said Berril. "How did you three even happen?"

"We were at school together."

"What?" Berril stayed confused.

Phex thought this probably not a conversation they should be having while everyone else stood around, staring at each other and not talking. The acolytes had no idea how to start negotiations without Kagee, and the diarchs were not helping, just staring at them and smiling like fools. Phex noticed that they held each other's hands tightly.

Kagee looked at Berril. "It's like potential training. The

elite families send their children to be educated together, in the same place. It's a boarding school that was designed to encourage planetary unity. Also, it's the safest place on Agatay. No one wants to bomb a school if *everyone's* kids are there. In reality, the factions just persist within the school, with a few notable exceptions. In our case, we became both the exception and lovers, despite split factions."

"How?" wondered Jinyesun.

"We shared a common interest and it brought us together."

Phex tilted his head and examined the diarchs carefully. They hadn't spoken yet so he didn't know their pronouns. But they looked about Kagee's age and far too young to be planetary rulers, especially if they were elected. Perhaps Agatay practiced scionism for inheritance, like the ancient monarchies? Nevertheless, if these two were Kagee's age and had access to the infonet, even on an isolated planet like Agatay, that meant pretty much one hobby was the most likely. "Bet I can guess at that *interest* you shared."

"I bet you can." Kagee gave a sarcastic grimace.

"The divinity."

"You were early converts?" Jinyesun looked very proud of Kagee, its crests puffed with pride.

Even Fandina was opaque with pleasure. "Were you the first on this whole planet?"

"Not sure. We had to hide it, after all. We started a secret divine club. We were so young and naive."

Phex puffed out a sharp breath, like a Dyesi laugh. He stared hard at the two diarchs, who were clearly trying to follow the conversation in a language they barely understood.

Phex intentionally switched to Galactic Common. "Kagee, what have you done?"

Kagee sucked his teeth and switched to a strongly

accented version of Common, which was probably his native tongue. "Apparently, caused a dome to be built."

"How else were we to get you back? You left us to become a fucking god, you absolute pustule," said one diarch, language identifying her as female.

"Seriously, Kagee? You ran away so far, you thought you might as well become immortal?" said the other one.

"Not that we aren't proud." The female had bolder features than Kagee – a wider mouth and a slight hook to her nose. Her voice was strong too. Not beautiful like Kagee's, but powerful. She'd never sing colors but she could probably command armies.

"I always knew you'd make for an amazing god," said the other diarch. His personal pronoun use identified him as male. He was shorter and slenderer than Kagee. Phex thought he looked like he could become a light grace – he gestured with his hands while he talked, quick and sure.

"Hi," said Kagee. He looked entirely embarrassed, for the first time in Phex's experience.

Phex spared a thought for the poor Dyesi who were about to be very confused. If they had objected to Phex and Missit, how were they going to cope with Kagee and this situation? Essentially, the divinity had been invited by an alien species to occupy their home world because the two rulers of that world wanted to fuck one of their gods. How ironic. Missit would have found the whole thing hysterical.

Sacerdote Chalamee did the crest-wiggle equivalent of clearing its throat. "Demigod Kagee, would you be so kind as to introduce us?"

Kagee shook his head, amused at himself. Then he did something odd: he introduced himself to the space, as one would with the Dyesi, only he did it in his own language. "Kagee Setset-Four, high cantor of divine pantheon Asterism, former proxy to the Deduct Faction. I am familiar with this place although I have never lived here."

"Kagee, what are you...?" asked the male diarch.

"You invited us here, remember. This is how it's done." Kagee's voice was flat and firm.

The two diarchs nodded vigorously.

"Of course. We are honored to be visited by both the Dyesi and the gods and" —the female diarch looked hesitantly at the bodyguards flanking Asterism— "um, whatever they are."

Kagee said, "You may think of them as divine proxies. Now hush or this will take all day."

Both diarchs went wide-eyed and quiet.

Phex was amused. Apparently, Kagee was a bossy bit of sour no matter who he was with – ex-lovers or current rulers, it didn't matter to him.

Phex quickly stepped forward. "Phex, low cantor of Asterism. I have no faction and am a stranger to this place." He clicked at Fandina.

The Dyesi adjusted its body language and straightened its crests. It said, first in strongly accented Galactic Common and then in formal Dyesi, "Fandina, sifter of Asterism. I have no faction and am a stranger to this place."

One by one, the rest of Asterism did the same. Then the three acolytes and finally the bodyguards. Only Quasilun did not perform an introduction.

Once they had finished, they all stood around awkwardly for a moment before Kagee said to the diarchs. "Your turn."

The female quickly said, "Miramo Conmet-One, first Modal, Diarch of Agatay. I, uh, live here."

The other ruler said, "Levin Retmor-Nine, first Endant, Diarch of Agatay. I live here too." And then carefully, as if not sure if it would be well received or not, he added, "Welcome to our planet, our capital, and our home."

"This was your idea, Lev, wasn't it?" accused Kagee, not even bothering with any more ritual or diplomatic talk.

"What is your high cantor doing?" the sacerdote asked Phex. As if Phex could control Kagee.

Phex thought the Dyesi had rather asked for this. So, he didn't answer, letting them stew in the mess they had created.

"Lev was always better at planning and strategy than you were, Kagee. What did you expect? He plays the game to win, and you're as much a pawn as the rest of us." Miramo clearly wasn't one to humor Kagee's abrasive personality.

"Still, how did you two climb all the way to the top without me around to kill for you?"

"You'd be surprised how far one can get without actually dealing out death," answered Levin, dropping Miramo's hand and moving hesitantly toward Kagee.

All the bodyguards in the room shifted notably.

Kagee gave a micro head-shake.

Levin stilled in his tracks.

Kagee said, "I'm surprised. You're saying you made it to the top *legally*?"

Levin winced. "More *organically*. Just because Miramo and I don't kill indiscriminately doesn't mean others share our scruples."

"Are you the last survivors of your lines?" whispered Kagee, grey skin paling noticeably.

"It's not that bad."

Kagee looked at his feet, then up with pained eyes. "And my family?" He bit his upper lip.

Phex moved close to support him if needed. Berril moved to his other side, for comfort. Kagee probably didn't notice, but hopefully he felt their presence.

Miramo twisted her jaw, uncomfortable.

Levin said, "You're it. All that's left."

Kagee closed his eyes and pressed his palm to his forehead. But he did not sway and he did not look surprised.

Phex bumped up against him gently. Kagee leaned slightly into him. Phex crossed his arms and looked away, not wanting to embarrass his friend.

Both diarchs glared at Phex. Like he was taking something from them. Phex gave them a baleful stare back.

Berril petted Kagee's arm.

The diarchs *really* didn't like that – both of them moved subtly forward, posture proprietary.

Phex put out an arm in front of Kagee, like a bodyguard, and shook his head at them firmly.

"My faction has dissolved?" Kagee guessed, voice strong and steady.

"Scattered. They still act up on occasion, but essentially, they're no longer relevant. They've a few small enclaves in the lowlands, but you know the lowlands – more concerned with survival than warfare. The Deducts are essentially neutralized as a political threat."

It was hard to tell from Kagee's expression how he felt about this information. His face was a neutral as a Dyesi crest – he could have been a diplomat and not a god.

He nodded, then said, "If you two are allowed the lead at such a young age, that means the factions are *all* weak and diminished. It must have been a bloodbath for a while."

"We lost a lot of proxies, too."

"Are there enough breeding-age adults left for planetary survival?" Kagee wondered.

Miramo laughed. "The elites may have to marry down for a while, but we mostly took each other out, like idiots. Amusing, no?"

"I am no longer surprised that you two managed to take power, you basically outlasted everyone."

Levin wiggled his eyebrows. "We were always good at flying under the radar, it's how we survived at school. Remember? We actually focused on recruiting more and more to the divinity and playing politics as a hobby to spread the colors. There's a whole divine movement now. *Make song, not war.*"

"Cheesy."

Miramo said, tone unexpectedly shy, "I have a baby too."

"We have a child?" breathed Kagee, his pronoun telling. He may have called them his exes, but he still thought of them as somewhat his.

"Liera Conmor-One." Miramo's smile was all pride.

"A little girl?" Kagee's tone was soft and yearning.

Levin said, "She's very cute."

"She'd have to be, with your genetics." Kagee complimented them without flirtation, just stating facts.

His face had gone to stone and he was clearly making an effort to recover his customary hard shell. Kagee usually wore grumpy sarcasm like an imago's skin, shiny and protective. It clearly wasn't working at the moment. He'd been shaken by the news of a child.

Levin and Miramo both blushed, a shadow of darker grey to their cheeks. Phex hadn't realized the Agatay could blush. Kagee never seemed to.

The acolytes had clearly had more than enough of this Sapien nonsense. They had divine business to discuss, and childhood reunions and family reminiscences could only be allowed to go on for so long, even with the leaders of a host planet. Phex was a little surprised that they'd permitted even this much.

"Diarchs," said Precatio Ohongshe in Galactic Formal,

"may we discuss the dome and perhaps see the site? Would you be wanting a satellite or a planetary construct?"

Kagee said to his exes, "You're absolutely *certain* that you want to invite the divinity to establish a presence here?"

The diarchs looks at each other. Miramo said, "The divinity brought us together even as it took you away. Asterism, your group, these past few months, here on Agatay – it has moved hearts and minds."

Levin added, "I don't think you realize, Kagee, what you have done for us as a god. For Agatay to see what you have become and what you are to the whole galaxy. Even only on the infonet. Even though it's not under a dome *here*. People are addicted to your beams and your vids. As a god, you've given Agatay something we never had before."

"Planetary pride," said Miramo.

"And a stake in the wider games of the galaxy. It feels like we count for something in the universe for the first time. It feels like we *matter*." Levin's expression was earnest and his eyes were fixed on Kagee's stony face.

"We have an actual god."

"People off Agatay remember that we exist."

"Or learn of us for the first time."

They way they spoke, one after another, was so in synch. Like cantors harmonizing. Had they practiced this speech or just talked about it so much with each other, waiting for Kagee to come home to them?

Miramo paced a little, hands moving while she talked. Those hands were as delicate and fine-boned as Kagee's, but she wore no rings. "And Asterism is *good*. Your music is catchy. It's played on broadcast systems all over the world now. At home and in public. 'Blue Mirror' has become a kind of planetary anthem. Then because you were touring with Tillam, everyone started listening to them, too. And you know Tillam has a huge back catalog. Now the divinity is just *everywhere* on Agatay. In less than six months, it went from something we had to keep secret, an underground movement among the youth, to something no one can avoid." Miramo shook her head in wonder.

"This dome, honorable diarchs?" pressed Ohongshe, who clearly spoke the best Galactic of the three acolytes.

"It seemed like the logical next step for us. Plus, we wanted Kagee to come home." Levin said this as if it were all perfectly natural. "If only just to perform for his people." There was an ache to the way he said it. As if those people owed Kagee a favor. As if making worshipers of their planet was a means of making reparations to this one person whom he had loved and lost.

"And your wars?" asked Quasilun, suddenly and apparently out of the blue.

"Things are calm right now, have been for a few months. That's why we thought now might be a good time to build a dome," explained Miramo to the imago.

"How can you guarantee its safety? Our safety?" wondered Kagee.

"We can't, of course. But we'll assign an entire platoon to the site, and things really have been very quiet recently." Levin was earnest with hope.

"We aren't claiming it's safe here. You're wise to bring your own proxies in such numbers." Miramo nodded to acknowledge the bodyguards and Quasilun.

"With no domes, there's no fixed yet, but there is still risk of assassination attempts," said Bob to Itrio.

Kagee said, in full threat-assessment mode. "The greatest threat is probably to me. If what they say is true, I'm the divinity's figurehead here on Agatay. Secondary threat is to any of you who look the most alien. The more you look like an Agatay, the lower your risk will be. Phex is probably the safest of us all."

Phex didn't think he looked that much like a local, but he could see Kagee's point. Much to his relief, that also meant Missit was probably relatively safe from assassination too. The relief in that thought prickled his skin, then turned his stomach. He forced himself to consider who else would be protected by their appearance. Tern. Fortew. Then he realized that no one had yet asked about medical facilities for Fortew.

The diarchs were clearly accustomed to conversations concerning safety and defensive protocols.

The Dyesi however, were not. Ohongshe said, "May we ask you quite bluntly, diarchs, do you *believe* in the divinity?"

"No. Not exactly." Miramo was cautious – she looked and sounded a lot like Kagee in that moment.

Phex wondered if that was an Agatay cultural trait – frankness mixed with circumspection and wariness.

"Why a dome, then? You know you'll have to convince a huge portion of what's left of the population to visit it. And a dome only holds so many at a time." Kagee rocked back onto his heels, thinking out loud. "There's a reason the Dyesi go in for smaller copula and cafe domes first, you know? So the performances can be beamed, not live, to start. Jumping into a full dome right away, that's a bold move. What's your political strategy?"

"What are you doing, high cantor?" hissed Calator Heshoyi at Kagee, crests flattening back. The Dyesi was afraid Kagee would scare the diarchs off.

Kagee shot back quickly in Dyesi Formal, "One dome for a whole planet? Small population or not, is that really the best opening tactic to spread and encourage worship?"

"You're worried our enemies will try to take it out?" suggested Levin.

"You're not? A big symbolic target like that?"

"Acceptance of the divinity is not falling along faction lines, Kagee. *Everyone* is listening. In a strange way, the fact that your family and faction no longer exist has made you that much more popular as a god. People can believe in you without being accused of betrayal or alliance. You are our world's first neutral option."

"That is exactly what makes for the best gods," said Sacerdote Chalamee, as if that should be obvious.

Kagee nodded, wincing but understanding. "Uniqueness? Or the curse of being the last one left alive?"

"Don't be fatalistic, it never suited you," said Miramo, sharper with Kagee than any of his pantheon would ever have dared to be when he was in *that* mood.

Phex was impressed. He was also moved to speak. "You just told him that his whole family has died."

"But he hated them," said Miramo.

"Sometimes, that makes it worse," said Phex, tone mild.

"What's he to you?" Levin snapped out fast.

"Jealous?" wondered Kagee, idly.

"Yes. Look at him."

Kagee glanced up at Phex and then snorted. "You know I prefer small and sharp-tongued." He seemed to be comfortably switching into some other mode all of a sudden. Relaxed. Unlike the Kagee Phex knew. Flirting?

They were getting glimpses into the Kagee who had been in a relationship. The Kagee who had allowed himself, once, to love fully and without hesitation. The Kagee who had come to Divinity 36 full of prickles and boobytraps because he had run away, leaving his safety net behind.

Phex said, "Better to ask what I am to him." He gestured to the pantheon. "What we are."

"And what is that?" Levin looked militant and angry, as if Phex had challenged a claim of some kind.

"We are the ones who stitched back together that which you unraveled," said Phex.

"He *left* us, not the other way around," snapped Levin.

Phex didn't think Kagee was the type who fled without a very good reason.

"Could we please talk about this in private, later?" asked Miramo.

Kagee said, "Ha. That won't be allowed."

"Why not?" The diarchs were *not* happy about that statement.

Kagee gave an evil sort of smile. "Gods aren't allowed to be sexual."

"What?!" Levin clutched at his chest in an overblown mockery of shock.

"Don't tell me you've been *celibate* since you left us?"

Kagee looked morose. "Tell me about it."

"*You?* Really?"

Kagee nodded with compressed lips. "It's a Dyesi thing. They're messed in the head over sex and romance. Price you gotta pay to become a god."

"How absolutely tragic," said Levin, looking more shocked and upset with this nugget of information than he had when talking about Kagee's dead family. "I mean, we read about the fact that gods weren't allowed to date, but no *sex*, at *all*?"

Phex began to suspect that Agatay might take sexual proclivities a little too far in the opposite direction. No wonder Kagee was grumpy all the time.

Kagee raised both hands. "Once again, you're absolutely certain you want a divine dome built *here*?"

The diarchs said in unison, "We're sure."

Kagee turned to looked at the acolytes, speaking in formal Dyesi. "And you are still absolutely certain that you want to build one?"

All three clicked at him.

Kagee swiveled to look at Quasilun. "And you, imago, do you have any thoughts on this matter?"

Quasilun was both interested and amused, crests puffy but stance wary. "You know it's not an imago's place to interfere with the expansion of the divinity. It is the nymphs' game and we do not play it."

Kagee sighed. "Yet here you stand, with us, on a world entirely new to the Dyesi. Well, if I am the only one who thinks it is a bad idea to build a dome on Agatay, I am clearly outvoted." He looked at his former lovers. "Seriously. How can you even think of allowing alien technology here?"

"You sound like your mother, Kagee."

Kagee shook his head. "Well, if you believe in the divinity *that* much. I guess you're in charge now and it's your choice."

"We believe in *you* that much, Kagee."

"You're ridiculous."

"We always did."

Kagee looked at his feet, then back up at them, eyes narrowed. "Did you know they had me sterilized? Turns out none of us Protans are *born this way*, it's *done* to us. It doesn't come along with being colorblind, they just don't want us to procreate."

"What?" Both diarchs looked genuinely shocked.

Kagee was clearly relieved. "Good. I'm glad you didn't know."

Miramo said, "Can it be undone?"

Kagee rolled his eyes. "Apparently, very easily. Or so the alien medics tell me."

"Your pardon, diarchs, but we appear to have gotten off topic yet again," Precatio Ohongshe interrupted.

Miramo laughed in delight. "How could have I forgotten how much work it is to have a productive conversation with Kagee?"

Tyve said, "I know, right? Imagine having two of them."

"No?" Miramo looked at the Jakaa Nova in delight.

"Oh, yes. Phex is even worse."

Phex and Kagee exchanged glances. How had this situation pivoted to them under verbal attack?

The precatio said desperately to Levin, "*The dome*, diarch?"

"Ah, yes. We thought, since it might be a draw for others to visit Agatay, that building it on the outskirts near the space dockyards would be best. Of course, you noticed our landing bays are old and little used? We have no regular off-world visitors and no satellite colonies."

"Why do you have landing bays at all, then?"

"We did have both, once, a long time ago."

The acolytes were disposed to be pleased with any crumbs they were offered. "Might you show us exactly where you want the dome built?"

"We will leave that entirely up to you. The surrounding territory is not utilized nor contested nor even claimed by any faction. There's no useful mineral deposits or farmland in the area. You may do what you wish with it." Levin called up a topographic map on his wrist ident.

Phex noted the Agatay seemed to prefer bracelet tech for infonet access. Only, theirs curved around and over the back of the hand. It was stylized and very pretty, ideal for displaying holograms.

The precatio made a recording of the location and then bowed. "If there's nothing else, we will take our leave now."

"But we have yet to finish our conversation," protested Miramo.

Precatio Ohongshe insisted. "We have much to prepare and the pantheon must practice."

That was a lie.

Asterism really couldn't do much more until they had a dome to rehearse in. With only a keystone and Phex and Missit constantly mis-harmonizing, there was hardly any use in trying anything until they had access to a proper dais again.

"Could you leave Kagee behind? We promise to take good care of him." Levin was not above begging.

"Apologies, diarchs, but that would certainly not be possible."

Miramo and Levin both looked deeply disappointed.

Kagee laughed at their sad expressions. "Celibate," he reminded them, "For nearly two years. While you two faffed around and took over a planet. Just think how I feel."

"To be fair, sweet-cheeks, you did become, ya know, a *god*." Miramo was fun – Phex was beginning to really like her.

"Flattery will get you everywhere," said Kagee, flirting again.

"Will it?" Levin looked hopeful.

"Well, no actually, because, ya know, gods don't do that."

"So unfair," said Miramo sadly.

Phex could not agree more.

The acolytes were already moving away, the bodyguards looking uncomfortable and restless, wanting the gods to follow – nervous about the increasing gap of separation in their diplomatic party.

Phex exchanged glances with his pantheon.

As a group, they turned and trailed after the Dyesi, leaving the diarchs behind.

"I like your exes," said Phex.

"Cuties!" agreed Berril, bouncing along happily on Kagee's other side.

"I'm sure they didn't mean to break up with you," added Tyve, needling.

"Ten minutes of chatter and you're taking their side already?" Kagee grumped.

"Well, they're much nicer than you are, hon." Tyve's grin was sharp-toothed.

"Look on the bright side, Kagee. At least your drama has pulled Phex out of his funk," said Berril cheerfully.

Kagee said, "You all suck," and meant it.

"What did we do?" wondered Jinyesun.

"You do realize your stupid celibacy restriction is objectively ridiculous to basically every other species in the whole galaxy, right?" explained Kagee.

Fandina's crests wilted. "Well, we kind of do *now*."

Jinyesun said in Galactic Common, looking rather proud of itself, "I think this is the first time a dome is going to be built because of a galactic booty call."

Kagee looked genuinely shocked.

Berril had a fit of giggles.

Phex swallowed down a snort of amusement.

Tyve threw an arm about Jin's waist. "You treasure, where did you pull *that* phrase from?"

"Did I use it right?" Jinyesun dropped back to Dyesi casual speech, both embarrassed and pleased.

Tyve looked back at Phex. "I do believe we're corrupting them, darling. There's hope for you yet."

Phex doubted that was the case – Asterism's two sifters were special among the Dyesi. Open-minded. He really wanted more than anything to go back to the ship, cuddle Missit, and listen to him talk and analyze everything. But

Missit hadn't been with them and they wouldn't be allowed to cuddle.

And Kagee had been wrong about everything.

Phex realized then that he hadn't sneezed, not once. Apparently, he wasn't allergic to *all* planets.

And a dome was about to be built on Agatay.

Back aboard the *Nusplunder*, Asterism was once more confined to quarters like disobedient children. Only, this time, Kagee was in trouble as well as Phex. But with the acolytes focused on the new dome, and only bodyguards guarding the door, Asterism did have a chance to talk freely.

Kagee scrubbed at his grey face and flopped back onto his cot. "Aye-ah, this is a mess."

"You still don't think it's a good idea to build a dome on Agatay?" asked Berril.

"It's something we always talked about, the three of us. Bringing color to Agatay. When we were kids at school together, we had to find illegal recordings of performances and watch them in secret. We always talked about a future where gods were welcome and performed on Agatay regularly. But I thought that was just childish imagination, all bubbles and stardust. We thought we could use the divinity to change people's minds about opening up to the stars. As if the divine could *actually* materially alter the oppressive system under which we lived. Those were stupid, fanciful, optimistic dreams. How can they still have them? They're grown-ups now. How can they still be trying to make that happen? They rule a planet. They have a child!"

Tyve said, "To be fair, you went away and became a god

and gave them new hope and new reason to try. Even the ability to push that very agenda."

Phex added, "This could be all considered your fault."

"Phex, anyone ever tell you that it's a lot nicer when you actually don't say anything?"

Phex made a rude gesture at Kagee.

"When you were a kid, you *wanted* the Dyesi to come. You wanted to spread worship. You wanted the divine *here*." Jinyesun was saying that, more to remind Kagee than anything.

"I was a *child*, but even I knew we needed something to pull us together as a planet. Some shared thing that we all loved. Rather than constant infighting and hate."

"You're angry that *you* became that thing?" pushed Phex. A part of him was kind of enjoying needling Kagee.

Kagee stood up to strip out of his top robe and threw it hard at Phex's head.

"A shared passion for music rather than a common enemy?" Berril sounded like she was wondering if that really worked.

"I told you we were naive children."

"It has worked with religion in the past," pointed out Tyve.

"Until another religion came along and they fought each other over *that* instead."

"Yes, but dead gods and old religions are not as powerful as the divinity." Fandina spoke with utter conviction. Dyesi immovability.

Kagee glared. "I refuse to defend my infantile ideology."

"Do Miramo and Levin really believe this will work? Do they really think the divinity can unite a planet and stop civil war with one dome?"

Kagee shook his head, but in confusion, not rejection. "I don't know."

"Is the divinity a plague that takes over or an act of benevolent enlightenment?" wondered Phex, because he had been wondering that for a while now.

"It is art," said Jinyesun, as if that should explain everything.

"Can't art be both?" said Berril.

Kagee sighed. "And what about the fixed? Do we spread beauty and love in truth, or are we spreading something worse alongside? Will my people suffer or thrive under your domes, Dyesi?" He stared hard at Jinyesun and Fandina, who wilted a little. Then he cut them some slack. "But do I care, when Agatay rejected me first?"

He turned and looked at Phex. "What do you think? Since you're being so talky right now. How would you feel if this were the Wheel?"

Phex frowned. He had never considered going back home for any reason. Ever. He had certainly never entertained the idea of the divine in his home sector. "The Wheel would never permit a dome."

"I said the same thing about Agatay, once. And now look at us. So, if for some strange reason, the Wheel did welcome the divinity?"

Phex didn't have to really think about that. Even though he had his own doubts about the divinity and the Dyesi. Even as he hated the acolytes for separating him and Missit – the Wheel was a thousand times worse. "I think anything that diminishes the power of the Wheel is a good thing. But it would be a war of ideology – the Wheel, after all, is also a religion."

"That's not helpful, Phex."

"You didn't ask me to be helpful."

Kagee sat back down on his cot, leaned his elbows on his knees, and glared. "Okay, you arrogant soup ladle, be helpful. Tell us, for a change, what you *really* think."

Phex felt exposed, but also, this was something he'd been pondering. This was something he might have talked to Missit about, and only Missit. So as not to scare his pantheon. But he didn't have Missit to talk to anymore. He had no more access to the jaded stability of a great god. And he was running out of desire to guard his tongue in care of others' feelings, even his pantheon. "No offense, Jinyesun, Fandina, but I think we do not know the agenda of the acolytes. Of the nymphs. Or of the Dyesi. Assuming the nymphs act independently of the imagoes, which Quasilun's attitude implies. We aren't allowed to understand the true nature of the divinity even as we proselytize it. Therefore, you have only your own experience to pull from, Kagee."

"What do you mean?"

"Simply put, have you enjoyed *your* time under the dome? Is it worth it to you, the divinity and the sacrifices you have made to become a god? Have the Dyesi made your life better? Would you do it all over again?"

Kagee looked surprised. Then thoughtful. "Yes. Without question."

Phex nodded. "Me too." Everyone there knew he also meant Missit. That he was thanking them, in his way, for having looked away for some small time and allowed them to be together. Allowed him to be foolish. Allowed them a kind of grace.

Phex glanced around, forcing himself back to numbness, not thinking about Missit, focusing on his pantheon.

Berril was nodding earnestly, Tyve smiling her confirmation as well. Jinyesun and Fandina looked somber but grateful to be part of the conversation.

Phex clicked *and* nodded – after all, they'd been speaking in a mix of Dyesi and Galactic Common since they got to Agatay. "Let's do it, then. Let's bring the colors to your people, Kagee. Let's risk the dome and be damned for it."

Kagee nodded. Then his face crumbled.

Phex had been waiting for that. He sighed and levered himself out of his own bunk.

He picked Kagee up even as the cantor muttered an objection. He sat and cuddled him on his lap as if he were Missit. Tighter, though, squeezing him. Grounding him.

Kagee shuddered and heaved in his arms, searching for tears and not finding them.

"They are all dead?" he asked, into Phex's shoulder, words like a sharp spatter of hot fat, one after another.

"They are," said Phex, squeezing harder.

Berril and Tyve made weights on either side of them, both reaching to rub Kagee's back.

Fandina reached down a hand to gently touch the top of Kagee's head.

Jinyesun came to stand close and cup the back of his neck.

Five points of contact. Five hopeful comforts.

But how do you comfort someone for something like that? Phex wondered. *How does anyone heal when they are the only one left?*

It was like being alone under a dome: nothing would work properly, and no matter what Kagee did, no matter what his pantheon did, nothing ever would work again. Not in quite the same way.

8

DOME OF SIX GODS

The divinity built its dome.

Phex found the process fascinating. He'd never seen anything being built from scratch before, let alone a dome. They did the scaffolding first and then the interior. The keyskin and its clones were fitted overhead, niches blocked out in between. It wasn't going to be a very big dome. It didn't need to be. Phex had seen photos on the infonet of testudines. He thought a dome being built looked a lot like a turtle shell, turned inside out.

Phex wondered if they built the inside first so the pantheons could practice or it if was always done this way for ritual reasons. It was certainly odd for Asterism, to sing inside an unfinished dome – light leaking in, builders and drones crawling all over. But they did it, because it was the best option they had to practice in.

They did lose one day of rehearsal because of rain.

Phex had heard of rain, of course, but never experienced it before. Water simply falling from the sky all willy-nilly like that, the earth muddy – it all seemed frankly messy and wasteful. Especially when his pantheon traveled all the way to the planet's surface only to be told it was too slippery to grace.

Planets were crazy, illogical things.

The exterior construction of the dome was loud. This dome was being designed to match local preferences and topography. The outside would be built of tight-fitting boulders, big and fortress-like. These had to be quarried and dragged around and chipped and such.

The Dyesi used a combination of the *Nusplunder*'s ship's complement, carrier drones, and local labor. Those locals were clearly nervous and cautious around the aliens. For the first two days, the Agatay kept stopping and staring at every Dyesi who passed. The arrival of the gods caused a near-riot. But they calmed down faster than Phex would have expected, and did as requested. They seemed grateful for the work. Kagee said it must have been a hard few years, if even the stone masons were desperate.

The Dyesi called it Dome 6, which Tyve in particular found confusing.

Finally, she worked up the courage to ask Calator Heshoyi, who was overseeing construction, why such a low number.

"Acolyte, why *Dome 6*? Isn't there already a Dome 6 built a long time ago?"

"It got destroyed," explained the calator, curtly. It was busying eating its evening meal, presumably prior to going back to work. The drones, after all, did not need sunlight to operate, and the Dyesi, at least, could work fine in low light. Agatay had three very bright moons.

"War?" wondered Tyve.

"Of course not!" The Dyesi actually looked deeply offended by the very idea.

"I thought you said domes *never* got destroyed," accused Kagee.

The calator's crests flattened. "It was an entirely unavoidable natural disaster. Even the divine cannot control earthquakes."

Meanwhile, someone had finally remembered to ask about Agatay's medical facilities.

Asterism learned, through the ship's gossip mill (aka Bob), that Fortew had been transferred to the planet's best medical facility, high up in the mountains somewhere, well versed in the treatment of crud lung. Everybody was left to hope and pray to dead gods, since the living ones were obviously useless.

Asterism spent some supervised time on the infonet conducting beamed congregation services. They had been absent for too long, and the divinity worried their newly established worshiper base would diminish for lack of cultivation.

They dutifully did their godly duty to the cause, individually and as a group. The worshipers responded well and it seemed much of the gossip about Phex fighting on the dais, and his possibly intimate relationship with Missit, had entirely faded. During the time they'd folded across the galaxy, no less than eight other divine scandals had popped up. Phex wondered if some of them were manufactured by the divinity to distract from him, or was that idea self-aggrandizing? Regardless, he was relieved he didn't have to enact damage control anymore.

Asterism's worshipers expressed concern for them, being so near the quarantine zone. But true believers respected the need to spread the love for the divine as far as possible. They were proud it was Asterism getting to Agatay first. They were happy for Kagee, that he was visiting his home world, and tended to ask him lots of questions about it whenever he was in the beam. Mindful of the diarchs' expressed interest in opening the planet up, Kagee made sure to extol Agatay's natural wonders and assiduously avoided the topic of civil unrest.

This seemed to work. Searches, keywords, and companion interest in what limited information there was on the planet increased exponentially.

Phex thought the galaxy might have a new issue on their hands as a result. With too many visitors to the area, contact with the quarantine zone was likely to increase. Agatay would have to institute some kind of space force to help safeguard and control incoming traffic.

When Phex mentioned this, Kagee found the idea laughable.

"We have no spaceships. I mean no military-grade ones or ones capable of fold. There are a precious few transports and unmanned larger drones for satellite landing and mineral collection, but we have never been a people who explored off-world. Anything in space, orbiting Agatay, tends to be pointed at enemies on the planet, not off of it."

"How did you ever manage to escape, Kagee?" wondered Tyve.

Kagee laughed. "You don't know how I was recruited?"

"No, we've never talked about it."

He shook his head, silver hair rippling. "It's embarrassing. I made a recording of myself, singing. Gods, was I *bad*, too. So was the recording. I mean, I had to do it in my old dorm room after hours and thought I'd be caught the whole time, if not by the monitors, then by Levin or Miramo."

"And the Dyesi got ahold of it? How?" Berril asked, flopping over with her head in Tyve's lap.

Tyve petted her hair idly.

"I circulated it through this really small worship group I was part of, one of those micro servers cultivating devout enthusiasm. Not even a proper divine forum. I can't even remember which god it centered around. Maybe Tarloun? Some high cantor or another. The believers there just got crazy excited about helping the divinity discover a new cantor. Plus, they really liked my visuals. They got behind me and started spreading the recording anywhere they could on the infonet. Eventually, some acolyte or another must have seen it and brought it to the attention of the divinity."

"They sent a transport for you?"

"Nothing so dignified. There was a trading vessel passing just close enough." He nodded at Tyve. "Jakaa Nova. I hopped an Agatay mining ship, which took every cent I could liquidate for the bribe, and the traders met me at a local asteroid belt. Even all that trouble, and the divinity put me through the audition process." He pursed his lips. "I guess it all worked out in the end."

"You didn't tell Miramo and Levin that you were going to try for godhood?" asked Berril.

"Of course not. I thought it was a stupid pipe dream and they'd be so disappointed when nothing happened and I returned home a disappointment."

"So, it *was* you who ran away," accused Tyve.

"Not exactly. They're both older. They graduated and left our school first. I was alone by the time the recording got picked up. They're both highly placed elites from more important bloodlines and established factions than mine. They outranked me in every way – age, status, and then also, I'm a proxy. Aborted bloodline, sterilized and useless except to kill. Delineated is a bit like being outcast. They had already left me behind in every way that matters on this planet. I didn't leave them, I left Agatay, and my family, at that godforsaken school. I never had any intention of staying in that hellhole without them."

Phex snorted. That was such a Kagee way of thinking about it. That his beloveds were leaving him behind anyway, so he'd leave entirely and completely, and punish them with his absence.

"You're an idiot," said Tyve.

Kagee muttered, "They never told me they had plans to keep me with them. Even if they did, it wouldn't have been possible. That's not how our world works. I would have had to stay at school without them for years. Then when I graduated, I would have had to go home and proxy for my pustule of a cousin against everyone else, including them. Working counteragent to their families and factions. I might have even been sent in, at some point or another, to kill one of them. Better to get out."

"You absolutely were the one who ran away." Berril sat up and glared. "I am *very* disappointed in you." She was trying to be fierce. It was adorable.

"Does that count, when I actually did become a god?"

"Now you're proud of yourself?" Berril crossed her arms in a tiny imitation of Phex.

Kagee threw his pillow at her.

Fandina said, "Get moving, you lot, it's time for practice."

Phex stood, relieved – practice was something to do even if it was coupled with the pain of having to interface with Missit. At least he got to see him, check up on him.

They left their quarters and joined Tillam at the transport ship.

The two pantheons made awkward small talk during the flight, mostly the Dyesi and the graces. Phex snuck little glances at Missit's face. The golden god seemed less angry these days and more just exhausted all the time. He wasn't sleeping, again – there were dark smudges under his eyes.

Missit looked away whenever their eyes met. Phex was hurt and grateful each time. He wanted to ask about Fortew. He wanted to make sure Missit was eating properly. He wanted to sit behind Missit and pet his hair. He wanted to cuddle him in his lap. He *wanted* and didn't *do* anything.

But the dome showed their tension.

Gods couldn't lie under a dome.

Phex worked with Tillam for the first half of each rehearsal in the new dome. The rest of Asterism just sat around, playing games, stretching, and otherwise entertaining themselves. They were only demigods, after all, they could wait. Sometimes, they tried watching Tillam's dome, but they quickly gave up doing that. It was brutally ugly.

Phex and Missit struggled to work together – even under a true dome, it showed all around them. Their voices remembered the harmony, but their bodies were stiff with each other, and they weren't allowed to be close. Phex was discovering that it was nearly impossible to sync godsong properly without actually looking at his cantor partner.

Phex hadn't realized how much a pantheon depended on body language and relaxed intimacy, how much he had to watch the other five on the dais in order to react and respond appropriately.

The dome Tillam produced when Phex and Missit could not bear to look at each other, let alone touch, was a catastrophe.

Oh, it was still a dome.

It was still skinsift and glory.

But the patterns were formless and the colors muddied. There would be no godfix from this kind of display. It was like something made in the dome by mere potentials – not a real pantheon.

This was the opposite end of the spectrum from when Phex and Missit had weaponized their voices. Although, when he had the energy, Phex did worry about songbruising Yorunlee or Melalan. He thought Missit would never be so far gone he wouldn't try to balance and help Phex control his voice, but Missit's control was weak. Phex may be lonely and aching, but he still sang with too much power, because that was the only voice he had to sing with.

The acolytes were in despair over the whole thing. No possibility of godfix from their best pantheon, plus a new population to convert – it was a nightmare.

Asterism, on the other hand, after Tillam had gone back to the ship, did absolutely fine. In fact, their dome was only getting better and stronger. Phex being a little tired from one full rehearsal already and Kagee being oddly relaxed now that he was back home rendered their singing more harmonious than it ever had been. Asterism's new song was going over well, too. They were proud of it, having created it on their own, and that pride also translated to the dome.

The acolytes were frustrated. They could not understand how demigods were outperforming major gods. How Phex and Missit, who'd once sung together so smoothly, had become something broken. They had exterminated the pest of a love affair in their midst, only to find it was the sustenance upon which Tillam had survived.

The pantheons continued like this for most of the second week of dome construction, while the exterior of the new dome was put into place.

Meanwhile, the two diarchs and their massive security detail made a point of visiting regularly – partly to publicly acknowledge and politically throw support behind the project, but mostly to see Kagee. They truly loved to watch him perform. Their eyes glowed with pride, and they made no attempt to hide their affection for Asterism's high cantor.

Unlike Phex and Missit, the two diarchs did not have to play by divine rules. As worshipers, they were allowed to love a god, although Phex was pretty certain the Dyesi did not fully understand the form that love would inevitably take. Levin and Miramo would not stop trying to get Kagee alone. And Phex suspected that, given half a chance, Kagee would let them.

Phex thought Asterism would need to come back to this planet and this dome regularly, for it was clear it would be difficult for Kagee to stay away for very long. Trust Kagee to pick planetary leaders for an assignation. Not that the three ever had any downtime to actually *do* anything, but Phex wasn't a nymph. He could see what Miramo and Levin wanted, and it wasn't just to watch Kagee sing.

Miramo even brought their daughter at one point. The little girl looked a good deal like Levin, small and sweet-cheeked. She had an even temper and her parents' appreciation for the colors. Unfortunately, her screams occasionally indicated that she did not, in fact, feel as affectionate toward Kagee's voice. Or maybe it was Phex's voice she disliked. In this, she was like the murmel. She was cute when she waved her hands excitedly, but otherwise, Phex thought her rather formless and raw, like ingredients rather than a meal. Nothing about her had come together yet into anything interesting or warranting his attention.

"You are *so* not a baby person," accused Tyve, as if this were a major character flaw.

"Apparently not," agreed Phex, who'd had very little contact with infants during his lifetime. He saw no reason to change that. Certainly, Liera Conmor-One wasn't helping to alter his good opinion, and from all reports, she was deemed an *easy* baby. Whatever that meant.

"Do you want kids someday, Mr Phex?" asked Miramo, offering him a crunchy snack thing.

The diarchs had brought food with them as well as the baby this time. Asterism was taking a brief break to socialize and nibble. The Dyesi didn't seem to mind. If anything, they encouraged it – gods luring rulers into worship was an act of conversion. This was simply a very casual version of a VIP congregation. Phex suspected that if Miramo and Levin tried to disappear into one of those pretty new niches with Kagee, the acolytes would put a swift stop to it, though – rulers of an entire planet or not.

Phex didn't know how to respond to that, so he said nothing. A tactic that usually worked well for him.

They were chatting as a group. Asterism had not changed their general opinion on the diarchs over the ensuing days. They collectively liked them and collectively felt like Kagee was as much, if not more, responsible for the breakup. That is, if they were broken up, which Levin and Miramo seemed to think wasn't the case.

"I like your new song very much." Levin offered Kagee a bite-sized nibble wrapped in a pickled leaf.

"Isn't it good?" Berril bounced – she was eating a fried dough ball that had been soaked in syrup and flower blossoms. It was a local delicacy and currently one of her favorite things in the universe.

"Can you show me that twirl move that you do?" Levin asked Berril. "The one where your foot kind of moves up your leg as you spin?"

"Ooo, certainly, come over here." Berril waggled a hand at him and marched toward the dais.

Levin casually passed his baby to Kagee and joined Berril

in spinning about happily. He was light on his feet but not good enough to be a grace.

Phex shook himself out of godly judgment. That wasn't the point – they were just having fun. When had he become the kind of person who assessed everyone he met for possible pantheon status?

"He's not very dignified for a supreme leader, is he?" Kagee's eyes were soft on his ex before he turned his attention to Liera, making a funny face and bubble noises at her.

"Says the man who currently looks like a complete idiot." Tyve popped a piece of fruit into her mouth.

"The new godsong is good. You created it yourselves?" Miramo was enough of a divine worshiper to have a basic understanding of how the pantheon system worked.

"I like the new song too," said a new voice from the dome entrance. Missit came wandering inside to join them. Bob dutifully took up residence just outside the open doorway. Quasilun was already standing on the other side.

Phex hid his shock. He'd thought Missit had left with the rest of Tillam. Had he been watching the whole time? Surely not. Phex would have noticed.

"Where did you come from?" asked Tyve.

"I was visiting Fortew."

"Ah. Are the facilities nice?"

Missit glanced at the diarchs from under his lashes, spoke carefully, "Excellent, actually."

"We may be the backwater of the galaxy, but hundreds of years of war and we know how to put a Sapien body back together. We put our very best doctors on his case," said Miramo. "He is a god, after all. We have a regrettable amount of experience treating crud lung."

Missit clicked, then remembered this was Galactic

Common and nodded instead. "Fortew said that. He said he feels like he is in safe hands. It's just that I flew over fighting on our way, or at least sabotage of some kind. Buildings on fire in the foothills. He's not in any danger, is he, at that hospital?"

"It's inside a mountain for a reason. It could be completely cut off from the rest of the world and still maintain standards of care. The facilities are geothermal and equipped to run for up to three months in isolation: water, food, supplies, staff. We believe in caring for our sick and injured. Don't worry. He's safe there. Plus, that fire you mention was only a handful of rebels, already suppressed."

Missit nodded. He did not look entirely reassured. He'd probably been told all this already. But then, Missit was always a little nervous when he was separated from Fortew for any length of time – let alone by a significant distance. Also, he'd been raised among the Dyesi – this would be his first experience with widespread violence.

Levin joined them again, apparently having learned the spin to his satisfaction. "I understand Fortew's case is quite advanced. You should brace yourself. Even we can only do so much." His voice and face were sympathetic.

Missit said, "I've been bracing myself for well over a year now. It doesn't get easier, even as it gets closer."

"No," agreed Levin with true understanding, "It never does, if you love the person."

Phex watched the diarch's eyes. *He's lost someone he adored to crud lung at some point.*

Kagee started singing softly to the baby in his arms, who was going heavy-lidded and boneless. He was singing Asterism's new song, "Moon Made."

"It really is pretty," said Miramo. "Reminds me of a lullaby from when I was a child."

Kagee stopped singing to say, "Yes, I took some inspiration from that one."

"You wrote it?" Levin was clearly impressed.

"I wrote *some* of it," Kagee hastened to correct. "It's a collaborative effort."

"You wrote most of it," grumped Phex.

"Kagee is the best at composition, though," said Tyve, who never skimped on praise when it was warranted.

"He's good," reinforced Phex. Everyone was vested in encouraging Kagee's gift for composition. He didn't love being up on the dais as much as some of the others, but he did have a talent for creating godsong in the first place.

Kagee dipped his head, embarrassed.

Missit, who'd been listening quietly and not eating, spoke up. "Can I try it?"

"You want to sing one of *Asterism's* songs?" Jinyesun was startled into informal Dyesi.

Missit nodded.

Phex wondered what Missit thought he was doing. Why?

Tyve said, "I don't wanna if you're gonna be as bad with us as you are with Tillam."

"Tyve!" said Berril, truly shocked. "It's not Missit's fault!"

"Are you saying it's Phex's? Because he does just fine with Kagee. Better than fine."

"Well, no, of course not."

"It is no one's *fault*," said Phex. Because it wasn't. It was their situation, and the empty space left between them that could not be filled with sound for it had once been filled with feelings, and the two were not the same shape.

He wasn't sure what Missit wanted to prove. But if Missit wanted to try singing a new song with Asterism, then Missit could do whatever Missit wanted. Just because they were no longer together didn't mean Phex could cut off the part of him that needed to give Missit everything. He might have switched off as much of himself as he could, but that instinct to care was too much a part of his nature. If Missit wanted to sing with Asterism, Missit could sing with Asterism and damn the consequences.

Kagee stayed off the dais, cuddling the now-sleeping infant. The rest of Asterism and Missit took up position.

They were still workshopping the new godsong, since this was its first dome. It had been written and developed without one. The grace parts were still weak, since gracing was always the last bit to be perfected. But it was shaping up to be something rather special.

Phex took a breath, nervous, and then they started.

Missit was good. Better than good. Not as good as Kagee for this song, but he knew the high cantor parts better than Phex had expected. He wondered how Missit had picked it up. Had he been listening to Asterism practice, outside in the hallway of the ship, when Phex hadn't noticed? Had he sat there, with his bodyguard, leaning against a bulkhead, just for the opportunity to hear Phex's voice?

Probably.

"Moon Made" was one of those songs that leaned on low cantor more than normal. Kagee had written it with Phex in mind to carry the weight of the colors, because he wanted to really play with and stretch Phex's voice. It was unusual for Missit to take the back seat to low cantor in any song – certainly, that had never been his dynamic with Fortew. All of Tillam's songs were high cantor forward, because Missit was just that good. Also, Missit was just that famous. With Fortew, Missit led and Fortew followed. Pantheons always tried to field their star player – it was what the worshipers wanted, after all. So, "Moon Made" was not the kind of song that Missit ever normally got to sing.

Since they had been rehearsing it before the break, Phex was comfortable enough to partly forget it was Missit and not Kagee with whom he sang. As a result, they sifted the dome remarkably well. The patterns were not amazing, but the colors were true and the results were nowhere near as ugly as they had been with Tillam earlier that day.

Phex saw the acolytes, who had been taking a break as well, suddenly regroup and pay attention, facing the dais.

Phex wondered if he *wanted* this to go well. If it was okay for him and Missit to sing together like this, or if that somehow worked against them as a couple. Had they been subconsciously punishing the Dyesi by failing the dome? Unable to work together not because they *couldn't* but because they *wouldn't*, rebelling against the divinity separating them? It was possible, of course.

Or perhaps it was just that Asterism was more accepting about everything than Tillam.

Tillam was old and inflexible. It had been hard work for Phex to join them, and he'd relied on Missit as a bridge to the rest of the pantheon. Without Missit's support, Tillam could not accommodate Phex's cantor. Asterism, by contrast, had relaxed enough around the elder gods to be gracious when Missit joined them. They were young enough to be flexible with a different voice.

Or perhaps it was all on Phex – he was just more comfortable with his own pantheon around him.

Whatever the reason, "Moon Made" went well, so they did it a few more times through with Missit. On the third try, that odd stillness settled over the dome, everyone holding on to the breathless quiet after the final note. The bodyguards were carefully not watching, earmuffs on. The acolytes were watching too closely. The only others in the audience, the three Agatay, sat entirely entranced. Kagee looked as smug as Phex had ever seen him. Miramo and Levin looked, well, godfixed by the beauty.

It wasn't as good as it was going to get with Kagee, but it was certainly better than anything Phex and Missit had done recently with Tillam.

Phex looked at Missit, wondering what had changed.

Missit looked a little like he wanted to cry. "Again?" he suggested.

"I don't think… Are you okay?" Phex asked, truly concerned.

"I don't think you're allowed to talk to me about something that isn't divine."

Phex's hands flexed at his side with the urge to reach out and gather Missit close. Support him.

"No, I know, but Missit, what's *wrong*?"

"What's *right* anymore, Phex?"

"What are you two doing?" came a call up from the acolytes below.

Missit's mouth twisted. "Let's just sing again, okay? If it's all we get to do together."

Phex realized that was what had changed. Something, maybe seeing Fortew, maybe an epiphany of some kind, had forced Missit to realize that this was all they got to have together anymore. He would take this small bit, singing with Phex, and cherish it, because as much as it hurt, it was a tiny sample of what they'd once had. The taste of his favorite dish without getting to eat the whole thing. But at least it was still the same flavor.

Phex nodded, agreeing with this sentiment. He too would take the crumbs, if that was all he got. If it came packaged with the hurt of longing, it was still worth the price.

"Sing with me, then?" he said.

They sang it again. It was a lot more like Sapien singing and a lot less like Dyesi cantor. It was more a duet than their usual roles in a pantheon.

They sang "Moon Made" just as a song, neither of them really caring about what the graces did or how skinsift worked or the dome around them. They sang it for each other and their mutual obligation to create art.

Phex found his face was wet near the end, and in the audience, three Dyesi stood frozen, and he thought if they could cry that maybe they would be crying too. Instead, they were simply inert.

Quasilun did not let them finish.

That dual-tone bell-like voice cut though the godsong, breaking it open and leaving the dome empty and the acolytes unmoored.

Imago power.

It was executed simply and painlessly right there from the doorway. Quasilun hadn't even left their sentinel position at the entrance, although Bob had disappeared completely outside, presumably to avoid any possible dome effect – like any good bodyguard.

Quasilun's cantor stopped shortly after theirs did.

The three acolytes folded down, cut free of fugue, limp with the loss.

Quasilun said, not sounding angry, just firm, "That is not the way to do it, little ones."

Phex bowed his head and said in frozen register, "Apologies, imago."

Missit stared back defiantly and said nothing. He scrubbed angrily at his eyes.

"Wow," said Levin from the audience. "Is that godfix?"

"Yep," said Kagee, handing back the sleeping baby.

"Why was it so sad?" asked Miramo. "I thought godfix was supposed to be euphoric and amazing. Transporting."

"Wasn't it?" asked Kagee, picking up some chewy meat thing and eating it – ignoring Missit and Phex and their messiness on the dais.

"Well, yes, I guess," agreed Miramo, "but also sad. I didn't realize godsong could be that sad. It wasn't when *you* were up there."

Kagee said, "Phex and Missit are complicated."

"Complicated?"

"Like we three are complicated."

"Ah."

Kagee was reaching for another meat cube when there came a sudden ratchet of noise and shouting from outside the dome. It barely leaked into the now mostly soundproofed space. They only heard what they did because the dome wasn't finished.

Then the dome shook.

Violently.

And then a huge portion of it exploded inward.

Kagee yelled. Others screamed.

Berril deployed her wings and lifted into the air on instinct.

Tyve dove for their sifters, grabbing Fandina and Jinyesun both and flattening them to the dais with her on top.

Phex grabbed Missit, turning to shield him with his own body.

He barely noticed Kagee doing the same, shoving himself forward to cover Levin and the baby.

Kagee had been right all along.

Someone was indeed bombing a divine dome.

9

BY THE SKIN OF OUR SONG

The dome partly collapsed. Bright sunlight streamed in, reflecting off huge clouds of dust. Phex coughed and looked around, squinting against the grit in the air. A pile of rubble blocked the door.

Fortunately, they had Bob and Quasilun on their side. Bob explained later that the local military had immediately taken out the drone that was bombing them and deployed a troop to track down the source. He and Quasilun had worked hard and fast to get at the pantheon now trapped inside the partly collapsed dome. The diarchs' private security were equally motivated.

Phex wasn't sure how long they were stuck inside. It was dark and stuffy on the dais. He couldn't see anything beyond his immediate vicinity. The natural semi-pearlescent grey glow of a completed dome wasn't working yet. The panels hadn't been hooked into the local grid.

There were a few screams and yells at first, but that subsided into desperate panting and soft whimpers and the wailing cry of a single baby.

Phex ran his hands quickly all over Missit's body, "You okay?"

Missit gave a little hiccoughing whimper. "I can't think when you do that."

"Missit!"

"I'm good, really, fine. Are you hurt?"

Phex ran a mental check over himself. Something large, possibly one of the carapace panels, had hit him in the upper back. He was pretty sure he'd have a spectacular bruise there, but he didn't think anything was broken. Blood was running down the outer portion of his right arm – a fractured bit of rock or something similarly sharp had cut his bicep open, but it was probably already clotting, given his crazy effective genetics. Certainly, it was no blade wound.

"I'm okay," he said. He stopped touching Missit but stayed crouched over him. If they were caught, at least he had the excuse of continued protection, since the dome was no longer stable. Plus, he realized there was a heavy weight of some kind leaning against and on top of his lower legs, cool and smooth. Another panel, maybe? It seemed too heavy for that.

"Kagee," he yelled, "check in."

Kagee said, "We're okay. I think Miramo has a broken arm. Stop crying, you big baby, you've been through this before."

"It hurts, you pustule," replied the diarch, her voice very much full of pain.

The actual baby was still screaming at the top of its tiny lungs.

"The child?" Phex asked.

"She's just shocked and surprised," explained Levin's voice.

"You all right, Lev?" he heard Kagee ask.

"Topping," said Levin. "Like a day at the races."

Phex tuned the three Agatay out. "Berril? Tyve?"

Berril said, "I'm good, managed to avoid rockfall. I can fly out the hole in the dome if I need to. I'm staying to help and keep you company." He saw a bright flash and the glory of her beautiful wings as she flew from one person to the next, checking.

"We're fine," Tyve said, answering for her, Jin, and Fandina. "Missed most of us. Luck of the Dyesi. I can see from here, the acolytes look okay too."

Phex hadn't asked about them.

Kagee said, "I don't mean to say I told you so, but *I told you so.*"

"Yes, yes, you're very smart," shot back Tyve.

Quasilun and Bob must have cleared the entrance at that juncture because the imago's double-barreled voice echoed through the inside.

"Nymphs!"

All five of the Dyesi present in the dome said automatically, "Unharmed!" practically in unison. It was weird.

"Gods? Diarchs?"

"Nothing serious," said Tyve. "Maybe one broken bone."

Missit whispered while the others exchanged information. "Phex? Not that I'm complaining, but why are you leaning on me so much?"

Phex realized one of his legs had gone numb from the knee down. Too much weight on top of it, he supposed. Also, the cut in his arm had not clotted as expected.

"Missit, please roll out from under me," he instructed. "Quickly, now."

"Phex!" Missit's voice rose to high-pitched panic and he didn't do as instructed.

Phex felt himself begin to collapse. He twisted desperately as his arms gave out. Lurching sideways as best he could, so that he and the weight resting atop him crashed to the side, away from Missit. He landed hard on one shoulder, the weighty object still on him. Phex hoped nothing had landed on Missit. The god was screaming in earnest now.

Phex heard the tremendous panicked crashing of an enraged cyborg hurling things out of the way.

He worried about the stability of everything. Extractions from a collapsed building should be done carefully, shouldn't they?

There was a flurry of white wings above and around him and Berril's sweet concerned voice. "Phex?"

From some far distant place he heard himself say, in a very annoyed tone and using decidedly informal register, "Again?"

Then there came that stupid crashing roaring in his ears followed by blessed silence and red darkness.

Phex was beginning to think one of the recurring patterns of his life would be waking up in the medical bay on some alien world, sticky with bandage spray and good intentions.

He looked around.

This time, it seemed to be a proper large hospital. It was rock-walled and huge but well lit and clean, with that certain smell all medical facilities always have, no matter the place or species – disease, injury, bile, bleach, and soap.

He wondered idly if his headache, queasy stomach, and dry mouth were from blood loss like last time, or if he had the more valid excuse of being hit on said head.

This time was a little different because there was the pretty face of a smiling Agatay medic in front of him. Phex decided that he definitely thought the Agatay were sexy as a species. He wondered what Kagee would say to that, if he told him. He wondered what Missit would say.

Missit.

Right, the dome. There had been a bomb. And then a collapse.

"Is Missit okay?" he croaked. He closed his eyes, even though the face above him was pretty, because this hospital seemed awfully bright. "My pantheon?"

"Aw, what a sweetie. He wakes up worried. Anesthesia does that to some patients." The medic's lyrical pronunciation of Galactic Common was almost as pretty as his face.

Kagee's voice came then. "Everyone's fine. You're the putz who ignored two gaping wounds and half a dome on top of you."

"Liar," said Phex, because Kagee was obviously exaggerating.

"You forgot about the bang on the noggin." That was Tyve's mild voice from somewhere near Phex's feet.

Phex was a bit pleased about that – at least he'd passed out legitimately this time.

"Missit is spitting mad," said Berril from his other side, opposite Kagee.

"He is unharmed?"

"Are you stuck in some sort of loop? I told you, he's fine and you're the injured numbskull." Kagee's voice rose. "Has his memory been affected? Medic!"

"No. Calm down, proxy," said the medic, calmly.

"It's just Phex being Phex, Kagee," added Tyve.

"Fandina? Jinyesun?" Phex called out for his sifters plaintively, because he hadn't heard either of them speak yet. Not that the Dyesi were the biggest talkers in his pantheon, but still, had they been hurt?

"Quasilun took them and Missit back to the spaceship. Agatay isn't equipped to handle Dyesi injuries."

"They're injured!"

"Not visibly and they said they were fine, but the imago was in a panic that they might be internally bleeding or skin damaged. So, the acolytes decided they needed a full checkup."

"Missit too?"

Kagee growled, "He's fine, Phex. Gods!"

Tyve explained. "He was angrier than I've ever seen him because he wasn't allowed to come with us and keep an eye on you. Tried to throw godhood around. Quasilun had to carry him under one arm like a big golden spitting-mad spud. There was kicking involved. Bob came with us, though. Say hi, Bob."

"Hi," came the cyborg's slightly tinny voice.

"You're sure he wasn't hit? When I fell to the side I couldn't protect—"

Tyve said soothingly, "Be reasonable, Phex. You think Bob would have let Missit go with Quasilun if Missit had been hurt in *any* way?"

That was reassuring. Phex's worry subsided slightly. Apparently, he was the only one stupid enough to have been injured. "So, I'm the only idiot?"

"Yes, you are," said Kagee, firmly.

"He's different, isn't he?" That was a less-familiar voice. Phex's brain grappled to place it. He was annoyed with himself. He was a cantor – he should be able to identify voices even with his eyes closed.

Levin. His brain finally came up with a name.

What was the diarch of Agatay doing hanging out with Phex in a hospital? He cracked a lid. *Ouch. Bright.* "Were you hurt, Diarch?"

"No." Levin's cheerful face appeared in his line of sight.

"Then why?" Phex's own voice kept cracking. Someone offered him some water. *Berril?* "Hi, birdie," he said, sipping gratefully.

"Why am I here?" Levin lowered out of view again, presumably sitting on something. "Kagee was freaking out and we thought things would go more smoothly at the hospital if I threw my weight around a bit." Levin switched to talking to someone else, presumably Kagee. "Is he always like this, your low cantor?"

"Weird?" suggested Kagee.

"Yes."

"Yes."

Tyve said, "He's our sun, what do you expect?"

Phex's fingers twitched on the blanket covering him, soft and silky. Nice. He liked it. Like Missit's pajamas.

"Sun?" Levin pressed.

"There's a lot about the divinity and how pantheons work that's not put out on the infonet or divine forums for worshipers to know about – for security reasons, among other things," explained Kagee, sounding pompous.

"What's *sun*?" Levin pushed.

"Overprotective, self-sacrificing meathead, with absolutely no sense of self-preservation and a propensity for injury," explained Kagee.

"Ah! I see," said Levin. "Are you one of these suns too, then?"

"Hell, no. I gave that crap up when I became a god."

"Occasionally, he makes very rare exceptions," said Tyve, humor evident in her tone.

Phex said, "You are all very talkative. Some of us got hit on the head."

"See what I mean? *Meathead*." Kagee was grumpier than usual, even for Kagee.

"At least Missit is okay," said Phex, drinking more water.

"How long have Asterism's low cantor and Tillam's high cantor been dating, then?" asked Levin casually, as if it were a perfectly natural question and a perfectly natural situation.

"Oh, we don't talk about *that*," said Tyve quickly.

Phex was very grateful there were no Dyesi in the room at the moment. Then wondered when was the last time he had been anywhere, at any time, without at least one Dyesi nearby. Maybe there was an acolyte present and it was just out of sight and staying quiet.

"Right. You all are supposed to be celibate." Levin's voice was full of teasing amusement. "How's that working out for a bunch of horny Sapiens of prime breeding age?"

Kagee snorted. "As badly as you might imagine." At least they were talking in accented Galactic Common.

"You gotta get that regulation relaxed," said Levin, spoken like a true ruler.

Kagee said, "We're working on it."

Are we? wondered Phex.

"Good, you gonna date us again once you figure it out?"

"I'm a god, you two are the diarchs of a planet, it'll never work." Kagee was actually being sensible.

"Bah. Niggling little details."

"Levin, you are an unwarranted optimist." There was something in Kagee's tone that came off as almost soft. Was that affection? His voice made it very pretty. Calming. Phex liked it.

"Warranted optimist, thank you very much. We got us a dome, after all." Levin seemed like a bit of a troublemaker, for a supreme ruler.

"And now you've gone and lost part of it. I told them

someone would make it explode." Kagee had every right to be smug for a change.

Levin's voice went dark and serious. "Trust me, we are looking into *that*."

Berril said, still at Phex's head and offering him more water, "I heard the acolytes talking when they were climbing out. Apparently, the keyskin wasn't impacted. They'll start cloning new panels immediately. Construction shouldn't be delayed. They were in a deep state of shock, though. This really seems to be the first time a dome has ever been targeted."

"They're going to persist?" Kagee sounded amazed.

Berril said, "More than that, Calator Heshoyi said it wanted to get Dome 6 up and running even faster or it might happen again."

"As if it somehow it won't happen after the dome is complete?" Kagee's tone was incredulous.

"They still believe it's impossible, even though Agatay just proved otherwise," said Tyve. "Sometimes, the Dyesi really do seem insane."

"Only sometimes?" said Bob, unexpectedly.

"Bob should know," croaked Phex. Bob would have been dealing with this for years, much longer than Asterism. The cyborg had once said Tillam was Bob's second pantheon detail. That could mean decades working for the divinity.

Levin said, "We took all possible preventative measures, but this is not unexpected. Frankly, we thought they would opt for something bigger than a mere drone strike."

"How could you invite a dome to be built if you knew this kind of thing was possible?" Berril sounded unhappy and disappointed.

Levin said, "Honestly, this was just a little bump, no one was seriously hurt."

"Phex is lying right there!" Now Tyve was annoyed.

"I'm fine," croaked Phex.

"Holy divine shrimp balls, you are *not* fine! You are an absolute nutjob," yelled Kagee. "Shut up and go to sleep."

"I was trying," grumbled Phex. "You all keep talking."

"You people are fun," said Levin. "Are all gods this cool? I want to be a god. Berril taught me that spin thing. Can I join your pantheon?"

"Levin." Kagee's voice was firm. "I've enough to deal with with this rocksock, don't you start."

"What's a *rocksock*?" wondered Tyve in a soft aside, probably to Berril.

"You're no fun anymore," Levin said. "What happened to that light-hearted pretty-boy I fell in love with and kissed silly under the akatt tree?"

"You must be thinking of someone else."

"Oh, right. I *am* thinking of someone else."

Phex realized he was never getting back to sleep. He opened his eyes fully, wincing, head blasted with pain. "Can we go back to the spaceship?" he asked plaintively. "I want my bunk and my comfort ladle."

"Comfort *ladle*?" Levin clearly thought he had misheard.

"Don't ask," said Kagee.

"You can't go yet. They haven't finished all your tests," explained Berril.

"Are they running bloodwork?" asked Phex.

"Yep," said Tyve.

"*My* bloodwork? Have they freaked out yet?"

"Yep."

"Stupid genetics." Phex turned his glare on Kagee and Levin. "You two, go flirt somewhere else and let me sleep, then. I had no idea Kagee could talk so much faff, but I certainly don't need to hear it."

Kagee stood, frowning fiercely. "Yeah, yeah. Missit really is fine. Freaked out about you, but fine. Not one perfect golden hair was out of place. Happy?"

Phex shut his eyes. "Sleeping now."

Agatay medical facilities really were top-of-the-line. They had Phex bandaged up and healing accelerated into almost-perfect condition by the end of the day.

Back aboard their spaceship, he got a good night's rest, cuddling the ladle, and a full meal. After that, Phex was told by a surprised acolyte that he'd been cleared to climb back on the dais. It'd take more time for the rubble to be cleared, though, so the two pantheons were prescribed a few days of rest.

The Agatay medics had lost their minds over Phex's bloodwork and healing capacity. They'd taken multiple samples of most liquid bits of him that they could get. They were ex-core and so they'd never seen anything like Wheel work – genetics triggered to perfect the human immune system, heighten physical abilities, and appearance? It was all crazy to them.

They wanted to know if they had his permission to synthesize some of his blood and maybe hormones and a few other fluids. Phex didn't care – he had no proprietary interest in the stuff once it left his body. The rest of his pantheon thought that he should be more discerning, but Phex kind of liked the idea of Wheel tech being in the medical system of an ex-core planet. It was pure irony.

Levin had promised rich rewards to Phex for his service to Agatay's medical industry.

Phex had told him not to be absurd.

When the diarch insisted, Phex asked if the goodwill could be passed on to Fortew.

Levin had called him a *precious ducky* and said he'd do

exactly that. Then Phex had been discharged. Unfortunately, Asterism didn't get to see Fortew before they left. Unlike Phex, he was actually sleeping.

Phex wasn't certain if it was Missit singing with Asterism or them going through a dome collapse together, but somehow, they got their cantor working properly again.

When Phex next climbed onto the dais with Tillam, something had shifted in them as well as on the remade dome. He and Missit were able to harmonize once more. They could meet each other's eyes. The artificial distance between them, formed of Dyesi regulation and heartbreak, had narrowed metaphorically, if not literally. Phex didn't know why, but Missit trusted him again and so did his voice.

Or maybe it was Phex who trusted Missit.

The Dyesi changed the dome-building design. A full stone edifice could not be completed in time for the first performance. But that first performance *must* happen on schedule. So, instead, they constructed a temporary exterior of fabric and foam, to shield for sound and light, with plans to put proper fortifications in place later. They added that they thought that "later, they might not need them, and they could build something really beautiful instead." Or something equally absurd.

Security, bodyguards, and the military advisors weren't pleased with this decision.

The new temporary dome exterior was an even flimsier structure. But the acolytes made the point that the first dome had been easily breached. If local weapons already outstripped Dyesi construction materials, there was no way to build a dome completely defensible by Agatay's standards.

Better to go the opposite, something incredibly lightweight, practically insubstantial, that at least, if it collapsed, was much less likely to crush and kill those inside.

Because it was the divinity's decision in the end, the locals could do nothing but relent. Phex wondered if the Dyesi worried about the loss of a keyskin, or if that too was considered an acceptable risk.

Tillam and Asterism had run through two complete rehearsals without incident, and they were ready for Dome 6's first public performance.

In terms of personnel, the protective measures instituted by the diarchs on opening night were massive. It felt like there were more troops outside the dome than there were worshipers within. Air and land for miles around was under protective cover both in terms of manpower and drone and all possible tech that stretched between the two.

The Dyesi insisted that all those with an interest should get to experience a dome performance. The pantheons were told they would do two additional shows, each one for half the standing military at a time. Three performances in a row. They would have to delay the other scheduled performances for rest and recuperation. Especially if each new wave of worshippers came with even more military. They were tripling the number of performances. Phex wasn't sure Fortew could do it. He wasn't sure he could.

"Don't forget the proxies," Kagee reminded his exes.

"Why would you do this?" Levin asked. Both diarchs were hanging out in the vestry before the opening performance. Their baby was not with them, this time.

"You don't think soldiers deserve entertainment, Diarch?" asked Jinyesun, carefully.

"Yes, of course, but shouldn't the bulk of the elite be first? Why should they have to wait on the military? The leaders and decision-makers – isn't that the best way to spread the songs of gods?"

Fandina said, "Never discount the fighting force of a planet."

Phex was confused. That seemed like a very un-Dyesi attitude.

One of the acolytes said, "The divine is open to all who are interested in the color and the light."

"Well, then, shall we bring it to them?" Phex stood, adjusting his costume in the long mirror.

Berril came to stand next to him. "We look good."

Phex nodded – she was right. "Yes, we do."

Kagee came over and joined them, preening. "Good enough to start a whole new religious movement?" They were about to be the first gods ever to perform on Agatay.

Phex looked at him, assessing. "Well, maybe not you."

"Meathead," said Kagee without rancor.

Jinyesun said, "That's Sapien platonic affection, right? Expressed as an insult between friends?"

"Very good, Jin!" said Tyve.

Jinyesun's face speckled with pleasure and its crests puffed.

Fandina said, "Let's go, shall we?"

They all fell into line behind the sifter, Phex bringing up the rear. He looked over to the other vestry where, presumably, Tillam was waiting for their turn. Then he looked quickly away so that the acolytes, who were hustling the diarchs out and into the congregation, could not see the longing in him.

It may be a fragile thing with an air of impermanence to it with its strange foam-and-fabric exterior, but Dome 6 turned out to be a wonderful dome.

The resulting performance was truly one of the best

Asterism had ever given. Their new song was well received and their colors and patterns were brilliant. Almost every one of their songs had at least one moment of godfix.

Perhaps it was the congregation. Under a dome, the worshipers were always warm, but Dome 6 was full of those who believed primarily in Asterism – because Kagee was one of *theirs*. These were also new converts to the divinity, full of enthusiasm. Young the way Asterism was young. These were worshipers who never thought they would be lucky enough to visit a real dome, let alone see gods live and in person in their lifetime on their home planet.

Or maybe it all had to do with the newness of the dome.

Or perhaps it was something else entirely. Asterism had been practicing with this one keyskin for months, including during transit. Maybe it, and its clones, somehow had become friendlier to the pantheon that had lived with it for so long. Perhaps Dome 6 itself *liked* Asterism and felt an affinity for the demigods.

Whatever the reason, the Agatay worshipers reacted strongly to their first dome. This was a culture that showed appreciation vocally. Phex might have guessed that after meeting Levin. The Agatay screamed and clapped and roared. In the throes of godfix, they were awed and silent, almost struck dumb into stillness like the Dyesi under fugue. But the rest of the time, they were very active and vocal.

They gasped when Berril's wings burst forth. They cried with the beauty of Tyve's grace.

To give them godsong was a privilege. Phex felt the magic of that dais like it was a living thing coming from his own skin. As if he were the sifter, not Jin or Fandina. He tingled with the joy of it. His flips were that much more spectacularly high. His low cantor just a little more resonant.

Kagee fairly glowed with pride, to be in front of his own

people, but also at how much those people were giving back to their gods. How much love Asterism could feel pouring off them.

It was a truly amazing experience.

Phex had never really been moved by a performance before Dome 6. For the first time, he understood what Missit had tried to explain to him. The joy of being able to give an experience like that out into the universe – not as a job or as a duty but as an act of creation, an act of love.

Phex left the dais euphoric and exhausted but also looking forward to getting to do it again with Tillam after the intermission.

That had never happened to him before. Performing, for Phex, had always been an obligation – this time had been a pleasure.

Tillam's performance was just as good. Even without Fortew.

The worshipers were almost as excited for an established famous pantheon of major gods as they had been for their local favorites. The honor of having the great Tillam open their first dome was palpable. The fact that Phex of Asterism (the planet's favorite pantheon) was performing with Tillam was largely considered a point in Tillam's favor. Agatay wasn't like the rest of the galaxy. They didn't see Fortew's lack as a flaw. Instead, they saw Phex as Tillam's gain.

Even Tillam, jaded and tired and sad and crumbling, rallied under a dome that enthusiastic. Even they could be impacted by worshipers with so much passion for the divine. No one could perform untouched under such circumstances, not even Yorunlee.

Tillam executed a near-perfect performance as a result. The congregation sobbed audibly during "Five" and cheered with utter abandon during Tillam's biggest hits. Godfix washed over the gathering in waves. Phex was certain the beam of this dome would go down in divine history as one of the best. It had to – there was no way it wasn't special.

Afterwards, even Quasilun looked impressed.

Then, the next day, they got up in front of two rounds of soldiers, one after another, and did it all over again.

And then, after a day of rest, they got up in front of a new massive congregation of tens of thousands of worshipers and did it *again*.

Twelve official performances were planned in all. But with added daytime events for the standing military, it would probably end up being thirty-six.

The divinity intended to make good use of their new dome. They wanted to get as many people in and out of it as they could – maximizing a new worshiper base. They wanted the whole planet converted as quickly as possible.

They were using Asterism and Tillam ruthlessly to do it.

There was more to do to spread the divine as well. There were VIP congregations and standard believer congregations and outreach. These took a lot more effort than normal, since vast numbers of security were required and the bodyguards were in a heightened state of tension and awareness. Phex was *never* without his whip scarf. Kagee *always* wore his rings. Kagee's rings, at least, garnered a lot of respect. Everyone on Agatay knew what they meant. Also, he'd gotten refills of the neurotoxin.

The Dyesi were convinced it was still far too soon for any fixed to have developed on Agatay, but the bodyguards were still worried. It was their business to be wary. Dome 6 was very effective, causing considerable godfix. Plus, they didn't know the exact nature of godsong's impact on the Agatay psyche. Fixed weren't well understood. All anyone knew was that the more godfix exposure in a given population, the more likely mental collapse and the higher the percentage of fixed. Simply put, the more true believers, the more fixed came out of those believers. It was a matter of ratios. And with Agatay, the bodyguards had to face the possibility that a fixed might spring up with highly specialized military or assassin training.

In addition to their performances and congregation obligations, Asterism was invited to attend various political dinners with the diarchs. Elites came to town to experience the dome, and Miramo and Levin were obligated, as the rulers of the planet, to entertain them appropriately. Having gods attend these feasts was considered a show of power.

At the recommendation of the acolytes, these meals were always the day after a performance. But that meant Asterism had little excuse not to attend. Still, usually two acolytes opted to go instead of Jinyesun and Fandina. It was assumed, quite rightly, that most of the elites couldn't distinguish between Dyesi, so the acolytes could pretend to be demigods.

Phex was beginning to realize that most nymphs saw their skinsift cohorts as more delicate and fragile than average. Dyesi gods were to be protected whenever possible. Phex was fine with that – let Jin and Fandina rest and be safe. At least some of them could.

Kagee had to go. He was by far the biggest draw. Phex went because he worried about Kagee's safety, and Tyve went because she was Tyve. Berril went because the others were already going and she genuinely had a good time socializing at *any* party, even if it was for work.

Kagee flirted blatantly with his exes. If the acolytes noticed, they couldn't really do anything about it. Phex envied him the fun openness of it. Perhaps the Dyesi thought it was just an Agatay socio-cultural thing. They were certainly a very flirty population. Phex grew accustomed to rejecting a dozen or more propositions every feast.

Finally, he asked Kagee how to do it properly, since it didn't seem to have any impact.

Kagee laughed. "You don't have to be polite about it. Low population numbers and generations of codified non-monogamy, remember? On Agatay, suggesting a sexual liaison is like the Dyesi introducing themselves to every flipping room they enter – habit. If someone thinks you're hot, they'll ask for sex. If you think they're hot, you say yes. If anyone isn't game for any reason, it doesn't happen. It's not complicated, it's just a compliment."

"How does an actual long-term romantic relationship happen, then?" asked Berril, whose own culture was full of ritualized courting and arranged marriages.

"We generally only marry for political gain or alliance. I suspect that's why Miramo and Levin made it official. Romantic partnerships are different. They are for household or children or love or all three. They're about loyalty and compatibility – like a pantheon."

"You and Levin and Miramo, what was that then?" Berril pushed because Kagee was being so forthcoming.

Their high cantor smiled nostalgically. He was definitely softening the longer they stayed on Agatay. Unexpected, that. "We worked well together, actually. I mean we were young and dumb and outcasts at school. We were brought together by a shared love of the divinity, but we stayed together because we genuinely liked each other. Enjoyed each other's company. Found each other attractive."

"You're still in love with them," accused Tyve.

Phex was glad she had said it so he didn't have to.

"Of course. I just unraveled the threads, I never cut them."

Phex wondered if threads of affection really could stretch across a galaxy. He wondered if he and Missit would always be connected in some small way, even when star systems lay between them. Probably.

If there were a way to cut their threads, would he?

It was all going okay.

Dome 6 hadn't been bombed again. The colors were beautiful. The worshipers were plentiful. The divinity was delighted.

Phex was exhausted. He was doing both pantheons every other day, sometimes two or three times. He was attending dinners and congregations. He was too tired to do much else but sleep and eat and miss Missit. He felt constantly adrift, like there was a part of him that needed to hold Missit regularly so he could pull himself back together. So he could gather up all the bits of himself he gave out on the dais.

All along, he'd thought that Missit needed him for centering and solidity. Turns out, it was the other way around.

10

VAULT OF GRACE

During the VIP congregation after their fifth performance, it became clear that Agatay had more than just pantheons visiting them. Worshipers were now crossing the galaxy on pilgrimage to follow their gods, quarantine zone notwithstanding. And one Sapien couple looked oddly familiar.

The pair was older than most worshipers. Phex thought, for a brief moment, that these were the leaders of a different nation or continent on Agatay, drawn in by the divine. But they hadn't any kind of aura of authority or feel of diplomacy about them. Instead, they were relaxed and snidely superior – probably intellectuals of some kind. Exoplanetologists or astrobiologists, perhaps?

They were not dissimilar-looking from the Agatay locals, except that they weren't grey. In fact, they were a lot more gold-tinged than silver. No Dyesi fancy work was glossing them up, though. They weren't made metallic by artifice. And one of them had awfully familiar flecked eyes.

Phex turned to Jinyesun. "What are Missit's parents doing on Agatay?"

"Those are Missit's parents?" Kagee glanced up at Phex's words. He was sitting on Phex's other side, making his mark for an excited believer.

"Who else would they be?" wondered Phex.

Jin turned away from an enthusiastic supplicant with a polite excuse and tapped open the infonet to check. "Agreed. Those two certainly match the photos we have on record. Of course, all core humans look alike to me."

"You have access to an image record of Missit's birth family?" Kagee was looking at Jin, impressed.

"They once lived on Dyesid Prime, of course we do." Jinyesun became much less impressive with one simple sentence and a crest-wilt.

"Why are they standing in *our* believer line? They do know Tillam isn't here, don't they?" Kagee smiled up at his next supplicant, addressed them. "Hello, pretty, who do I mark this for?"

Phex hurriedly made his mark for the patient believer standing in front of him, tried not to be distracted. But those were Missit's *parents* standing over there – he was bound to be distracted.

He watched out of the corner of his eye as all three primary acolytes moved to intercept the newly arrived couple. They extracted the golden pair from the supplicant line and hustled them off into one corner of the reception room. There all five began an intense conversation, in fluent Dyesi. It made Phex nervous. He really wanted to eavesdrop. He couldn't tell from the crests whether this intensity was being dictated by excitement or annoyance – the acolytes' body language remained controlled and neutral. Phex had grown to expect nothing less from Ohongshe, Heshoyi, and Chalamee. As acolytes went, they were three of the best, oldest, and most experienced he'd encountered during his time as a demigod. Phex was wise enough to see that, even if he resented them punishing him for the sin of loving someone.

Phex focused on his line of worshipers. After they had finally all been greeted and marked, Asterism was granted time to socialize. Or, to be more precise, Asterism was strongly encouraged to do so. Phex made his way directly, and as politely as he could, to the group in the corner. He had things he wanted to say to Missit's parents. Probably things that were better said in private, but he wasn't certain if he'd get another opportunity.

Phex managed to introduce himself politely enough.

"The honor is all ours," said Missit's mother, obviously delighted to meet him. Her Dyesi was the best he'd ever heard spoken by a Sapien – including Missit.

His father added, "We are very interested in Asterism's work. Your rise has been meteoric, and your reputation exceeds those of previous demigods at the same career point, by an entire order of magnitude. Statistically, Asterism is either an outlier or you're pioneering a new trend in divine expansion." He made a nuanced clicking noise of shocked respect. It was not a sound that Phex himself had mastered. "A demigod pantheon being used to enlighten a new planet is truly remarkable."

"Thank you?" said Phex, because what else could he say?

"How would you explain your unprecedented reach and impact?" asked Missit's mother, presumably continuing her research right then and there.

"Are you two here to *study* Asterism?" Phex hazarded a guess, a little shocked and upset on both Missit and Tillam's behalf.

Missit's father looked conspiratorial and jocular. His smile was crooked exactly like Missit's, and Phex hated that. "Sort of. We are here to witness the opening of a new dome on an ex-core planet and ascertain how quickly enlightenment takes to transmit though a population of this particular genetic type."

Missit's mother added, "We are very excited by the small population size and violent tendencies of Agatay. This is an unprecedented opportunity to clearly track *the effect* of enlightenment in terms of both distribution and speed." Like most academics, they seemed to enjoy nothing more than discussing their own research.

"You're not here to see Missit?" Phex pressed.

Missit's father laughed. Actually *laughed*. "Ah. Well. That will be nice, of course. But not necessary. Tillam isn't very interesting to us anymore. Highly reliable outcomes with their godsongs, godfix, and performances at this juncture. They're good for an organic baseline but nothing more. We can predict the statistical probability of conversion, enlightenment, and side effect from Tillam. We can calculate with an accuracy of plus or minus ten percent for any new Tillam godsong."

His mother added, "Frankly, they're boring to us." She brightened. "However, we did see a recording of your vintage duet performance with our son. Now, that was *very* interesting. We understand it managed to cause fugue in the caves. No pantheon needed. Our boy has such a powerful voice. We're quite proud, of course. But what he can do in a cave was always remarkable from the very beginning. You, on the other hand – how did you happen? Your public-facing bio of record is very sparse."

Phex said, grappling to understand. "You never stopped studying the Dyesi, did you?"

"Certainly not! We were the first embedded anthropological musicologists on Dyesid Prime. Our life's work is the study of godsong."

"Then why did you leave the planet?" Phex narrowed his eyes at them.

"You're awfully curious about us, demigod Phex, for a young man we've only just met."

The acolytes had been following the rapid back-and-forth with interested crests and wide eyes. Calator Heshoyi looked like it intended to say something at that juncture.

Phex switched to Galactic Formal and said quickly, "As opposed to your curiosity about me and mine?"

Missit's parents looked at each other. His father said, still in Dyesi, "The reports underrepresented your personal aggression." He leaned forward and stared at Phex. Up close, his face was more pointed than Missit's and his eyes harder. His golden skin was worn and rough, like unpolished stone. "Were you not enlightened when you were recruited, Phex?"

"I was never a worshiper." Phex assumed that was what they were asking. He'd never heard the word *enlightenment* used in this way – except maybe once by acolytes.

Missit's mother had a tighter smile than her son. "Really? Now I'm even more curious as to how you happened. You're not from divine space originally, are you? Even though your bio says you're Attacon."

Her question was pointed, like she knew something.

"What are you implying?" Phex asked, sticking tight to Galactic Formal.

"I was a linguist before I became a musicologist. Did you know? No, why would you. Your Galactic is accented with archaic. You aren't from Hu-core, and I highly doubt you come from the quarantine zone, assuming there are any ancient humans left inside. That only leaves one option."

"Oh?" Phex narrowed his eyes, impressed despite himself.

"Wheel. I did my master's thesis on the accents of the

different Spokes." She leaned back, crossing her arms, looking impossibly smug.

Phex was intrigued. He'd had no idea he had an accent that indicative. He also hadn't realized that enough recordings of Wheel-folk speaking had leaked for one ex-linguist to identify him by it.

She continued to impress. "Your family line is armiger, right?"

Phex shifted, suddenly uncomfortable in his own skin. He'd always assumed he was progenetor stock – elite blood. Perhaps based on ego or hope or having so many genetic triggers. But armiger made more sense. His size, those intimidation features, the power in his voice, the way all his triggers were for physical fitness. He was an engineered soldier. Warrior stock. And apparently, the right ears could hear it in his accent. He'd been off the Wheel longer than he'd been on it at this point, and still his past cut at him with surprise wounds.

He switched back to Dyesi, even though his mastery of the language was poor by comparison and put him a weaker position talking with Missit's parents. "Why exactly did you two leave Dyesid Prime?"

"Oh dear, no more pretty archaic accent for me?" Missit's mother's lips twitched, amused by Phex's obvious discomfort.

But Missit's father answered Phex's question. "We left because our research pivoted to focus on what godsong was doing once it left the planet. The caves could teach us nothing more. We became fascinated by enlightenment. We had to follow the divinity into space. Dyesi do not get enlightened, they don't need to be."

"You left Missit behind because you got *bored*?" Phex struggled to keep his tone neutral.

Missit's mother didn't seem insulted. "Ah, well, that was a long time ago. If I remember correctly, we needed to run years' worth of analysis, and then there was the pressure to publish. But we had gathered all the data that we felt we needed from Dyesid Prime. No need to stay there. Isn't that right, dear?"

Missit's father pursed his lips. "Yes, I think so. Didn't we win our first Scholar Emeritus Award for that paper?"

"You're right, dear, we did."

As if academics would ever forget such circumstances. Phex stopped himself from sneering. "What about Missit?"

"He wanted to become a god. He has always known his own mind very well. Strong-willed." Missit's mother wasn't being defensive, simply stating facts.

The three acolytes seemed to be getting a little bored. But they couldn't quite figure out a polite way to divert the conversation.

Phex's voice dropped low and he pressed on. "You left him behind on an alien world?" How old was Missit when he first took to the dais with Tillam? Ten, maybe? Which meant he had been eight when he entered the divinity as a potential.

"He was *fine*. He said so at the time. I remember, don't you, dear?" Missit's father looked at his wife.

She nodded, misty-eyed with nostalgia. "*I'm gonna be famous,* he said. *Your work is more important, Mama.* He was always very mature and understanding for his age."

Missit's father clicked. "Such a brave little man. Old soul, you know?"

"Do I *know* that?" Phex's face felt stretched and cold. He wondered if *old soul* was code for *easy to abandon*. He wondered why he, of all people, was reacting so badly to this information and attitude.

He thought about the way Missit always came looking for

him. From the very beginning. In a crowd. At practice. In the dorm. In his bed. How Missit warmed his feet between Phex's legs when they cuddled at night – even when his toes weren't cold. How Missit crawled into his lap if Phex sat still long enough. How Missit sang high cantor always assisting low cantor, twining their voices, for balance and support. How he threw himself at Phex time and time again, in multiple ways. Leaping off the dais and into space, trusting Phex to catch him.

Missit's parents had tossed him away as if he were broken – all the while calling him *strong* to justify it. Missit had built godhood out of that, but no wonder he felt like molten metal in Phex's arms. The unwanted always tried to shape themselves into something desirable, with no understanding of what that could be, having never been shown it in the first place.

Phex should know – he was formed and formless in exactly the same way.

He wondered what metal he felt like to Missit, hot and bleeding through golden fingers. Was he burning silver or cold, poisonous mercury? Should he have said to Missit, *You have me and I will not abandon you*?

Clearly, he had no right to say any such thing and be believed. Since he *had* abandoned Missit. Was he any better than Missit's parents if he too had let the divinity separate them?

Kagee's voice interrupted the conversation then. "Phex, come with me." Kagee's hand was on Phex's shoulder, grip hard and firm.

Phex looked down at him, startled. *What was he doing?*

Then Kagee, of all people, said, "It's nice to meet you, Missit's parents. I need to steal my low cantor away now." But he hadn't introduced himself.

Missit's parents pouted but Phex barely noticed. Kagee was acting so weird.

"Why are you extracting me?" he asked as soon as it was safe to say something.

"You looked like you wanted to kill them."

Phex tilted his head, considering. "You would know."

Kagee up-tilted his chin. "Exactly. So, *did* you want to kill them?"

"Probably."

"Why?"

"Because they made everything I couldn't do for Missit that much worse."

Kagee didn't pry, just licked his lips and nodded. "So, what are they doing visiting my home world?"

Phex felt his jaw tense, so he made an effort to relax it. "They're studying godsong here. Our godsong. Something to do with xenomusicology – about Asterism, and Agatay, and the new dome. It's called *enlightenment*, and they want to watch it be born on a new world in a new population."

"Is it something to do with the fixed?"

Phex wrinkled his nose. "I suspect it's kind of the opposite. I didn't really follow."

"You should have paid closer attention!" Kagee sounded anxious and sharper than normal, even for him. Why, when it was just the divinity expanding as always? Did it really matter to Kagee that anthropologists wanted to watch Asterism lead the conversion? Or was he afraid for Agatay itself, which he purported to dislike?

"I was busy trying not to kill them, remember?"

"Still, this is important." Kagee frowned fiercely.

"Why are you mad at me all of a sudden?"

"This is something that impacts my people directly, Phex! *My planet.*"

"I thought you hated it here."

"I did too. I was wrong. Clearly. So, this enlightenment? What is it? What is it *doing* to Agatay worshipers?"

Phex hated to disappoint him but: "I have no idea."

Kagee growled in frustration. His gaze shifted to Miramo standing and chatting animatedly with Berril and two awed worshipers in a corner. Levin wasn't attending this event.

Phex looked at the floor. "Missit's blasted parents seem remarkably forthcoming about their research and remarkably interested in Asterism because of it. We might get more out of them on enlightenment if we engage them in protracted conversation. Which I was trying to do when you pulled me away."

"*Protracted conversation*? You?" Kagee sneered.

"I was thinking of siccing Tyve and Berril on them."

"See, you can be smart."

"Should we invite Missit's parents to visit us and conduct oral interviews in an act of benevolent graciousness?"

"Phex, you got evil when I wasn't looking. Well done."

"Thank you."

"It's crafty. I like it."

"Let's talk to the acolytes when we get back to the ship. See if we can officially arrange it. Also, I need to tell Missit that his parents are here. I doubt they saw fit to inform him themselves."

"You promise not to kill them?"

"How about a light maiming?"

"You can't maim your boyfriend's parents. Not done."

"Boyfriend?"

"You're not fooling anybody."

"I certainly hope I'm fooling the acolytes. Show me how your deadly jewelry works and maybe I'll just poison them."

"My baby boy is all grown up and getting vicious. I'm so proud."

"Just one ring?"

"No, but I applaud the thought."

Phex crossed his arms and relaxed slightly. He liked having Kagee back on his side. He looked around, surprised to find that his ire had cooled. He was peckish, too. Were there snacks?

"Get them out!" That was Quasilun's voice, instantly recognizable and booming out over the congregation.

Itrio's voice came next. "Phex! Fixed!"

Phex and Kagee swung back-to-back.

Phex checked for the rest his pantheon. Quasilun was standing in front of Jinyesun and Fandina. Tyve and Berril were under the care of Bob and two other bodyguards. Itrio was wading through the confused gathering toward Phex and Kagee, who had accidentally isolated themselves in an effort to have a private conversation.

They couldn't tell which of the several dozen VIPs in that room was fixed. But there was a writhing lump of local security personnel to one side that Phex assumed had the fixed at the bottom of the pile.

Itrio came bouncing up. "Already neutralized, but it's a good excuse to get you all out of here."

"That was fast," said Phex, who hadn't even unwound his whip scarf.

Itrio said, "It's not good, though. It was an Agatay fixed. They shouldn't be that far gone already."

"I guess the acolytes miscalculated."

"I guess they did." Itrio looked dour. "Wouldn't be the first time."

Phex glanced over the crowd. He was taller than most Agatay, so it wasn't difficult. Missit's parents were easy to spot. They were recording everything, wrist idents out, faces intent.

Phex wondered how much trouble he'd be in if he just whipped his scarf out at them. Just a little scratch. They had abandoned their child to the divinity in order to better understand that divinity. Missit had suffered two-fold for his godhood, yet still gone on to become one of the greatest. How had he not become bitter? How had he become the capricious, good-humored golden child that Phex had once held in his arms?

For the first time, Phex understood Kagee's anger on his behalf. Kagee had hated the Wheel for what it had done to Phex. But the Wheel had done it out of indifference. Carelessness. Missit's parents had done it intentionally. For the divinity.

Was the divinity truly to blame for everything?

They docked back on the *Nusplunder* to find Tillam waiting for them.

"We heard that a fixed attacked. Are you all okay?" Missit was shifting his stance from foot to foot, his eyes on Phex, but he carefully addressed all of Asterism with his public concern.

The murmel around his neck trilled in a way that was both affectionate and instructional. Presumably trying to calm his anxiety.

"That was fast," said Tyve. Her brother scooped her into a hug. She batted at him in affectionate annoyance.

"Tern likes to follow local news whenever we're in orbit," explained Missit.

Tillam's light grace tilted his head almost sarcastically.

Phex couldn't think of anything more unpleasant than local politics, in any corner of the galaxy. Tern had weird interests.

Kagee pushed through Tillam and into the spaceship's hallway. "Word travels fast on Agatay. The divinity can't keep a lid on things here. We still have an old-fashioned radio broadcast system. It isn't infonet-dependent." Kagee said this without changing languages, like he meant the acolytes to hear.

Phex and the others followed aboard.

"I bet they aren't letting this beam out to the rest of the galaxy," said Zil in Galactic, arm around Tyve's neck as they walked.

"Certainly not. The divinity always suppresses info on fixed attacks," Kagee replied in Galactic Common, his accented Agatay dialect more pronounced than ever.

Phex thought back over his conversation with Missit's parents. He looked at Zil, wondering if he would understand. "It's too soon, though, isn't it?" He also switched to Galactic, aware now that he spoke it with an archaic accent. Wondering why no one had ever told him. Wondering if that was one reason he'd been mocked on Attacon.

"Too soon for what?" asked Tyve.

"Agatay to have fixed." They were speaking rapidly. The acolytes and sifters were confused about what was happening.

Phex said quickly and directly to Missit, "Your parents are in orbit."

"My *what*?"

Tern moved to Missit's side in a show of support. Phex was pathetically grateful for this.

Dimsum made a little squawk noise and then patted Missit's cheek with one tiny hand.

Kagee added, "They're here."

Phex explained. "They were at the VIP congregation.

They had a long conversation with the acolytes. And me." He kept his gaze steady on Missit's face, looking for signs of sorrow or stress. The murmel was doing the same.

Missit just looked confused. "At the meet-and-greet for *Asterism*?"

"Well, Tillam isn't hosting VIP services, just us," said Kagee, trying to mitigate the offense.

But Phex thought that wasn't fair. Missit deserved the truth, not platitudes. "They *are* here for Asterism. Apparently, they find something about us worth *studying*."

"Not Tillam and not me?" Missit understood the implications.

Kagee banged Phex on the shoulder with a closed fist. "Why are you being mean about this?"

"I'm being truthful. He needs to protect himself."

Missit looked at Phex far too fondly. "Of course you would think that."

Phex made a face. "No insult intended, but I don't like your parents at all, Missit."

Missit beamed at him. "That's the nicest thing anyone has ever said to me."

From behind them one of the acolytes said, "Why are they talking in Galactic?"

Another said, "This is a Dyesi ship, proper linguistic respect should be observed."

Phex puffed out a breath, ignoring them. "I'm about to disappoint you. Again."

"Again? Disappoint? What? Phex?" Missit was adorable when he was confused.

Phex stared at him hard, wondering if Missit could see the pain behind his question. "We are gods, should we meddle?"

Missit relaxed a little and gave one of his old familiar smiles. "Phex, gods always meddle, it's part of our charm."

Phex nodded rather than clicking. "You'll remember you gave me permission?"

"Permission? Phex, what is going on?" Missit's eyes got big and scared.

Phex had to hold both his arms tight to his sides to stop himself from reaching out. One touch and that fear would have dissipated. Missit in his arms and his own itchy, numb anger would be mitigated.

They simply didn't work as acquaintances. They barely worked very well as themselves anymore. At some point, they had traded bits of identity. Now, to be apart left them with gaps unfilled, like a sauce that had curdled.

Phex glanced back at the acolytes, who seemed to be waking up to the fact that Phex and Missit were engaging in an intimate conversation, whether alone or not, whether touching or not. Phex and Missit were focused on each other.

Phex quickly turned his back on the great god and addressed Sacerdote Chalamee directly. "Those two academics wish to interview Asterism."

The acolytes stopped crest communication at this direct verbal attack. They stilled all movements, confused.

"You should invite them aboard to interview us." Kagee doubled back to join Phex in the face off.

"For science," added Phex, with a quieting gesture at both Tyve and Jinyesun, who looked like they wanted to protest. Or at least like they might make a fuss in order to find out what was going on.

Missit's face was a picture of confusion, hope, and betrayal. He obviously wanted to see his parents but also had no idea how he felt about them inside his own territory. And he had no idea why Phex, of all people, would want to invite them aboard the *Nusplunder*.

The acolytes exchanged confused crest-wiggles. Finally,

the sacerdote said, "Of course we welcome the Scholars Emeritus, but are you certain? Asterism is in the middle of a performance cycle. Normally, outside interviews are for publicity, not research. Have you the time and the energy?"

Phex didn't have anything else to say to them. He gave Missit an apologetic wince.

Missit threw his hands up in the air and then stormed away, frustrated.

The murmel stood on his shoulder, levered herself up onto her back legs by leaning on the top of Missit's head, and chittered at everyone angrily.

The rest of Tillam followed. Yorunlee was last – it paused next to Phex.

"He's not eating properly," said the sifter.

"You think I can't see that?"

"You're not going to do anything about it?"

"What can I do?" Phex knew the frustration was coloring his tone into insult – with Yorunlee, of all Dyesi, the stiffest and the meanest. Jinyesun plucked at his arm in silent warning.

"You started this. You were warned not to." Dyesi stubbornness was as set in stone as the caves they inhabited.

Phex curled his lip, as if he'd ever had a choice where Missit was concerned. "Yet here we are. Do you have a solution?"

Yorunlee's crests went stiff for a long moment. "It's a risk, but when they finally come for you, ask for *truth in fungi*."

"What?"

"Just remember the phrase."

"*Truth in fungi?*"

Yorunlee clicked a harsh, annoyed confirmation and then glided aggressively after the rest of Tillam.

Phex ignored the acolytes who were trying to get his attention and just walked away to Asterism's quarters. After a brief hesitation, his pantheon followed. He heard Fandina and Jinyesun reassure the acolytes as to their willingness to be interviewed by scientists.

As soon as they were inside, Kagee said, "We can explain. And Berril and Tyve, we are going to need your help. But we must wait until we have privacy."

The rest of Asterism clicked agreement and, since it had been a long day, began their evening rituals of hygiene and ablution and bed.

Late that night, after lights were out when the bodyguards were pacing the hallway but probably not the acolytes anymore, Kagee explained.

"Phex and I are too blunt, so we need Berril and Tyve to take point with the visiting scholars."

Jinyesun sounded crestfallen. "Why not me?"

"Because we have an agenda. Missit's parents are highly educated Sapiens, they may speak like Dyesi but they aren't. We must approach with our best social manipulators. They're academics, Tyve, use flattery."

Tyve clicked. "Like a trade negotiation."

"Why me?" wondered Berril from her top bunk.

"You're cute and everyone likes you." Kagee didn't like to compliment anyone except Berril.

"Phex wanted to invite Missit's parents to interview us, but actually we want information from them?" Fandina sounded wary but not unwilling.

"For Kagee," added Phex.

"For *Kagee*?"

"This has nothing to do with Missit?" Jin pushed.

"Nothing," agreed Kagee.

Both sifters clicked in tones of profound relief.

Phex said, just to make sure they knew, "I would never ask you to betray the divinity." Because he wouldn't. If he were to betray the divinity, he would do it alone and try to leave the rest of Asterism out of it, especially his beloved sifters. It wouldn't be fair to involve them. Not that he intended to betray the divinity.

Not yet, anyway.

Phex added, to make his point, "To be kind to Missit, I would never have invited them aboard at all. I doubt he wants to see them."

"You think Missit does not desire to reunite with his breeders?" Jinyesun sounded truly shocked.

Phex grappled for a way to explain that the Dyesi would understand. They seemed to have such clearly defined relationships between the life stages. How to articulate the Sapien concept of *family*? Especially when he himself had only an outsider's understanding. "Missit wants them to be what they cannot be."

"What is that?" Fandina asked.

"Parents. So, maybe I should have said that I don't think he *should* want to see them. Best to limit exposure."

Fandina huffed. "Sapien familial relations are so complicated."

Jinyesun moved them back to the main topic at hand. "What does Kagee need from *Missit's* parents?"

Kagee said, "Godsong causes something called *enlightenment*. Apparently, this is happening faster on Agatay than normal because of Asterism. Or that's what Phex gathered from talking to Missit's parents. It's what they are here to research."

"Phex talked?" said Tyve.

"For a while. I stopped him."

"Why?" asked Berril.

"He was about to stop talking and start hitting."

"Fine, keep your secrets." Tyve sounded more amused than annoyed. "So, you want Berril and me to find out what Missit's parents think is going on here?"

"Yes."

"Because this is your planet. And your exes are in charge of it." Tyve was quick on the uptake.

"Versus the divinity." Kagee made it sound like war, which Phex thought was very Agatay of him.

"You make it sound unpleasantly combative," said Fandina. Mirroring Phex's thoughts in a way that he would have believed impossible for a Dyesi.

Phex was overwhelmed by a grave suspicion. "Fandina, do you and Jin know what this *enlightenment* theory is?"

Fandina was very careful. Phex could hear it in the precision of its words, even if its crests were out of view. "Not *as such*."

"But you have some idea?" pushed Kagee.

"We aren't sure how Sapiens would phrase it." Jinyesun came to Fandina's defense.

"Is it third beauty?" asked Phex.

Jin's tone went flat. "Not exactly. It's a concept for which there is no translation. But if the Scholars Emeritus are trying to research it, they might have reached an understanding in such a way that Sapiens could comprehend without offense." Its pronouns changed, indicating it was talking directly to Fandina. "I think that would be a good thing, don't you?"

Fandina's tone softened. "Would it? Is it usually better when Sapiens know the truth, or will they willfully misunderstand like always? Sapiens also seem to specialize in that."

Phex had to agree with that assessment. Especially where the Dyesi were concerned.

Kagee said, "Okay. So, we talk to Missit's parents and see

what we can find out. Then you assess if we comprehend in the way that you think is correct? Test us? After all, we're gods, we have a better understanding of the Dyesi already."

"If you don't get it, no Sapien will?" suggested Fandina, slipping into amused informal.

"Exactly," agreed Kagee.

The two sifters clicked.

Phex relaxed. All of Asterism was in agreement. Missit's parents were going down.

11

THE FIXATION HAS BROKEN

The acolytes set up the interview between Missit's parents and Asterism with very little fuss. Apparently, they were disposed to favor scholarly research, especially when dealing with abnormal planetary reactions to the divine. If they could figure out why Agatay already had its first fixed, they wanted to. It might guide better, more controllable results on the next ex-core planet. Or mean they should stop using Asterism for first divine conversion. Or Phex assumed that's what they hoped to find out.

They wanted to know if this freak occurrence was the result of Asterism or Agatay, or a combination of both.

First, however, Asterism had another performance to get through.

It went as well as the previous ones. Again, for Phex, it was made magic by the enthusiasm of the congregation. Their willingness to immerse themselves in godsong was unprecedented. They were so responsive. They gave back so much adulation and love.

Phex was touched and a little awed by how much he enjoyed the experience because of them. Not just with

Asterism but with Tillam as well. Being a god was not so bad, if this was the kind of thing he received in return. Missit's face during their cantor together was pure joy. The golden god forgot everything when he performed for a crowd like this. He could forget being separated from Phex, his parents suddenly appearing, Fortew's illness. It all faded in response to the congregation. Or, at least, it seemed like it did from Phex's perspective.

They experienced a kind of feedback euphoria that surprised Phex but bolstered Missit. This kind of show was obviously one of the things that had kept Missit going over the years. It was probably one of the things that made him great, to love them back for *this* feeling. Phex wasn't there yet. But for the first time, he thought he could get there. With Missit. Because of Missit.

There was an impossible promised future when their voices combined. It was a thing that could bring joy for years if it were allowed to explode as starburst. Not just to the audience but to Phex and Missit. There was a togetherness to them on that dais that went beyond voices. Only Missit and Phex could make space for all the facets of beauty and love at once, for each other and their worshippers, like all the colors of the dome. Phex enjoyed the promise of it while it was happening. But afterward, when he left the stage and could not touch Missit and had to pretend that he no longer cared, he resented the divinity. They saw only the beauty as it swirled above them but ignored the promised future in it. What right had they to limit love by confining it to such a temporary, superficial thing as beauty?

There was another fixed in this congregation. Another one. Already. She was dealt with easily. One in ten thousand was a perfectly acceptable ratio, explained the acolytes while informing them of the breach.

They waited to tell them until both pantheons were back on the *Nusplunder* with none of them the wiser to the fact that their performance had not gone seamlessly.

Sacerdote Chalamee said, consulting some notes on its ident, "In fact, at your current conversion rates, Asterism, it is almost expected."

"The fixed was for one of us again?" asked Phex. "Which one?"

His question was ignored.

The sacerdote also didn't say anything about this being too soon for Agatay to have fixed, or the dangers of fixed surfacing in a population of highly trained military.

Instead, it reminded them that security was already as high as it could get for this dome. And they had no intention of stopping the performance run for any reason.

Phex wasn't surprised. If the bombing of Dome 6 hadn't stopped them, nothing would.

Phex didn't know if Kagee made a point of mentioning the risks to his diarchs, but they took it upon themselves to show up, one or both, even more often than they had before, at as many of Asterism's events as possible. Their added presence meant added security for the gods. Phex had no doubt that's why they did it. They were worried about Kagee. The fixed may not be actual assassins, but on Agatay, assassins were commonplace. The diarchs had established protocols for dealing with them. They were not above activating those protocols on Kagee's behalf and, by extension, the other demigods. Also, how bad would it look if, while hosting their very first tour, a god died on Agatay?

Missit's parents made the very grave mistake of opting to interview Asterism as a whole pantheon rather than one-on-one as individuals.

Phex supposed it made a crude kind of sense. After all, they performed as a group and had the most impact that way. But Missit's parents did not realize how coordinated in their social defenses Asterism could be, as a group, either. Especially when they wanted something. Information, for example.

"Did you enjoy the performance in Dome 6?" asked Berril politely, before the scholars could even call up their notes and begin the interview. She was good – it was exactly the kind of thing one talked to musical anthropologists about. Berril's cute little face was openly winsome, charm dialed up.

Missit's father was instantly taken in. "Aren't you just as adorable as your believers claim!"

Missit's mother, on the other hand, actually answered Berril's question. "We did indeed, thank you for asking. Observing enlightenment in its nascent form is always a privilege."

"Is it? How nice."

Missit's mother dropped Dyesi formalities rather quickly for someone chatting with gods. Phex supposed she was their elder and they were only demigods, but still. It might be considered rude. "Indeed. And Asterism seems particularly effective on Agatay. We are currently trying to understand why that might be. And that is why we're excited for this interview. Shall we get started? You don't mind if this is recorded, do you? Of course you don't. You're gods, you're accustomed to being recorded."

Phex thought that was true but presumptuous.

"How can we help, honorable scholars? What exactly do

you wish to understand?" Tyve donned her best most efficient tone.

Kagee and Phex stayed seated to either side of the graces, with the sifters on each end. Kagee looked sullen, but that was normal. Kagee didn't have very good control over his facial expressions. Phex tried to look less grumpy than normal, making an effort to relax his posture and soften his lips.

The two scholars fired questions back and forth quickly.

"Is it your unique combination of talents?"

"Something about your cantors? Or are your sifters particularly potent?"

"Or is it possible that Tillam is providing some kind of assist? Is it something to do with Phex singing with both pantheons at once?"

"There's a lot of unique things about Asterism. Unusual species, for example. It makes the variables particularly difficult to isolate."

"Of course, we are accustomed to such difficulties when working in the social sciences."

Asterism stayed quiet – they didn't know the answers to any of these questions.

Finally, Jinyesun said, "Honorable scholars, those would seem to be elements best studied in the field as outside observers. How can interviewing us help with such things? Although we are more than willing to try."

Missit's parents exchanged glances. "We think Kagee might be able to offer insight, as a native to this planet and *also* a god."

Kagee said, "I can try, of course, but I don't quite understand the nature of your research. Or what is so unique about my people as compared to other worshipers. I mean to say, what is a *normal* reaction, if you consider Agatay and Asterism abnormal?"

"Would we use the word *normal*? How about *average*?" Missit's mother was gentle in her reprimand.

Kagee only clicked.

Missit's father cleared his throat. "Our original hypothesis was that on a highly violent ex-core planet like Agatay, the impact of godsong would be mild to start with a much slower growth curve than average. But it seems as if the opposite is occurring here. Dome 6 is activating a much stronger nascent enlightenment from the moment godsong commenced under the dome. It is baffling."

"Enlightenment?" Berril was gentle and innocent with her curiosity.

The man looked at his wife. "I suppose Asterism might need to understand, in order to properly assist with our research." He turned back to Berril. "It is a culturally proprietary secret, you understand? The Dyesi are not open about this, for obvious reasons. The divinity might be seriously curtailed in its attempts to expand if *enlightenment* becomes common knowledge."

"And yet you are being allowed to study it?"

"We are Scholars Emeritus," said Missit's mother, proudly.

"And we granted the acolytes the right to review all our data, findings, and results before publication," added Missit's father, much less proudly.

Phex leaned forward, tone carefully neutral. "You may consider us safe repositories of knowledge. Who could we possibly tell?"

Tyve said, "Our access to the infonet as content providers is severely limited by the divinity."

"We are gods, after all," added Berril, in an attempt to mitigate the sting. "It's all about image."

But Missit's parents, who had put their child into the very system that muffled him even as it made him great, had no particular concern or critique to offer on the nature of godly autonomy.

They were xenoanthropologists, after all. So far as they were concerned, all potential gods, and resulting pantheons, had willingly put themselves into the divine system. If that position included being taken advantage of by the Dyesi, it was the price of cultural immersion. Potentials, demigods, and gods had joined the divinity not as worshipers but as proselytizers. Pantheons were missionaries. It was how the divine system worked – no one understood that better than Missit's parents.

Phex never really felt like he'd traded freedom for godhood. He'd been subconsciously pursuing safety at the expense of liberty his entire life. He didn't mind having his actions monitored or limited in order to become a god.

Or, more precisely, he *hadn't minded* until the Dyesi separated him from Missit. Now he hated it. Now he, who had sacrificed his autonomy for security, finally understood that he'd once had autonomy at all. He'd never realized how important it was, until he suffered because of its absence.

Missit's mother said to her husband, "How do we explain? Tillam would have noticed but Asterism is too young. Barely demigods. You need experience to recognize enlightenment."

"We just have to try, dear."

"True. They seem like smart kids." She sat back, face thoughtful.

Phex realized for the first time that Missit's mother was small and lithe like Missit. His bone structure must have come from her. Age and inactivity had placed a layer of fat and stiffness over the woman's skeleton now, but the liquid was still there in her bones – had she once been a dancer? Or had she too picked up Dyesi double-jointed elegance from her time living among them?

"Have you never noticed that the higher the per-capita number of domes in any sector of space, the lower the local incidents of violent crime and the more unlikely conflict is to occur within or between species? Especially among younger generations? The same age bracket tends to become worshipers regardless of sector of space, and they always also become *calm*. Some might even say *unnaturally relaxed*."

Phex frowned. Thinking hard. Was it Tern who had said something about this? How the younger generations of his people just didn't care to argue or fight anymore?

Tyve sat upright all of a sudden. "It's happening with the Jakaa Nova *now*. Take my sister as an example. Are you saying this has something to do with the divinity?"

"Is your sister a worshiper?"

"Yes. Of course. Tillam. Has been most of her life. Zil is her adored older brother, after all."

"Well, she is just one data point. Anecdotal at that. Prior to her teen years, would you have called her as violent as the average Jakaa Nova?"

Tyve laughed. "More so. She bit anything that would hold still long enough for her to toddle up to it. Screamed all the time. A lot like the murmel. I still have faint claw scars on my ankle from when she crawled up to me and just swiped, for no good reason."

"What you're describing is just a single example, but when compounded over millions, it's a known effect." Missit's father spread his hands broadly. "Enlightenment."

"You're saying godsong has an impact on worshiper

psyche? Calming them all down or something?" Kagee was leaning forward, fascinated. He looked the least smug Phex had ever seen.

"On the *Sapien* psyche specifically, yes. And it originates with godsong and, most powerfully, godfix. Live and in person under a dome is best. The more godfix experienced by a worshiper, the more likely they are to be nonviolent in their actions, choices, and careers going forward."

Phex turned to look at Jinyesun.

The sifter looked very still and very impassive.

Phex turned to the other side and Fandina. The same. Did they know about this enlightenment?

"The Dyesi are pacifists," he said. This was an accepted universal truth. Somewhat mocked by many other cultures. And yet...

Kagee followed Phex's line of thinking. "Are you implying that the divinity has an intentional mass *pacification* effect?"

"It's a bit more complicated than that, kind of soporific and mellowing, but essentially, yes." Missit's mother was smiling softly. "Places with more domes and cupolas have less interpersonal violence across all parts of society. Not just political conflict. They show less civil unrest, fewer incidents of mob destruction, and no mass shootings. Even more interesting, it seems to work on a micro scale. With sufficient exposure and among long-term worshipers, domestic violence drops to levels lower than any in recorded history, so do all forms of sexual violence and bullying, not to mention emotional, psychological, and verbal abuse. There even seem to be fewer serial killers. It may also act as an antipsychotic. Although that is a difficult data point to track. Still, we've found that the impact of godsong is culture-wide and occurs in all worshipers of all ages and demographics. Although, since most worshipers are teens, they experience the most profound effect. Godfix seems to impact a Sapien's sense of security and well-being. It encourages changes in career and other lifestyle patterns. It affects how worshipers vote and whether they choose to enlist in a military. The best word we could come up with, that the Dyesi accepted, was *enlightenment*."

Missit's father added, "This enlightenment is remarkable. Statistically, we've discovered that places where the divinity is most popular have the least amount of suicide, conflict, and war. We've now become particularly interested in how enlightenment takes root initially. How much time is required to reach cultural saturation? Which is why we were so excited to come to Agatay."

"You're saying you expect Agatay to become *peaceful*? Because of *godsong*?" Kagee's face was blank with shock. He looked more shaken than Phex had ever seen.

Phex tilted his head at Berril. She instantly shifted closer to Kagee. Pressed against his side to offer wordless comfort.

Missit's father clicked. "Indeed. And faster than normal. Under most circumstances, we believe it takes a decade of exposure before any kind of major change is recognizable in the surrounding society and culture. Because younger worshipers must grow up and begin to procreate. But on Agatay, it appears to be happening exponentially fast. Within days, not years."

"How do you know?" Kagee was very intrigued.

"Because of how quickly your people have produced fixed."

"What do the fixed have to do with it?"

"The fixed seem to be an unfortunate side effect of enlightenment. In a small percentage of any given population, godsong has the opposite effect on the psyche. Or it's possible it is a kind of allergic reaction, we aren't sure."

"Explain," barked Phex, not minding his tone as he ought. Tyve pinched him. But this was important.

"The more worshipers, the more fixed, you know that, right? Well, the more worshipers, the more enlightenment too. Thus, the more enlightenment, then the more fixed. Of course, correlation is not causation but it is statistically predictable. For every ten thousand true believers in a god, there are one to three fixed in the mix focused on that god. Fortunately, the fixed do not turn their violent tendencies on the general population. That would be truly terrible, since that population is no longer equipped to defend itself. Instead, they refocus on their godly obsession."

"So, we gods suffer the consequences of enlightenment?" Phex wanted this very clear.

"We also reap the rewards of worship. We are, after all, *gods*," pointed out Jinyesun, still carefully neutral. Unusual, for his friend to challenge Phex's opinion. Jin's crests were folded back slightly, as if it expected to be scolded.

Phex was dying to know what their two sifters really thought about all this. Had they known all along? Before they came to the divinity? As skinless? Were they ignorant or complacent or supportive?

Tyve stood up, began pacing. She was a grace – she processed stress through physical activity. "Are you saying that the nymphs are sacrificing us gods to promote galactic peace?"

"That is one way to look at it," admitted Missit's father.

Jinyesun said quickly, "But that is why the divinity has taken so many steps to protect us." Jin, clearly, was supportive of the enlightenment agenda.

Phex was unconvinced. "Even though the Dyesi do not

understand violence, you hire bodyguards and block their ears against conversion."

"Bodyguards cannot be allowed to become enlightened," agreed Kagee. He and Phex stared at each other for a long moment. Gods couldn't, either.

Which is why Phex refused to learn the names of Missit's parents. He still wanted to kill them. He was not a pacified person.

Kagee turned to Fandina, tone demanding and desperate. "The Dyesi know this is happening. Have *you* always known?"

Fandina's crests folded and its cheeks specked – embarrassed confusion. Finally, it said, tone and body language acknowledging that this was neither an excuse nor a defense, "*Enlightenment* is the honorable scholars' term, not ours."

"Why did you not at least tell *us*?" Kagee demanded of both sifters, gesturing to include the four non-Dyesi of Asterism. "Are we not your pantheon? Do we not deserve the truth, at least? The truth of what we really do to our worshipers? To my people?"

The sifters remained wilted and mute, but Phex understood. The Dyesi had been telling them, in their way, all along. They had always called it *the divinity*. They called godsong *beautiful* in their language. As devout pacifists, would they not see peace as the ultimate beauty? Would they not see the divine as a *lack* of pain? Had they not said all along that beauty and love were the same thing? What could be more loving than to stopper up hate and violence all around the galaxy? To repair what they perceived as the main deficiency in all cultures they encountered – the wildly ugly desire to hurt themselves and destroy others?

Phex said, "For the Dyesi, the divinity is the enlightenment it causes, and it always has been. They are the same thing. No need to explain a truth self-evident. Why would they think this is something we must be warned of? They believe everyone should be less violent. Should hurt each other less. There is nothing wrong with that, is there?"

"You support this, Phex?" Tyve asked, confused and uncertain and needing her sun.

"I need to cook noodles and think about it," said Phex. Because he did. Just because he understood the Dyesi perspective didn't mean he agreed with it.

"Of course you do," said Kagee, annoyed with him for some reason. He turned back to Missit's parents, "Every time we spread godsong, we are spreading enlightenment without realizing?" He glanced at Jin. "Well, some of us are ignorant of the impact."

"You are disposed to think of this as—" Jin hesitated, clearly crushed. "—underhanded?" It almost whispered the word.

"Are you not taking advantage of us gods?" Kagee wondered.

Missit's father clearly liked a bit of an intellectual debate. He cocked his head at Kagee. "If this is merely what the divinity always does, isn't that a little like drinking alcohol and then getting angry at the booze when you get drunk?"

"No, because we all know that drinking can make you drunk. Worshipers don't *know* what the divinity is doing to them. And we didn't know it was alcohol when we gave it away on the dais." Kagee was sharp.

"Okay, not alcohol, then, something less poisonous. How about this: doesn't the perfect meal or talking with a friend make you feel better? Before the divinity, didn't listening to the right music make you happy? How is this different?"

Kagee looked around the group. All of Asterism was clearly puzzled and a little hurt. They needed time to process.

The high cantor said, firmly, "You're not here to defend the divinity but to ask us questions. We have instead quizzed you on the subject of enlightenment. Our apologies. But now we are at your disposal."

Phex wondered what Kagee's tactic was with this switch in topics. But he supposed they had learned what they needed, too, from Missit's parents. There was no point in further debate. Now Asterism simply had to get rid of them as quickly as possible. Which meant giving them what they wanted.

Missit's mother said, "Well, I hope you can see from your own questions and moral quandaries why the Dyesi are so reluctant to share the truth of enlightenment."

Phex could see it all very clearly indeed. "Does Missit know any of this?"

Kagee glared at him.

Missit's father looked amused. "He has never been particularly interested in our research, poor dear. He was never was very smart, you know? That's why we encouraged him to go into entertainment rather than follow us into academia."

Phex had a sudden wish for his own enlightenment, since he was now fantasizing about throttling the man sitting across from him. "And so, you allowed him to become one of the Dyesi's most effective tools, unknowingly?"

"We *allowed* him? It was his decision."

Phex tilted his head back and looked at the ceiling and thought about hand-pulling noodles and satisfying ladle shapes.

Missit's mother said, suddenly interested for some reason, "You're awfully protective of our boy, demigod Phex. Do you think he would care that his godsong causes enlightenment? We always assumed he'd not mind. He does so enjoy being a god."

Phex wished he could ask Missit that very question. He couldn't predict how Missit would react. He suspected Missit's parents didn't, either, for all they claimed the contrary. They were the type of people who, outside of their research, only predicted the outcome they wanted.

Phex and Missit had never had a conversation about free will or war or cultural resets. They hadn't talked philosophy or political theory. They had been too concerned with the taste, and smell, and feel of each other. With thoughts and conversation around who they were as individuals, and what they could become as gods. Hopes, and dreams, and pantheons, and performances had occupied their thoughts as innocent art, untainted by intent. Because they were young, dumb children with the gift of song, and no thought to question how it was sent out into the universe. They'd never considered what it was doing – cantored pollen riding solar winds through the stars. They hadn't even considered the repercussions of their own godhood until they'd been taken away from each other because of it. They'd thought only in terms of what the divinity made them do each day, beneficial or arbitrarily abusive. They'd never once wondered what the divinity was doing to its worshipers.

That was their moral failing, not the Dyesi's.

Phex had no idea what Missit thought on the matter of enlightenment.

Kagee said again. "How can we help you with your research, Scholars?" He did not use the prefix *honorable*. Kagee wasn't like that. "What do you want to ask Asterism?"

There was something in his tone that woke Phex up from his musings.

Kagee was being *genuine*. He had switched allegiances. He really did want to help Missit's parents with their research. He wanted to help the divinity. He was being *nice*.

Kagee nice was a truly terrifying thing.

Phex thought, but did not say of course, that the Agatay susceptibility to enlightenment might have something to do with the enthusiastic willingness of the worshipers. How could he, of all people, articulate a performer's sixth sense about an audience? Scholars would probably receive such information as the mere creative feeling of an artist. It wasn't scientific. It was sensation.

Plus, Phex was pretty sure he didn't want to help Missit's parents.

But he did mention it to Kagee, right before they took to the dais the next night.

Kagee looked embarrassed but agreed. "I had noticed there was something better about performing here. I thought maybe it had something to do with these being my people and mostly my believers. But if you feel it too, then it's not just me."

Phex clicked.

Kagee looked at the others.

Asterism was stretching while they waited for the dome to settle and their cue to begin. The bodyguards and acolytes were mainly distracted with security measures or pre-show preparations.

Berril and Tyve clicked too.

After a pause, so did Jinyesun and Fandina.

"You don't think it's just that this is the first planet to predominantly believe in Asterism?"

Phex could see Kagee's point. "At first, yes, but I get the same feeling when I'm up there with Tillam. There is something special about Agatay worshipers. I think Tillam would agree." He left unspoken that fact that he couldn't personally confirm this with Tillam, since he and Missit no longer talked.

Tyve shifted, restless. "I agree with Phex. I don't know how else to put it, but it's as if they just *want* godsong more here. They're so excited for the sensation of godfix."

"They feel it deeper," said Phex.

"It makes it a lot easier for us," added Berril. "I always love gracing, but this dome is special."

As if to emphasize her point, the congregation roared as the dais lit up in anticipation of gods manifesting.

Asterism took to the dais as worshipers screamed and fainted in excitement. Some of the faces Phex could see were wet with tears of joy or just an excess of emotion spilling out. They hadn't even started singing yet.

They began their first godsong, amazed to hear most of the crowd singing along. Seamlessly, Asterism moved from one song to the next. Even their most recently released godsong, Agatay had already memorized all the words. In a language that wasn't even theirs.

Asterism ended on a flourish to resounding approval. The dome, an airy, fragile, impermanent structure, vibrated with the sheer volume of Agatay's approval.

As quickly as they could, Asterism made their way off the dais to the safety beneath it. Berril first, in flight. Then the others. Phex, as always, last. Making sure his pantheon was safe but also giving his believers what they wanted with a spectacular running flip down the side of the dome.

There was some kind of chaos at the bottom involving most of the bodyguards.

It was a marker of Asterism's resiliency and regular exposure to the fixed that this barely registered as a danger. Most of them didn't pause to see what was going on, just moved fast, obeying acolyte orders.

With all of his pantheon out of sight down the passageway in the safety of the caves below, Phex, of course, checked out what was happening. But it was too chaotic to understand. There seemed to be some kind of fighting.

Itrio was guarding their exit and gestured at him aggressively to follow the others.

Phex might have gone to help, but he knew that his presence would be more distracting for the bodyguards than useful, so he ran after Kagee.

Behind him he was shocked to hear Quasilun's bell-like tone sing out. The acolytes in his peripheral vision jerked in puppet-like response. The imago was activating the nymphs to fight? That seemed excessive. Perhaps it was worse than he thought. Was he getting jaded about their safety?

"Keep moving, Phex," yelled Itrio at his back as if she knew what he was thinking.

It didn't sit well with him but he did as ordered. Quite apart from everything else, Phex couldn't afford to be injured right now. He had to go back up on that dais with Tillam in only a few short minutes.

12

LIVE FOR THE DOME, DIE FOR THE DOME

Asterism joined Tillam in the vestry deep beneath the dome.

Tillam already knew that something had gone wrong, since only one bodyguard followed Phex down and Itrio looked extremely tense. She took up a defensive stance in the doorway. Anyone coming after them would have to go through her in a one-on-one fight. Phex didn't give good odds to *anyone* under those circumstances, not even an Agatay proxy.

Itrio pulled her earmuffs off but didn't turn to look at them.

"Fixed?" asked Phex.

"Yes, but multiples all at once." Her eyes remained focused on the passageway.

"Coordinated attack?" asked Zil, disbelieving.

"Yes, it seems so. Or just one big terrible coincidence. Frenzied, too."

"Has that happened before?" Tyve asked.

Her brother answered her. "Not to Tillam. In divine history? I don't know, better ask the acolytes."

"Would they answer us?"

"Probably not," said Jinyesun. "There's no record I can find." Of course Jin was already checking via its ident.

Phex joined the loose circle formed by the two seated pantheons. Everyone was tense. Even Melalan, who Phex had thought unflappable, had slightly wilted crests. Phex settled himself easily into one of the couches. Found himself instantly with a lapful of Missit.

Missit's hands were on both sides of his face, forcing him to look. Phex was drowning in flecked gold.

"What are you doing? Get off." Phex ordered even as he wrapped his arms around Missit's slim waist and squeezed. It had been way too long since he'd gotten to do that.

"There's no acolytes."

Phex grimaced but agreed it was license to indulge. "Quasilun activated them."

Missit shivered. "It must be really bad. Are you okay?"

Phex ran a thumb over one shimmery cheekbone. "To my shame, I barely noticed. I assumed it was the usual, just one fixed, and that the bodyguards had it covered. But then I heard Quasilun's cantor, so I figured it must be bad."

"Maybe the imago was ordering them to flee, not fight."

"Then you really should get off my lap, they'll be here soon." Phex dropped his arms and pressed his body back into the hard wood of an Agatay bench.

Missit trailed his fingers over Phex's face and neck, not looking away.

Phex felt self-conscious. He was sweaty from Asterism's performance, but Missit never seemed to mind that. Never had. He always pounced, saying that he liked the salt on Phex's skin.

Phex looked away from all that gold, up at the ceiling cut into the rock above them.

Reluctantly, Missit stood and walked to Tillam's side of

the circle, sat next to Melalan on another piece of aggressively square wooden furniture, hugged his knees to his chest, kept his eyes on Phex.

Everyone was staring at them.

As usual, Missit had taken on all the focus in the room.

Phex said to Kagee, breaking all his own rules in order to deflect attention, "You know what I don't get? Shouldn't Agatay have *fewer* converts and fixed because of protans?"

Kagee stared at him. Grey eyes blinking, eyes that couldn't see color. Or couldn't see most of it. "You're right. This really doesn't make sense."

"Should we tell Missit's parents?" asked Phex.

"What?" Missit twitched.

"We should at least look into whether any protans are being converted. That would be unusual, not to say unlikely." Kagee gnawed at his lower lip. "I'll asked the diarchs to look into it."

Phex clicked approval.

"What are you two talking about?" asked Zil.

"Protans?" queried Tern, struggling to get his mouth around the alien word.

Phex said, because he knew Kagee was embarrassed, and he had no intention of outing his friend for something he perceived as a defect, "There should be a larger-than-normal percentage of individuals on Agatay immune to godfix, and therefore fewer fixed overall. But instead, we're getting more fixed than normal."

"Why?" pressed Zil.

Phex recited it monotonously, as if he'd read it in a textbook somewhere. "Agatay has a genetic defect, propagated post planetfall, resulting in a high percentage of protanopia in the Y-chromosome-carrying members of the general population."

Melalan's crests puffed. "The people on this planet are *colorblind*?"

"Not all of them. Not even *most* of them, just a higher-than-normal percentage of the population, and mostly just blind to the red end of the spectrum." Phex said, glancing at Kagee to make sure he got it right.

Kagee, grumpy, added, "And mostly within elite families."

"Does the divinity know this?" wondered Yorunlee.

"Jinyesun?" Kagee looked at their sifter.

Jin only looked uncomfortable. The four sifters in the room exchanged a complicated series of crest-wiggles and body posturing.

In the middle of whatever that was, the rest of the bodyguards came into the vestry.

One of Bob's forearms was partly detached. A few of the others sported scratches and bruises. Even Quasilun looked rumpled – as much as someone hairless with almost no soft parts could look rumpled. The three acolytes were with them and seemed entirely unharmed.

Bob began attempting to reattaching the arm.

Itrio said, "We should cancel Tillam's performance."

"Those were Asterism's fixed," said Elder K, annoyed. As if it were Asterism's fault.

"Whose believers?" pressed Phex immediately.

"Mostly Kagee's," answered Elder K.

"How many?" Phex was immediately in protective mode.

"Six."

Fandina went over to see if it could help Bob with the arm.

"Coordinated?" Phex stood, then didn't know why he'd done that and sat back down again, the thick edge of the seat biting into the backs of his thighs through the thin material of his performance jumpsuit. Was everything on Agatay uncomfortable or had he become spoiled by Dyesi soft furnishings?

"Yes. Apparently, they met in one of Phex's believer forums." It seemed like Bob had managed some interrogation during the chaos. Phex wondered if that had something to do with the arm.

Kagee looked more stubborn than guilty. "Is it weird that I'm kind of honored my obsessives managed to organize a coordinated attack?"

"Yes, it's weird," shot back Zil.

Phex thought it was a classic Kagee response. From their amused looks, so did the rest of his pantheon.

There was a sudden disturbance at the doorway.

A new set of security appeared, local Agatay. Then Miramo's very worried face.

"You cannot come in," said Quasilun, tone expressionless, huge body moving incredibly fast to almost entirely block the entrance.

"Kagee, are you okay?" Miramo's voice carried easily, an orator's projection, not a singer's.

"I'm fine, Mira," said Kagee, not moving.

"Let me in! I need to see him."

"You cannot enter," reiterated Quasilun, immovable as any wall.

"But I am diarch of this planet!"

"A dome is consecrated space and its premises inviolable," insisted the imago.

Kagee stood and went toward the entrance, standing safely behind Quasilun.

"You have been listening to my songs. You're considered too risky," explained Kagee, no softness to his words for all they were spoken in his native tongue.

"Kagee!"

"Those who just attacked were *my* believers, Miramo. *Mine*." Kagee's face was pained when he said this, as if he were owning up to a personal sin. Maybe because she couldn't fully understand what fixed were, Kagee could be more vulnerable with her. Phex felt like that sometimes with Missit. To love someone meant sometimes trusting them with harshness.

"What does that even mean?" Miramo was now standing directly in front of Quasilun. Phex could see her fancy boots and the bottom of her robes through Quasilun's braced legs. She was too close, and he worried that her security detail had guns.

Kagee felt similarly. "Please go, Miramo. Now is not the time to flex your regency. This is a divine concern."

"But your pantheon was attacked! On my planet. In my dome."

"All domes belong to the divinity," said one of the acolytes. "We merely loan this one to your world."

Kagee said, ignoring the Dyesi, "My pantheon is untouched and remains perfectly safe. Did you forget that I am trained to kill?"

"No. Of course not. I'm just worried." She took an audible breath and stepped back.

"Imago, let her see me fully and then she will leave. Okay, Mira?"

"Okay. Yes. Please."

Quasilun stepped slightly to one side so there was a clear line of sight to Kagee – all the bodyguards in the room shifted as well but remained tense.

Kagee turned in a slow circle so Miramo could see that he was entirely uninjured.

She nodded, eyes softening. "Okay. What can I do to help?"

Kagee looked pained. "Nothing, sweetheart."

But Phex said, confidently, "Assign your proxies, not your soldiers, to protect this dome."

Miramo's attention shifted to him. "What?"

Phex moved to stand next to Kagee. "You have some on retainer, correct? Actual protans, like Kagee? You want to protect him and us? Assign them to us."

Kagee looked at Phex, actually impressed. "When did you get smart?"

Miramo didn't need to understand – she trusted Kagee implicitly.

"I'll recall the ones I can, immediately. I'll be back tomorrow with as many as Modal and Endant have access to."

"No need for overkill," said Kagee, meaning it.

Miramo was all diarch in that moment. "But I think there is. You're sure you want proxies, not crowd-trained military?"

"Not just proxies, specifically the *protans*. Protans are immune to godsong, Mira."

At least we think they are. Phex watched Kagee closely out of the corner of one eye. This was as good a way as any to test the theory. It certainly couldn't be any worse than normal planetary security.

"Really? How would you know that?"

Kagee tilted his head at her very slowly, then wiggled his fingertips, rings flashing.

Miramo cracked a smile. "But you're a god, aren't you already immune?"

"It's a working theory."

"You're risking your life and that of your pantheon on a theory?" Miramo was back to frowning.

"Every time we climb onto that dais, we risk our lives on a theory, it turns out." Kagee was thinking of enlightenment.

"When did you get philosophical?"

Kagee pointed at Phex. "His fault."

"I'll look into how to prove it," she said. "It's our population, after all."

"Assign protans, we'll figure it out soon enough," said Phex, done with discussion on the matter, diarch or no.

Miramo relaxed at this. Clearly, she was one of those who liked to solve for a given problem with action. She now had a task that might help, so she felt better about the entire situation.

Still, she gave Phex an inscrutable look. "He was mine first."

"Yes but he's mine now." Phex turned away and returned to the circle of gods.

"Hey! Hey," said Kagee. "I'm my own, thank you both very much."

Miramo ignored him. "I'm off, then. See you all tomorrow." She was almost cheerful.

"You're not staying for the second half?" Sacerdote Chalamee asked.

Phex started. He'd forgotten the acolytes were there. He wondered what they'd made of that conversation. What they'd understood of the rapidly spoken Galactic Common, of course.

Miramo stared at the Dyesi in shock. "You intend to continue with the performance?"

"We were just discussing that before you arrived," said Tyve, when the acolytes didn't answer.

Miramo shook her head and made a sharp hiss noise. "I have proxies to reallocate. And I need to go home. If I can't hug Kagee, I need to hug Levin and Liera. They're no Kagee, but they're what I have access to."

"Give them an extra hug from me?" suggested Kagee, with an ironic little smile.

Miramo nodded, looking like she wanted to cry – she certainly was a curious leader. Experiencing many emotions in such quick succession and hiding none of them. She whirled around and marched away, her security detail following her.

The bodyguards relaxed.

"Did the fixed say *why* they attacked?" Phex asked Bob.

"You want us to repeat the crazed ramblings of the insane?" Calator Heshoyi's crest indicated disgust, whether that was with the fixed or Phex's desire to understand them, or both.

Phex ignored the acolyte and, when Bob remained silent, turned to stare at Quasilun.

The imago gave the ear-crest version of a shrug. "This interests me not at all."

"I asked." Bob spoke up at least, punching the air with both arms to test the repairs. "One of them said they wanted to keep Asterism on Agatay and never let them leave. Force them to stay and perform only for them, here forever."

"See? Insanity. It's always insanity with the fixed," said Calator Heshoyi.

"Calator, may I respectfully recommend a modification in register?" Sacerdote Chalamee's tone was censorious, much to everyone's surprise.

Phex tried to remember a time, apart from his audition process, when he'd heard two acolytes disagree so openly. It was almost an outright argument.

"Nymphs." Quasilun sounded exactly like an adult reprimanding children.

"Low cantor, you can rest assured that we will conduct the full standard interview process later." Sacerdote Chalamee tried to placate Phex.

"Assured?" said Tyve, all sarcasm.

"Tyve," hissed Fandina, shocked.

"The fixed *coordinated* an attack!" Tyve was almost yelling at Asterism's sifter. "Against Kagee!"

Fandina's crests folded flat.

Phex quickly explained to his sifters. "She's scared. Sometimes, Sapiens react in anger to fear."

Fandina looked like it wanted to be the one to cuddle in Phex's lap.

Phex indicated with his chin at Berril, but for once, she didn't follow his suggestion, instead sticking close to Tyve.

Phex sighed and pointedly went to sit with his sifters on their bench, pulling one close to each side with his long arms. They were ignorant, not intentionally malicious. "I'm fine. Kagee is fine. We'll figure out what happened."

"Now you side with them?" Kagee accused.

Phex looked at his high cantor very hard. "Stop that." Fandina and Jin were Dyesi, yes, but they were also friends and colleagues and family.

Kagee instantly looked ashamed, then just as quickly covered it with his usual layer of cool arrogance. But he settled back.

Phex directed his gaze at Tyve. "This is not your call."

"You're gonna go back up there and onto the dais with Tillam, aren't you?" Her was voice raised high in shock.

Berril looked like she wanted to cry. "Phex, please." She spoke very quietly and in Galactic Common. Berril, who never objected to anything that Phex felt like he must do. Or *they* must do.

"Oh, birdie," said Phex, gentle as he could, "Tillam is also mine to look after."

"Are we sifting a dome tonight or not?" Zil's face was carefully neutral, but he was looking at his sister.

"Of course you are," said Precatio Ohongshe as if there were absolutely no reason why Tillam shouldn't go out there.

"Those were Asterism's fixed," reiterated Calator Heshoyi, as if that were an excuse.

"And yet one of Asterism sings with us these days. You're really willing to risk Phex?" Missit's voice was slightly muffled, since his chin was still firmly nested in his knees.

"All the fixed have been neutralized and taken into custody."

"Who is to say there are not more in that audience? Agatay seems unpredictable and dangerous in this matter." Missit remained speaking mostly into his legs, but he was being very clear and firm with his language and his register.

"That is statistically highly unlikely."

"And what is the statistical likelihood of a coordinated fixed attack?" Missit asked, again, tone carefully polite and entirely neutral.

Sacerdote Chalamee said, "The high cantor has a valid point."

"Thank you, acolyte," said Missit, dropping his register to informal in a sarcastic way – he meant it to insult.

From the wilt of the acolytes' crests, it worked.

"The divinity endures," intoned Calator Heshoyi.

"At the cost of its gods?" wondered Missit.

"Of course. You are, after all, the ones up on the dais."

Phex wondered if Calator Heshoyi had always been so callous. Or if it represented the philosophy of most acolytes.

"I object. In this instance, the risk is too high." Of all people, it was Fandina who spoke up.

"You challenge the status quo, youngling?"

"Agatay is clearly an aberrant worshiper base. Prior experience cannot be applied as a predictive measure of behavior," said Jinyesun, coming to Fandina's defense with facts, as expected.

Asterism's sifters looked nervous but unafraid.

"Agreed, but the dome must sift. It is the first divine mandate." Calator Heshoyi pushed back.

Missit stood. "If I don't go up, Phex can't either."

"Missit. Those were *Kagee's* fixed. Tillam should be fine. I should be fine." Phex tried to be both firm and gentle. At the same time, there was a small part of him that wondered if all this was something to do with his voice and not Agatay. Was this the same thing that caused him to bruise and burn sifters? Was he too powerful in the wrong way, causing extra fixed? Was it something he did to Asterism's sifters and, by extension, the dome that encouraged more than normal obsession? Saturation was his specialty. Was a grey planet with generally low color saturation more susceptible to his dome?

"You're the second most popular god on Agatay. The *second in all the divinity*. You think you're immune? No one is immune to fixed." Missit was barely looking at Phex but fierce about this. Tiny, protective, and terrified for him.

"Is your only real concern Phex's safety?" asked Sacerdote Chalamee.

Everyone but Phex nodded.

"I guess that's why I'm here, then," said a sweetly warm voice from the doorway, and the bodyguards parted to allow a small cloaked figure to enter the room.

He was trailed by an entourage of medical staff.

"Fortew!" Missit and the rest of Tillam leapt to their feet

and charged their low cantor, surrounding him with joyfully concerned welcome.

So it came to pass that Fortew sang low cantor with Tillam, not Phex, and the divinity was happy.

Everyone was happy, actually.

Except perhaps Phex, who missed singing with Missit. Up on that dais with thousands watching was the only time he got to really be together with Missit anymore. Twining their voices to sift the dome was the only intimacy they had as a couple. It wasn't exactly satisfying, but at least they did it together.

If Fortew was back, if somehow Agatay had managed to heal him, they didn't even have that anymore. The divinity would persist in separating them and all this would be over.

Asterism stayed in Dome 6 to watch from an observation niche. Certainly, it was a risk and they should have remained safely underground, but Tillam performing whole again was a miracle. They were demigods, but most of Asterism had started out as worshipers. Tillam was still formed of major gods, some of the greatest ever. It was an opportunity not to be missed.

And it was worth it right up until the end.

Perhaps even then.

Fortew's cantor was a little weak at times and his breathing audible to those who knew how to hear the spaces between notes and see the slight blurring in the colors. But Phex guessed the congregation was entirely unaware of the corruption in Fortew's lungs. It was made manifest only to other gods and to the Dyesi.

Missit had to work much harder than ever to carry the

weight of both cantors. But his voice never wavered. It stayed entirely true to his part and almost double-toned enough to carry low cantor as well as high. As if he really were an imago. Missit had been doing this a long time and he had learned a lot over the years.

Phex did not enjoy watching him struggle, but also, he knew that Missit both hated and loved it up there. For the first and last time, he was the foundation, the sun, the strongest by necessity if not inclination. As the youngest of his pantheon, it would feel like a privilege of love and time. He had earned this chance, not to shine – for Missit always shone – but to support.

That desire, Phex understood completely. So, he watched Fortew suffer and Missit glow with pride tempered by remorse and ached for both of them.

Afterward, the Divinity would issue an official statement that Fortew was just very tired and physically exhausted. That when he collapsed at the very end of Tillam's performance, it was simply a faint.

Apparently, medical privilege was a sacred right on Agatay. Apparently, if a god wanted to leave his sickbed and sing, the doctors had no right to stop him. The Agatay medics felt, quite strongly, that the divinity shouldn't stop him either. Last wishes were sacrosanct.

No one knew that they'd already told Fortew it was too late. His disease was too far along. Agatay may be accustomed to treating crud lung, but Fortew was still terminal. There was nothing they could do for him but honor his wish to sing one last time under a dome.

Fortew had paid his dues in that bed under a mountain on an alien planet, knowing he would never leave Agatay. He didn't want to spend his last days counting his time in doctors' visits and strangers' faces. He had told no one but Missit.

Missit had lifted up and carried that burden willingly, in a way that Phex knew would translate to guilt going forward but also honor. This was Missit's favorite person in the whole universe, and the golden god didn't know many things, but he knew how to love.

Phex understood that too. He would have done exactly the same for any one of his pantheon.

The final low cantor note of Tillam's last song was truncated. Fortew folded to the dais – a wilted, empty weight.

Missit watched him crumble, but his own voice did not falter. He did not run across the stage to catch his friend – only his eyes bled pain. He held high cantor exactly as he always had.

Phex found himself singing that last note for Fortew, for Missit, even though it did not work on the dome – it was trapped with him inside the niche.

Tillam had changed the set list, so that this time the final song was "Five." Of course it was. Because they were gods and performers who knew drama. Because "Five" had been written for this moment. As an epitaph.

Dome 6 went to grey.

Itrio did something she wasn't supposed to then. She took to the dais. She lifted up her charge and carried him, limp and unresponsive, down from the heavens and back to the mortal realm where he was now doomed to reside.

There was a hush in the dome – godfix, reverence, and confusion.

No one there really understood what had just happened, but they all sensed that it was a true ending.

Asterism mobilized immediately.

Leaving their niche with Quasilun, Phex, Tyve, and

Kagee took on protective roles as surrogate bodyguards. The mood in the dome was somber. Phex felt as if the likelihood of fixed appearing was slim for a change. They all made it safely back beneath the dais.

In the vestry, there was a kind of restrained chaos. There were three medics hovering over Fortew, but they weren't doing anything. There was nothing to do. The three acolytes stood to one side, crests completely flat, communicating in rapid formal Dyesi with each other and their wrist idents. The divinity was clearly unsure of which protocols to activate.

Fortew lay in waxy stillness on the largest wooden bench. He looked smaller than ever. All the mods the Dyesi had made to him over the years, skin and ears, hair and eyebrows, were suddenly startlingly obvious. Glaring additions of someone else's taste to the surface of an empty shell. It was as if they were still living even though he was not. The difference between god and mortal was scripted in his skin, editorial corrections made manifest in death. Fortew's body showed godhood like an archive – his flesh permanently sifted by a life spent in service to the dome.

Phex had seen the dead many times. Crudrats died all too often. He had little concern for Fortew now but for damage his leaving had wrought. He took in the results on Tillam quickly. Melalan and Yorunlee had crests flat and bodies caved, seated together but apart from everyone else. Phex did not know how the Dyesi grieved, but he guessed he was about to find out. Tern and Zil were wrapped together, rocking gently. He sensed Tyve and Berril heading toward them – graces grieving in motion.

Missit was a ball of trembling gold at Fortew's feet, curled at the end of that hard bench. He keened softly in high cantor pitch. The color, Phex thought, would be bright red, sharp and agonized. It might even burn a sifter's skin.

Phex considered the consequences, but he also decided in that moment that nothing else really mattered. Not the divinity, not the Dyesi, no rules, just Missit's song of pain like the whine of shattering of metal.

Phex ran to him, only to find his path blocked by the acolytes.

"Let me through."

"It is not your place."

"This has nothing to do with that." Phex was so frustrated, he yelled it at them. How dare they not understand what was required here? How could they be so callous?

"He is not yours to care for, sun."

"That doesn't matter when I am what is needed." Phex started to push his way through. Violently.

Quasilun was immediately there. Of course, protector imago. Asterism's bodyguard would protect them against everything, except other Dyesi. Phex did not want to threaten anyone – he just needed to get to Missit.

"Please," said Phex, who never begged.

Missit's head went up and he noticed Phex, the center of a cluster of iridescent elegance.

The bodyguards stood helplessly, unsure what to do.

Missit called out a desperate fractured version of Phex's name, and Phex entirely lost patience. He took down Quasilun because the imago was the only one who could effectively stop him.

"Apologies, elder," he said in frozen register, and then kicked as hard as he possibly could to the side of the imago's knee. He heard the crunch, and it could have been the carapace or it could be what it was meant to protect. Either way, Quasilun stumbled and crumpled to one side.

Phex pushed easily through the acolytes to Missit.

Fortunately, Quasilun didn't activate the nymphs to fight

him. Maybe the imago didn't want to, or maybe it was too surprised. And the nymphs were nonviolent – they wouldn't do anything to physically stop Phex without fugue. They couldn't.

Phex picked Missit up, then sat with the golden god still huddled in a tight ball, just now in his lap. Phex wrapped his arms as tightly as they could go around the slight, trembling body, as if he could physically hold Missit together.

Phex was liminally aware of the acolytes protesting. He heard them order them to separate, but he did not listen. The Dyesi didn't matter anymore. This had nothing to do with them.

He did look up when they ordered the bodyguards to pull them apart. Because Bob and Itrio were both right there, standing near the bench. But the bodyguards simply refused – Itrio with silence, Bob with anger, and the others with firm denial.

"We guard. We do not interfere in the personal lives of the pantheon," said Elder K, speaking for the group. This was not what they were paid for.

Phex glanced over at Quasilun, slightly worried he'd done real damage. But now that the nymphs were not under threat, the imago was simply standing to one side. Quasilun's crests were not folded. The imago watched the scene with interest, maybe sympathy, body language indicating nothing more than mild curiosity. Perhaps Quasilun was leaning more weight on one leg than usual, but otherwise, the imago seemed unharmed. When those big yellow eyes met Phex's, Quasilun gave him the Dyesi finger-flick gesture of respect.

The three acolytes crowded toward Phex, still arguing with him. Or trying to. Phex remained silent. He knew they weren't going to physically do anything, but they were being noisy and difficult. How could they not understand something so simple and necessary as comfort?

Phex turned and angled his torso, protecting Missit's grief with his body, as if he could buffer the sound of acolyte annoyance. He had no time to think of anything more – Missit held all his focus. But he felt the air shift and a dimness descend over him. A sparkling white hit his peripheral vision and he realized it was Berril.

Asterism's light grace interposed herself between Phex and the rest of the room. She spread her wings and created a tent over Phex and Missit, shielding them from the acolytes. Phex was grateful, for all he was caught up in Missit's pain. He would thank her later.

He heard Berril say, more firmly than she'd ever spoken before, and in a tone of informal Dyesi that brooked no argument, like an imago to a nymph, "You will let them grieve."

"They are not allowed to be together."

"Irrelevant," replied Kagee. Was he there too?

"Why *grieve*?" asked one of the acolytes.

Jinyesun's voice then: "Sapiens do not leave parts of themselves behind after death to color future generations. For them, death is a total ending."

Fandina added, "It is like a nymph or a skinless dying young. An emptiness is left behind with no record. It is a forever nothingness."

So, both of Phex's sifters were standing nearby too. They had looked it up, done the research, prepared for this moment when they would have to explain Sapien death to other Dyesi.

"It's like the void between stars," said Tyve. Her voice sounded like it was coming from farther away. Good, she was still with her brother.

Phex hugged Missit even tighter, trying to fix the void between gods.

Missit's keening slowed and quieted, less ear-piercing. It became tiny pants of pain. They sounded like Dyesi laugher. Or maybe like the flip side of Dyesi laughter.

Phex shifted Missit a bit, relaxed his grip so he could rub circles on his back. But Missit whimpered and protested, and only uncurled himself enough to bury his face in Phex's neck, wrap his own arms as tight as they could around Phex's waist. Phex resumed squeezing. Missit needed to be held together right now.

Missit's face was cold and clammy against Phex's throat but not wet. He wasn't crying.

Phex had no words of comfort to offer up, not that Missit would have been able to hear them. But Phex never had words. For a man who spoke three languages fluently, none of them were his native tongue. His language was there in the strength of his arms and the warmth of his lap, in the part of him that wished it could be he who'd lost a friend. Because Phex was accustomed to death and loss. It was he, not Missit, who had the resiliency to suffer. But he could do nothing more for the golden god in that moment than be what he already was, a silent, empty satellite upon which Missit could land. He hoped what he had to offer, stone and dust, were enough for Missit to build a new foundation.

They stayed like that for a very long time.

Far above them, the dome emptied.

Agatay circled its sun and spun on its axis untroubled.

In the space between stars, beams of gossip raced along the infonet, and the divinity tried desperately to control the message of what had happened. Tried to deny truth that was not beauty one more time.

The dome stood grey and silent. In the quiet after godsong ended, it was, and always had been, a testament to the dead.

13

ABANDON ALL HOPE, THOSE WHO CANTOR HERE

Later, Phex struggled to recall exactly how they got back to the *Nusplunder*. He supposed there must have been a shuttle involved. He carried Missit the entire way – he remembered that much. He kept him curled in his lap, even when they had to activate safety webbing. Missit clung to him, wrapped around him like a murmel and weighing not much more. He'd lost weight since Phex had held him last.

The acolytes must have given up trying to separate them. The bodyguards refused to do anything. Besides, Phex turned out to be the easiest way to transport Missit back to the spaceship.

Phex did remember what happened after they docked. He remembered the bright, colorful lighting in the hallway, Missit still coiled around him, as if he'd just been caught after a grace. Golden arms strangled Phex's neck – long, slim legs were wrapped around his waist. Phex was accustomed to it or he might have felt stifled.

Unfortunately for everybody, Missit's parents were on the spaceship, waiting for them, and they had no idea what had just happened.

Phex had no clue what he should do under such circumstances. He only knew what he wanted to do.

"Your parents are here," he told Missit.

Missit didn't say anything, just clung.

"Do you want to go to them?" Phex asked. They were, after all, his parents.

Missit shook his head against Phex's neck, hissed a Dyesi negative.

Phex clicked acknowledgment, hoisted him higher, and then carried the god past the couple, ignoring them entirely. He didn't pause to think about it, just took Missit back with him to Asterism's quarters and his own bed. He knew that was the place Missit went to for safety. Or at least it had been from the start.

For once in her life, the murmel followed them docilely and curled up at the end of Phex's cot. Although she did give Phex a very dirty look.

Phex set Missit down next to Dimsum long enough so he could climb in after, pulled the blankets over both of them, wrapped his whole body around the god so Missit could suck at his warmth, maybe stop trembling. Maybe start crying. Maybe something – anything beyond the bereft shock.

Phex was aware of others following him into the room. He sensed his pantheon moving around the tiny space. He didn't hear Tyve – she was probably still with her brother. Someone put two flasks of water near his head. Berril or Kagee, he guessed. Then he caught flashes of iridescent blues and realized it was his sifters. The Dyesi were looking after him. Jin and Fandina had learned not to understand Sapiens but to accept them. Which meant Kagee and Berril were probably guarding the entrance against intruders.

Then the acolytes arrived. Or tried to.

"This is not Missit's correct sleeping accommodation," he heard one of them say.

Kagee replied, "Who are you to claim Missit's relationship to a space? Did you hear his statement when he entered?"

When had Kagee become so clever with Dyesi culture? Of course the acolytes could say nothing to rebut that. Missit had made no statement, because he belonged there.

He heard Missit's parents' voices then, their command of Dyesi aggressively perfect. "What is wrong with our child? What is he doing in a demigod's bed? What has happened to Tillam?" As if they really cared. As if they really were interested in Missit and not just the consequences to the divinity.

Kagee and Berril did not possess Phex's bitterness or resistance to familial connection, so they let the scholars enter. He heard them claim stranger status with Asterism's quarters. As they should.

Phex shifted onto his back so he could watch them. Missit stayed buried against his side, face hard in his neck, back to the wall. He wasn't trembling anymore and he was a little warmer. He was very still but he also wasn't sleeping. He was holding himself motionless, as if when he moved or spoke some part of him would disintegrate.

Phex watched the two Sapiens who had brought a great god into the universe. Watched them do battle with the idea of a child that they had created but not protected. Watched them reap the consequences of their own hubris with inaction. They could do nothing. They *should* do nothing. They had nothing to offer their offspring anymore. Missit would never turn to them for any reason. He did not care that they were there. When they died, he would not still himself for one second of their passing.

They, of course, did not know this or him.

Missit's father reached a hand down to offer some kind of physical sympathy, touched Missit's tangled hair.

Missit flinched away, plastering himself, if possible, even closer to Phex.

Phex grabbed Missit's father's wrist and gently but firmly tossed it away.

His mother stood a little off, one fist pressed hard against her mouth.

"Ah, I see," said Kagee. "Sorry, Phex. I didn't realize."

"They gave him away," explained Phex. Because Kagee would understand *that* entirely.

But it was Berril who turned fierce at the information, pointed face gone pale, looking up at Missit's mother. "You're not welcome here," she hissed, informal Dyesi, insult intended. She tried to use her tiny presence to press both Missit's parents back out the doorway.

Neither of them budged. Berril was, after all, not very intimidating. Neither was Kagee, for that matter. Kagee could flash his rings as much as he liked, but Missit's parents had no idea what threat the glittering silver represented.

Jinyesun asked gently, "Are not breeder pairs reassuring to the grieving process of Sapiens?"

"Depends on the relationship," explained Kagee.

"Isn't the relationship inherent in the word *parent*?" Poor Jin was so easily confused by humans.

Kagee hissed in annoyance. "Not every parent-child relationship is the same. Procreation doesn't necessarily indicate care or affection."

"How bizarre," said Fandina.

Kagee said to Missit's parents, "You should leave this to Phex."

"What is Phex to our son?"

"A great deal more than you, evidently" was the most

Kagee would give back. Kagee had learned circumspection at some point. Phex wondered if his high cantor had gotten that trick from him, or the Dyesi.

"But clearly he needs us!" claimed Missit's mother.

Kagee said, "Maybe he did once, but now he needs Phex."

Phex spoke then, keeping his voice soft, mindful of Missit's ear resting on his chest. "You lost all privileges through neglect." Missit made a little whimper, so Phex stopped talking.

"He's still our child. We want to help. We want to understand what has happened."

Kagee said, "For that you must speak with the acolytes."

Missit's mother made a move as if she too wanted to touch her son, console him somehow.

Berril unfurled one wing and formed a barrier of shimmering white between them. "It's good that you maybe want to repair what was broken, but now is not the time."

"But—"

Kagee lost patience. Of course he did. "Get out!"

"Honored scholars" —Fandina was using formal Dyesi and all polite protocols, no doubt its crests were positioned perfectly— "let the pantheon handle this for now. There is nothing you can do here."

Phex couldn't see beyond Berril's wing, but he had to assume Missit's parents left the room. Someone else came inside, though, announced a relationship to the space as a formal visitor.

"This is highly irregular," said Calator Heshoyi.

Fandina's voice then: "This is a Sapien grieving process, acolyte. Please let them be. I assure you, nothing romantic or physical will occur. This is purely comfort."

"How long is such *comfort* required?" pressed the calator.

Kagee's tone was not polite, although he stuck with formal register. "You mean how long will Missit need Phex? Forever, probably."

"That is not a permanent solution."

"No? You might want to consider making it one." Kagee was remorseless.

"Berril," Phex said, keeping his voice soft, "I don't think the wing is necessary anymore, thank you."

"Oops, sorry, Phex, I forgot." The sparkling white disappeared.

Calator Heshoyi occupied the entrance to their quarters, holding the heavy curtain to one side near Phex's feet. Kagee was standing braced in front of the acolyte, Fandina next to him. Jinyesun was at Phex's head, next to Berril. Behind the acolyte, Missit's parents and Quasilun stood in the hallway.

Phex presumed the other acolytes were off dealing with the political and public-relations nightmare incurred by the death of a great god in an active pantheon on a dais in front of millions of worshipers.

Phex wished it were one of the other acolytes visiting them, though. The calator always seemed the least sympathetic to Sapien foibles.

A standoff ensued. Had this been a bunch of Dyesi, there would have been a lot of crest-wiggling. But as it was Kagee and Calator Heshoyi, it was mostly just glares.

Finally, Kagee said, "Come back in the morning, see how things are then. For now, we will take care of him."

"But the rest of his pantheon?"

"Yes, exactly. You should be thinking about all of Tillam. Shouldn't you?"

Calator Heshoyi looked startled at being called to account by a mere demigod. It immediately turned and walked away. Presumably to Tillam's quarters.

Asterism's quarters fell into silence.

After a long while, the hallway cleared and the curtain fell. The rest of Asterism went about their evening hygiene rituals. What else could they do?

Tyve didn't return. She would sleep next to her brother tonight, Phex suspected.

He shifted until Missit was lying half on top of him, arranged their legs so Missit's toes were tucked between his calves.

Eventually, Missit relaxed. Phex knew it was an exhausted sleep, not a lessening of emotion.

Phex stayed awake all that night.

So that when Missit woke up and sobbed like a tiny child in his arms, he was ready for it.

So that when Missit woke again with eyes sore and still leaking, snot-covered and hating himself for the mess that he was, Phex could carry him into the hygiene chamber and clean them both up as a much as possible.

He bundled Missit up in Tyve's robe and carried him back to bed. Held him while he chattered with a cold that wasn't coming from the room.

Stayed awake so that when the morning came, Phex could swing to rise with Missit. Walk him back to Tillam's quarters. Watch as he climbed into Tern's open arms. Pass him over to one who understood better, who had known Fortew just as long and loved him just as deeply. One who had also lost his low cantor and his partner and his friend. Rather than Phex, who had known Fortew only as some transient, frail god, impermanent and fragile, and dangerous in that he could hurt Phex indirectly through Missit.

He met Tern's bloodshot eyes over Missit's back.

They exchanged slight nods.

It wasn't Phex's scheduled time but he went to the kitchen

anyway – insisted on helping to prepare breakfast with the first-shift cooks. When they objected to a god lowering himself to sous-chef, Phex only stirred porridge and ignored them.

When the time came to serve, he used his best ladle, reassured by the shape and weight of it in his hand.

Kagee, Berril, Fandina, and Jinyesun found Phex in the galley when they came for breakfast.

Phex was wearing nothing but house slippers and his sleeping robe with an apron over it.

Kagee sat at the counter. "Thought you'd be here."

Phex plonked a bowl of porridge with shredded meat and pickled vegetables in front of him, plus a mug of what passed for tea on Agatay. Kagee loved the beverage. Phex thought it tasted like cleanser smelled, but at least it was caffeinated. He'd already had four cups.

"Did you sleep at all?" asked Berril.

Phex shook his head, gestured with his thumb at the big pot of tea behind him, then went to fetch her a bowl of porridge. Berril got local nuts and dried fruit sprinkled on top of hers, plus a dish of some kind of sweetener that apparently came from insect vomit – planets were so weird – so that she could add more sugar if she needed to.

One of the other cooks had already served Fandina and Jinyesun.

"How's Tyve doing?" Phex asked.

"We checked on Tillam before coming here," Berril said between bites. "Tyve is looking after them as best she can. I'll go back as soon as I've eaten, take them some food. Not sure if they'll eat it, though."

"Missit was still sleeping?" Phex pressed.

"Yes."

He turned to Jinyesun. "Will Tillam's sifters be all right?"

"Better than the Sapiens. Especially Yorunlee."

"We feel differently about death," added Fandina, baldly.

"Yes. You're callous." Kagee gobbled his porridge. There was an edge of respect to his tone that Phex suspected had to do with growing up in a place where lots of people around him died all the time. Better to be callous under circumstances of civil war.

"Death isn't an ending or a failure to live longer, it's just the next life stage." Jinyesun tried to explain, but Phex suspected Berril, at least, would never understand. Didn't really want to.

Berril looked quickly around. "Are we unmonitored at the moment?" No acolytes were present, and no Quasilun either. Only one bodyguard, Bob, who was sitting alone, slumped in a corner. All the rest present were ship's staff and crew.

"They're probably recording the room and us. They could review it later," said Kagee.

"That's okay, this is time-sensitive not content-sensitive." Berril still switched to rapid-fire Galactic Common. She didn't want to make it easy on the divinity. "Phex, if they ask you to leave Asterism and join Tillam in Fortew's place, what will you do? What will you decide?"

Phex thought that question assumed he'd be given a choice. He thought *that* would be highly unlikely. In fact, he hoped he wouldn't be given a choice. He hoped the decision would be made for him. Because either way, he'd lose – either he'd leave Missit finally and forever or he'd leave his pantheon. He didn't want it to be *his choice*. In the one case, he got to stay with Asterism but never see Missit, and in the other, he lost Asterism but stayed with Missit while simultaneously being forbidden from loving him. He had no idea which scenario would be worse.

"They haven't talked to me about it." A part of Phex hoped the acolytes would make good on their threats and simply kick him out of godhood altogether. He'd held Missit in his bed all night long. Perhaps that was enough of a breach to get him sent back to obscure mortality. He'd rather be a barista on a forgotten moon than either alternative now before him. Maybe he could just stay on Agatay. Did they have baristas? He should ask Kagee.

"But everyone knew this was likely to happen," said Kagee, annoyed as ever.

"Perhaps the divinity dwells in denial." Phex looked over at Jinyesun.

His sifter said, "I suspect that they have multiple strategies in place for all eventualities, including this one, and that they are activating them now."

Fandina's crests flexed in a very telling way. And Asterism immediately turned to look in the direction the sifter had indicated.

The three acolytes had entered the galley. They made their way immediately over to Phex.

Phex took off his apron and let them escort him away. He wondered what they would do if he insisted on taking an emotional-support ladle with him.

Of course, Phex thought the acolytes were going to reassign him or at least inform him of their decision on the matter of his future pantheon. Permanent placement with Tillam or stay the low cantor of Asterism. Surely, they could not leave the two pantheons in limbo for long.

Instead, the three Dyesi led Phex to a part of the spaceship that he'd never seen before.

It was a small, dark room, cave-like and somewhat hostile-feeling. There were no carapaces or panels – this was not a dome or a practice room. But it still had that feel, a sense of being made by, of, or for imagoes. The floor and walls were covered in some soft material, as if constructed of the same material as the ubiquitous puffy Dyesi furniture. It was like walking inside a massive couch.

Phex announced that he was a complete stranger to this space and then stood awkwardly just inside the entrance while the acolytes, all familiar with the room, entered after him. In the eerie unison of ritual, the thee Dyesi sat down on the floor, backs against the bulkhead across from Phex.

After a moment, Phex sat in the middle of the room, legs crossed, facing them.

They stayed like that for some time in silence, staring at each other. Phex couldn't read intent from body posture, skin speckles, or crest behavior – it was all neutral. If they wanted him to do something, they would have to instruct him verbally.

Finally, Calator Heshoyi's crests folded and it impatiently tapped its ident. "Where are you?" it asked in frozen register.

A few minutes later, Quasilun entered the room, announcing complete familiarity with the space. Phex wondered if the imago slept there. Then he wondered if the imago slept at all.

Instead of sitting with the other Dyesi, Quasilun stood near the entrance, like a proper bodyguard, arms loose and relaxed, a careful observer. The imago's body language was different from normal but far too complex for a mere Sapien to understand.

"This was your idea, imago, and now you object?" Precatio Ohongshe asked, more curious than upset.

Quasilun said, "Was this my idea? The divinity is nymph business. Why would you listen to me even if it were?"

"You have a point." Calator Heshoyi was using frozen register but in a way that was more abrupt and annoyed than Phex had ever heard.

"I want to be on record. This is a risk to the demigod that I don't believe is worth taking, especially under such circumstances as a dead cantor," said Sacerdote Chalamee. "We have no idea how a Sapien brain will react. Studies are not conclusive but they also are not positive."

"Your objection is noted," said Quasilun.

Phex wondered what they were going to do to him.

"As the challenger, Chalamee, you will administer verity and monitor."

The sacerdote was clearly prepared for this, because it leaned forward and passed Phex a small packet containing a gummy candy of some kind. It was white and nondescript, about the size of his thumbnail.

"Swallow that but do not chew it."

Phex did as instructed. It had a slight mushroom taste, earthy and bitter, highly unpleasant. And Phex normally rather enjoyed fungi.

"Try not to throw up," advised Calator Heshoyi, unhelpfully.

They sat in silence and stared at each other for another long spate of time.

The gummy sat in Phex's stomach. And then his gut got excited, not butterflies or anything, but as if the part of his brain that felt emotion had been moved to just beneath his sternum. It warmed into enthusiasm and optimism, even affection for the acolytes across from him. Phex was suspicious of the sensation – he'd never felt affection for an acolyte before.

Then, without Phex doing anything, the walls of the dark puffy room around him started to move. He didn't notice at first because it was so dim, but then they shivered a bit and began to wiggle – like an excited Dyesi crest. It was very disconcerting but not frightening. It was like looking at reality through the surface of heated oil.

What was he cooking?

Was the ship turning into a wok?

"There is nothing wrong with the *Nusplunder*, this is your brain."

Apparently, Phex had spoken his confusion with the wiggly walls out loud.

Also, he had to assume he'd been given a mind-altering drug of some kind.

Charming.

Phex had no experience with such things, so now he was suspicious of what he might say or do.

No doubt he would embarrass himself, but he did want to share the warm excitement he felt in his belly.

"You'll be fine. We are interested in truth, not humiliation."

So, he was saying everything he thought out loud as he thought it.

This was not going to go well.

"Yes. That is the point. We have questions for you and we need you to actually answer us for a change."

Phex tried not to think of anything.

Like that would work.

The three Dyesi across from him were behaving very strangely.

They were melting into and then away from each other, like they were patterns on the dome.

Like they were them but no longer made of flesh, skin-sifting reality.

He thought they should stop pretending to be liquid gold.

They were not gods.

They were not Missit.

Was it not rude to be formless?

They also smelled of the musty underground soil of Dyesid Prime.

"Interesting," said Precatio Ohongshe. "I wonder why he smells the caves right now."

"Probably something to do with the taste of the verity."

"Shall we begin?"

They hadn't already?

Now they were being both rudely formless and lazy?

"He's very chatty for one of the few Sapiens I've ever met that ordinarily holds his tongue."

"Isn't that normal? Don't we all swap personalities after consuming verity?"

"You're saying this is his true beauty?"

Phex wanted to know why they were talking about him as if he weren't right in front of them.

Although Dyesi was such a pretty language.

Did they not remember that they had taught it to him?

"Quite right, we should begin."

Phex thought that was silly – they had begun. Why were they dancing around, talking about eating truth?

There was some huffing at that.

Someone had made the Dyesi laugh.

It was probably Phex.

The Dyesi were always laughing at him for some reason.

"Tell us about Missit, Phex."

Phex had stopped being able to distinguish between the three Dyesi.

It wasn't his fault they kept oozing into each other like mashed spuds.

Maybe that didn't matter, since they were all just different facets of the divinity and the divinity wanted to separate him from Missit.

"We actually don't want that. Your behavior drove us to it. Together, you two give the best dome in divine history. It is annoying to us that your Sapien hormones have to complicate divine matters."

Phex wasn't sure what to feel about that but he decided to be insulted.

Was that what they thought it was?

Just hormones?

That was unfair.

It trivialized both the fact that he wanted Missit and the facts that he liked him and needed to be near him.

As if desire could be divvied up and prioritized.

As if sexual need and emotional resonance should be put in different caves.

As if they did not swirl together, colors and patterns, neither greater nor lesser and both necessary.

As if low cantor ever worked without high.

As if only one Dyesi could sift a dome.

"This isn't working. He just says everything without filter."

"He's angry with us. With the divinity."

"Phex?"

Phex was angry with them.

At these children of a dim underground world who brought color to the galaxy but did not understand the depth of it.

"He is a lot more brutal than I would have guessed."

"He sings honesty under verity like he sings the dome, all power and no subtlety."

"Phex, what would you say to Missit if he were here now?"

Good question.

Phex had been unable to say anything all night, because he didn't know the right thing to say.

What could someone like him, with so few words, say to Missit, who had lost one of his pantheon?

One of his great loves?

One of his own?

His sun.

The worst possible thing that could happen to a god had happened to Missit.

Phex had had his own pantheon for so short a time, and already that would feel like losing one of his senses.

Like going blind.

What words were strong enough to fill in the void left by a whole person?

Was it like a dome that could be filled with cantor?

Did words exist that were powerful enough to bring color to a vacant heart?

"Try. For Missit."

Phex thought he would like to say, "Missit, it is not your fault."

He would tell him, "Missit, you are still loved, not just worshiped. There are those around you who, like Fortew, see beneath the gold.

"Missit," he would say, "There are many hands around to hold you when you melt. There always have been. Not just Fortew. Not just me. You can find form in the fondness of friends. Missit, you do not need to burn yourself to ash on the

dais, paying penance for being the one who survived. Missit, you have not lost Fortew. You have not left him behind. It is Fortew who has gone on ahead."

Phex's mouth felt warm, saying Missit's name.

The taste of it was filled with memories, like a food he'd eaten as part of that idyllic childhood he never actually had.

He really was speaking all his thoughts out loud.

Well, these things happened.

Who was he to think he could keep secrets from the divinity?

"Do you have secrets that you keep from us?"

Not intentionally.

Not anymore.

But sometimes, the acolytes surprised him with what they didn't know.

"What do *you* want, Phex?"

He wanted Missit.

Just Missit.

More than anything else.

More than divinity or pantheons or to belong to a planet.

He wanted to fill his mouth with warm gold every day, because of Missit's name.

Because of Missit's body.

Because of Missit.

He wanted fill his hands with silk and melted metal that did not burn.

He wanted to fill the Dyesi with the same shame they'd made him feel for that desire.

He wanted to punish them with understanding, but also, he wanted to forget.

"I'm sorry," he found himself saying over and over again to the Missit who wasn't there.

Who Phex knew wasn't there but also, for some reason, felt was sitting just out of his eyesight.

This was all Phex's fault.

He had known before they began that they shouldn't.

That he and Missit together would have an end point, sooner rather than later.

He had known Missit was relentless and irresistible, yet he had not even tried to say no.

He had been weak and pathetic, grasping something beautiful for the very first time in his life just because he wanted it. Because it had been gifted to him.

Something offered only to him.

He, who had never had anything that really belonged to him, let alone something so special as another whole person's love.

He had known all along Missit would never pause them.

Missit wouldn't resist anything Phex wanted.

It was Phex, the custodian of caution, who had been careless with both their hearts.

He had failed them both with his wanting.

And in failing them, he had failed both pantheons as well.

And he had failed the divinity.

Failed the Dyesi.

The Dyesi, who had actually been the first to want him.

Phex's face was wet and he wiped at it angrily.

His throat was sore.

Had he been shouting?

Missit's name was ringing in his ears.

What language had he been speaking?

"Dyesi. You've been speaking Dyesi."

"Is it my native tongue now? If I spoke Dyesi after eating verity," Phex asked, out loud, intentional this time.

"You realize what's happening?"

Yes. But in the way that he knew he was still on a spaceship orbiting Agatay, but also didn't really believe it anymore. In the way that this whole journey to godhood, from the moment the Dyesi appeared in his cafe, had been one long hallucination, but also beamed out into universe for all to see.

"What is reality, anyway?" he heard himself say, voice ringing in his own ears. Sobering.

The walls were beginning to solidify, just as quickly as they had gone all wobbly. The three Dyesi across from him were once more distinct from each other.

He let his head loll forward. He was still crying, as if his eyes were an outlet valve for all the things he still could not say.

"It's still in effect. We can continue."

14

A SKINSIFT IN DISGUISE

Phex sat quietly. He was sobering quickly – as fast as he'd gone under, he was coming back to reality. But he decided to pretend he was still out of it. Partly out of embarrassment, partly out of curiosity to see what the Dyesi would ask him next. Why had they put him through that? Did they want him to expose himself? Which part were they after?

Ohongshe said, "We were worried it was obsession, but this cantor is not fixated. It's definitely the third beauty. We should not have doubted the imago."

Phex stared at the hands in his lap, his own, but they felt very far away – still, he could follow the different acolyte voices easily now. Each one somehow represented a different tone of iridescence and different sound of sifted skin. All that training under a dome, and he saw sound as color even when it was only spoken words. Or maybe it was the lingering effects of the drug.

"Is that possible? He may be a god but he's still only a Sapien." The calator was skeptical.

"They are both very young." Phex wasn't sure if the

sacerdote was making an objection or a mere statement of facts.

"Only Missit *acts* young," said the calator.

The sacerdote's voice was soft. "We must recognize that Missit's behavior is, in part, because we ourselves never allowed him to be young as a Sapien is young. Instead, we made him a god."

Ohongshe said, "Phex, I think, was never skinless either. Perhaps that is why they are so drawn to one another."

Phex figured they had underestimated how fast he metabolized drugs. He was now entirely sober and aware of their conversation, but it didn't feel like he was *meant* to be. He kept his head lolled forward and tried to pretend he was still incapacitated. He no longer wanted to constantly vocalize his thoughts, so they would probably figure out that his silence meant sobriety soon.

The sacerdote made an annoyed hiss. "I do not think age is a factor in this particular instance. You have heard and seen and felt what they can do to the dome. You can't possibly think that beauty is limited by anything when it contains within it all the infinite colors of the universe?" The Dyesi added the linguistic particle of mild disapproval.

"Even though they are both Sapien?" the calator shot back.

"The fact that we all experience beauty differently does not negate that fact that we all experience it." That was Quasilun's voice, dual-toned and sarcastic.

Phex started. He had forgotten the imago was in the room with them.

"Even accepting that this is the third beauty – can we allow it between gods?" The sacerdote did not acknowledge the imago and continued speaking in low register.

"Allow? When is beauty allowed or not allowed, especially by the Dyesi?" Ohongshe took offense at the question.

"Is it not the very definition of our domain?" protested the calator.

"Beauty is in the soul of the sift, but never forget that we cannot change the colors ourselves. We need others for that. We need cantors and graces. This is not for us to allow or not allow. The godsong is theirs. It is something they give to us." Sacerdote Chalamee sounded almost impassioned.

"He's gone quiet," Calator Heshoyi pointed out.

Phex glanced up from behind lowered lashes. The calator was staring at him, suspicious.

But Ohongshe was inspired by debate and pressed on. "Then isn't proximity even more dangerous for them? Like for the fixed?"

"I suspect that any distance we enforce has been and will be more damaging. Difficult to tell with Sapiens." Sacerdote Chalamee would not commit.

"So, we vote?" the calator pushed. "This one seems to have survived verity."

"I vote in favor. Soulsift is sacrosanct." Ohongshe said immediately.

Phex wasn't certain what was happening, but he felt that Ohongshe was on his side. Even on *their* side – his and Missit's. If such a thing existed anymore.

"I vote against. The risk is too high, they are both gods." The calator would stick to divine caution – it was in its nature.

The sacerdote who had been, all along, the voice of questioning logic said, after a long tense moment, "I vote in favor. The risk is not ours to take, it is theirs. We should see what they become, together, if soulsift is in play."

"You are willing to allow this breach merely out of curiosity?"

"I allow it out of wonder. Beauty is, of course, love, but did you forget that love, in and of itself, is also beautiful?"

"You sacrifice Tillam and risk Asterism. Both pantheons are in play."

"Tillam is fading. If not already grey."

The calator said, "Very well." It looked at Phex.

Phex straightened and met its huge eyes.

"You're already sober?"

Phex clicked.

"Amazing metabolism."

"So I have been told."

"His voice isn't even slurred. Remarkable." That was Quasilun from behind him.

Phex ignored the imago and asked, "Which pantheon do I go to?"

"Is that what you thought this was about?"

Phex had no idea. He'd just spent the last half hour touring alternate planes of existence as a result of some strange Dyesi mushroom. "If not that, then what decision have you come to? How have my private thoughts clarified anything?"

"The blue demigod is *not* happy with us," said Precatio Ohongshe crests puffed with amusement.

"Sapiens are so cute when they're affronted," agreed Sacerdote Chalamee, sounding genuinely fond.

The calator said, "Phex, you and Missit may be together."

"Together *together*?" asked Phex, desperate.

The acolytes clearly did not want to elaborate.

Finally, Sacerdote Chalamee said, "Yes. As you Sapiens would have it. As lovers or partners or whatever label you would like to labor under, and in all the ways we nymphs do not understand and would rather not contemplate. You must not let it impact the dome or your pantheon. Prove to us that this was the correct decision. That exceptions can be made for third beauty."

Phex clicked earnest agreement. He would do everything he could to prove their faith in him was justified. Faith in Missit. Faith in both of them. Faith of the divinity.

"But *which* pantheon?" Phex pressed.

"Whichever one is in the dome."

Phex clicked. Clearly, they were not yet ready to solve for the absence of Fortew. He would take what he could get – an unexpected blessing.

"I will not fail," he said formally, because he couldn't. This was a new kind of grace, and he had to learn to dance it according to their tune.

"Gods willing," said the acolytes, all three as one.

Phex wondered what he had gotten himself into. He had just made a promise based on Missit's behavior. Missit, who was flighty and capricious and a true god. Missit, who was deeply in pain.

Missit, who he could go to now and hold and no Dyesi would stop him.

Phex ran from the room.

Missit was more present and aware than he had been. He noticed when Phex came into Tillam's quarters and responded with more than just fierce desperation when Phex hugged him.

"What are you doing here?" Missit asked, voice damp with suppressed pain, like it was drowning.

Phex felt a little strange inside Tillam's domain. Missit always came to him in Asterism's room.

Missit always came to him. Period.

"They're letting us be together." Phex couldn't think of a less blunt way of putting it. Why was he always so bad with words?

"What?"

"The acolytes, they say we can date or whatever... unless you don't want to?" Perhaps this was too much right now. He was the one excited. He was the one who had run to talk without thinking. He was the one who wanted. Too much, right now? Stupid to tell Missit when Missit was suffering and already had enough buffeting his emotions. Perhaps Missit would hate him for intruding on his misery with selfish need. Phex panicked, began backing away. He should have waited.

Missit grabbed his face. "What is going on?"

Phex bit his lip. Remembered the divinity had injected new fillers recently. Stopped. "The acolytes gave me this mushroom gummy to swallow, and then the walls wiggled, and they asked lots of questions, and I pretty much told them everything I was thinking, and in the end they decided we could date."

Missit looked less exhausted and grief-stricken and more fiercely angry. "They gave you *verity*?"

"Yes. That."

"But that can kill Sapiens!"

"Evidently not all Sapiens." Phex looked around.

Tillam's quarters were messier than Asterism's. He wondered if that was because Fortew had been away so long. Were suns usually the tidy ones in a pantheon?

"Phex, honey, and I mean this in the nicest possible way, but I really don't have the energy to deal with you being terse. You need to tell me everything that just happened. I know it's hard, but please? Just this once."

Phex puffed out his breath. He was already feeling taxed from talking so much to the acolytes. Plus, the rest of Tillam was *right there*. They were huddled together in pairs on their bunks – Tyve and Berril with them. That was a lot of people listening for him to just talk. But Missit rarely asked him to do something contrary to his nature. And Missit was already dealing with so much. Phex didn't want to add to his stress. But he did want Missit to know that they had been given grace. Even if it came off as selfish, this one time.

So, he told Missit what had happened. Perhaps not everything the Dyesi had asked him, nor everything that he had said in reply, because he couldn't remember a lot of it. But he remembered the gist.

Missit listened in silence to Phex's halting speech and embarrassed recitation of all his wrong words that had miraculously resulted in the best possible outcome. He did his best, and Missit was more patient with him than anyone had a right to expect.

Everyone else stayed silent too.

Missit contented himself with resting against Phex with an ear to Phex's chest, listening to the deep rumble and the steady heartbeat underneath. He petted a lock of Phex's hair that had worked loose and was lying across one shoulder and down his arm.

"Third beauty, really?" Yorunlee spoke when Phex finally finished.

"Can Sapiens truly experience extended soulsift?" Melalan was skeptical too.

"A better question is, can Missit?" Yorunlee replied.

"You always trivialize my feelings." Missit sounded like

this was an old complaint. He also sounded petulant and quite young.

Yorunlee huffed at him fondly.

Melalan asked, "They voted and *all* three agreed?"

"Two of the three." Phex felt Missit relax entirely against him for the first time in a long while.

"Then it's official, they spoke for all the divinity. They really are letting us be together." Missit's voice was bright with gold.

"Will they go public with the information?" Phex asked. Not sure how he felt about being out in the open about dating the most famous god in the galaxy.

"I doubt it. Publicity nightmare. Why? Do you want to be public about us?" Missit asked.

Phex couldn't tell from his tone of voice how Missit felt about that idea, so Phex said cautiously, "I'd rather not. That seems needlessly messy."

"Yes. You're a very private person… for a god." Missit didn't sound upset.

"Are you mad?"

"Of course not. I understand you more than you think."

Phex only clicked at him and cuddled him close.

Missit lounged against him, bonelessly melted and his.

Phex took a deep breath. "Tell me about what it was like back then, when you first formed Tillam." *When you first met Fortew.*

And so Missit began to talk about the beginning. The things that Phex knew because he had read it in Tillam's bio and on the divine forums, but also the things that were not recorded by the divinity for public consumption. Funny little stories. How Tillam had been formed using a much different process than Asterism.

The rest of Tillam contributed comments and thoughts.

Then Tern was telling a funny story about Fortew and the first time he swam in an ocean. Then Zil was telling a different story about the time he took Fortew back to his home spaceship to meet his family.

So, while Phex held Missit without fear of discovery, Tillam shared memories like wedges of cake and sips of corrosive dark, sweet and bitter, comfort and warmth. This was an oral record that time had given only to them, of a person who now only existed only as love left behind.

Phex wasn't certain if it was healing or healthy, but Missit's face was less frozen. He began wiggling and squirming more like he usually did when sharing a bed.

Phex thought those were good signs.

Eventually, Phex got up and went to the galley and brought back mugs of warm beverages, passed them out. Because he knew Tillam's preferences now, just like he knew Asterism's.

At some point, Berril left.

Fandina and Jinyesun stuck their heads in. Came inside and listened for a while, then just as politely left.

Even the acolytes checked up on them.

And so they whittled away the day, sharing and weaving stories together like godsong knitted into a dome colored only by memory.

When Phex returned to his own quarters at the end of the day, Tyve came with him. They thought it was, perhaps, a good thing to leave Tillam alone now. The great gods needed to sink into the reality of being five instead of six and learn if they worked together without Fortew. Five was an ugly number.

"How are they doing?" asked Kagee.

"Not great but also not so bad," said Tyve.

Berril was bouncier than was appropriate. "Yes, yes, but can we talk about the fact that Phex and Missit have permission to be a couple?"

Tyve looked to their high cantor. "Kagee, did you hear? The acolytes tested him and decided it was soulsift and therefore permissible."

Phex raised his eyebrows. That was one way of putting it. He puttered about their quarters, tidying while Tyve and Berril relayed to the rest of his pantheon what had happened. He let the graces answer Kagee's questions, smooth out Jinyesun's confusion, and revel in Fandina's approval.

All too soon, there was nothing for him to do. Lacking a kitchen, and missing it, he sat on his bunk, waiting to see if he was needed. Wondering if they should go practice, maybe do some stretching.

Much to Phex's surprise, Jinyesun came over and sat next to him, leaned against him. That alone wasn't unusual, just rare, but then the Dyesi put its head on Phex's shoulder.

"What's this about? You okay?" asked Phex, using the informal to make sure Jin knew he was worried.

"Nothing like that. I just like it."

"It's a south-caves thing," explained Fandina. "They're very crowded, more affectionate than most Dyesi."

Phex remembered his own cave experience and the way the Dyesi slept in big piles together. It seemed the nymphs on their home world were, in general, a lot more physically demonstrative than off of it.

"But Jin has not been like this before." Phex stayed stiff and confused. Was something really wrong with his friend? Had he missed something important because at first he'd been stuck in that weird floaty space where nothing could touch him because he'd lost Missit? And then he'd been coping with Missit's grief. Had his lover caused him to neglect his pantheon worse than normal? Perhaps the Dyesi had been right all along and no one should be allowed to have both.

Fandina huffed in amusement and pointed both crests at Phex. "You're a safe Sapien now."

Jinyesun snuggled in slightly, in a way that reminded Phex a little of Berril.

"Safe?"

"Sapiens tend to lust after us, and that's uncomfortable for nymphs."

"You're worried any gestures of affection will be perceived as flirting?"

Fandina clicked an affirmative.

"But because I'm now officially allowed to be with Missit, it's okay?" Phex guessed. "You can't be accused of leading me on or anything?"

More clicks.

Phex felt compelled to say, "You know not all romantic relationships are monogamous, right?"

"Should I stop?" Jin didn't move.

"No, it's fine. Strangely enough, I find the Dyesi completely resistible."

Kagee chuckled.

Fandina asked, "Is yours monogamous, with Missit?"

Phex frowned. "I don't know. We've never defined any of it." It had been illicit and then it had been secret and then it had been broken.

"It is," said Missit firmly, appearing in the entranceway with a dramatic swipe of the curtain. "He's mine. I'm his. We already have to share each other with pantheons, and worshipers, and believers, and fixed, that's complicated enough to balance without adding additional lovers into the mix."

Phex felt something warm and golden unfurl through him, seeping into his blood like tea in water. Whatever it was, it was changing the flavor of him, staining his bones with comfort. He couldn't drag his eyes away from Missit's flecked eyes.

Kagee's voice was husky with amusement. "Missit is a jealous god."

Phex considered how he felt about this. Decided he liked it. The idea that Missit chose him out of a million possibilities and wanted to keep Phex for himself was a first in Phex's life. Even the Dyesi had only granted him citizenship so he could be part of the divinity, so he could be shared. That was *use*, not affection. Missit wanted to keep him for himself, and that was unique in the universe, just like Missit.

Missit's eyes were big and pleading. Phex hadn't realized that he had a choice in this matter. He drowned in flecks of gold. The warmth inside him spread even more. Was Missit melting him? "Good."

Missit leapt into Phex's lap. Which only made Phex feel lighter. Or maybe that was the melted gold now running through him.

For the first time, Missit's warmth was not a danger – there was no possibility of being burned. They were matched now, the perfect mixed beverage, warm in a way that brought comfort, not risk. Phex had made space for himself by always knowing, always offering drinks to others. For the first time, he realized that he'd never chosen one for himself. He'd never determined which was his favorite. Yet here it was, in his arms, in Missit form – nourishment. Happiness.

Jin murmured a protest. The Dyesi was still resting on Phex's shoulder, and Missit had jostled it.

Phex shifted Missit so he could accommodate both. He tucked a lock of hair behind one pointed gold ear, thinking that they probably needed snacks, and that Tyve looked amused and Fandina confused, and Kagee was glaring at them affectionately, and that each one of his pantheon was a pinpoint of warmth too, like Missit, like stars. Maybe that was living, filling the spaces between them. Perhaps Phex had crossed a galaxy for this moment.

It was worth it.

Berril's sharp little face was delighted. "It's nice to be able to openly witness how much you two love each other."

"Soulsift," said Jinyesun, also pleased. "And from a Sapien in *my* pantheon."

Phex said, in Galactic Common so he could separate the two words, "It's beautiful, but I don't know if it is actually love. I never have." Did one *love* the atmosphere that kept him safe from the vacuum of space?

Missit looked crushed.

Phex couldn't help that, so he pushed on. This was why he was normally careful with words. "Missit is just my reason."

"Reason for what?"

"Continuing."

Fandina looked like it understood exactly what he meant. "That is beauty in its third form. It is dangerous because it renders the other forms of beauty irrelevant. It becomes all you can see. Like the dome for worshipers. Like that one god for a fixed."

"And that makes it a kind of love?" Phex wondered.

"That makes it a kind of hope." Fandina looked almost wistful.

"Are they not the same thing?" Jinyesun did not shift from leaning on Phex. But, like it always did, it explained.

"There is this place deep inside all of us where hope and love and fear are rolled together. We Dyesi call it beautiful because it is. It is also the unmaker, you will lose some of yourself to it. I am one of the few who believe that it is also glorious."

Phex sighed and looked at his hand on Missit's shoulder. Dark blue starkly contrasted to Missit's skin. Should it not also be gold right now? He wondered why he'd been denied skinsift. Why had he not been born to a species that showed the world its colors instead of having to feel them all the time? "I read somewhere once that if you have never been loved, you do not know how to give it."

Fandina looked odd, crests almost wilted – not sad but somehow sympathetic. "You're a god, Phex. All you get from worshipers is love. You think you don't return it, there under the dome?"

Phex winced, considering the congregation and its needs and the way they fed off pantheons on the dais. Thinking about the fixed, spat back out as hateful exceptions – were they manifestations of divine fear? He considered what his voice was doing to the sifters and the dome, and what the divinity was doing to the Sapiens that consumed both. Phex was pouring out love and it turned into what? A weapon of peace?

Fandina continued. "You think you don't serve love up to your friends, your pantheon, your lover? You think Missit doesn't feel it from you? You think he chases you without encouragement? You are the only person who can't see it. You send out love the way you send out song, in all the colors at once."

"I don't feel very loving." Was love this warmth skin-sifting his veins to gold? Were all the things he was scared of losing – Missit, the divinity, his pantheon – to be treasured instead of feared? Were the things he had resisted because they were beyond his control actually instruments of his own happiness? Did they tether him home?

"Of course you don't. Did no one tell you? Dyesi are tone-deaf. We do not really hear music, we only manifest it. Just because you know how to create a thing doesn't mean you know how to feel it. Beauty is not in what you experience, it's in how you impact others."

Phex absorbed that for a moment.

Jinyesun pressed three fingers to Phex's temple in the Dyesi caress of affection. "We, your friends, we understand little bits of what happened to you. You've parceled out nuggets of information about your past. We've talked about you and put things together. None of us really understand what it's like to live as a refugee. But *our* lack of empathy doesn't make *you* stunted. Whether you realize it or not, you love us, and we feel it."

Phex frowned. Was it possible to love without realizing? Was this how friendship worked? To sing at someone's skin until it became beautiful when he could so easily bruise instead? To catch them when they leapt, every time, in every performance, at exactly the right note, when he could so easily drop them? To hold melted gold in his arms because he knew it would not burn? Was love just trust in a different pattern?

"That is not the kind of love Missit wants from me." Phex said, a bit unguarded, a bit too trusting.

This time, Missit didn't mind his bluntness. "Yes, it is."

Tyve spoke up then. "It's still love. That your love takes physical form – don't wince, it's not like you two are exactly subtle – that it's expressed one way does not diminish it or make it any less a thing of connection."

Fandina said, "We Dyesi do not trim love to fit belief – it is the other way around."

"But the divinity told us we couldn't. You sifters told us to hide. And the acolytes separated us." Missit sounded upset and tired.

"Because none of us understood."

Evidently, Phex hadn't really understood either. Now he realized that in avoiding connection for fear of its severing, he had hurt himself the most. He now knew one thing without question – the golden warmth was a good thing and his previous numbness was not.

Phex felt the solidity of Missit on top of him as a newly minted precious thing, no greater or lesser for its intensity then the quieter gentle weight of Jinyesun's head on his shoulder.

Jin, who had been his first Dyesi friend. His first friend at all, really. Jin, who had joined him in the kitchen on Divinity 36 without ever intruding. Jin, who asked questions because the answers helped it better understand Phex. Jin, who handed out facts like precious gifts. Jin, who took on a foreign nickname as if it were an honor, even as the single syllable diminished it in the eyes of other Dyesi. Jin, who was no longer afraid to touch him. Jin, who had, apparently, spent a long time wanting to be cuddled and not asking for it, because of fear. Jin, who had watched Tyve and Berril and Missit crawl all over Phex and never thought a Dyesi could have the same.

Both weights, Missit's and Jinyesun's, were things Phex loved. People he loved. How dare Phex dishonor them by being afraid? By trying to rename it something lesser?

He said to Missit, explaining the Dyesi to someone who had lived with them many times longer and yet still didn't understand, "The nymphs made the rules that hurt us to protect themselves – acolytes and sifters. From us. They may be older in years, but by life stage, nymphs are still children. All species in the galaxy want to protect their young." Even though those exact regulations had driven the sifters of every pantheon into loneliness and isolation. The Dyesi too had sacrificed to become gods.

"Fandina, come here," said Phex.

His other Dyesi flew across the room, cuddled Phex's other side. The tiny bunk groaned under all the weight, even as Phex warmed and glowed with it. He may not be able to tell them that he loved them, but this way, they knew.

15

THE DOME IS SALVATION

Because this was the Dyesi, every tour stop meant a mandated number divisible by three. But with all the extra shows on Agatay, Phex had entirely lost track of the number of divine events they'd participated in. Asterism was informed by the acolytes the next morning that they still had one more performance in Dome 6.

Of course, Tillam wouldn't be performing, so Asterism was trying to come up with a full set of nine songs. Twelve would be better. They had seven ready, but they would have to cover a few of Tillam's songs to make up the full requirement. It was generally felt that would be considered gauche since Fortew had just collapsed in that very dome. When the truth of his demise came out, Asterism would suffer the flames of the forums.

It was surreal to even consider the fact that they still had to get up on that dais. When someone had died there. Not just *someone* – a *god* had died.

Yet Asterism boarded the transport shuttle like they had many times over the past few weeks, and traveled to Agatay to Dome 6 and readied themselves to perform despite all misgivings.

It did not matter to the divinity what had happened before. Today the dome must be sifted. Always the dome must be sifted.

Now they all knew why.

Now they all knew why the acolytes had insisted on the soldiers getting their own performances. Why they wanted to expose as many people on this violent planet as possible to godsong and its pacifying impact.

But something was very wrong in Dome 6 when Asterism arrived.

It had nothing to do with Fortew.

It was the result of a different kind of death.

The dome was intact, but they were told by a scraggly squad of militia that the capital had been badly bombed. The diarchs were in hiding and the standing army was in tatters. This was not because they could not fight but because they no longer had the will to do so.

The dome had done its work too well. The places on Agatay where the divinity had not yet reached had been able to take advantage of the enlightenment that exposure had engendered in those they had reached already.

Kagee was furious. He pointed his deadly hand at the three acolytes. "You changed the balance of power on my planet."

The three Dyesi looked guilty, scared, and worried. "This was not our intent."

Kagee growled. "I know, I know. Normally, enlightenment takes much longer. Well, not here. And we all get to witness the carnage wrought by instant pacification."

"And we understand why it is meant to take time. It should

only change Sapiens slowly. Agatay was too fast." Calator Heshoyi was obviously upset by this lesson, but the dome's impact was out in the world now – it could not be retracted.

"You were the ones who insisted on building Dome 6." Kagee was worried about his people.

"But it was your diarchs who invited us," replied the calator.

"And you liked the idea at the time, Kagee," added Phex, not siding with the divinity, but not as firmly against it, either.

The Dyesi had no way to predict what had happened there. And Kagee *had* liked the idea of his people getting enlightened. Phex had seen that in his eyes. Kagee did not get to rewrite his own culpability because the outcome was undesirable.

"People have died, Phex!"

"People are always dying here, Kagee. You told us that."

"I don't know whether Levin and Miramo are okay!"

Ah, now they were getting to the crux of the matter. Kagee was actually worried about his loved ones.

They were inside Dome 6 but not underground and not on the dais. Just standing and looking up at the grey panels, the massive structure empty around them.

Kagee began pacing. "Gods, there's Liera, too! She's only a baby."

Phex said, "We had them summon all their protan proxies. Remember? All the colorblind can still fight. They will protect your diarchs."

"Us proxies are assassins, not soldiers."

"You are also bodyguards. Your kind will save your diarchs, Kagee. Stop panicking, you know better." Phex hated to be sharp at a time like this, but it was what Kagee needed. He was spiraling, and usually he was the most predictable among Phex's pantheon and the most dependable as a result. Spiraling could not be allowed.

His high cantor swallowed audibly, deadly hands clenching and releasing at his side – flexing poisoned threat. Kagee would not admit that Phex was right, but his anger did cool, became more internally directed. "I should have known this would happen. Of course peace in one part of the planet only means vulnerability to invasion."

Phex said, "Do we know exactly what happened?"

Bob relayed a litany of information gleaned from conversing with the small cadre of remaining military still at the dome. The few who had not fled.

In retrospect, it had been unwise to enlighten their only real defensive force. But then again, the warriors of any society were the ones who needed enlightenment the most.

Phex had no idea how converting Agatay might have been approached differently. The Dyesi had acted as per usual with a new planet. There was no point in remorse or regret. Asterism was now caught up in the middle of a civil war, allied with the country whose defenses he and his friends had destroyed with song. There was no way around it: the divinity was at fault.

The acolytes had intended to bring peace and had, instead, wrought destruction.

Phex gathered from Kagee's accented Galactic Common that the only other occupied continent of Agatay had seized the opportunity of a capital city distracted by visiting gods to attack. They'd managed to unify several disparate factions under a rebel warlord – their initial invasion had discovered a major city unexpectedly vulnerable and oddly passive.

Now they were mobilizing an occupying force. Most of their fighting population, which on Agatay meant any capable adult, was on the move. The mountain territory held by the diarchs was considered the most desirable territory on the planet, and they intended to take it by force.

Essentially, a transition of power was now occurring.

Kagee explained and then made a decision. "I'm going to them."

"What?" The acolytes were confused.

"To the diarchs. They'll need every proxy they can get to keep them safe. Did you forget that's what I originally trained for?"

"Kagee, think this through." Tyve had also trained as a warrior once.

But Kagee was looking at Phex. "I don't expect you to come with or to help me, of course. But I also don't expect you to stop me."

Phex only sighed. "Did I say I would?" He understood. Of course he did. Miramo and Levin were Kagee's Missits. Just like Phex, Kagee had lost them for a time, only to return and find them still waiting for him. And Kagee was no refugee. He had the option to return home. So, when he finally did, and found love still waiting for him, his loyalties were bound to be divided.

Phex, facing up to the looming prospect of choosing between Missit and Asterism, felt a great kinship to Kagee. He too would eventually be compelled to make a choice.

Kagee didn't look at the acolytes or Asterism's sifters. Or Berril. He focused on Phex and Tyve.

"I'm going to them," he said again, and there was nothing anyone could do to stop him.

Quasilun or the bodyguards, Phex or Tyve, any of them might have physically tried to restrain him, but they weren't going to. A few of the bodyguards looked like they wanted to, but oddly, the acolytes didn't order Kagee stopped.

"Take a tank," suggested Phex.

"Of course. I'm not a complete idiot."

"Good luck." Tyve was not giving her blessing, but she wasn't standing in his way, either.

"Try to stay alive," advised Phex.

"You too." Kagee left the dome at a run. Phex wondered if his high cantor could actually drive a tank. Probably, knowing Kagee.

Phex turned to the three acolytes. They were looking to Quasilun for guidance. This was, after all, not something they'd ever had to deal with before. The protector imago was the only voice of authority they had when faced with an invasion on an alien world.

Precatio Ohongshe said, "What now, imago? I suspect there will be no performance tonight."

"You think?" Phex huffed, imitating Dyesi laughter.

"We get out. Go back to the ship. Leave orbit immediately."

"But Agatay will fall," said Sacerdote Chalamee, crests back in horror.

"It will be first major failure of the divinity," added Calator Heshoyi, and even it seemed shaken by the idea.

"And all *our* fault." Precatio Ohongshe's crests wilted – its iridescent skin was almost completely dull with depression and horror.

This was a heavy burden for a nonviolent species to bear. It was possible that the Dyesi had inadvertently destroyed an entire Sapien world. Worse, these three acolytes had spoiled a pristine record of continued expansion.

Phex watched them grapple with the consequences of one massive miscalculation.

Quasilun said again, "There is no divine fix for this situation. We must leave. Protect ourselves and Asterism."

Phex said, "There is another solution."

"Phex." Tyve's voice was full of caution.

"The enlightenment of Agatay has been almost instantaneous, correct? On the ones we managed to godfix with live colors?"

"It has."

"So, we just have to get this invading army under a dome," said Phex, like it was that simple.

"Impossible," said Quasilun.

"Godfix should, theoretically, stop them in their tracks." Phex persisted.

"Are you insane? How could we do that?"

Phex turned to the scared-looking military squad that had stayed to protect Dome 6. Their captain was standing close to the entrance, constantly checking her ident for updates. There was another woman at the back who was in possession of some ancient piece of technology called a *radio*. It crackled regularly with status reports from the capital.

"How much danger are we in right now?" Phex asked.

The captain clearly appreciated a question she could answer. "I doubt the dome is much at risk anymore. They'll focus on taking out the city center. And their army is still on the approach. The mountain passes are not easy. They won't be anywhere near here until sunset."

"We have time?"

"You have time."

Phex turned to his sifters. He'd been waiting to ask this, and now he had good reason. "Jinyesun, how does it work? How does skinsifting a dome have such a profound impact on Sapien psyche that it changes the personality of a generation? Putting aside why it has such a rapid effect on Agatay, please explain to me what actually happens under normal circumstances."

The acolytes made murmurs of protest.

Phex turned to them. "To fix a thing that you broke, I must know how it worked originally."

"We don't know for certain." Jin ignored the acolytes and answered Phex. They had always been close, but since yesterday, Phex felt even closer to his sifter. Asterism had become Jin's cave now. If it came to a choice between Phex and the acolytes, he was certain Jinyesun would pick him.

Jin continued. "Research would need to be done by *Sapiens* on enlightened Sapiens, and the divinity has never allowed that. Missit's parents are the closest we have ever gotten."

Phex nodded – he'd feared as much. "Do you at least know how the dome tech and skinsift interact? What causes transmission? How does the color move from skin to dome?"

Jinyesun clicked. "You know that in the caves, cantor is used by imagoes to control large numbers of skinless and nymphs? Skinsift is a visual pheromone, a reaction to sound. The carapaces of imagoes, dead or alive, act as amplifiers. The domes rebroadcast those pheromones, brighter and more intense."

Fandina added, "We have a vomerocular organ rather than a vomeronasal one." It tapped at its brow ridge.

Phex had no idea what that meant but he would look it up later. "There is a kind of hormonal drug in the color and pattern itself when combined with the sound?"

"Yes." Jinyesun's crests puffed, pleased Phex was following the explanation. "Most Sapiens, so far as I understand, transmit pheromones as scent, but ours are a combination of visual and auditory. You know imago skin hardens as they age, reflecting sift but no longer sifting itself? It sympathetically responds to the pheromones of nymphs. Even after they have died and the imago skin hardens into a carapace, it still responds. And so we invented the domes."

Precatio Ohongshe said, sounding like it was reciting something, "Skinsift visually activates monoamine neurotransmitters in hominid brains. In a low, modulated dose, it is pacifying and addictive. It's particularly effective on Sapiens. And apparently overly effective on Agatay."

"So, you *do* know how it works," said Tyve.

The acolyte clicked.

"And the domes synthesize this?" Phex was focused on the end game.

"Yes. The great domes, the ones for live performances like this one, use the keyskin and cloning tech. They are as close to the caves as we can get off Dyesid Prime – very powerful. The cupolas are less effective, since they are entirely synthetic."

"And that's why us gods aren't affected."

"Exactly. A pheromone impacts others, you cannot, after all, be attracted to yourself. Not in that way. You can think of becoming a god as developing a kind of immunity."

"But we are human, not Dyesi."

"You are *mostly* human. Learning a new language changes the way you think, but also it changes the shape of your brain, what aspects of it you can access. It's the same for cantors, what you have learned to do has changed you mentally *and* physically."

"Becoming a god changes our brains?"

"Both the shape and the way they work, yes. How you process and receive sound and color."

"And the fixed?"

"Ah, yes, we're still studying that one. But it seems to have the opposite effect. And yes, it also has to do with the Dyesi pheromone. It seems they have…" It considered a long moment. "…an allergy."

Phex thought that was a mild way of putting it. He, who

sneezed because of pollen, had never sneezed his way into killing anyone.

"Why are we having this conversation now and not leaving this unsafe place?" Quasilun did not care if Asterism understood how domes worked. The imago was not vested in the divinity and its secrets.

Phex stared at the bodyguard. "Give me six more minutes."

"You are such a difficult god."

Phex's skin prickled. He'd successfully fought Quasilun once, but then he'd had the element of surprise. He did not think he would be victorious a second time. Plus, all the bodyguards were there. Their priority, in the absence of Tillam, was to keep Asterism safe. That meant getting them off this planet. They too wanted Phex to stop talking and leave.

So, Phex became verbally cruel to get what he wanted. "Imago, your nymphs made a grave mistake, and people are dying as a result. Have died. This is more than just a god being sacrificed to a fixed. More than just Fortew collapsing on the dais. You let us visit a planet at war because the acolytes thought they could *fix* it. You let your children play with lives, and we all lost."

Quasilun's crests, usually so impassive, wilted slightly.

Calator Heshoyi said, "We did not know what would happen here."

"Ignorance usually results in violence with Sapiens," explained Tyve. She too sounded harsh.

Berril was looking lost and scared. Jinyesun and Fandina were carefully neutral, but their crests were tilted ever so subtly in Phex's direction.

"It never has before," shot back the calator.

"That is luck, not skill," replied Tyve. It was something Kagee would have said.

Phex thought about what he'd just learned. If visible pheromones had once been used by imagoes to control nymphs as well as sound, to push them into violence that was anathema to their nature, then that would explain why the nymphs were so vested in controlling the violent tendencies of the galaxy. Since they were no longer called upon to become cannon fodder, they needed to make absolutely certain no one else ever would be, either.

This, what was happening now on Agatay, was their worst nightmare.

"Agatay's population has a large percentage of individuals immune to godsong, and therefore it should have less fixed, not more, did you know that?" asked Phex, because he needed to get the acolytes on his side.

"What? Why?" Calator Heshoyi seemed annoyed by this information.

"Agatay proxies are mostly protans, like Kagee."

"What does *that* mean?" asked the sacerdote.

"They are colorblind. They would be unaffected by the dome."

"What?! How did we not know this?"

Phex said firmly, "Your ignorance is not relevant. Except that there are more fixed than normal, when there should be less."

"We need Missit's parents for this," said Berril.

Phex thought of his own genetic triggering. He thought about the fact that he was allergic to the atmosphere on planets. A side effect of being triggered with only space-station life in mind. "Perhaps it's the flip side of the same genetic defect?" he suggested. "Perhaps those who are born on Agatay and aren't protans are somehow more sensitive to color, hyper-reactive to the skinsift pheromone. Perhaps that is why enlightenment spreads so fast here. That would explain why there are so many more fixed. But also, it would explain why one dome managed to change the entire balance of political power."

Phex paused, but everyone was just staring at him – they still hadn't figured it out.

Finally, he said, "Doesn't that mean one dome can fix it?"

They simply needed to expose the rest of Agatay to godsong. Or, at the very least, the majority of Agatay's population. Specifically the invading army.

If that army would not come to the dome, then the dome should go to them.

"Let's move it," Phex said.

"What?"

"Dome 6. Let's pick it up and move it over them. Wherever they are. This army that's invading."

"I'm sorry, what?" Calator Heshoyi was startled into informal speech.

Phex gave a very human shrug. "We have a construction ship, after all, full of heavy lifting drones. Can we not just use them to raise the whole dome into the air? It's only foam on the outside, after all. We can't take the underground bits, of course. But we don't need those. Just a dome and a dais."

Tyve was intrigued. "How do you propose we handle the dais?"

"Same again. Construction drones. We can program them to stay coordinated so that the dais is spaced exactly as normal. It shouldn't feel any different to us. Maybe a bit..." He paused, considering. "...bouncy?"

"The dais is made of stone."

"But it doesn't have to be. Just build a portable one, like a wooden stage. There are plenty of trees on Agatay, right? Or use some of the plastic in the hold of the ship, it's a construction barge, after all. So long as it's exactly the same shape and size as a regular dais, we won't care."

It was Quasilun who said, "But you'll be performing in the middle of the air – just floating up there."

Phex supposed that would seem scary to someone born and raised underground. But he'd grown up in space.

Tyve too. She was looking almost excited. "So long as everything is the same size and distance that we've been working with since we got here, it should be fine. The performance patterns are easy. We have everything memorized. We'd have to float quite high. But I think it could work."

The Dyesi were having a hard time understanding.

Fandina said, "But what if we fall?"

Phex considered two sets of worried crests. "Well, you two could have your feet strapped to the dais, if you liked. We can modify our group dancing sections."

Fandina and Jinyesun exchanged crest-wiggles.

"We don't move all that much. It's not us I'm worried about." Fandina touched Phex's arm, concerned. "You do tricks. You run up the walls. You spring off the dome and flip to land back on the dais. You're willing to do this high up in the air?"

Precatio Ohongshe said, "Can you imagine a god plummeting from the sky to his death?"

Phex was offended. "When have I ever fallen off of a dais? When has any god ever fallen off of any dais under any circumstances? Are you mad?" Certainly, Phex had never been a very good crudrat, but he wasn't clumsy. He was still a god! This was taking things too far. He actually felt insulted.

"Aren't you afraid of heights?" asked Sacerdote Chalamee.

"No." What an odd idea.

"And what about the rest of your pantheon?" The sacerdote was clearly worried, but at least one acolyte was considering Phex's hare-brained scheme.

Tyve said she would be absolutely fine. The two sifters agreed that if they had some kind of safety strap and were stationed in the middle of the dais – which they already were most of the time – they too would feel okay.

Sacerdote Chalamee turned to Berril.

Berril gave him a funny look. "I have wings, remember? It's what I do, fly. In fact, if anyone does fall, I can catch them."

Phex said, "I don't think Missit will mind, either."

"Missit, what, Missit?" Berril chirruped.

Phex cocked his head. "Tillam's Missit. Who else do you think will be singing high cantor with Asterism? Kagee is not currently available, and the invading army will be here by nightfall. We need to float the dome as quickly as possible."

The three acolytes, the bodyguards, and Quasilun just stood there, dumbstruck, staring at Phex.

"Okay," said Phex. "Remember, Missit and I are even more powerful as a duo than Kagee and I. We all sift domes, but Missit and I can cause not just godfix in Sapiens but fugue in Dyesi. That means more visual pheromones, right? And isn't power what's required most right now? We need as much godfix as possible, and from a distance? Isn't Missit the logical choice?"

"Will Missit do it?" wondered Tyve. "Isn't he still, ya know, incapacitated?" She was referring to Fortew.

"Of course he'll do it," said Phex. Because he would.

Missit loved the dais. More than willingness, right now he probably needed to sing more than anything else. It would be good for him. Distracting. Missit lost himself when he performed, lost all fear and sorrow. Especially with something so unique as a floating dome, an army to stop, and a civilization to save.

Could there be anything more distracting?

Phex, being practical warrior stock and knowing the Dyesi wouldn't consider weaponry, felt compelled to add, "We are banking on enlightenment occurring quickly since projectiles are a big risk. We can go high enough to avoid fixed, but we can't go high enough to avoid bullets."

The three acolytes consulted with one another for a long time.

Eventually, the sacerdote turned to Phex. "We approve your plan."

The bodyguards all looked shocked. Phex was not surprised. The acolytes had already shown themselves ever willing to risk gods in pursuit of mass enlightenment.

Even Quasilun seemed surprised by this decision. "You wish to repair what you broke. But more, you think if this works, you could introduce the concept of mobile domes elsewhere."

"Of course." Sacerdote Chalamee gave a cheeky crest-wiggle.

"Clever child." The imago actually sounded impressed.

"If this works, we will have turned a catastrophe into an opportunity for even greater enlightenment," said Precatio Ohongshe, sounding a little like it was trying to convince itself.

While they spoke, Calator Heshoyi was already beaming the *Nusplunder* above. It was requisitioning all the drones, programmers, supplies, and builders required to turned Dome 6 from stationary into mobile.

Then Precatio Ohongshe opened a beam to Missit.

Missit wanted to talk to Phex about this idea, and then also to Itrio.

DOME 6

Phex explained his plan.

Missit thought it sounded insane but also lots of fun. His voice was full of the kind of excitement Phex hadn't heard since the caves.

Itrio tried to dissuade him. The bodyguards wouldn't be able to accompany them up in the air. They could, of course, occupy niches, but there would be no fixed to protect them from. Easier just to leave the bodyguards behind. Itrio hated that idea.

It actually worked.

The hardest part was simply separating the dome from its foundation. But the impermanence of the sprayed-foam exterior worked in their favor. It was a lot easier to break the ties that bound Dome 6 to the rocky mountain earth than it had been to build them in the first place.

The drones were easy to program. It was a simple matter to link them all in a coordinated, stable pattern so that the dome simply rose up into the air, in one smooth movement, like a transport ship taking off. The new temporary dais wasn't pretty, but it would do the trick. Or, to be more precise, allow Phex to do tricks. In order to maximize the colors and not interfere with the view from far below, they constructed the new floating dais out of clear, hard plastic.

The builders had taken Asterism at their word that no one was afraid of heights.

Fortunately, when Missit arrived, he thought that it was *delightfully scary*.

Drones lifted it up too, and also managed to match the spacing perfectly. It was exactly like being inside a regular dome on a regular dais, just high up in the air.

They did a practice performance a couple feet off the ground. After that went well, the whole thing rose up, higher than the tallest dome Asterism had ever been in, and then they practiced the whole performance again. Far below they could see the small crowd of military and bodyguards and those who had come to help with Dome 6's transformation.

Phex could not make out the faces of anyone, they were so high up. But he imagined he could see some pretty exaggerated crest-wiggles from the acolytes.

All things considered, Asterism did fine.

Phex enjoyed it. It was like a normal rehearsal, just not exactly. He thought he would enjoy the actual performance even more. With no possibility of fixed attacking, he would be able to fully relax for the first time ever under a dome.

This was going to be fun.

The workers controlling the drones consulted with local military on the subject of munitions range and had a good idea on optimal height. The risk was still there, but they could try to avoid *some* of them. Now all they needed to do was wait to find out exactly where the invading army was located.

It was Berril who thought of simply trying to raise Kagee on the infonet. They tried a divine private beam first, but when that didn't work, they jumped to one of the local networks.

"You're still planetside?" Kagee's voice was very annoyed. "Seriously?"

Phex relaxed.

"Are you okay?" Berril asked, Kagee's tiny grey face floating above her wrist.

"I'm fine, birdie. But shouldn't you and the divinity have folded your pretty little booties out of here by now?"

"Did you find your diarchs?" asked Berril.

"I did and they're fine. We are a bit busy at the moment."

He got distracted by something and looked away from the beam.

"Can you give us the exact location of the invaders?" Berril asked.

"Why do you need that? Never mind, I won't ask. Phex had an idea, didn't he?"

"And it's a good one."

"Of course it is. Why am I not surprised?"

"Because you're a smarty-pants too," replied Berril cheerfully.

Kagee said, "Here's the last coordinates we have. Assume the intelligence is about an hour behind. They are definitely headed toward the city center." He sounded like a soldier, not a cantor. It made Phex suddenly sad.

"Okay!" said Berril, "Thanks, Kagee."

"Put Phex on for a moment."

Phex stuck his head over Berril's shoulder so she could patch him in.

"Don't get yourself killed, either," said Kagee.

"This is gonna be fun," replied Phex.

"I'm scared. You look like you actually believe that."

"Just you wait," said Phex. "Look out a window if you can, toward city center, just after sunset."

"What are you doing, Phex?" asked Kagee, all wariness.

"Putting on a show, of course. What else can we do?"

Asterism stopped an army in its tracks with godsong.

Truth be told, Phex wasn't actually convinced that they could do it, not even with Missit, right up until the moment that they did.

He thought the distance might be a factor. He thought the

dome might be too high, too far away. He thought maybe they miscalculated the immediate effect that godfix had on Agatay. He thought there were many, many things that could have gone wrong. Although him falling off the dais was certainly not one of them.

But it actually worked. And, of course, none of them fell.

The dome hovered over the amassed invading army bellow, and that army looked up in confusion, expecting threat and finding beauty. A few of them cowered or took cover, thinking that the dome was a massive weapon of some kind. Instead, they were blasted with amplified cantor and the colors of a dome from far above, small but not too small, showing them all the bright patterns of possibility.

They were stopped in their tracks. Riveted by the pure, unsullied glory. And none of them shot up at it.

The dome moved sedately around and above them, making sure to catch everyone that it could. Accidentally, this herded the audience closer and closer together, until they all stood as one tightly packed massive group, heads back, mouths open, staring up at the dome – godfixed. Absorbing the song. Feeling the enlightenment.

The dome moved closer.

Phex and Missit did not even try to hold themselves back. There were no acolytes to worry about fugue. There were no fixed within range to worry about attack. They need only protect Jinyesun and Fandina from songbruise and -burn. Phex and Missit had been working successfully together for long enough to be seamless in their harmony. They used cantor to push the dome as they never had before.

Missit let himself go as bright as he wanted. They were high enough up, the dome could become a sun. And it did. Missit could become a sun, for some short time. And he did.

Phex let himself coil fractals across the panels like waves

crashing over, with no fear of overwhelming the congregation, because this congregation needed to be overwhelmed.

After six songs, the army below had forgotten why they marched.

They began to stumble and sit, weak-kneed with awe. Some cried. Others collapsed on their backs, so taken by the beauty, they had nothing left but to stop themselves from thinking for a while.

Perhaps there were a few protans among them who were confused, who got to see what it was like as an outsider. But there were not enough of them left to continue the invasion.

After nine songs, Asterism stopped.

Cheers and screams erupted from below. The army was now just a blob of dark against a nighttime mountainside. The dome hung above them like a chandelier, dangling from the stars. They had experienced something entirely new and never before attempted. Something unique. Something awe-inspiring and enlightening and truly divine.

And they had been saved.

16

THE DIVINITY ENDURES

It would have been one for the history books, if books still existed. As it was, the beam of Asterism's aerial dome on Agatay was considered one of the best ever produced by a demigod pantheon. It was a sensation – even if the sticklers said it was too short a performance.

Dome 6 didn't stay floating forever, of course. It landed back on its original foundation. Resting exactly as it should over the excavated warren of vestry and passages. Perhaps there would be more shows there. But Phex doubted it. Already the builders were planning new ways to make it click in and fasten, like a lid, so it could be popped off and released to float again. Agatay, after all, had more than its fair share of fixed – it would be better if the dome were not, in fact, fixed permanently to the earth itself.

It simply made more sense to do performances not just aboveground but up in the air. Not only did it eliminate the risk of fixed attacking gods, the congregation numbers would no longer be limited by building capacity. The divinity had been irrevocably altered by the idea of the mobile dome. By the popularity. By the sensation. By the practicality.

The Dyesi had shot footage from below, of their first floating dome. For the first time in years, the acolytes weighed in with opinions on the divine forums.

Dome 6, the dome of all skies, was already famous. Already worshipers from off-world were planning to make pilgrimages to Agatay to visit it. The premier dome of its kind. Already the Dyesi were planning to build more. The divinity was strategizing which planets and places and continents would be better served by a mobile dome. Already acolytes around the galaxy were assessing pantheons for gods who could take to the skies. Already things were changing.

The divinity was evolving.

Asterism and Missit returned to the *Nusplunder* victorious.

Missit was elated, even as the post-performance letdown brutalized his psyche with the memory of recent loss.

What was left of Tillam was waiting for them. The older gods had kind words for Asterism. There was no envy in them for demigods piloting a new style of art. They were too tired for that. There was no anger at Asterism for performing when Tillam simply could not. For stealing their thunder. For stealing Missit to launch a new divine beauty into the galaxy. They had no need for envy from their lofty perch, broken though it now was.

Tillam saw that the sorrow on Missit's face had been mitigated by novelty and challenge. They knew their youngest well. They knew the golden god and his capricious ways. They knew he healed with distraction and attention and glory. They knew that of all of them, Missit was the one who still loved the dais the most, floating or not, with an unparalleled joy. It was what made him famous. They were not bitter for one of them moving on to greater things when they had already attained the pinnacle of what had once been possible together.

Tillam swept Missit toward their quarters to clean and debrief. To spend some small time taking comfort in his success, because they were not jealous gods. They knew better than to hold court with petty thoughts when history had been made by one of their own.

Missit trotted away with them and then paused halfway down the hallway. He whirled on one foot, elegant even after such a performance as this, taxing in its novelty. Even exhausted and heartsore, his bones stayed liquid.

He ran back at Phex.

Phex knew he would do it, so he braced his stance.

Missit leapt into grace, tossing himself carelessly into the air in one of the moves from their duet. Phex caught him easily, whirled and dipped as the choreography had dictated.

"What you want?" he said, setting Missit back on his feet.

Missit was all crooked smiles and sad eyes. "I'll come back to you tonight. After I spend some time with Tillam."

"I never doubted it."

"That was fun, Phex, that idea of yours."

"It was, wasn't it?"

"We did a good thing tonight, didn't we?"

"We certainly did a beautiful thing." For the divinity, that would count as *good*.

"I like singing with you, Phex."

"And I like singing with you."

"Okay I'mma go now."

"You do that."

The golden god walked after the rest of his pantheon, backward so he could watch Phex the whole way.

He ignored the murmel streaking, and shrieking, toward

him. She climbed up his leg and torso, and onto his shoulder in a serpentine flash of blue.

From far away he shouted, almost in high cantor, "I'll be back in your bed tonight. You know why?"

Phex sighed and didn't say anything.

"Because I can!" sang out Missit.

Tyve came to stand next to Phex. "He's going to be impossible about that, isn't he?"

"Until he trusts that they really won't stop us, yes. Probably even after, simply because he can."

"You chose that," accused Tyve.

"I certainly did not. *That* chose me."

"Just like the divinity," said Berril, grinning up at him.

"I suppose so. Very demanding, the lot of you."

"What'd I miss?" asked Kagee, coming in from one of the other docking bays. His long hair was tied tightly back, and he was wearing a set of Dyesi armor in gunmetal green. Phex didn't realize he'd ordered one, but he wasn't surprised.

"Yay, good," said Berril clapping. "You're back."

Phex evaluated Kagee quickly for injuries. He looked none the worse for a day spent protecting the rulers of a planet at war.

Kagee saw Phex do it. "I'm unhurt. A little bruised, but it turns out I remember all my training. I forgot how much fun it is to really *fight*."

"Your family is okay?" asked Phex.

"My family?"

"The diarchs and their child."

"They aren't my family."

Phex gave him a dour look. "Liar."

"We've been separated for less than twenty-four hours, Phex, and you're still the most annoying person I've ever met." Kagee turned to stride toward their quarters – Asterism trotted to catch up and grouped around him.

"So, what happened with the show?" Kagee asked without slowing, marching like a general.

"We flew a dome!" crowed Berril. "Like a massive bubble in the sky."

Kagee nodded. "So I heard. You're crazy, you know that?"

After that, it was a perfectly normal evening for Asterism – dinner, rotation through the hygiene chamber, bed. Just another winding-down from just another performance, nothing special. Jinyesun explored the forums to see about reactions to their strange new beam and their crazy new dome. Reported the best bits to them all in an excited voice with puffy crests.

Universally positive about Dome 6. But the worshipers were mixed on Missit singing with Asterism instead of Kagee. They had reacted poorly to Phex singing with Tillam initially, too. Worshipers never liked changes to their pantheons. But this time, it didn't seem to be quite so bad.

It was thought of as Missit *slumming it*. And Kagee's believers were obsessed with figuring out why he had not been singing high cantor that night. Why had Asterism had to use a different god? Missit's fans were equally obsessed with figuring out why he might lower himself to perform with demigods.

But mostly, the forums were filled with just that, confusion. Maybe even a little worry. There were no haters. Not yet, anyway.

Largely, it was considered a one-off situation. Impressive and fun but never likely to happen again. The floating dome. Missit singing with Asterism. Kagee disappearing. All of it was considered a novelty. It was exciting enough in its uniqueness for many to entirely forget that only a few nights earlier, Fortew had collapsed on a dais.

Worshipers had very short attention spans.

They were done with Agatay.

For the time being, anyway.

The divinity did consider adding three more performances. Just Asterism. Using the floating dome, trying to convert as many stragglers as they could. The acolytes even discussed it with Asterism and the diarchs of Agatay. Was it necessary? Or had they managed to enlighten most of the more violent elements of the population with that one spectacular show?

The diarchs said they thought it was enough. They had a lot to do, after that stalled invasion, to unify their population. They thought additional performances might be too distracting. Diplomatic negotiation should now take precedence. Agatay was, in the end, a very small planet and a very small population. Getting ever smaller.

What the diarchs didn't know, unless Kagee had told them, was that decline should reverse going forward. Agatay might actually be able to expand a little. Survive the horrors of itself and its past. Thrive.

Phex asked Kagee about that later.

"Did you tell Miramo and Levin the truth about enlightenment?"

"No."

"Will you?" asked Berril.

"Probably. I don't know. Will they hurt for having done such a thing to their whole planet? For having invited it here? Is it a violation to take away violence from an entire population without telling them? Should anyone feel guilty for that? Should we? Should I? I don't have the answers. But I will ultimately choose to protect them. It's a matter of whether I think the knowledge will hurt or comfort."

"Do you blame us?" Phex asked. Because they had been the ones, in the end, to close out the fate of Agatay. It was a world of worshipers now. It belonged to the divinity.

"How could I? It was the best solution at the time. And it brought peace."

"At a fair price?" wondered Phex.

Asterism's two Dyesi remained quiet. They had always known what the divinity did. They did not question the cost of enlightenment. They didn't even notice it was being pitted against autonomy.

"We face a moral quandary," Tyve explained for Jinyesun's benefit. "We have the ability to stop people from fighting, but they also become addicted to us. We are being used to impose the Dyesi agenda of nonviolence on all Sapiens who believe in us, and that means they do not have any choice but worship."

"It is a question of free will," said Phex.

"And what do you think?" Fandina asked him.

Phex huffed. "Having never experienced free will, I think I am not qualified to judge."

"Berril?" Fandina looked at their light grace.

Berril was not a complicated creature, and the Shawalee had been early adopters of the divinity. She had been born to an enlightened planet. "I think it is a good thing. I don't mind spreading enlightenment."

"Tyve?" Fandina turned to their dark grace.

The Jakaa Nova was less confident. "I don't know. My parents run a medical ship. In another life, without divine influence, that would have been a warship. I would have *had* to fight. And I am no fighter. But is my lack of bloodlust also because of divine influence? Do I have purpose because of them, or was I an outcast originally because of them? Do I like what the Jakaa Nova are becoming? And even if I do, is that because they are becoming more like me or because they will be more accepting of me?"

She made an exasperated face, and gestured with her claws for the others to stop focusing on her.

"Does that help you decide, Kagee?" Fandina asked.

Kagee smiled, kindly and not sarcastic for once. "I was never in doubt. I like it. I like that this was done to my planet. And I like that Asterism did it. I have no compunctions around the enlightenment of my own people. I truly believe we would have destroyed each other and ourselves in the end. There was no stopping our spiral – no peace possible on Agatay any other way. This is it. This was our salvation. Unconsciously, I think my diarchs knew this too, and that was why they invited us. Perhaps, as a protan, I am not a fair judge, since there was no chance I could ever be enlightened, but still. I believe that this is a good thing." Kagee had his own kind of faith in the divinity, one that sprang from desperation.

Of all of them, Kagee turned out to be the most devout, in the end. Even Jinyesun and Fandina had gone from a place of faith to questioning as a result of their pantheon. Kagee seemed to have moved the opposite direction. But, Phex supposed, in his awkward way, Kagee loved Agatay. And more than anything else, he wanted to see it thrive.

"Aren't you afraid we have set up yet another disparate power struggle? After all, you protans are likely to be the only ones left who can fight. Isn't there a risk that proxies will take over?" Tyve asked.

Phex had been wondering the same thing.

"The disenfranchised rising up? I think that unlikely in the short run, especially if no one knows the specifics of enlightenment. Also, there really aren't very many of us. And for now, we will be occupied, defending against fixed. Besides, the divinity is already planning to recruit bodyguards from protan ranks. Proxies will start to take work off-world. But I suppose it could pose a risk over the next few decades. It's one of the reasons I'm considering telling the diarchs the details of enlightenment."

"You don't have much time. We'll be leaving soon," said Jinyesun.

Kagee clicked. "They're coming aboard tonight, for a kind of diplomatic goodbye party."

"Unusual?" wondered Phex.

Jin answered, "To invite aliens onto a divine spaceship? Very. But then again, this is an unusually big ship, and the diarchs are known true believers as well as planetary leaders. Tillam's bodyguards will still be very much present."

Fandina wiggled its crests in amused mockery. "I hear that the acolytes are in a tizzy. They have never had to host an actual *party* before. They'll be running around all day tomorrow, preparing."

Accordingly, the next night, the diarchs of Agatay, with only two proxies for protection and no additional entourage, were the first leaders of an alien world to board a Dyesi spaceship.

Agatay was generating more than its fair share of *firsts*.

It reminded Phex a great deal of the first meet-and-greet party he'd ever attended, on Divinity 36, surrounded by other potentials. It boasted a table of intergalactic delicacies and a milling throng of alien confusion. Maybe not so much alien anymore. At least not to Phex. What did one call familiar aliens? People.

This was smaller and more intimate, including only the diarch delegation, Asterism, the three acolytes, and Tillam's bodyguards. Also, Missit's parents were in attendance. Which probably explained why Missit was not.

Everyone behaved themselves admirably and the diarchs did well – not wincing even once at the strange Dyesi food, too sour and too bitter, or the strange Dyesi drinks that were the same. Luckily, Kagee stuck by them and gave fair warning. In fact, Phex overheard him explaining many things he had learned about Dyesi culture and the divinity to his lovers, so Levin and Miramo never made a single social gaffe.

"We should make you minister of protocol," Phex heard Miramo say at one point.

At which Kagee actually laughed. Apparently, that was a hilarious idea. Phex wondered if he had ever heard Kagee laugh before.

Kagee was relaxed in this environment. This was all easy for him. Being with his lovers, explaining how his world now worked – there was no pressure, he could only excel. He was comfortable in both worlds – the one that was newly forming between the diarchs and the divinity, and the one the Dyesi had handed him.

Phex envied him that.

While Phex watched his friend introduce the diarchs to yet another member of the *Nusplunder*'s crew whose name Phex had never learned, Missit's parents approached him.

Phex got very nervous. There was no way for him to be as comfortable as Kagee with any of this.

"We understand you are sleeping with our son," said Missit's mother.

Apparently, the acolytes had seen fit to inform them of specifics.

Phex crossed his arms and looked down at them, silent.

"For how long?"

"Since the beginning." Phex could answer that. Because Missit had climbed into his bed to sleep there long before they had done anything more than that.

"I bet the nymphs hated that," said Missit's father. Trying to sound – what? Sympathetic? Cool? Calm? What was he doing? "When they eventually found out."

Phex cocked his head.

"How did you persuade them to let you stay together?" asked Missit's mother.

"I'm persuasive," replied Phex.

"You're an odd one, aren't you?" Missit's mother was clearly annoyed. Just as Missit occasionally got perturbed by Phex's taciturn nature. Except this time, Phex was doing it on purpose. Missit's parents may have revealed the secret of enlightenment, but Phex didn't feel like he owed them honesty in return.

Kagee might owe them – after all, it was his planet that had been saved with Phex's knowledge.

But Phex felt no such obligation.

He only did what he was told to by the divinity. He did not feel guilt over the theft of free will when he had none of his own.

Perhaps that was why he spoke so little. He didn't want to give anyone free access to his thoughts, because he had already given away everything else.

"Where is Missit now? Why isn't he here?" asked Missit's father.

Was this Phex's future, people always asking him where his boyfriend was? Was that part of what it meant to *have* a boyfriend? Had all his singular pronouns become *us* and *we*? Was he supposed to always keep track of Missit now? To be fair, he did that already. But still, this was Missit. Willful and stubborn with no sense of self-preservation. Phex had his work cut out for him. Did this mean he would have to excuse, or at least explain, Missit's behavior to others? What insane future had he consigned himself to?

"Missit is with Tillam," said Phex, curtly, "Where else would he be?"

"I could have wished my son chose a lover with less attitude." Missit's mother was very annoyed.

"It's a good thing for me, then, that it was his choice and not yours."

"Well, actually" —the academic was back in her voice— "it was the divinity's decision in the end, was it not?"

Phex was oddly annoyed that she knew so much about their situation and could use it against him.

Suddenly, Kagee was standing there with his diarchs. "Honorable scholars, may I introduce you to the Diarchs of Agatay, the rulers of this planet, Levin and Miramo?" Kagee said in Galactic Formal.

Missit's parents turned politely to engage with the rulers of a whole planet and new key players in the broad political scope of the divinity. Phex, if not forgotten, was at least deemed much less important.

Phex gave a Kagee a grateful nod.

Kagee, of course, looked smug.

"You research the divine presence?" asked Miramo of Missit's mother.

"Indeed we do."

"How wonderful. We are great advocates of the art form."

"I understand it is immediately effective and impactful on your planet, and apparently, the results have been quite innovative. How did you conceive of the idea of a mobile dome?"

Phex escaped before he could be dragged into *that* conversation. Let Kagee and the diarchs claim invention of that particular trick. Phex did not want to take credit or responsibility.

He sought refuge with the rest of his pantheon, who were hovering near the table of snacks, at the sugary end, because Berril was hungry.

"Anyone need anything to drink?" Phex hoped one of them wanted something that wasn't being provided so he could sneak away to the galley for a while.

"Oh, look, it's the hero of the hour," said Tyve.

"The savior of Agatay," said Berril.

Dear gods, was that what they were saying? Who? The bodyguards? The proxies? The acolytes? The divinity?

"Are they actually telling everyone that the floating dome was *my* idea?" asked Phex in horror.

"Oh, yes, they are." Tyve wiggled her brows and popped a bit of fruit into her mouth.

"It has been decided that it is good for our *brand*. Asterism's, I mean. To be seen as innovators rather than upstarts," explained Jinyesun.

"Well, poop," said Phex, meaning it.

And so that rumor took flight. Phex became somewhat infamous for having conceived of a floating dome first. *First* was always given an extra burst of respect in the creative field, especially among Sapiens.

Phex gained believers because of it. Asterism gained worshipers on the back of that and their performance in Dome 6.

The flames of hate in the divine forums turned entirely to embers.

Speculation about Tillam's silence and Fortew's collapse returned, but Asterism and Phex were no longer being blamed for whatever was happening with the great gods.

It was to be their last night orbiting Agatay. The divinity was preparing to move on, ever expanding. It had done all it deemed necessary and sufficient – this time around. There was another pantheon en route. Another six gods ready to try out the galaxy's first floating dome, ready to keep the divinity alive. Ready to keep the population of Agatay alive.

There was an odd stillness in Asterism's quarters that evening.

"Where's Missit?" asked Kagee. And there it was, Phex's new pronoun in action. The *us*. Even his pantheon thought of them as multiple.

"His parents are staying over tonight. He decided to actually talk with them this time."

"He didn't want you there?" wondered Berril.

Phex had offered. Missit had said only, "It will be all right. The knowledge of you is enough, and I think I need to do this alone." Phex hadn't understood. And because this was something about the parental relationship, he probably never would. He could only accept.

"I don't think *want* mattered," was his reply to his pantheon. He could tell from the ensuing silence in the dark that the others didn't understand, either. He wondered about their relationships with their parents. He had never asked. It had never occurred to him to ask.

Kagee had been very quiet ever since bidding goodbye to his diarchs after the party. The three of them had hugged for a very long time. Levin's hand had fisted the robe at Kagee's waist. Miramo's hand had rested on his neck, intimate and proprietary. Unwilling and unable to let him go, they had stood together – holding the last note on a dais.

It would be harder for Kagee to leave his lovers this time. Now that he knew they still wanted him.

Which is how Phex knew what Kagee was going to say, when he eventually spoke, because he himself would have made the same choice. Phex had made that choice, under verity, before three acolytes. Kagee was simply braver about speaking the truth. He didn't have to be drugged into it.

"I'm not going with you when you break orbit tomorrow."

Berril gasped. Phex heard the rustle of her climbing out of her bunk and into Kagee's. "Noooo!"

Her wailing was muffled. Kagee must be hugging her. Good.

Tyve said, "You're breaking up with us?"

"This is why gods aren't supposed to date." Fandina sounded sad.

Phex, who knew better now, replied, "That's not really why."

"Well, it is one of the reasons." This time, Fandina sounded sulky.

Jinyesun said, "You are sure about this decision, Kagee?"

"No, of course not. But I never did stop loving them, and if you asked me to weigh the cost, I love being a god less. Also, this way, I can help the reconstruction. I can help my people rebuild, newly enlightened. I can help them better than anyone, because I understand the divinity from within."

Berril whimpered.

"You could even co-rule. After all, you are a god," said Tyve.

"Or I will once have been." Kagee's tone was neutral. Phex could tell the high cantor wasn't sure he wanted that kind of power, although they all recognized that it was just another form of fame. "Celebrity counts for a lot, in politics," Kagee admitted.

"Especially divine celebrity on a galactic scale." Tyve had seen much of the galaxy – she understood such things. "And with Agatay opening up, you being famous will help diplomatic relations of all kinds."

Kagee groaned.

"And you can help them cope with the protans, without revealing why you need to," suggested Jinyesun, showing a depth of understanding that Phex hadn't really expected from a Dyesi but should have from this one.

"And I understand proxy training, too," Kagee agreed.

"But Kagee, you're *our* high cantor." Berril's voice was plaintive. "What about us? What about Asterism?"

"I don't want to hurt you, birdie, but I can't think of a better way. I don't want to leave Mira and Lev, certainly not right now."

Silence descended for a long moment.

"You're not saying anything, Phex." Kagee's tone of voice was weird and flat. What did he need?

Phex was thinking about how happy Kagee had looked at that party. How easily he handled Missit's parents. How skilled a diplomat he actually was. How much he loved Levin and Miramo and their baby. How good he was at showing it.

"I'm not surprised," Phex said.

"Of course you aren't. You probably knew I was going to do this before I did."

Phex took another educated guess. "You had the Dyesi reverse your sterilization procedure. That's where you were this afternoon."

"You're so annoying." That was Kagee for *agreement*. "You all are." That was Kagee for *affection*.

"We love you too," Phex replied, knowing Kagee was

annoyed because they wanted him to stay. Because they needed him. Because they loved him. They were making an already-hard choice that much harder.

Asterism was silent for a long time after that. In the dark of that tiny cabin, resolving brave faces and voices. Carving away at the wobble and the thickness that sorrow wrought so Kagee couldn't hear it when they spoke again. Understanding but also giving up. To fight this decision would only hurt Kagee more. Much as they felt pain, Asterism was not a pantheon that cut away at the cause of suffering. Only Kagee ever did that. And he was leaving them.

Phex felt a weight and then Jin crawling in next to him on his bunk.

"Just until Missit gets here," said the Dyesi.

Phex made room.

A shifting in the bunk above, and he knew Fandina had climbed in with Tyve.

Asterism was grieving.

"You could at least get mad at me. But instead, you are all compassion and understanding. It's so frustrating." There was Kagee, lashing out as expected.

"What good would that do?" asked Phex, because he *was* angry. But it was anger at the situation, not Kagee's choice.

"Why should Phex be mad?" asked Missit, the light flashing in from the hallway briefly as the curtain was swept aside. Then darkness again.

"I'm leaving Asterism and staying behind on Agatay." Confessed Kagee.

"Are you really?" Missit's voice was carefully neutral. "Why?"

"Because Agatay needs me more."

"That sounds like something Phex would say." Missit

paused at the side of Phex's bed. "Hello, there's a Dyesi in my bed."

"Phex's bed," corrected Kagee.

Of course, he was wrong – it was Missit's bed now, too. Phex felt that impossible warmth under his skin again, that he got to have that reality. That somehow, them loving each other was allowed to be true.

Missit said, "I suppose this will make my decision easier."

"You're making this about you?" accused Kagee.

Missit lashed out, fast and hot. "Well, I, at least, can say with confidence that I won't miss that personality of yours."

Phex thought that them snapping at each other was good, better than depression and sadness and the anxiety of immanent separation. He also understood what Missit meant.

Phex had always worried it would be him having to decide between Tillam and Asterism, between lover and family. Fortew had even asked him about it once. If Phex had to pick between Missit and Asterism, who would he choose? Between passion and comfort? Between love and friendship? Phex had never been prepared to make that choice. Unlike Kagee, he wasn't strong enough.

Turned out it was never going to be his decision anyway but Missit's. Missit and his marriage of over a decade. How old was Tillam, twelve years now? Marriage to five other beings, now four, who adored him. Who had raised him from child into god, in their way. It was Missit who would have to decide between Phex and family.

But Missit was unexpectedly wise about it. Perhaps that was the difference that age had given him. The ability to boldly risk safety and stability. Phex was too new to both – he couldn't face the possibility of letting anything go.

"You plan to leave Tillam and join us as high cantor? Take Kagee's place?" Fandina finally understood.

"Tillam would keep going – for me, if I asked them. Without a sun. Perhaps they'd even let me pull Phex into Tillam – destroying Asterism in the process. But Yorunlee is going yellow. And Tern just seems tired all the time. The joy of the dais is gone for them. The colors gone dull. Even Zil talks more about his family back on their medical ship and the good deeds they do, how much benefit he might provide as a famous face for their charity work."

"*Going yellow?*" asked Berril.

Jinyesun explained, standing up and ceding its spot in Phex's bunk to Missit. "Instar is coming. You can see it in Yorunlee's eyes. Sooner rather than later. If you've informed the divinity of this decision, Missit, that must be why we are leaving orbit so quickly. We've got to get to Dyesid Prime as soon as possible, get Yorunlee back to the caves before it's too late. I'm surprised it held out this long. It must be so relieved."

Missit climbed in next to Phex. Tucked cold toes between his calves. "You are not the first to say that."

Phex thought that it wasn't fair to be so happy to have Missit join Asterism and so sad to lose Kagee at the same time.

Ultimately, Phex was the one who had won. He got to have both Missit and his pantheon. Kagee was being sacrificed for that happiness. Kagee, the last to join Asterism. Kagee of the bitter tongue and flashing rings. Phex's enemy and then his cantor and then his friend. Phex already missed him. The void he would leave behind was not one that could be filled back up with Missit's love – for it was the wrong color and the wrong pattern.

But at the same time, Phex was elated. Missit would be

his high cantor. Asterism's high cantor. Missit, the golden god of gods. His Missit.

How could the two things exist inside him so entirely and so fully at the same time? How could joy hurt this much?

This must also be how Missit felt. Missit, who was losing his pantheon but joining Phex's. Getting to be with Phex, getting to start fresh and stay divine and stay a god.

They were both losing and loving in the same breath. Stars and voids swirling together.

Missit's voice had been steady and calm, but his face against Phex's neck was wet.

Phex shifted and pressed their foreheads and then cheeks together, both sticky and damp. Sharing salt and pain and happiness.

This time, it was not Phex holding Missit as he cried. It was them holding each other while they both did.

The next morning, they said their goodbyes to Kagee.

The divinity must have agreed entirely with Missit's decision. With Kagee's, too. With everything. Because they made no protest – in fact, they made no appearance. The acolytes did not even bother to see Kagee off.

Phex wondered if this had been their endgame all along. If they had always intended to keep Missit and retire Tillam. If that was why Missit had been allowed to sing in Dome 6. If that was why they had been encouraged to cantor together in the first place. If that was why they were allowed to love each other.

Agatay sent up a transport, one of the very few spacefaring vessels that they had. Ancient tech and very clunky but serviceable.

Kagee, with his pile of belongings, stood in the docking bay looking delicate but determined. "I'll see you when you're next on tour. Agatay will be on the list?"

"Always," said Phex, meaning it. "You're the custodian of the universe's only floating dome, we have to come back. We started it."

"They made me sexton." Kagee sounded a little surprised.

"You're an acolyte now?" accused Tyve.

"Maybe something halfway in between?"

"Send us your godsong compositions?" asked Fandina.

"Who else would I give them to?" Kagee was, as always, annoyed. "The divinity already put me under mandate on the matter." At Phex's concerned expression, he added, "It's a good contract, they're paying well."

The murmel, wrapped around Missit's neck, chose that exact moment to scream at the top of her little lungs.

"Not gonna miss that." Kagee glared at her.

The murmel looked faintly embarrassed and stuffed one tiny paw into her mouth.

"Come sing high cantor with us when we return?" suggested Missit, magnanimous in victory.

"You'd let me?"

"Of course, they were your pantheon first. You may have fallen back to earth, but you're still a god."

Kagee nodded. "For a short time, I was one of the best."

"Keep singing so you don't forget how," ordered Missit, dictatorial.

Jinyesun said, "They say you never forget the dome once you have been inside it. But for the gods, it is the dome that never forgets us."

Kagee looked even more annoyed, which meant he was touched.

To save his friend further aggravation, Phex hustled his

pantheon out of the docking bay. He looked back as the door closed behind them. A proper door, one of the few the *Nusplunder* boasted, because it had to seal tight against the vacuum of space.

Phex wondered if it was effective enough to seal away Kagee's guilt. He wondered if he could shut such a thing against his own guilt. There would always be, between Phex and Kagee, the knowledge that in the end, they would choose lovers over godhood. For two such different people, they shared this one profound belief. So, Kagee got his diarchs and his home world, and Phex got his Missit and his pantheon.

Phex thought he had the better end of the deal.

No doubt Kagee felt the same.

Kagee boarded the ancient transport with no backward glances or fond waves – that was not his style. Phex caught one last gleam of his many rings as he manually lifted the boarding ramp and shut it behind himself.

They watched as the port opened and the transport was sucked into space. Watched as the fuel cells kicked in and Kagee left them forever.

Phex felt like his heart was opening up to the void, and it hurt, but that pain was a beautiful thing.

Guilty or not, Phex and Kagee must both live with the consequences of choices. And because they felt no lack of love from any quarter for having made the difficult decision, they both *could* live with those choices.

Phex picked Missit up and twirled him just because he could. He kissed him softly. Because he was allowed to do that, too.

"Phex, you're smiling as you kiss me," said Missit, pleased and cheerful.

"I'm always smiling when I kiss you," said Phex.

Agatay disappeared behind the *Nusplunder*, swallowed up

to become one of many planets, and then one of many stars. The divine spaceship folded toward the Dyesi sector in careful stages. It would take longer than anyone liked to get home.

Missit practiced with Asterism.

Tillam did not practice at all.

Yorunlee took to its bunk in contemplative meditation. None of the Dyesi seemed surprised by this, just driven by an increased sense of urgency to get back to Dyesid Prime.

Zil, Tern, and Melalan actually hung out with Asterism quite a lot. Letting the demigods freely pick their brains and ask for advice about godhood and celebrity. Watching Phex and Missit flirt with tolerant approval – seeming to take pleasure in their joy. Not just that they could be together, but that how there was no inevitable end point to that togetherness. Phex felt a little like Tillam was handing over care. They had raised Missit and now it was Phex's turn.

The elder gods were taking time to make plans for their mortal futures. Melalan was thinking about some new aspect of the divinity, perhaps becoming a prior, producing shows and building domes. Tern wanted to travel, not tour but really travel. He wanted to stay for long periods of time on exotic worlds. Zil's parents' medical ship was heading to liaise with the *Nusplunder* and pick him up. Phex would get to meet Tyve's extended family. That would be interesting.

Asterism practiced with Missit every day that they could. Several times, Phex caught the acolytes watching, sometimes just one, sometimes all three. Whatever they saw clearly pleased them – they always left with puffy crests.

Phex had no idea how they planned to announce Tillam's retirement, Fortew's death, or Missit's reassignment. No doubt they had some strategy in mind. No doubt it would cause a fervor and a fuss. No doubt the divine forums would flame and the believers would be in uproars. Worshipers would grieve the loss of such a great god as Fortew, even as they blamed Asterism for stealing Missit away.

But they had been through gossip and drama before. It would all shift and fade, like the colors from the dome.

They would spend some time back on Divinity 36 in the familiar building there. Phex would get to play in a real kitchen again. He would learn all of Missit's favorite drinks. He would introduce some of the new snacks that they had encountered on their travels to the acolytes. They would watch the new crop of potentials practicing and competing for their own place among the stars. Phex would feed them, too. Asterism would be the seasoned old guard now. The famous ones. The youngsters would look upon them in awe. The members of Asterism would stick their heads into practice rooms and pretend they were wise.

Asterism would move from demigods to gods, probably faster than other pantheons. Because they had Missit. Because they had invented a whole new kind of dome. Because for all that Asterism was a controversial pantheon, they had effective godsongs that encouraged godfix, and that would only improve with every new dome they performed in. Because Phex and Missit together were the most powerful cantor pair in the galaxy. And eventually, the whole galaxy would know that.

Phex would get his own statue. The personality chip would cause issues, for it would be as grumpy and uncommunicative as he was. No one would ever steal Phex's statue. His ladles would become famous too. They would be branded and sold to fund more divine expansion. They'd probably bring out a gold version, in honor of Missit.

Missit would wallow in the joy of performing once more. With Tillam, it had become work. Because of Fortew, it had become painful. With Asterism, it would be fun again. He was already brighter on the dais when they practiced together. He already burned more gold in Phex's arms.

They had a new godsong to work on. One of Kagee's compositions. He'd left it with them, saying that he thought it would suit Missit's high-cantor style much better than his.

And it did.

The new song would make for a beautiful dome. It would become one of their most famous, beamed out into the galaxy on a billion different feeds. Phex could feel that in his bones. It would bring amazing colors and patterns to all the domes across space and time, cupolas and the new mobile ones, too. It would fix Sapiens in their tracks and make Dyesi huff with joy. It would bring them to Berril's home world at last, where she would get her chance to shine. It would cement Missit as one of Asterism and yet still a great god. It would remind one deadly grey assassin on a planet far away that he had made the correct choice. It would go on rotation in cafes until it became just one more background song among many – for a barista on a forgotten moon to mark his shift by.

The teenagers who listened to it would flirt and steal Missit's statue and dream of becoming gods themselves. And some lonely child on some rocky satellite would fall in love with peace.

fin

Thank you so much for joining me on Phex's journey. It has been a pleasure sharing it with you.

If you're curious about crudrats, there is a companion book to this series called (unsurprisingly) *Crudrat*.

AUTHOR'S NOTE

Thank you so much for picking up *Dome 6*. I hope you enjoyed the final installment of Phex's story. If you would like more Tinkered Stars or have a favorite character you want to see more of, please say so in a review or tell a friend. I'm grateful for the time you take to do so.

Join my newsletter, the Chirrup, for sneak peaks at cover art, sample chapters, and insight into what I'm writing next. Find it and much more at…

GailCarriger.com

ABOUT THE WRITERBEAST

New York Times bestselling author Gail Carriger (AKA G. L. Carriger) writes to cope with being raised in obscurity by an expatriate Brit and an incurable curmudgeon. She escaped small-town life and inadvertently acquired several degrees in higher learning, a fondness for cephalopods, and a chronic tea habit. She then traveled the historic cities of Europe, subsisting entirely on biscuits secreted in her handbag. She resides on the edge of the Pacific, surrounded by fantastic shoes, where she insists on tea imported from London.

Printed in Poland
by Amazon Fulfillment
Poland Sp. z o.o., Wrocław